MUSES AND MONSTERS

ROSE GRAVESTONE

DKS PUBLISHING LLC

CONTENTS

To all the girlies who read love triangles and think (or scream at the page):

"WHY CAN'T SHE JUST CHOOSE BOTH?!"

Carson Ajax and Seth Balor are ready to show you that their girl can choose both and reap numerous rewards from that choice.

Author's Note

Hello lovely reader and thank you for picking up Muses and Monsters! I very much hope you'll enjoy this story.

Before you dive in, a few warnings about content that might not be to everyone's tastes:

- Eating disorders are discussed and at times displayed on page.

- Graphic depictions of a campus serial killer's activities and the state of the victims.

- MFM.

If none of these themes are a problem for you, go on and get started! I think you'll have a lot of fun on this twisty ride.

Prologue

Carson Ajax

"Remind me why I agreed to come here, again?" My best friend asks from beside me, sulking in his lush velvet seat as if we're at a mortuary rather than one of the finest theatres in the state.

My eyes scanning the patrons in the main auditorium below the box I share with Seth, watching as they settle into their seats in preparation for the performance, I say dryly, "Wipe that scowl off your face, you ungrateful fuck. Do you know how much tickets for box seats here cost?"

Seth Balor, my reluctant friend and even more reluctant companion, answers, "Well over three grand each. What's your point? This is a production hosted by college level dancers, not professionals. The directors are teachers, and the stagehands are students. The fuck am I gonna see here that's consequential?"

I roll my eyes, casting him a sidelong glance. The performance we're attending is not just put on by college level dancers, it's put on by dancers who've been handpicked from around the world for their talent and invited into a very selective, very elite four-year program. Somebody who hadn't danced professionally by the time they grew pubes wouldn't even be considered as a candidate; every single girl and boy in the program is the real deal, and the list of alums has some world-famous names.

The fact that Seth and I happen to attend the same university that is home to this dance program—though we're in entirely different studies from the finer arts—combined with my father's copious yearly donations to the aforementioned program means that I'm obligated to attend at least one or two of the performances that the department puts on throughout the year in affiliation with the best theatre in the vicinity of Greywood.

"Get that stick out of your ass, Balor. Aren't you artists supposed to appreciate all art?" I ask, smacking the top of his head with a rolled-up pamphlet of tonight's performance; a contemporary take on the traditional ballet Sleeping Beauty.

"I'm a double major in science and engineering," Seth says flatly.

"Who spends half his nights locked in his apartment, working on his newest painting or sculpting project," I point out.

At a fresh twenty-one years old, Seth is already acknowledged as a polymath by the scientific, engineering, and artistic communities worldwide. There is absolutely no denying the guy is a genius, with several of his paintings and sculptures on display in museums around the world, a few of his inventions having already been patented and introduced to commercial marketplaces with insane success, and one of his invented chemical formulas getting classified by a three-letter government agency that was very disappointed when Seth turned down their job offer last year.

"Exactly; sculpting and painting. When done properly, both take a deeper understanding of engineering, geometry, anatomy, and even physics. The sort of dancing our school's program teaches isn't even classical ballet, which means it requires no knowledge of the finer arts and might as well be nomadic."

I shake my head, lowering my voice as the lights dim on the walls and the ceiling, signaling that the show's about to start. "You're a fucking snob. I should've come alone."

The only reason I'm here is because my father sent me a very clear email last week as to which school functions I'm expected to attend this upcoming school year, in order to reflect properly on his shiny, philanthropic public image. An oil tycoon with an international trade empire and more money than he can spend in five lifetimes, my piece of shit sperm donor is not the sort of man to take no for an answer. He's not even the type to ask a question; he issues orders and expects everyone around him to obey.

I thought bringing Seth along might ease a modicum of my irritation at my forced attendance, but he's proving to be in the mood to goad me tonight. As someone who I often suspect is a certified psychopath, when Seth decides to drive someone up the wall, he doesn't fail. His response to me dragging him here is to make me regret it—appropriately Machiavellian of him.

"Yes, you should've," Seth purrs darkly, not bothering to lower his voice even as the stage lights come on and the curtain rises. "Next time you'll remember that and leave me out of it."

"Psychotic bastard," I mutter, pulling at the knot in my tie to loosen it. It feels like it's approximately five thousand degrees in here with all the bodies, even though Seth and I are well above the masses, and I do not look forward to sweating through my suit. I don't look forward to this bullshit any more than Seth does, but I'm keeping my complaints to myself.

The orchestra finishes warming up in the pit below the stage, falling silent as dancers wearing costumes that vary from traditional maid garbs to Victorian dresses fill the stage, creating a chaotic display of color and clothing as they take their spots. At the back of the stage is a large white screen serving as an electronic backdrop, on which words form, telling the audience about a king and queen beseeching an evil fairy queen to bless them with a daughter, but forgetting to show their gratitude for her wish-granting, prompting the evil fairy to plan a terrible revenge.

A beat of silence passes, and then the orchestra breaks into classical Tchaikovsky as dancers start moving gracefully across the sparsely decorated stage. Men and women interact together along with a doll meant to represent the baby Princess Aurora, and I watch with distant detachment and a steadily growing sense of boredom. The dancers are good, without a doubt, but I've already seen this adaptation twice in the two years I've spent at my university, meaning good dancing isn't enough to hold my attention.

"At least the orchestra's good, and this modern bullshit stuck with the original score," Seth mutters, crossing his arms and leaning his head back, shutting his eyes. "I think I'll let it lull me to sleep."

I snort. "You do that, man. I'll be picking which dancer I'm fucking tonight."

If I'm forced to park my ass in this chair for two hours, I'll accept a warm—and preferably flexible—female body beside me tonight as payment. One thing I'll give dancers; they are eager to please, especially when your last name alone could make or break their career.

Seth lets out a puff of laughter. "Of course you will."

The dance progresses, quite different from the original Sleeping Beauty ballet, but nothing I haven't seen before. Frankly, none of the talent on stage is eye-catching enough to keep me entertained. Maybe Seth has the right idea; the music is nice enough to put me right to sleep.

Just as I'm settling back, ready to nap my way through the rest of this waste of time, a prickle of what feels like static electricity rolls over me, perking me up as if I got a cold bucket of water thrown on me. I glance at Seth, surprised to see him also suddenly sitting up and alert, his eyes glued to the stage with interest for the first time since he sat down.

Looking to the audience below, I note that everyone seems to have perked up at the new, vibrant energy that fills the entire auditorium. My eyes find the stage in time for the barren space to be graced by a single dancer—Princess Aurora, now suddenly turned from a baby into an adult. My bottom lip finds its way between my teeth as I get my first look at the star of tonight's performance and, I swear to god, the temperature shoots so high I have to wonder if a volcano isn't about to spontaneously erupt out of the ground beneath me.

As this dance requires, Aurora wears a beige mask over her face to make it look as if she's faceless as she's passed between the evil fairy queen and the queen's two minions. The small, lithe dancer playing Aurora wears a diaphanous, lacey white dress that hugs and presents her breasts through a corset while flowing down her hips and stopping above her knees. She has, without a doubt, the single best body I have ever seen on a stage or anywhere else for that matter, complete with mouthwatering curves and luminous fair skin that glows under the stage lights. Her dirty blonde, multicolored and layered hair is pulled away from the mask covering her face at the sides and flows down her back and around her shoulders with each of her movements.

Even with her face hidden, my breath catches in my throat—it seems she has this effect on the entirety of the audience, as well, because one glance around tells me that the previously half-interested patrons are now all watching the stage with rapt attention. Seth is squeezing the arms of his chair so tight his knuckles are white while staring at her.

I know that true performers have the singular ability to captivate an entire audience—I've heard about it and even experienced it once or twice—but the way the faceless Aurora on stage moves isn't just captivating, it's mesmerizing.

The scene shifts as a new batch of good fairies arrive to fight the evil queen away from the princess, and the good fairies create a faceless boy to help lift the curse the evil queen has already put on the young princess. Even with the addition of new dancers—ones with talent too, as the prince moves almost as gracefully as the princess—all eyes remain glued to the dancer playing Aurora, who's now resting motionlessly on the side of the stage, having succumbed to the evil fairy's curse.

I watch, absolutely ensnared, as the prince approaches the princess and puts his hand on her shoulder to roll her onto her back. The entire audience holds their breaths as the prince leans down to place his nonexistent face on the princesses in a decidedly odd imitation of a kiss—considering neither of them have visible lips—and even that manages to look beautiful, because directly after, Princess Aurora jerks upright and is back to dancing, this time facing down the evil queen.

I stare at the blank mask covering the principal dancer's face as she continues to dazzle everyone around her, desperate to see what's under the mask. It becomes a physical chore to keep from marching onto the stage and removing the mask myself just to satiate my burning curiosity. I know I haven't seen her before—I'd recognize that body for sure—which means she's a freshman. For a freshman to land a leading role in the dance company's start of the year performance... if I wasn't seeing the power this girl commands on stage, I'd laugh at the thought.

The music ends after a final crescendo, with both the faceless boy and princess being carried off to opposite ends of the stage, and then out of sight into the wings.

I glance at Seth again, seeing that his attention is still glued to the stage. The glimmer in his hazel eyes is disconcerting, because it connotes interest, and Seth doesn't get interested by anything that isn't of his own invention. It's especially disconcerting because I've already decided I'm going to be fucking the new girl tonight, and I'm not interested in competition from my closest friend.

He meets my eyes, and at the same exact time, we both call, "Dibs."

***

Seth Balor

I eye the closest thing to family I have in the world, wondering whether or not it'd be appropriate to throw him out of our box and into the auditorium below to demonstrate how serious I am when I call dibs on the dancer that had the entire auditorium enthralled for the first act of the show. I've been friends with Carson for years and we've gotten up to some shit together, but he should know better than to challenge me once I've set my mind to something. Perhaps a ER stay would do him some good; remind him why we stay on good terms with each other, because if we were on bad terms, one of us would already be dead.

Before I can turn my thoughts into actions, the theatre is plunged into darkness. When the stage lights up again, the dancer playing Princess Aurora is back on stage—wearing the same, sinful white dress as earlier—except this time, she's unmasked, and my heart starts to race at the sight.

Everything about her is perfectly proportioned and symmetrical. Her face is a delicate oval shape, with a slightly upturned button nose in the center, and wide crystalline eyes that are a mixture of arctic blue and wispy grey, the color clearly visible even all the way across the auditorium. Her lips are heart shaped and full; her cheekbones are high in a distinct way that hints to Eastern European heritage; her brilliant white smile reveals dimples on either side of her mouth. She looks like a walking, living, breathing masterpiece, created with the upmost attention to detail.

What calls to me most, though, isn't the angelic beauty she emanates from without, serving as a beacon to a creature as dark and twisted as myself. It's her eyes. They're bright, shining, and exulted as she performs, but there's a weight behind them that catches my interest. As blonde and bright as she might appear, everything within me knows that I'm staring at a fellow tortured soul.

For the briefest moment, her eyes flick over mine. There's no way she could possibly see me through the stage lights blinding her, but the jolt that goes through my entire system at that one look is enough to tell me that I'm not just observing a fascinating being; I've found my muse.

Following the thought, a chilling calm flows through me, one that startles me intensely because I'm never calm. As much as I try to release the ball of tension that lives, ever-expanding within me, I can never fully succeed—I'm always restless unless I'm exhausting myself with work. Now, though, it feels like I've found a sliver of nirvana in the world. The tension inside me subsides as I watch her dance, and I release a soft breath of laughter, because as hesitant as I was to come here tonight—Carson had to call in a favor for me to agree, and I had every intention of making him miserable regardless—the evening is turning out more fortuitous than I imagined.

I take my phone out of the pocket of my pants, pulling up the camera and starting a video as I zoom the frame closer to the stage. I know any images I pull from the video will probably end up blurry and unsatisfactory, but I intend to convince my muse—whoever she is—to pose for me in real-time, so that won't be a problem. The only reason I take a video is out of curiosity as to whether or not I'll feel the same pull I do now later tonight, when my muse is no longer directly in front of me. And, of course, because her dancing is like nothing I've ever seen—something everyone else in attendance seems to be in agreement with. It'll be interesting to slow the footage down and watch her technique frame by frame. Pocketing my phone after I have a thirty second clip, I return my full attention to the show.

Ballet is a beautiful art; graceful, lithe, precise, and requiring endless amounts of self-discipline. Contemporary dancing, on the other hand, is more often than not a ridiculous spectacle of limbs and flesh. That's why I'm in no way a fan of Greywood University's dance program; it strays from tradition and classic, devolving into chaos and unruliness.

The way this girl dances, however, makes me rethink my opinion. While much of this performance takes sequences from the choreography of the original Sleeping Beauty ballet, there are also more modern dance styles and variations incorporated, and my muse fluctuates between the two flawlessly.

The storyline is quite different from the original ballet; along with Aurora being faceless in her first several dances, the prince charming grows up to be the palace gardener, the evil fairy queen dies early on and is replaced by her vengeful son, and the timeline spans from gothic-era to modern day.

After Aurora's been cursed to eternal sleep by the evil queen's son and the prince-charming-gardener is immortalized by a good fairy so that he's alive to resurrect Aurora once it's time, the screen behind the stage announces that the timeline has skipped forward 100 years. Dancers dressed as Gen Z fill the space, taking selfies in front of the overgrown castle gate where Aurora is rumored to still sleep.

Then, the scene turns interesting; the evil queen's son watches over a sleeping Aurora, pining for her to wake up. He goes as far as to dance with her limp body and try to kiss her to awaken her. The aesthetic of a Dracula looking character carting around a blonde angel in a flowing white dress is darkly pleasing, and I know my muse is going to end up as the misplaced angel in some twisted, bloody paintings I'll create.

When the immortal-gardener-prince finally finds Aurora and kisses her, effectively awakening her, the evil queen's son has his minions take the prince out of sight so he can take credit and appear as a hero instead of the villain he truly is. He proceeds to drag Aurora off stage, despite her obvious protests and attempts to run. Watching my Little Muse wriggle and struggle, I feel a particularly unusual phenomenon occur; my cock starts to stiffen beneath the fabric of my dress pants, until it's pressing against the zipper painfully. It's not unusual because I'm impotent, it's unusual because arousal is always a conscious decision for me, not a subconscious bodily response. Several feelings wash over me in quick succession; surprise, indignance, irritation, followed by a burning need to know more.

I allow my gaze to flick to Carson for a moment, depriving myself of the sight of my muse in order to assess my friend. Obviously, I am not the only person she has an effect on, which serves as a cold consolation.

Carson's eyes are stuck to her, sharpened like a predator, and I can see he's every inch in hunt-down-and-fuck mode. For someone who goes through more condoms in a week than a prostitute does in a month, I must say, Carson looks particularly keen on this one. Usually, one of crook of his finger accompanied by the golden-boy smile has any girl in a mile radius throwing herself on his dick, so he doesn't often get locked onto a single target. The fact that the current target also happens to be my newly discovered muse does not go over well with me at all.

I don't particularly care if he fucks her; despite my hard-on, my interest isn't sexual, it's purely artistic, but the way Carson's looking at her is proprietary enough to raise my hackles. He doesn't look at conquests that way—it's too focused, too possessive. While I wouldn't give a shit if he decides to have her as his next one-night-stand, I would give a shit if his pursual of her interrupts my plans for her.

Already, three separate ideas for paintings and several sculptures with her as the star are starting to form in my mind, meaning I'm going to commandeer a good deal of her time once I've convinced her to pose for me, and Carson will not get between me and my art. He should know better, and if he doesn't, a motherfucker's about to get a painful reminder.

I kick his leg with my foot deliberately hard, and hiss, "If you want her, fuck her tonight and get her out of your system. After that, she's mine."

Carson's head turns towards me with eerie slowness, a dead ringer for Annabel from those killer-doll movies. When his eyes fixate on mine, they're gleaming with challenge, and I understand that I would've done better to keep my mouth shut.

My fuckup is confirmed when he mutters with deepening interest, "Is she, now?"

Carson knows me better than most, which means he should know damn well to back the hell down when it comes to getting between me and something I want. Right now, what I want is unfettered access to immortalize the breathtaking muse still dancing her heart out on stage with whatever medium strikes my fancy. If Carson is feeling difficult, he could viably get in the way of that, and I don't particularly want to have to kill the only person I consider a true friend in this world. I know from experience I'd get away with it, but the idea of harming Carson irrevocably leaves a sour taste in my mouth. Contrary to some opinions, I don't get violent unless it's necessary.

What's a way around this that wouldn't require first-degree murder? Letting my gaze run over Carson, I realize that all I need do is allow him to dig his own grave. Possessive look in his eyes or not, I have never known Carson to sleep with a girl more than once, and most don't appreciate feeling like they're just a warm hole.

Take away the challenge I've posed to him and his interest in the dancer—which always subsides once he's gotten a girl in bed—and I doubt he'll give her more than a day of his time, which might or might not leave my muse in need of comfort. Comfort that I will be most glad to provide.

I relax in my seat, allowing a small smile to play on my lips as I return my attention to the performance. It's nearing the end of the show, and I have a long night of plotting ahead of me. I watch my Little Muse as she dominates the stage, turning heads and probably breaking the hearts of every single audience member through the sheer power behind her movements. Yes, I think I'm going to spend ample time getting acquainted with my newest object of interest.

Things will fall into place; they always do when I have anything to say about it, and I certainly have something to say for spending some time with my vibrant Little Muse.

CHAPTER ONE

Eliana Pierce

A chorus of congratulations rings through the overcrowded dressing room, as every single person who's part of this dance program—and therefore a de facto member of the affiliated company, Greywood Dance Co.—has made their way back here to celebrate a successful performance night. Even those who weren't cast in the show have filed in for the unofficial dressing room afterparty. The small room is already bursting with costume racks and odd out props here and there, so squeezing an additional thirty people into a space meant for a dozen is just asking for claustrophobia problems.

The structure of the show that was just performed was very unusual—the entire thing was put together in the last four weeks, from casting to blocking to costumes to rehearsals, which meant absolute chaos for anyone who'd made it onto the cast list.

I shrink closer to April, the one friend I've made since coming to campus a month ago to attend the pre-year retreat for the dance program. Like me, she's here on a full-ride scholarship, which is a far cry from our ridiculously wealthy peers. She's also the only other freshman who made it into the cast, and with a significant role to boot. Ironically, my only friend played the evil queen whose goal was to put me in an eternal sleep.

April's absolutely stunning—somewhere in the vicinity of 5'7, a good four inches taller than me, she is *all* long limbs and sheer grace. With pin-straight black hair, golden skin, and gorgeous almond eyes that hint to her Asian heritage, my first impression upon meeting April was a healthy dose of apprehension—she's one of the best dancers in the company, and so gorgeous it's hard not to feel a bit ugly next to her. Then she took my hands in hers, told me that scholarship girls need to stick with each other, and asked if I'd be willing to work on techniques together. That was all the invitation I needed to glue myself to her side, and in the last weeks alone, she's already proven to be a true friend.

Aside from keeping the bitchier girls in the company—who don't like that two freshmen got roles in the first show of the season—in check, she's stuck by my side and isn't put off by my quirks. In short, I already adore her.

April threads her arm through mine, giving me a bright smile that's at total odds with her wicked queen makeup and costume. "We fucking killed it. I've heard dancers who do well in the first show are guaranteed to get recast throughout the season—we're gonna have offers from companies coming out of our asses by the end of the year."

When I first auditioned for the show, I had no expectations to even make it into the cast, as freshmen rarely make it into any productions. Evidently, some of my past performances in high school had already caught the eye of the ballet masters assigned to the dance department, so I made it into the second round of auditions before even meeting my instructors.

I have never felt fear in my life like I did when my name made it onto the cast list, as the leading role, no less. Primarily because—aside from this being the biggest role of my life with only four weeks to prepare—it made an enemy out of every girl in the dance program. Nobody's direct in their distaste of me, of course; it's all fake smiles and laughs in front of my face, but I know that I'll have to watch my back for the rest of the year.

"Did you see how many scouts were in the audience?" I ask April, trying to ignore the seven female glares boring into us, coming from varying points in the room.

"I saw one from New York City Ballet—this program isn't a joke," April responds. "Your pas de deux's with Sean were absolutely *golden*, I wouldn't be surprised if other schools try to steal you away now. You gotta promise you won't leave, though. I can't be the only scholarship girl among these bitches."

A startled laugh bursts out of me as I squeeze her arm in the crook of mine. I appreciate her praise on my individual ballet dances with my kind-of prince charming on stage. "I won't abandon ship, I promise. Completing Greywood's dance program opens up every stage in the world for a dancer; I'm not giving that up, even for School of American Ballet."

Besides, while ballet is my first love when it comes to dancing, it isn't my only. I love when directors and choreographers mix ballet with contemporary dance styles to make the stories we tell with our bodies more modern, beautiful, and accessible to the masses. Greywood's program, while boasting of some of the best ballet masters in the world, isn't *just* focused on ballet, which is why I ended up choosing this university.

Out of the corner of my eye I spot Andrew, who played the evil queen's son, make his way through the crowd of bodies, coming towards me and April. Knowing that he has a massive thing for April and not interested in getting stuck between their flirting, I tell April, "I'm gonna head to my dressing room and then back to the dorms for the night—I'll catch you on Monday?"

She smiles, untwining our arms and squeezing my shoulder. "You're lucky the star gets an entire room to herself, babe. Go on, I'll be wallowing in overcrowded misery here with the rest of the plebians."

With a laugh, I thread my way through the crowd and manage to only get pulled into a fake congratulatory hug twice before finding the door.

As soon as I step out into the hallway, I nearly collide with a member of stage crew—a sophomore technician who grabs my arm to steady me before flashing me a smile. "You were amazing out there, Elia. One of the patrons—son of some big shot, goes to our school—was asking Mr. Sanders about you."

I tense. I've been in the limelight on and off since discovering my ardor for dancing before I'd hit double digits. My mother was so excited to have a talented daughter—one she could hide her own failures behind—that she spared no effort in pushing me towards a career of dancing. Once I picked up traction in local studios, I started attending dance competitions and getting cast in ballets, and from there, my entire life became focused on my art.

To my mother, it was her way to stardom; to me, it was an escape. It still is. The unfortunate part of being an ambitious dancer is it tends to attract attention of stuck-up snobs who make sport out of fucking their way through dance teams and companies. To say I'm not in the mood to deal with that after sixteen hours of rehearsal followed by the biggest performance of my life would be an understatement.

Sensing this, the crew member says with a chuckle, "Don't worry, Sanders sent your admirer off. The coast is clear."

With a breath of relief and murmured thank you, I make my way to my dressing room. Though the space is small, it belongs solely to the star, which is a slice of heaven after being surrounded by bodies. I make short work out of changing into street clothes, grab my hardback copy of *Pet Sematary* from where it lies next to a bag of makeup on the vanity counter, and take a seat in a rickety rolling chair, resolved to read until the theatre is emptied of people and the coast is clear for me to sneak out unnoticed.

People like April *live* for the attention that comes with performing—for me, it's my least favorite part. While I love telling stories with nothing but movement, I don't love all the scrutiny that comes from doing so successfully. Ergo, I use every trick I can to avoid the worst of it.

Half an hour later, I've made good headway in my dozenth reread of this book, and the sounds of footsteps in the hall have died out, telling me that just about everyone's gone and it's my turn to go home. I pick up my cross-body, *very* old dance bag, draping it over my shoulder as I walk to the entrance, flick off the light, and swing open the door to the room. With my nose still buried in my book, I don't realize there's someone standing *right there*, and find myself crashing face-first into a rock-hard chest.

Several things happen at once. My book falls out of my hand, landing on the floor with a distinct crack. I tumble backwards, clutching at air and panicking that my career will be over before it's even begun with a single ill-fated fall. A strong hand grips my wrist and pulls me into the same chest that sent me tumbling in the first place. Because

I'm startled and it's late and the theatre should be empty, I shriek as I practically throw myself away from the stranger and into the nearest wall, gasping while trying to calm my racing heart.

Warily, I glance at the guy that just nearly gave me a heart attack, and my breath gets caught in my throat. Everything about him is golden, shiny, and polished; from the crown of lush golden hair that decorates his head, to the glittering blue eyes fixed on me, and down to the obscenely expensive-looking charcoal grey suit he wears. For a second, I feel like I'm staring at a sun god, about to be blinded.

Then, I remember that just because privilege wears a nice suit and looks pretty doesn't make it anything other than a ball of privilege. And this guy *reeks* of privilege. He also nearly took ten years off my life.

"Excuse me," I snap, glaring at Golden Boy, "but what the *fuck* is your problem?"

Eyebrows slightly darker than his hair inch up. "Pardon?" He looks genuinely surprised.

"You could've taken me out, standing there like a creep!" I say, aware that my voice is rising until it's close to a shriek. "What the hell were you thinking?"

I bend down to snatch my book from the ground, only to have it plucked from my hands by the dude that is now asking for a slap to the face—*nobody* messes with my books and walks away unscathed.

"I was thinking that I needed to see the girl who captivated hundreds of people every time she stepped on stage, and now I'm thinking that I can't believe a girl who looks like you had her nose stuck in a Stephen King book."

That raises my hackles. I know I'm not ugly; I spent my entire childhood on rigorous diets planned by my mother that landed me in the hospital from exhaustion several times. I've spent the last many years honing my body by dancing at least six hours a day, from the time I could walk, and not being allowed to eat any more calories than I'd burn. Having a nice body does not, in any way shape or form, indicate a person's reading abilities.

The fact that this asshole just said he can't believe a girl who looks like me reads good literature honestly makes me want to sucker punch him. The only problem there is that he's a good foot taller than me, has around a hundred pounds on me, and could probably crush me like a grape.

That realization makes me acutely aware that it's around midnight, and I'm stuck alone in a hallway with this guy. That might not be the safest scenario. Despite what I've said and my dislike of the perfume of wealth that clouds him, I don't get creepy vibes from him, which bodes well.

I extend my hand in front of me, ready to be done with this and get out of here. "Give me my book."

Gleaming blue eyes lift from the novel and lock on mine. "What will I get in return?"

I let out a puff of astonished laughter. Is he actually *propositioning* me? "You know what? Keep it. I'll get another."

I most certainly *won't* get another, because every spare penny I have goes towards school and dance supplies. My savings from working as a ballet instructor for children over the last several summers are just enough to cover what I'll need for my time in college—I don't have room in my budget for indulgences.

Feeling resentful that my urge to get out of here is strong enough to part with a treasured book from one of my favorite authors, I turn and stomp down the hall, ignoring Golden Boy and everything he represents—mainly, someone who could easily buy his own book because his parents spare him no expense, while my dad fucked off when I was a toddler and my mom spent the child support he sent monthly on herself for *years* before having the good grace to drop dead. Right now, the very concept of this male offends me. *I guess I'll be putting my university library card to use sooner than expected.*

Golden Boy catches up to me before I can make it halfway down the hall, falling into step beside me.

"I've offended you," he observes calmly.

Angry and exhausted, I stop in my tracks and whirl on him, shoving my finger in his chest. "You won't give me my book. That puts you at the top of my shitlist. So, unless you want to see what happens when a dancer gets mad, kindly *fuck off.*"

Chapter Two

Elia

"I'd *love* to see what it's like when you get mad," he responds instantly, taking a step towards me. "I have a feeling it'll be even more passionate than your dancing."

"Ugh!" Seeing that reacting won't get me anywhere with him, I continue forward, ignoring him as best as I'm able to even while he follows me through the darkened theatre and towards the exit.

"I'll give your book back if you agree to go out with me," he says suddenly, as we're approaching the front door.

I pause in reaching for the handle, casting this stranger that has more nerve than anyone I've ever met an amazed glance. The fact that he'd even *say* that...

I say with a saccharine smile, "I'm sorry, but I don't go out with strangers that accost me outside my dressing room after a performance, steal my book, and then follow me around like a damn stalker.

Whoever you are, you look like you'd get any girl you want with one of those crooked smiles—go find them, because I'm *not* interested."

He blinks several times, appearing lost for words, his grip on *my* book tightens until his knuckles turn white, and I have to say, seeing the golden boy charm drain away—making room for confusion and anger at being denied—is immensely satisfying.

"My name is Carson Ajax. I'm a Junior at Greywood, business major." He offers me another grin. "Why don't you tell me your name, so we can get past the strangers phase and to the good stuff."

"Tempting as that sounds, Ajax, I'd rather stay strangers. The fact that you were waiting for me outside my dressing room without even knowing my name..." I trail off, shaking my head with astonishment. He must lead quite a charmed life.

"I didn't say I didn't know your name, I said why don't you tell me your name. That's the formality when two strangers are getting acquainted, right, Pierce?"

Hearing him call me by my last name jogs my memory of what the stage crewman told me earlier. "Are you the guy that was bothering Sanders about me?"

Carson scrunches his face. "I wasn't *bothering* the director, I was *asking* about the most talented dancer I've ever seen. If anyone else's parents donated as much as my father does here, believe me, they'd have been backstage asking about you too."

The strange compliment is wrapped in a reminder that Carson Ajax is the characterization of the sort of people I dislike most: the 1% that considers themselves better than the rest of the world simply because they're rich.

"I'm not sorry to tell you, bits and pieces from others are all you'll ever hear about me, because I have zero intention of getting stuck with you again. For the love of god, please, let me walk home in peace."

His head cocks to the side. "Walk? Home? If you mean back to dorms on campus, I'll have to insist otherwise. It's late, and if I remember correctly dance dorms are over two miles away from here. I'll drive you."

I snort. "I'll risk the dark."

I swing open the heavy glass door that serves as the entrance to the theatre, but before I can step out, slender fingers curl around my bicep, staying me. Carson's grip is cool, strong, and radiates with such authority, I instinctively freeze.

"You're not walking back to campus," he informs me flatly. When I turn my head towards him and open my mouth to tell him that yes the hell I am, he puts a finger to my lips. "You're tiny, unarmed, and practically a glowing target for a late-night mugging, or worse. Your performance tonight has proven that you're also the best our school's company has to boast of, which means I'm honor-bound to make sure our star doesn't end up as a statistic. I don't give a shit what you think about me, I am taking you home. I'll even give your book back as consolation. Now, will you comply, or do I need to drag you like a naughty child? Hint: naughty girls get punished."

I swallow, the sound of my throat clicking audible, feeling myself wobble from the power he radiates which, coupled with his innuendo, sends heat scorching up my cheeks and neck.

The truth of the matter is that I have absolutely no interest in walking home; if it wasn't so late that public transport's closed for the night, I'd have taken the bus. And although everything I've seen so far of Carson makes me detest him, sharing a car compartment with him for five minutes in exchange for my book *and* a safe way back to dorms is just the smart thing to do. Granted, I won't be safe from him, but I'm not terribly worried he'll try anything, even with his teasing punishment comment.

Carson's told me his name, and I recognize his last name from some news stories about an oil tycoon. My director knows he was looking for me, so if Carson decides to murder me in a ditch somewhere, he'd be caught, and Golden Boy doesn't strike me as the kind of person to leave any evidence behind if he commits a crime. I can sense his interest in me, but I don't sense any malice.

Squaring my shoulders, I say, "Fine. But if you're a serial killer, I'll have you know that there's video evidence of us leaving together, and my director knows you were asking about me earlier. So at least I'd spend my afterlife happy knowing you were in prison, wearing a horrendous orange jumpsuit and eating slop for the rest of your life."

Carson stares at me for a moment, before throwing his head back and roaring with laughter. The sound is loud, carefree, and surprisingly mirthful—so much so I almost want to smile in return. Almost, but not quite.

"You're really something else, Princess, aren't you?" he asks me, releasing my arm to wipe a tear from his eye.

I scowl. "Don't call me that."

He grins. "Why not? I think it's appropriate, considering the first time I saw you, you were enthralling hundreds of people playing the role of an infamous princess."

"I danced the part of a mythological princess for a few hours—that does not make me one." I cross my arms over my chest, tapping my foot. "It's late and I'm tired, so either kill me or take me to the dorms, dude."

I don't mention the fact that my feet are *killing* me after tonight, and I'll happily spend the next hour with my legs in an ice bath. Another reason to take a ride—even from this asshole—rather than put myself through *more* pain.

"Sure thing, *Princess*," Carson taunts, opening the door for me in a poor imitation of a gentlemanly move.

I cast him a wary glance as I step through the doorway and into the chilly Vermont evening. Fall has just started, and in this part of the states, that means nights get *cold*. I'm only wearing an old hoodie over leggings to protect myself from the chill, which isn't much good against the wind.

Teeth chattering, I clutch my bag as I follow Carson in the direction of the theatre's parking lot. When he stops in front of a sleek blue Tesla, I have to stop myself from snorting because I should've figured the rich golden boy drives the golden standard of luxury cars. Instead, I snap a photo of the license plate with my cell and shoot it off in a text to April, along with instructions to send this to the police if I turn up dead tomorrow.

"Are you seriously texting someone a picture of my license plate? If you're that worried I'm going to kill you, why accept the ride?" Carson asks with a half-smile, guiding me to the passenger side door with a hand on the small of my back.

"You have my book and, like I've said, I'm tired," I respond, watching as he finds the handle hidden in the smooth door.

I startle as it opens upward rather than outward, jumping back and accidentally pressing my back against his chest. His hands catch my waist to steady me, and I feel the distinct bulge of his erection pressing into my lower back. My cheeks flame, hidden by the darkness, but something strange also happens—I feel heat pool low in my belly. Maybe it's because I haven't had sex since dumping my ex at the end of senior year, or because sex with him was never really that appetizing anyways, but I'm suddenly scorching hot despite the crisp breeze.

I throw myself into the passenger seat to get away from the feeling, because *no fucking way* is the first guy who manages to turn me on in months going to be a trust fund brat. I respect myself too much for that.

"Careful there," Carson says, watching with amusement as I scramble to orient myself on the cool leather.

The car is more ostentatious than any vehicle I've ever ridden in, and I kind of feel like I'm sullying the fine interior just by being here. Carson doesn't seem to mind, though, as he shuts my door for me and rounds the car, sliding into the driver's side. When I reach for my book, he drops it in his lap with a sly smile. "You'll have to wait until we're there for the prize."

He turns on the car, making a huge center screen to the right of the steering wheel light up, and then quickly turns on the heating before peeling out of the parking lot. He doesn't ask for directions, but I don't expect him to, since it's common knowledge where all the program dormitories are.

Greywood doesn't just specialize in its dance program—it offers several other prestigious programs that give students a chance to work in their chosen profession while attending college, so that they can launch their careers as they learn.

"Is Pet Sematary your favorite Stephen King book?" Carson asks out of the blue.

I glance at him out of the corner of my eye. "One of them," I say vaguely. If pretty boy's going to try to start small talk, he'll have to do better than that.

He nods, not taking his eyes off the road. "Did you know King sat on it for four years before releasing it?"

Is that all he's got? If he's trying to convince me he's a Stephen King fan, he'll have to do better. "Yeah. He based the book on a road he lived near for a while, where a lot of animals lives got taken by speeding trucks. Kings' daughter's cat actually died that way. His son almost got hit, too. So, when King wrote the book, the theory is he felt like it was too close to reality and macabre to publish."

"The speculation is he published it to get out of a shitty publishing contract he'd signed when he was younger," Carson finishes, nodding.

This time, I don't glance at him out of the corner of my eye—I face him full on. Anyone who'd watched the movie Pet Sematary could know the fun fact that King held off on releasing the book, but only a true fan would know the details that Carson just spewed. *So, the pretty face and trust fund might also have a brain.* If I had time to spare, that unusuality might interest me.

Carson turns the car off the highway and pulls up to the campus gates, which automatically open as a hidden camera somewhere recognizes the university pass hanging from the car's rearview mirror.

Before I can think it through, I ask, "What's your favorite of his?"

"Children of the Corn," he responds instantly. "Or Carrie."

I tilt my head to the side, considering him. "Why?"

Carson shrugs. "Children of the Corn just goes to show how King can weave such a deep, thrilling tale in a few dozen pages. As for Carrie, what better horror characterization is there of the classic high school experience? Everyone strives for acceptance, and it's almost always dependent on circumstances outside of our control whether or not we achieve it."

Carson pulls up by the curb in front of the program dormitory building. It's a large, twelve-story structure, as it houses students from all of Greywood's programs. It also gives each student an individual, albeit tiny, room.

"I'm pretty sure I technically have an allotted apartment somewhere in there," Carson says, tipping his head at the building.

I raise my eyebrows at him. "You're a program student? I thought you said you were a business major."

He smiles. "Aren't they the same thing? I'm in the business program, which technically makes me a business major. I spend work hours at one of my dad's company buildings in the city."

The reminder of his privilege serves as a cold splash on what would've otherwise turned into a surprisingly pleasant ride. I give Carson an icy, tight-lipped smile as I hold out my hand expectantly.

Seeming endlessly amused, he makes a show of picking up the book from his lap, examining the cover for good measure, and finally handing it to me. When I move to take it from his hand, he tightens his grip. "I want to see you again."

I snort. "And I want a stack of gold bars so I can build a pyramid and see if I can summon some aliens. We can't all get what we want, dude."

"I *will* be seeing you again, Princess," Carson clarifies. "I'm offering you the courtesy of choosing the time and place. Otherwise, who knows when I might show up?"

"My vote is for *never*," I snap, retrieving my book with one hard yank, opening the car door, and slipping out.

Not giving Carson a chance to speak again, I offer him a half-hearted wave, slamming the car door shut and turning towards the entrance of the building. Before I can make it to the door, the car window rolls down, and Carson calls out, "I guess I'll figure out the when and where, then. I'll be seeing you around, Princess." With that, he drives off, leaving me with a hanging jaw and boggled mind.

Chapter Three

Despite being so exhausted from the last four weeks that I'm ready to sleep for the next year, the afternoon after the first show of the season, I drag my ass out of bed and take a bus into the city.

I've been wanting to explore the city near my university since getting here a month ago, but I've had absolutely no free time since getting cast as Aurora, so this is my first chance to really familiarize myself with my home city for the next four years. I asked April if she wanted to come with me, but she informed me she planned to stay in bed for the next forty-eight hours, only coming out to use the bathroom and get food, and maybe to wander the campus later. I'd probably be doing the same things if there wasn't a museum I've been keen on checking out in the city; *everything* aches as I step off the moderately-crowded bus and onto the sidewalk. My entire body is sore in the way it only gets after a hectic, brief rehearsal period leading up to a performance.

Still, I stifle my wince as I trot across the street and up to one of the most notable museums in the area. Growing up in ballet, pain was a regular companion; ballet masters are cruel and pitiless in the way they drill their ballerinas. Bleeding feet are a common occurrence after a long day of pointe, as are bruised and battered bodies from particularly brutal rehearsals or the occasional tumble. If there's one thing that can't be denied about dancers—ballerinas in particular—it's that they know how to push through *serious* pain, so some soreness won't stop me from checking out a local museum that's home to several impressive displays.

The building is large, with faux marble pillars holding up a courtyard roof in front of it, and a grand double doorway that marks the entrance. Round stone tables are sporadically placed around the courtyard, all of them having already attracted crowds of people enjoying the sunny day.

Another perk of going to the best university in the state; my university ID grants me access to most museums, libraries, and theatres in the area for free. Greywood is affiliated with several artistic centers, so students receive enviable privileges—and I don't have to scrounge up twelve dollars for a ticket.

I follow the crowd of people through the doors and into the entrance hall of the museum, feeling my mood brighten at the beauty that surrounds me. The room is large and bright, decorated with tones of beige and cream. Stone benches litter the polished floor, and a velvet rope marks off the line for the ticket booth on the far-left side of the room. On the right of the room is a café, which I cast a single longing glance at before reminding myself that I can't afford to get a coffee no matter how much I crave one and joining the line of people waiting to buy a ticket.

I scroll through my school schedule on my phone as I wait in the queue, trying to figure out if there are any gaps in my classes and dance company times where I could squeeze in teaching a few classes. There are plenty of dance studios for youth in the area, and I've heard from April that they're happy to pay Greywood dance program students to teach some children's classes. Especially if those students have already made it onto school cast lists, meaning they're the real deal.

Finally reaching the front of the line, I hand my school I.D. badge over to the salesman through an opening in the opaque window that separates us, and he hands it back along with a wristband and map of the museum. They have a particularly enticing Renaissance collection on the second floor, which is where I decide to start.

The Renaissance wing is made up of several interconnected rooms with polished wooden flooring, walls, and light fixtures. Lights shine above and below each painting, statue, and figurine. Each of these pieces were created at the hands of some of the most talented artists to grace the earth in the last millennium.

I take my time examining each work, reading the plaques that explain the artists and origin of the items, appreciating the intricacy and beauty of every single work. As I'm examining a sketch of Michelangelo's depicting the overly muscled torso of a man, a deep voice from beside me says, "Michelangelo drew that when he was learning to sculpt at the Medici gardens in Florence. He taught himself about the human form by studying dissected corpses to better understand our muscular structure."

A chill raises the hairs on the back of my neck as I turn my head in the direction of the smoky, rough voice edged with an undefinable darkness. Two hazel eyes meet mine, belonging to one of the most intimidating people I've ever encountered. Everything about him is overwhelming, and too much—too much muscle packed onto his body, straining the material of his grey cashmere sweater, too much intensity in those endless eyes, too much *power* attached to a single being. It feels like all the air's been sucked out of the room around me.

I understand exactly what deer in headlights experience now. The primal knowledge that they're in life-threatening danger which causes them to instinctually freeze rather than do the smart thing and run. I don't know *who* the man staring at me like I'm his next meal is, but I do know that the weight of that gaze is not something I'm cool with shouldering.

Also, were his first words to me really talking about an artist dissecting corpses? If his demeanor didn't already advertise *walking red flag*, that would.

And yet, as I look over him, I have to admit there's something… compelling, for lack of a better word, about this man. He looks college age—the Greywood I.D. hanging out of the pocket of his slacks confirms it—but something makes it difficult to look away from him. Maybe it's the common sense of not turning my back to an obvious threat, but there's also an intrigue that keeps me glued to my spot instead of getting the hell out of here.

I clear my throat, trying to reach for enough composure to string together a sentence. "Dissection of corpses was common during the Renaissance—probably because the lines that previously distinguished art, science, and religion started to blur during the time. DaVinci dissected corpses as well, if I remember correctly. But he wanted to understand the machinery that gave us life from a scientific standpoint, whereas Michelangelo seemed to believe that God made us as we were and wanted to capture God's creation with as much truth as possible." If at all possible, the man's eyes sharpen on me even more, and my nerves kick into overdrive, causing me to babble aimlessly.

"I once read that Michelangelo believed marble was God's best creation, second only to man. A lot of his art is centered on God and the bible, which historians believe is due to him attending the local

Florentine priest's—Savonarola's—sermons when he was young. His interest in human anatomy was in a bid to better understand divinity. Da Vinci was more scientifically inclined, though, and his religious beliefs are still a source of debate."

At the end of my rant that's essentially a collection of random facts I've collected in my lifetime of being an art nerd, I glance around to see if anyone else had the misfortune to witness me make a fool of myself. Thankfully, everyone in this wing seems to be too focused on the art to pay others much attention, so I only have an audience of one for my embarrassment.

"You know the Renaissance." The stranger says the sentence like he's discovered a mythical unicorn.

He still hasn't blinked or looked away from me in the entire time since he first spoke, which is more than a little unnerving. It's also difficult not to stare back, because his eyes are bottomless and have too many colors to count. Browns ranging from mocha to chestnut, greens ranging from forest to emerald, and even flecks of grey sprinkled through. More than their uniqueness, I feel like his eyes are drilling a path into my soul, which is *not* a pleasant sensation.

"Well... yeah," I say simply. The Renaissance gave birth to one of my favorite dance forms; of course I've made a point of studying it. Not to mention the fact that art history has always been a passion of mine; if I didn't dance, it'd be my main focus. As is, I still intend to study it this year, even though that means my schedule will be unimaginably busy.

The stranger's eyes finally peel themselves off of mine, only to slowly travel down my body, millimeter by millimeter. His attention is like a physical force—it honestly feels like phantom fingers are following the path of his gaze as it travels over me, sending a shiver down my spine. His eyes linger on my neck, breasts, waist, and legs, as if he's committing them to memory. Getting eye fucked so blatantly in public makes me feel more than a little dirty.

Still, I take the opportunity to study him back. Last night, Carson was like the personification of the sun. Whoever *this* is, he is the personification of a luminous moon in an eternally dark sky. His skin is so fair it almost borders on vampiric, yet it glows in a way that leaves no doubt he is alive. His hair is dark, just like his eyebrows and eyelashes. His cheekbones are pronounced, and his jawline is so sharp it could cut diamonds. Everything about him is elegant, gorgeous, and perfectly proportioned; that's exactly what makes him too much. That sort of perfection confined to one being is intimidating, especially when it's shrouded with darkness.

Finally locking his eyes back on mine, he tells me, "I was in attendance of Sleeping Beauty last night. You're the best dancer I've ever seen."

Well, *that* came straight out of left field. Through a solid decade of dancing on stage, I've never found myself in a situation of being approached by audience members twice in a twenty-four-hour period. Usually, the cast talks to any enthusiastic patrons in a designated time slot after the performance; dancers on my level don't get sought out beyond that.

I blink slowly at him. "And you noticed me in the museum and thought... hey, let me tell this dancer about how the artist who's sketch she's examining would dissect corpses? Are you *trying* to scare me off?"

He responds, "You're not scared, though, even though you know you probably should be. I like that."

I nod my head sagely. "If I were trying to lure in unsuspecting victims, I'd like it if they presented themselves as horribly naïve, too.

On that note, I'm going to do the opposite of every dumb girl that gets killed in the movie first and walk away from the danger."

I turn to walk towards the next piece I haven't studied yet, a sculpture held in a glass case; the guy follows me step for step. As I'm not willing to let him crash my enjoyable day at the museum, I ignore him while I examine the plaque beside the sculpture.

"Carson told me you were funny, but I didn't believe him," my new shadow comments from beside me. As the meaning behind his words, that he's spoken to *Carson* about me, dawns, I whip my head around to stare at him.

Chapter Four

"You know the tool that gave me a ride home?" I demand. It makes sense; they both have an almost aristocratic wealth about them. Whereas Carson's was glaring and in your face, this guy is more understated, but there's no denying from his clothes, shoes, or watch that he's well off.

"If he was a tool, why did you get in his car?" he responds coolly.

I let out a quiet groan, stifling the urge to bang my head against the nearest wall. "I got in your friends car because it was cold, late, and he was holding my book hostage. Also, if he wanted to kill me, he wouldn't have left video evidence of us exiting the theatre together, which I reminded him of."

"He could've hurt you instead of killing you. He's rich enough to get away with it. Did you consider that before getting in a stranger's car?"

Okay, now I'm *really* pissed. A random guy who happens to go to the same university as me does not get to judge me on my life decisions. I've been around enough shady men to pick up on when they want something from me that I'm not willing to give, and that wasn't the vibe I got from Carson. He was interested in convincing me to give myself to him; not in taking me regardless of my sentiments. I know the difference.

Instead of giving this male any more of my attention, I pop my headphones into my ears and turn on a classical playlist to drown out this asshole so I can enjoy my time. Despite no longer being able to hear his patronizing bullshit, I feel his presence, which stays no more than five feet from me as I move from room to room. My shadow doesn't attempt to interrupt me or strike up conversation again, seeming content to hover in proximity while I go about my business. I don't waste time telling him to go away; if ignoring him isn't getting the message across, saying it won't make a difference. He seems like the type to thrive on reactions, so reacting to his presence would get me nowhere, fast.

He must follow me for the better part of two hours as I go from floor to floor in the museum, all while pointedly ignoring him. What surprises me is how comfortable the silence is, coupled with the fact that if he hadn't been a jerk, I don't think I'd mind walking around a museum with him for company, whoever he is. As jarring as his presence is at first, after a time it becomes almost soothing. Not because anything about him is comforting, but because I know without a doubt that he is the greatest potential threat in my proximity, yet nothing about his demeanor is threatening towards *me*. Intimidating, without a doubt, but not threatening.

Growing up in ballet teaches a person the value of body language; dancers understand better than all that nonverbal communication is often the most telling, and everything about this guy's body language and demeanor tells me that while he's obviously focused on me, it is not in a malicious way.

Still, that doesn't put me at ease, since a threat is a threat regardless of which direction it's aimed. So, when the aches in my feet become too much to bear and I know I'm due for an ice bath, I head straight for the entrance of the museum, hoping that my shadow will get the hint and fuck off.

He doesn't. As soon as we reach the first floor, he has the audacity to pull one of my headphones out. I stop dead in my tracks and snatch the earpiece from him, nearly ripping the cord in my haste because who the hell *does* that?

Before I can tell him where he can shove his bullshit, he says, "Let me buy you a coffee."

I blink, feeling like I'm in some weird imitation of groundhog day. I was just shooting down an overprivileged asshole last night; do I really have to do it again *already*? Shouldn't there be a limit on how often I have to go through crap like that in twenty-four hours?

I say flatly, "No."

He doesn't miss a beat. "Lunch?"

"What kind of person asks someone out when they don't even know their name? Do you have no manners whatsoever?" I snap.

He observes calmly, "I didn't get the chance. I thought it'd be polite to let you listen to your music and enjoy the art. Now that you're done, though, I'm taking my chance."

It looks like I have to spell things out here. "Let me make this abundantly clear so we have no misunderstandings; there is no chance for anything here."

He nods once. "I thought so, too. Watching you dance last night, I did intend to track you down on campus at some point—but only to ask you to pose for a painting or two." He pauses, assessing my reaction, which I imagine is startled. My first impression of him was more so someone who skins cats in their spare time rather than paints.

Or figures out how to destroy the world—I could see either with him. When I don't say anything, he goes on, "Then I saw you again here, but this time, I actually saw *you*, not just the dancer. It was fascinating. Of course, I want to know more. So, lunch?"

I throw my hands up beside me, exasperated beyond belief. "What *is* it with guys like you? Is getting turned down so unbelievable—"

My words are cut off when, quick as a striking serpent, his arm snakes around my waist and yanks me directly into his chest. If I thought I felt like a deer in headlights earlier, now I'm the deer that the hunter has his gun locked onto. The shift from casual—albeit deeply strange—conversation to swift, almost blurring action is discombobulating.

"Let me stop you right there," he tells me in the softest voice, reaching up with his free hand to tuck a strand of loose hair behind my ear, like a lover would. "There are no guys like me. Believe me when I say, I am one of a kind, and that is because I don't have a single kind. You are, too—I see that now. Last night, I thought you were the best of your kind—dancers—but now it's clear that while you might be the best contemporary dance has to offer, a dancer isn't the only thing you are. Is it?"

His voice remains soft, almost hypnotic, lulling me in and inviting me to agree. If I hadn't already dealt with some serious Machiavellian bullshit in my life, I might fall into his well-spoken trap like a fly gets tangled in a spider's web. As is, while I can't deny that his strange, almost psychotic charm affects me, it doesn't control me.

The scary thing is, I think it would control others. Those eyes, that face, that voice... I think whoever this man is, he could convince a priest to commit murder with nothing more than a few murmurs in his ear. People with such a potent ability to affect those around them are dangerous. And while some small part of me would like to crawl into this strange, magnetic creature's mind and dissect it, the rest of me knows that would be like pulling the pin on a grenade. I happen to like myself in one piece, thank you very much.

"To answer your question, my name is Seth. Seth Balor."

The abrupt change in topic gives me whiplash, and it takes a moment for me to catch up with his brand of crazy. "I asked your name?"

"Implied it by pointing out that you didn't know my name," he tells me. "Now, as I've been a good boy and kept my mouth shut and hands to myself for the last hours—which, by the way, was a herculean task of impressive proportion—why don't you tell me yours?"

His eyes flick down to my lips when I pull my bottom one between my teeth in contemplation. Giving him my name would be accepting whatever's going on here, but not doing so would only prolong it. If there is one thing I've learned in life, it's that sometimes the path of least resistance is the best way to sustain less damage in tricky situations.

Despite his intensity, I don't think Seth will hurt me. There is something very different about him—something that makes me suspect his mind doesn't function the way the rest of ours do. The way he described himself earlier—as being one of a kind because he doesn't have a single kind—is very interesting. The weight to his eyes, his strange sense of social situations and human interaction, everything about him tells me that he's distinguished from the rest of society. While that makes him fascinating, it also makes him comparable to a thunderstorm; beautiful, fierce, and potentially deadly.

I say slowly, "I don't think that would be a very good idea."

"Lunch? Or telling me your name? I already know it—I was at the show last night, remember?—but I figure that's part of the usual social repertoire between two new friends."

"Friends?" I echo faintly. This man is dizzying. Everything with him, including the lightning switches in topics, happen too quickly. "Are you sure you're one of a kind? Both you and Carson seem to have a propensity for being very forward."

Seth's eyes narrow slightly, and I'm fascinated as I watch the green in those orbs flare, until they appear more emerald than hazel. "I think the fact that you managed to snag both of our attention so swiftly is a testament to you being one of a kind. Now, tell me your name, and we can decide where you'd like to eat."

I'm starting to figure out that the only way to keep up with him would be to match his bluntness and sporadic form of conversation. "My name is Eliana Pierce, though you admit you already know that. As for where I'd like to eat, I've heard Parisian cuisine is delectable, but the odds of me tasting it are about as high as me going out with you. Take your pick from my dance company for girls you want to pose for paintings—it's a surprisingly common request—but rest assured it won't be me. Have a nice day, Seth."

With that, I twirl out of his hold in a practiced ballet move that's too quick for even him to stop, and continue on my way to the exit. This time, he doesn't follow. I won't deny that there might be a sliver of disappointment over that fact, but the more overwhelming feeling is that I just narrowly escaped a trap of some sort.

CHAPTER FIVE

I make it back to campus within the next hours, but instead of heading back to my dorm, I resolve to familiarize myself with the general layout of Greywood University. Despite already having been here for a month, I only know the arts area in the southwest corner of campus, home to the art-inclined departments and programs. Since I received my finalized school schedule this morning, I decide it'd be best to get an idea of how much sprinting I'll need to do between classes while trying to maintain a *very* ambitious schedule.

Greywood's dance program alone requires students to dance for six to eight hours a day, five days a week, and on top of that, I'm vying to get a bachelor's in art history at the end of my four years here—which means I'm in classes from six in the morning until four in the afternoon from Monday to Friday. That doesn't include evening rehearsals I'll inevitably end up in if I get any more parts in future shows—which, as April speculates, is all but a guarantee.

I had my guidance counselor squeeze everything academic together before 5pm so I could have time to teach classes and earn some extra income in the evenings, when I'm not in rehearsal. Completing the rigorous dance company requirements on top of an art history degree is going to be grueling, and I have no doubt I'll be ready to die at the end of each day, but it'll be worth it.

Getting a scholarship in both dance and art history was my condition for coming to Greywood over my other top choices, and while I didn't expect the university to accept, my high school guidance counselor was a friend and absolute bulldog in negotiations. Since I left her with several shiny medals attributed to my old school, she gave me a lot of help with college applications and making the decision that favored both of my passions, dancing *and* art history. I can't create art beyond dance, but I'm drawn to it on a level that transcends aesthetic appeal or objective attraction. To me, art—especially the older historical pieces—are living, breathing creations to be studied, learned, and revered. If dancing doesn't work out, I'd happily work in a museum.

I use the campus's dance building, known to most as dance headquarters, as the starting point for my self-guided tour. Armed with my schedule pulled up on my phone and campus map clutched in my hand, I sit at one of the wooden tables in the courtyard behind the dance building to map out the best routes so I can make it to all my classes on time. The dance building itself is a state-of-the-art facility, three stories high, that's home to the university's auditorium along with all of the studio spaces used for classes. Dancers are also required to take core gen ed courses, a dance history course, and a language course along with their physical classes. All of those additional courses, save for the language, are taken online and at a dancer's leisure, though we still need to get good grades to stay in the company.

I'll be spending the first half of every weekday here, from 6am-12pm, doing everything from bar work to blocking to rehearsal. The company puts on productions continuously throughout the year, so there will always be a show to prepare for along with rigorous sessions to iron out the finer points of each dancer's technique.

After six hours of dance, I'll have half an hour to shower and haul my ass either a mile to my art classes or two miles to my English classes. As a bonus, twice a week I'll have to find my way to a museum ten miles away for some course-required volunteer work. At least being in the city twice a week will give me the opportunity to teach some classes at whatever local studio I manage to wrangle a job with.

Staring at the shit I've gotten myself into for my first year at university—which will have the most challenging schedule—I wonder if some nutrient deficiency caused me to temporarily lose my mind when I signed up for this.

"Hey girlie," April's voice echoes through the courtyard, startling me. I glance over my shoulder to see her striding out of the back entrance of the dance HQ and towards me.

"Hey," I greet with a smile. "What are you doing here?"

April groans, plopping down on the bench beside me and leaning over to look at my map. "I figured if I want to be in dancing shape come Monday morning, I better get a few hours of practice in, even if it's just stretching. I'm just finishing up. You?"

I nod at my map. "Trying to figure out the best route around campus so I can make all my classes on time."

April wrinkles her nose. "We all need to take the gen ed courses, but why are you torturing yourself with art history on top of it? Will you even have time to sleep?"

When I told her my plans to get two degrees under my belt—dance and art history—in four years, she pleasantly asked me if I was a psychopath or had an abusive childhood. I told her in turn that I'm a realist. One bad injury could end my career, and no matter how hard I train to keep my body in top shape, there's no guarantee that I won't break a bone or tear the wrong ligament. If I only focus on dance, I'd have nothing else; if I have an art history degree, I could pursue my childhood dream of curating displays. If there's one thing that growing up with a totally neurotic mother taught me, it's that contingencies are a must in life. Very few things end up going according to plan in this world.

"I'll have time to sleep, but not much else," I admit. "I was just about to take a self-guided tour so I'm not totally fucked come Monday. Want to join?"

April's eyes crinkle around the corners as she smiles. "Sure. As long as you let me have one of your tea bags when we get back to dorms; the ones I got are shit, and I don't have room in my budget for another box until next week."

The woes of being a scholarship student. I gather my bag and tuck my phone into my back pocket, rising from the table. "Tea sounds like a fair trade for company. Have you heard anything from the studios in town?"

April's already sent out her resume and applications for work, as she had a little more time on her plate this last month than I did. Her role was still significant enough to take up most of her waking hours, but she wasn't always quarantined to dance HQ like the leads were.

April stands and joins me as I start on the path that'll take us deeper into the maze of campus. "I have, actually. Two of them called with offers for jobs this morning, for both of us."

I frown. "What do you mean for both of us? I haven't had time to send out applications."

"Yeah, babe, you were a freshman lead. You're not gonna get time for menial shit often, so I sent one on your behalf. I think mentioning that you landed Aurora straight off the bat made the studio owners more amenable to taking both of us."

I ask faintly, "Why would you do that for me?"

It's not often someone goes out of their way to help me or show me kindness; in fact, it's so unfamiliar, I don't know how to respond. I'm used to having to fight for what I have tirelessly, often swimming against whatever tide of complication is applicable at the time, and I'm yet to meet someone who'll throw me a life raft without an ulterior motive. In a world where greed and corruption are rewarded, it's difficult to find a decent soul.

April bumps my shoulder with hers. "Because you're my friend, and probably the only other real person in the company. In a place like this, that's sacred. I'll keep having your back, and I suspect you'll have mine in turn, too."

"I will," I promise. While the majority of me is prone to suspecting that true kindness doesn't exist without an underlying motive, as life has taught me, April doesn't reek of shallowness and vanity like most other people I've come across. That makes her a rare gem.

April nods. "Good. Let's figure out where all your damn classes are while I tell you about the job offers, and then I'm taking my tea bag."

Feeling warmed in my very soul, I agree, "Deal."

I steer us onto the path that veers to the right, taking us closer to the center of campus. The art department lies about halfway between the dance building on the southwest corner of campus and the annex in the center, and the walk is around a mile long. Odds are I'll end up running between my dance and art classes.

We end up walking for hours after I've mapped out the best routes and pathways, exploring the beautiful campus and enjoying the fresh air while it's still somewhat warm outside. April tells me about growing up with an immigrant family—half Asian and half Russian—the mindset of ambition for the sake of survival she inherited and how she thinks that contributes to her perfectionism in ballet. I in turn tell her a little about my psychotic mother, who very nearly killed me with her diets several times growing up.

By the time we find ourselves back near dance HQ, night has fallen, and I'm starting to shiver from the pronounced chill of the evening air. I only took a thin sweater with me this morning, which serves as poor protection from the quickly dropping temperature.

April seems to share my sentiment, because she says through chattering teeth, "I'm taking two tea bags. Consider the second a tax for freezing my ass off."

I'm about to tell her that so long as we stay friends, I'll give her all the tea she wants, when a glimmer in my peripheral vision catches my attention. I turn my head towards the flash of light, coming from a thick arrangement of garden shrubs that will bloom into roses come spring.

It's dark outside, and the lamp posts in front of dance HQ offers lighting that doesn't quite reach the bushes. I take a few steps in the direction I saw the glimmer come from, and finally make out what looks like the glint coming from a ring. Several steps closer and I see that the flashing jewel that caught my attention is connected to a pale hand, mostly concealed by the bushes.

The final step forward reveals that it's not just a ring on a hand; the hand is attached to an arm, which is attached to the nude body of a woman, *covered in blood.*

CHAPTER SIX

The next several hours are a blur, in which I feel like I'm floating around aimlessly in space and time with no solid tether to reality. The police are called, as are teachers and school administrators. It only takes ten minutes for the previously barren area to fill with people, all of them either here for the body or to find out how the body got here.

The body belongs to a fine arts female student—a painter, if I'm not mistaken, who was on campus early for a seminar. I'm not told the cause of death, but the glimpse I got of the corpse before it was taken away is enough to tell me that the death was not an accident, and whoever the girl is, she suffered horribly before dying.

As far as introductions go from universities to new students, Greywood is not making a good impression. Since getting to campus I've had my life commandeered by preparing for a show, found myself accosted by not one but *two* patrons of that very same show, and now—before the school year even officially starts—I've actually stumbled upon a dead body. *What the fuck is this place?*

It's a small consolation to see that nobody is taking the scene light-ly—the gathered crowd of spectators, made up of faculty, police, and students that have been drawn to the commotion all look stricken and shocked to their very cores. The pale faces and trembling hands are absolutely nothing compared to the storm of shock, dread, and bone-chilling fear taking over every cell of my body. While these people might be disturbed at whatever glimpses of the scene they managed to glean, they weren't the ones to find the damn body.

They also weren't the ones to have been sitting in this courtyard, alone, mere hours before, possibly around the same time a *murderer* was *disposing of a body*. The idea that I might've been in the same vicinity of a killer, totally unprotected and unaware, isn't something I'm prepared to cope with.

The police spend an hour extracting every drop of information I can give them in my witness statement, since I am the one who first saw the body. April was the one to call them because I was too shocked at the possibility that I very well could've been a victim myself to string together a coherent thought, let alone make a call. I wobble my way through answering their questions until they take pity on me and decide to leave me alone for the night, after giving me a phone number and instructions to call if I remember anything else.

Then it's my turn to be interrogated by the school president—who got called in for this fiasco—along with administration at dance HQ, who assure me that they'll take upmost precautions for my safety and that I needn't be afraid. Honestly, I think they're worried I'll transfer before the official start of school after tonight; since I have a standing invitation to some of the best dance academies in the world, Grey-wood is concerned I'll run away with tales of the horrors on campus. It'd be a lie to say I wasn't at least somewhat considering it.

Finally, once I've zombified from exhaustion, the dance program director—Moira, a stern woman in her fifties who wields so much command in her thin frame sometimes I swear the ground shakes from her voice alone—pulls me into dance HQ, leads me to her office on the third floor, and after seating me and bringing me a mug of tea tells me that the administrators have decided to pair me with another student on campus in order to help me feel safe, so that I won't feel compelled to leave the program.

I blink at her several times, feeling like there's slush instead of a brain floating around in my skull, not understanding the message. "I'm sorry, you're doing what?"

"Pairing you with another student, dear," Moira clarifies patiently, a placid smile pasted on her face. She's seated across from me, with a large glass desk littered with framed photos taking up the space between us. "It must've been rather scary to be the one to stumble upon that... *scene* earlier, and the administration wouldn't want you to feel uncomfortable coming to class. I understand there was some talk concerning the possibility that you and the killer may have been around the same place during the same time, and at Greywood Dance we take nothing more seriously than our dancers safety."

It sounds like she's reciting lines for an infomercial, but I don't dare say that to her. I also don't say that there is literally no way for me to ever feel safe on this campus or in this building again, or that no number of precautions would make me feel better.

Instead, with a smile and through gritted teeth, I say, "I appreciate the offer, but—"

"—I'm afraid it isn't an offer," Moira interrupts, lukewarm smile still in place. "In fact, we had a donor ask for an immersive glimpse into Greywood's dance program this year."

I could probably double for an owl at this point, staring at the program director with wide eyes and blinking endlessly while trying to wrap my mind around her words. I just found a dead body, and she's trying to talk to me about donors? Can she not see that my thoughts are still too much of a tangled mess to process complex notions such as school politics?

"I'm not sure I follow," I say slowly when she doesn't offer any more information.

Moira leans back in her office chair, looking suspiciously like she's hiding an eye roll. "One of our biggest donors has a son at Greywood. He's requested that his son shadow classes and rehearsals this year so that he knows his money is going to good use. The unfortunate situation tonight actually coincides with our donor's request quite nicely; you're in need of a protector to help you feel safe, and he's in need of a tour guide to show him the joys of our program."

Despite my cognitive function currently working at around the pace of molasses, I manage to comprehend that in the midst of one of the worst and most terrifying nights of my life, my program director is trying to pimp me out to make the program look shinier and better. She might not be selling me for sex, but she's offering my company to her own benefit. Once again, I begin wondering exactly what I signed up for in coming to Greywood.

It's not unheard of for dancers to have to rub elbows with donors to get an edge, but being assigned as a tour guide to a donor's son? Yeah, I've never heard of something like that happening.

Moira's eyes start to glimmer with nostalgia as she says, "Really, I couldn't have choreographed it better. Damsel meets prince, sparks fly."

I say with disbelief, "Are you actually comparing this tragic situation with a ballet?"

Moira's eyes harden. "Boy meets distressed girl, boy covets girl—the premise of every good ballet and just about every story ever written. Can you disagree?"

I can, but I see that doing so won't yield any desirable results, so I decide to keep it to myself. Instead, I say as gently as possible, "While I appreciate the offer and being considered for such an honorific, wouldn't it be better to pair the donor with an older student? They have more experience here and more time to dedicate to extracurricular activities."

Moira corrects me, "I'm not pairing the donor himself with anyone, dear. It's his son that will act in his place, as Mr. Ajax is a very busy man."

Hold on a fucking second, Ajax?

As in, Carson Ajax, trust fund brat who I got a ride home from last night? I recall his parting words—*I* will *see you again, Princess, I'm just offering you the courtesy of choosing the time and place.* The bastard must work *fast* to have gotten daddy to pull some strings this quickly. The reprehensible timing of this situation—coinciding with me stumbling on a dead body—is just the cherry on top.

I manage through gritted teeth, "What exactly is expected of me in regards to Mr. Ajax?"

Moira shrugs, not looking like she particularly cares. "Let him shadow you around campus, sit in on dance, watch choreography and rehearsals. I don't expect this will extend beyond first term, but you'll have someone to help you feel safe, and the department will get a nice bonus from his father. It's a win-win for everyone involved."

From her perspective, I expect it is a win for everyone. From *my* perspective, however, this is *not* a win. I came here to study contemporary and classical dance from the best teachers, choreographers, and masters in the country. I did not come here to play games with frat boys and do favors for the department. But, considering the fact that I've been on campus for a month and already got a lead role in the company's first show of the season, I figure now it's my turn to repay them by trotting around like a show horse for a donor's son. A man who happens to irritate me to an obscene extent, second only to his friend who I also had the misfortune to run into already.

"I understand," I murmur.

What I truly understand is that I have very little say in the matter. Unless I'm prepared to leave Greywood and accept one of my other school invitations, I'll need to play the donor game. And, despite the horrors I've already been subjected to on campus, I'm not keen on the idea of losing the best opportunity of my life simply because some bad shit is happening around me. My childhood taught me the value of perseverance under pressure. If staying at Greywood means consigning myself to spend time with Carson, then I'll pull on my big girl panties—and chastity belt, because despite his shortcomings, the man is as hot as it gets—and get the job done.

Moira inclines her head with approval, a thin smile on her lips. "Excellent. We'll see you bright and early tomorrow morning, Eliana, when you'll meet your new shadow for the term."

I leave her office in a daze, opting to take the stairwell instead of the elevator to the first floor. The walk doesn't help clear my mind; in fact, I don't know that there is anything that could pull me out of my haze. I'm swiftly proven wrong when, as seems to be the new standard, I run face-first into yet *another* person. This time, however, it's a police officer I collide with, instead of an errant schoolboy.

The officer looks to be somewhere in her thirties, with assessing narrowed eyes and thin lips pinched in concentration as she puts a hand on my shoulder to steady me.

"S-sorry," I mutter, stumbling back and giving my head a shake. My classical ballet training means my reflexes are impeccable—what is *with* me running into people these last days? Considering there's now a killer on the loose, it doesn't feel like a good time to lose focus of my surroundings. But, being as preoccupied as I am with the absolute madhouse that has been my life recently, it's hard to stay grounded. If I don't get my shit together, my dancing will suffer.

The police officer glances at the Greywood ID badge hanging from a lanyard around my neck, and upon seeing my name, softens. Evidently it's already circled around the department that I'm the unlucky fuck who found the body.

The officer offers me a half-grimace, half-pity smile. "Would you like an escort back to dorms, Ms. Pierce?"

Considering the night I've had, I say instantly, "If it wouldn't be too much trouble, yes please. I don't feel the safest walking around campus right now."

The police officer nods. "No, I suspect you wouldn't. I'll walk you, then—you're at the program dormitories?"

I nod, and the officer leads me outside, one hand resting on her belt near her firearm. I guess the events of tonight *have* rattled the community around here. The policewoman stops for a moment to speak with her supervisor, then proceeds to walk with me on the path that leads to my dorm building.

I manage to hold my tongue for the first five minutes, but eventually I can't prevent myself from asking, "Do you guys know anything yet? Cause of death? Potential suspects?"

The officer glances at me from the corner of her eye, considering my words. I very much doubt she counts me as a suspect for tonight's events, but that doesn't make the officer any more likely to share whatever preliminary speculation there might be about the murder.

I'm a civilian—a student who found the body no less—so I have no right to request information, beyond sheer terror driving me to gather what there is to know so I might better protect myself.

"I'm sorry to ask," I murmur, "it's just... whoever did this could've seen me. I'm scared."

My words hit their mark; the officer gives me a tight-lipped nod, seeming to decide that sharing with me isn't the end of the world.

She says shortly, "Cause of death is suspected blunt force trauma to the head, though we'll have to wait for the coroner's report for confirmation. From what I saw of the body and the chatter I've heard, we're most likely dealing with a male perpetrator—one who's done this before."

CHAPTER SEVEN

Those words reach deep inside of me, wrapping around my chest like a vice and squeezing until I feel like I can't get enough air in my diaphragm. She's just confirmed my worst fears and suspicions; that there is, quite literally, a crazy killer on the loose.

The officer must see the effect her words have on me, because she quickly backtracks. "This is all speculation, of course; we won't know anything for sure until the autopsy's completed." Just as she finishes speaking, we arrive in front of the program dorms. I stare at the imposing building, suddenly feeling unsure of whether or not I want to sleep here tonight. What if I'm sharing a roof with the killer? What if the killer is a student or faculty member?

"We've had the entire campus and all active *and* inactive buildings thoroughly searched in the last hours," the officer assures me. "Whoever the perp is, he's long gone—didn't stick around." She pauses, placing her hand on my shoulder in an awkward offer of comfort. I get the sense she's not the type to usually deal with rattled bystanders. "If you'd like, I could take a look around your dormitory, just in case."

Considering the fact that I'm having a difficult time forcing myself to walk up to the building and open the door—too frozen with fear—I nod jerkily, accepting the offer. I can tell the officer is just doing this to ease my mind, not because she suspects she'll find anything, but I appreciate the gesture nonetheless.

After taking a look around my matchbox dormitory room—even checking under the bed and in the closet, as if searching for monsters—the officer leaves me with her business card and instructions to call if I should see, hear, or remember anything of importance.

Not a minute after she leaves, just as I've sunk down on my tiny mattress, loud knocks that could double for gunshots sound at my door, alarming me. The alarm fades when I hear April's voice, demanding to be "let the fuck in so I can get all the dirty deets".

Amused despite myself, I make my way to the door and open it, stumbling back when she breezes right into my room as if she owns the place. Although she's wearing worn sweats and a hoodie, and we've both had one hell of a night, April is as stunning and collected as ever as she calmly interrogates me about everything that went down since the cops showed up and separated us for questioning.

Once we've exchanged our version of events and put together all the facts we could, we sit for several long minutes in silence, side by side on the floor with our backs to my bedframe, contemplating.

"I saw rope marks on the girl's hands," April says faintly. "Couple that with the wounds you saw, and..."

"Whoever did the deed is one sadistic motherfucker," I finish for her, shaking my head with bafflement. It seriously feels like I'm living in a twisted thriller movie of some sort, and the premise is not promising. "He also could've seen either or both of us."

"So, we're going with the killer being a he?" April asks.

"The cop who walked me here assumed so, and I'm inclined to agree. Just the act of carrying a body from point A to point B requires strength that few women are trained to have. Even a ballerina would struggle, and ballerinas are *strong*," I respond.

Despite the slender appearances of most ballet dancers, ballet itself requires immense strength and impeccable muscle control. A male ballerina probably could carry a dead body, but females are usually short and slim; it seems unlikely that one could've dragged around—let alone carried—the body.

April nods. "True enough. So, the summary of the situation is that we may or may not have been glimpsed by a murderer as he was dumping a body before the first day of school." Perversely, she grins through her entire statement. "I knew Greywood would be exciting, but I didn't expect to live in a murder mystery! If I wasn't partly scared for my life, I'd think this was awesome."

I stare at her blankly. I'm getting the sense more and more that April is a rather eccentric person with plenty of quirks; one of them is an apparent lack of sensibility, because in no world would this situation be awesome. I myself am partial to murder mystery games and movies, but this is neither a game nor a movie; it's my fucking *life*.

April's grin fades at whatever expression I'm wearing. She reaches over and grabs my hand. "Hey, whatever this is, I'm in it too. Odds are if the killer saw you, he saw me, so if either of us is fucked we both are—at least our misery will have company, hmm?"

I let out a weak laugh. "What is this place, April? What am I doing here?"

She squeezes my hand. "The same as all of us; learning to be the best dancer from the best dancers that have lived in the last several decades. I don't think anyone expected for us to have this start to the year, but it is what it is. All we can do is what we were born to do; dance."

I nod, unable to do or say anything else, because there's nothing left to say. In that moment, I shore up my strength and make my decision: I'm staying at Greywood. I'm the dance program's current star pupil; as long as I remain as such, which I intend to, I know the program will have no problem expending resources on my behalf. Although I'm not totally comfortable with the prospect of being shadowed by Carson, Moira was right in one thing: I'll feel a touch safer in the presence of a man who looks like he'd have no problem beating the shit out of someone and seems to have interest in me. I can use those things to my advantage. He might serve as an irritant, but there's no denying that—as long as he doesn't turn out to be a total douche—he'll make for a decent wall of muscle I can cart around with me to feel safer.

I'll bet this is the first time in a long time someone is using Carson for their own gain, especially without sex being part of the equation. He struck me as the type to have a different girl every night, which is why his continued interest in me is disconcerting. Maybe it's time to turn the tables and show *him* what it feels like to be the arm candy, the disposable body only appreciated on a physical level. I don't need his brains or even his company; I need his biceps as a deterrent to any roaming killer who might have gotten a glimpse of me.

Realizing that I haven't yet looped in April on that new development, I say, "On another note, Moira's pimping me out to a donor's son in return for a cash bonus to the company."

April's silent for a beat, staring at me with wide eyes, and then proceeds to burst out in gales of laughter, laughing so hard she actually chokes on her laughs, falling into a coughing fit. Watching her hack and cough, bent over at the waist and clutching her legs, I try to suppress a smile.

She says through wheezes, "Moira's—doing—*what?*"

I give her a brief rundown of my meeting with our program direc-tor, telling her that I'll now be Carson Ajax's official tour guide for first term, and mentioning our little run-in last night along with the fact that he drove me home. At the end, I say, "Considering your reaction, I'm assuming you didn't get an offer for a campus shadow to *help you feel safe?*"

Finally having caught her breath, April shakes her head. "No, I absolutely did not. Which means the situation is probably less about your safety and more about our company getting a fat check. Hold on, did you say Carson *Ajax*?"

"You're familiar with him?" I ask dryly

"No, but I know he's the business program's star pupil, and rumor has it he's fucked his way through half the girls on campus. So, the golden king of Greywood's set his eye on you, huh? That's weird. From what I've heard, he doesn't have to go out to get girls, they naturally flock to him by the masses. The fact that he's going out of his way to seek you out... I think golden boy might have a little crush, Elia," April responds.

I let out a puff of laughter. "More like I turned him down and he can't handle rejection. Moira implied that this whole thing's orches-trated by his father, but considering the fact that he told me he'd be seeing me again soon before driving off last night, I'm more inclined to think it was set up by Carson himself."

April lets out a low whistle. "*Damn*, girl, looks like you've got yourself a very sexy and ridiculously wealthy admirer. You gonna fuck him?"

I snort. "Absolutely not, which I made clear last night. I plan on using his physical appearance as a shield against any wandering killers, and that's all."

April considers me in silence for several beats, before nodding her head in approval. "Go you, sis. Since you'll be spending time with him, it'd be a shame not to use him for all his worth. The Ajax name carries a lot of weight in the dance world—they're patrons of several renowned companies."

I cringe. "He'd probably only help me out if I slept with him, and I'm not keen on whoring myself out in the literal sense."

April shrugs, pushing off the floor. "Fair enough. I wouldn't blame you if you caved eventually, though, considering all the time you'll be spending together. I've seen pictures of him on social media; that man is a dish. Anywho, I'm gonna try to get some sleep, I'll see you in the morning?"

I give her a half-hearted smile. "See you in the AM."

***

Monday morning comes around, bringing with it a jaded sense of enthusiasm for my first official day of college. I would be purely enthusiastic if I hadn't spent the night bathing in anxiety, my mind torturing me with images of the dead arts student I glimpsed and conspiracy theories surrounding her death until I decided to conduct obsessive and extensive internet searches as my own form of an investigation. My 5:30 alarm goes off just after I've finally fallen asleep, leaving me especially grumpy as I roll out of bed and tug on tights, a leotard, and pull a sweatsuit on top of it so I don't freeze on my way to headquarters.

Three knocks sound at my door just as I'm shrugging on the straps of my overly full backpack. Assuming it's April, I don't bother to check who it is before opening the door. We agreed we'd walk over to dance together; in the times that Carson won't be shadowing me, I intend to stick with April.

Staring at the many messages from people in the dance company asking if I'm okay on my phone screen—looks like word that April and I discovered a dead body outside of HQ has already made its way around the company—I swing open the door while muttering, "I don't know about you, but I got thirty minutes of sleep—"

I cut off when I glimpse expensive leather dress shoes decorating the floor outside my dorm room, attached to beige slacks that look tailored. April's feet aren't that big, and I haven't seen her wear anything other than jeans or leggings. My eyes slowly travel up the person standing in front of me, taking in a crisp white shirt under a beige vest and black overcoat, until my eyes lock with two familiar and overly mirthful ones. Golden boy apparently decided to get an early start to bothering me today.

"Are you *fucking* kidding me?" I whisper-yell, because while showing up at my dorm room at 5:50am is not what anyone could call socially acceptable behavior, I'm not going to wake everyone in the hall up by actually yelling. I'm not the inconsiderate asshole here.

Carson Ajax offers me the same brilliant smile he did when he was stalking me after my show. "Good to see you too, Princess. You were saying something about not sleeping? Anytime you want a cuddle buddy, I guarantee I'll give you the best night of your life." He pauses, his smile turning sly. "Sorry, I meant sleep. Best sleep of your life. You know, in a totally non-sexual way." He has the audacity to top that statement off with a wink.

The door across the hall opens, revealing April, who's dressed almost identically to me in her own sweatsuit. She looks from me, to Carson waiting in my doorway, and back at me. When I give her a pleading *help me* expression, she throws her head back with a cackle.

"Good luck with that, Elia," she calls out, closing and locking her dorm room before flitting down the hall, leaving me to the overgrown manchild in front of me.

"Elia," Carson repeats my nickname, a smile curving his lips. "I like that. It suits you."

I let out a long-suffering sigh, feeling my shoulders droop slightly. I knew I signed up to spend time with Carson when I agreed to Moira's proposition; I simply didn't expect him to show up this freaking early, let alone *at my dorm room*. How he even knows which individual room is assigned to me is beyond me, but it doesn't surprise me.

As unfair as it is, we live in a capitalistic society, which means money is power. The Ajax name is obviously *filthy* rich, which means it's also probably obscenely powerful. I imagine it wouldn't be difficult for Carson to find out a great deal about my life, and I find myself hoping he doesn't. I don't have any skeletons in my closet, per se, but I do have a past that I prefer to keep private, simply because I managed to escape it. I don't want to go back to it by thinking about it or even acknowledging it, and the idea that I'm faced with someone who might already know it or could easily find out about it doesn't sit well with me.

I snap, "Am I going to have to deal with you being a pervert all the time?"

Carson hums, tilting his head to the side as if he's considering it. He offers, "I *could* try to keep my innuendo to a minimum, but it'll cost you."

At this point, my tone is probably a good imitation of a grizzly bear. "I'm *not* having sex with you."

Carson's eyes twinkle. "I wasn't going to suggest it, but since you keep bringing it up, I'm starting to think *you* might be."

I don't grace that bullshit with a response, since I am most certainly not the one who keeps bringing it up. Instead, I push him out of my doorway with a hand on his chest, lock my dorm room, and start down the hall, hoping that he has the grace to go away but knowing better.

As expected, he keeps pace with me. "My offer was going to be the same as the other night. Go out with me, I'll keep a leash on my innuendo. Mostly. Probably. I'll try to, at least."

At the end of the hall, I press the button for the elevator repeatedly, as if that act alone will make it get here faster.

"I already told you I wouldn't go out with you, and in response you managed to pull some shit to end up as my shadow for the term. That doesn't make me keener to spend time with you."

Carson tosses back, "But it should show you that I'm determined, and good at getting what I want."

I say tiredly, "Look, Ajax, I agreed to this bullshit because I might be on a murderer's radar, and your appearance alone would make a criminal think twice about trying to snatch me off the street. I have no interest in you beyond the fact that a wall of muscle beside me bodes well for my protection."

Carson says, "Backup, you're *what?*"

CHAPTER EIGHT

The elevator arrives with a ding, and Carson follows me into it. As we descend, I tell him, "Check the news. A student's body was found right outside of dance HQ last night, by April and me. We were around that area earlier—before the body was dropped—so paranoia and common sense have made me wary."

Carson falls silent for a while as he clicks around on his phone, presumably to double-check what I've told him. I leave him to his research in peace, navigating my way out of dorms and through campus so I can get to dance in time. The first hour, from 6 a.m. to 7 a.m., is for warmups—not mandatory for all company members, but recommended for those who hope to get noticed for their commitment. As April and I have already gotten cast, that sort of makes warmups *highly* recommended, because sometimes masters and teachers will come in early to observe and take notes.

As soon as dance HQ comes into sight, my heartbeat triples, and for the briefest moment I'm thrown back into last night, when the now-deserted area was swarming with people, and the parking lot was filled with police cars. The early morning sun fades into a dreary night filled with flashes of blue and red, and I hear hushed, horrified murmurs from a phantom crowd. Along with a racing heart, my chest also decides to tighten with panic, making it difficult for me to get a full breath in.

Carson puts his phone away, casting me a glance of amazement. "This belongs in a Stephen King novel. New girl gets to campus, finds a body..."

"Don't forget the part where new girl is bothered by two friends who don't know how to take no for an answer," I add in dryly.

Carson's eyes sharpen at that. Seemingly to himself, he says, "Seth's already wormed his way in, has he? I thought I'd have more time to charm you."

"You have all the charm of a grey sprinkle on a rainbow cupcake," I inform him with a sweet smile. Despite my snark, I'm actually glad that he ended up stalking me this morning; if he didn't take my mind off the scene last night, I could've tumbled into a dark place.

I've always struggled with anxiety and restlessness, from the time I was a child. It wasn't until my teenage years, after some particularly unpleasant experiences, when I first experienced an anxiety attack. They've mostly tapered off over the years, and I've learned how to manage my stress so that it doesn't build into a panic attack, but I've had a particularly trying few days. Now is *not* the time to lose my cool, and surprisingly, Carson provides a distraction that makes it easier to stay grounded.

"So, you think Seth is more charming than me?" Carson's tone has changed from somewhat sharp to completely flat, in a way that makes me nervous.

I cast him a sidelong glance, startled to see that the charm we're talking about has disappeared—as if it were a construct of my imagination—and has been replaced by a stark intensity that makes me wonder if my initial read of golden boy was off. On the surface, there are absolutely no similarities between him and Seth, but the look he's wearing right now is similar to the one his friend had at the museum yesterday. Predatory, singularly focused, and far too intense for my comfort.

"Seth has all the charm of a serial killer," I respond, not even joking. Come to think of it, I could picture Seth as being a killer—it wouldn't surprise me whatsoever if he's taken human life before. He's just so... *dark*, and from the little I saw, so calculating, that I don't think anyone who got in his way or crossed certain lines with him would live to regret it.

As soon as the thought crosses my mind, it's followed by flashes of the body last night, and my exhausted and overstimulated mind jumps to conclusions that cause me to start shivering, and not from the early morning chill.

There have been an awful lot of coincidences in the last days, starting with Carson's entry into my life. Him seeking me out after the show was intentional, but what are the odds of me randomly crossing paths with his friend not twelve hours later? Followed by happening to be the one to find the dead body on campus?

Before I can start down a rabbit hole of debilitating fear, I take a deep breath and remind myself that thinking from a place of fear has never gotten me anywhere, but life experience has taught me that using logic does. Yes, the vibe I got from Seth was dark, but it was not—in any way, shape, or form—unhinged. Everything about his demeanor and body language told me that he's a man who holds total control over himself, and from what I saw of the body last night, the crime was not committed by someone who has self-control. The marks on the body look like they could've been made by a rabid animal.

While my impression of Seth didn't lead me to believe he valued human life, I also didn't feel unsafe around him at any moment. I've had to develop good instincts about people to survive the revolving door of abusive boyfriends my mother invited into our home, so I've learned to trust my well-honed judgement.

My instincts about Seth were that he was dark, potentially dangerous, extremely calculated, and not altogether normal, but not one fiber of me felt that he's the type to do what I saw last night. He'd only commit murder if it suited him, and I'm willing to bet my scholarship that he sees no appeal in snuffing out innocent life. Playing with people and manipulating them, yes, but not killing senselessly.

Besides, Seth has gone to this university for years; if he were a killer, more bodies would have dropped in the area in recent years. I spent a good portion of the night scouring the internet to see if there were any other reports of dead women in the entire state that could point to a pattern and indicate the killer being local, finding nothing applicable.

The fact that I'm rattled and sleep deprived enough to jump to outrageous conclusions worries me as much as it should, and makes me grateful that I'll spend the next six hours dancing on autopilot. Muscle memory makes up the majority of dance; I don't have to think or reason when in class, all I have to do is follow the teacher's directions. Getting out of my head will be nice, even if it won't last.

"You just got very quiet," Carson observes, following me as I push through the entrance to headquarters and walk through the lobby, heading for the stairwell. Jogging up the stairs should warm me from my morning chill, getting me ready for dance.

"I just weighed the possibility of Seth being the killer," I say honestly. If Carson's friends with him, he should understand the urge to do so; Seth comes off as a dangerous individual.

Carson barks out a laugh, following me as I trot up the steps. "What's the ruling? Is he guilty?"

I glance at him over my shoulder. "You're his friend. Wouldn't you be the better judge of that?"

"I'm curious what you think," Carson shoots back.

What's the harm in giving my analysis? It might spur him into giving his own, and if I happen to run into Seth again, I get the sense I'll appreciate any tips I can get. He doesn't seem to be the type of man who'll be easy for anyone to handle.

"I think while he's capable of taking a life, he's not the psycho who killed the girl from last night."

Carson's quiet after I speak, not offering any response. His quietness makes me nervous, so much so that I trip over one of the stairs and lose my balance, nearly face-planting. Carson saves me from that fate with an arm around my waist, using it to jerk me towards him and stabilize me. I'm once again pressed chest-to-chest with him, just like the night I met him, but this time I don't shriek and scramble away out of stranger-danger fear. This time, I stay still and stare into his eyes, trying to see if I can glean anything from them.

Authors, poets, artists and philosophers have often agreed on one key point throughout the centuries; that eyes are windows to the soul. I very much believe this, and since Carson isn't saying anything, I want to examine his expression. His eyes are narrowed in consideration and contemplation as they stare at me, the blue orbs of his irises appearing unusually intense in the fluorescent light of the stairwell. The flecks of black sprinkled across the blue are more pronounced right now, darkening the color of his eyes from arctic to midnight. Staring into them, I almost feel myself falling into a spell of some sort, forgetting all about my objective. A low heat starts to pulse between my legs the longer we stare at each other, because while I may have stayed still with the intent to see what I can read of Carson, the only thing reflected back at me in his gaze is pure, stark hunger.

"Keep looking at me like that, and I'll start to think you're sweet on me," Carson says, breaking the trance.

His words serve as a necessary splash of cold water to my system. I take a step back, holding my hand out in front of me when he tries to match my step and stay close. I need to remember one thing above all; I don't have time for distractions. I certainly don't have time for pretty trust fund brat distractions. I have four years to get two degrees under my belt, and I won't waste my time.

I demand, "Do I need to be worried about you and your border-line-psychotic friend?"

Carson replies with amusement, "You'll have to clarify what makes you worry. You caught both of our attention, which is unusual—usually when a girl has my attention it's purely for a fuck, and Seth generally doesn't pay attention to anything unless he decides to. You caught his attention without his permission or decision, and he is one intense motherfucker. We're both very intense when going after what we want, in fact. I don't know if that's a cause for worry, but you should be aware of it. I can tell you this for certain; we're also both known for being relentless and not backing down. So, unless you want to dispense with the bullshit and give into the chemistry that very obviously exists between us—which, by the way, I've never felt with anyone else before—I'll just keep upping my game until you do. I'm not known for backing down lightly. And, if I find out Seth's interest in you extends beyond artistic, I'm only gonna double down my efforts. So, should you be worried? That's up to you. But it's only fair I give you warning in advance, your life is likely going to change now that you landed yourself on both of our radars."

My lips part at the end of his little speech as I regard him with open astonishment. His bluntness is discombobulating, but what's more dizzying is how blatantly he's stating his intent. Carson comes across as the charmer, not as someone who would flatly inform me that he's going after me.

I'm equally shocked about the way he characterizes his friendship with Seth; Carson can obviously see that Seth is far from normal, but he appears versed in handling that abnormality. He also had no compunction essentially telling me that I'm in for one hell of a time, simply because I danced well and caught the attention of two men I'm steadily growing more and more wary of.

The way he's speaking, it almost sounds like he's willing to get into a competition with his friend over me—as if they have a bet or something going on as to who'll get me first. Seeing as I'm a person and not an object to be won, the concept of being pursued for the sake of what might be a game between two asshole rich boys does not sit well with me. I don't get the vibe from either of them that this is a game—from what I'm picking up on, Carson is surprisingly serious in going after me, and I'm no longer sure it's entirely about sex. But even if it isn't, that leaves one glaring question: why me?

My performance alone might've snagged their attention, but it shouldn't have kept it. Carson should've backed off when I definitively made clear that I'm not interested in him, but he hasn't.

I say, "You don't even know me. How could you be so dead set on going after me? We've technically only spoken twice, and both times I shot you down. Why go after someone who's unattainable?" My eyes narrow as realization dawns. "Oh, is it about the chase for you? Is that what this is? Because if it is, I'll let you know now, there is absolutely no universe in which I'll sleep with you, so your efforts are in vain—"

Carson cuts me off by pressing his index finger to my lips, just like he did that first night. Unlike the first night, butterflies made of both nerves and what I'm starting to fear is the beginnings of a reluctant attraction take flight in my stomach and chest, turning my breathing harsh.

The finger pressed to my lips starts to slowly trail across my cheek as Carson stares down at me, wearing an expression of contemplation. "I'm not here for the chase," he assures me. "If you want me to be honest, I'm not sure what I want from you. Do I want to fuck you? Of course. I'm not blind or stupid. But although I don't know exactly what I'm looking for here, I can tell you with absolute certainty it isn't just sex. I'll get you in bed eventually, make no mistake, but when I gave you a ride home I actually *enjoyed* your company and talking to you." The way he says the last part, you'd think that enjoying spending time with a woman is a foreign concept to him.

Looking him up and down again, I realize that it probably is. If Carson's usual repertoire with girls starts and ends with pursuit of sex, that tells me that his interest in me is because I'm offering him a novelty; a woman with the balls to turn him down and brains to stand up to him. Which means that eventually the novelty will wear off and his interest will wane; all I have to do is wait. The concept of him only being attracted to the novelty I represent hurts, because it reinforces the belief that my mother spent my entire life trying to convince me of: my only purpose and use in this life is to dance well and marry rich.

CHAPTER NINE

Carson

After our conversation in the stairwell, Eliana seems to withdraw into herself. She leads me to a studio space, sits me in the corner by the piano bench and tells me to stay there as if I'm a dog, then proceeds to ignore me while chatting with the other dance program students that are already here. After making a round across the room and saying hello to a couple people, she dumps her bag along the back wall and strips out of her sweats and hoodie. I suck my bottom lip into my mouth as the same body that's fucking *haunted* me since I first saw her dancing on stage makes an appearance. She's wearing a tiny leotard that outlines every curve of her upper body, from the perkiness of her breasts to her tiny waist to her flaring hips, and tights that show off just how toned and mouthwatering her legs are.

Landing myself a front-row seat to Elia's campus life was surprisingly easy. All I had to do was seek out the dance program director and mention that my father had interest in giving a bonus to the department if they could show me the money was going to good use. Moira was *most* accommodating when I mentioned that the bonus would be in the six-figure range. Since I haven't clued my dad into this—not like he would care regardless—that bonus will be coming straight from my bank account, but I don't mind. I've been working at my father's company for years, earning a nice income from it. Father's very accustomed to throwing money at problems he wishes to ignore. That extends to me.

Really, I'd probably have been willing to pay double, because I carved out an ideal position in Elia's life. She'll have to spend time with me, and I intend to put that time to use by convincing her I'm not whatever monster she assumed I was as soon as she saw my watch and the quality of my clothes. It's obvious Little E has something against wealth—so much so that a person being wealthy is enough to make her run in the opposite direction.

To someone like me, that shit is *unheard* of. Every person in my life—aside from Seth—is there because of my last name and my father's money. Superficiality is the standard among the upper class, so I know damn well that none of the people in my life are there for *me*, they're there for what I bring to the table. That's why girls chase after me; not even because they like the way I look, but because they see me as their ticket up. Elia obviously doesn't, which only heightens her appeal.

I wasn't lying when I told her I don't know what I want from her. Initially, I had every intention of fucking her; that was the motive and endgame. Then, I actually spoke to her, and quickly realized that while I still intend to bed her, I don't think this is my usual one-and-done situation, because she is not my usual fare. Sex has always been transactional to me; I get release, the girl gets a good time and to say she fucked Carson Ajax. At this point, I don't know why that's such an achievement as hundreds of girls have those bragging rights, but whatever floats their boats. With Elia, though, I don't know that I'll be ready to give her up. She's so shiny, witty, and fucking *unique* that I think I'll probably continue to be locked on her for quite some time.

The only problem there is that Seth has obviously noticed the same things about her as I have, and he seems to have also developed an intentness where she's concerned. He told me he didn't want to fuck her after the performance that first night, but she's already had a run in with him, and something's telling me that could've been enough to change his interest from purely artistic to something more. If that's the case, I need to find out soon and plan some sabotage. I am *far* from being done with Little E, and I won't allow him to get in the way of that.

I watch as Elia settles beside the same girl that abandoned her to me in the program dorms. Obviously, she's not holding a grudge, because they talk and laugh as they start stretching. Watching Elia bend and contort her body in some impressive positions, I feel my dick start to stiffen. *Shit, this is* not *the time or place.* I adjust myself as discreetly as possible, thankful when nobody seems to notice. The adjustment doesn't make me any more comfortable; my cock continues hardening against the side of my leg as I watch Elia until it's painful enough to make me wince.

Another dancer—a brunette with cunning-looking brown eyes—starts walking across the room and towards me. I give her a cursory up and down. Usually, her double D's, plump lips, and sultry smile would be enough to make up my mind to fuck her, and I'd be pulling whoever this dancer is to the nearest closet for a quickie. Now, however, watching her sashay over to me only has the result of making my erection go away. Probably for the best considering the setting, but it also deprives me of the sight of Elia lifting one of her legs over her head while the other remains on the ground in a *very* enticing version of a split.

"Can I help you?" I ask flatly as the other girl stops in front of me, tossing her hair over her shoulder.

She blinks, put off by my lack of interest, but recovers quickly with another sensual smile. "I heard a donor's son would be shadowing some classes, but I didn't know he would be so delicious. I'm Scarlett."

It doesn't take much to deduce that Scarlett is probably the mean girl/queen bee of the dance company. She carries herself with a confidence that comes from being the proverbial queen of the hill, and the way the other dancers gathered all glance at her in regular intervals, as if looking for direction, clues me in.

"Hello, Scarlett," I say monotonously. "If you don't mind…" I gesture for her to move out of the way so I can get my eyes back on Elia.

Scarlett glances over her shoulder at Elia, and when she looks back to me her eyes have a new hardness. "I heard you got paired with one of the silly little novices," she says sweetly, voice remaining inviting even while her demeanor is steadily changing to pissed. "I'd never question Moira's judgement, but if you want someone with a little more *experience* to show you the ropes, I'd be happy to help you in *any* way you might desire." Her emphasis on the words *experience* and *any* reinforces the fact that she's looking to fuck the golden boy of campus. She also seems to have some animosity towards Elia—probably because freshmen never get cast, and Elia ended up a lead.

I inform Scarlett, "I requested to shadow the best dancer I've ever seen. Thank you for the offer, but I'm very happy with Elia being my tour guide here."

Scarlett's smile drops, replaced by a scowl that contorts her features in a particularly unflattering way.

With a scoff, she says, "Well, if you ever want a *real* dancer to show you the ropes, I'll be more than happy to take *very* good care of you."

I only acknowledge that with a snort and shake of my head, causing Scarlett's cheeks to flame with indignation as she whips around and goes back the way she came. The dozen or so dancers strewn about the room all have their eyes glued to us, and most of the gazes are nothing short of shocked. Looks like I'm not the only person here who's used to getting what they want.

Elia and her friend are still stretching at the bar, but Elia's eyes are glued to me, laced with confusion. She looks from me to Scarlett with furrowed eyebrows, probably wondering along with everyone else why I'd turn Scarlett down. When her gaze settles back on me I give her a very deliberate and appreciative up and down, telling her without words that I turned down the queen bee because my interest right now is solely with her.

Her eyebrows draw even closer together, and she squints at me in confusion, as if she can't figure out what my game here is. Then, with a quick head shake, she returns to stretching and talking to her friend.

My phone buzzes in my pocket, drawing my attention. During school hours I have it set to do not disturb, save for a few select contacts, who's messages and calls still get through. I already know who's texting me even before I see Seth's name on the screen.

The message is concise and to the point.

Seth: *We need to talk.*

Considering that I haven't spoken to him since the night of the Sleeping Beauty performance, and I suspect he's been a busy bee in the meantime, I've been waiting for this text. I have a general idea of how our conversation will go. If Seth's interest in Eliana has deepened to personal, he'll try to get me to back off of her. I'll refuse, because

I haven't nearly gotten my fill of Little E yet. We'll probably argue, possibly physically fight, before reaching an agreement on how to proceed. How damaging that fight will be depends on what Seth's intent with Elia is. I don't give a fuck if he wants her to pose for some goddamn paintings, but I would very much give a fuck if he's going to pursue her the same way I am. If we don't come to an agreement on how to proceed, it's quite possible one of us will end up in the hospital.

I text him back swiftly.

> **Carson:** *When?*

His reply is instant.

> **Seth:** *Now. I'm waiting outside.*

A small smirk curls my lips.

> **Carson:** *I'm not home right now.*

Once again, he responds at once.

> **Seth:** *I'm well fucking aware. I'm outside of dance HQ, get your ass out here.*

Might as well get this out of the way now. If I know Seth—which I believe after years of friendship I do—he's already planned out exactly how he intends to proceed, and he'll tell me I can either get on board or find out what it's like to be on the opposite side of a battlefield from him. The problem with that is that I know damn well a battle between us would end up with one of us either in jail or dead; there's a very good reason we decided long ago to be friends instead of enemies.

I stand from my spot just as a dance teacher enters the room and calls the dancers to attention. As I pass, the teacher asks, "Is there a problem, Mr. Ajax?"

Money will afford a person a lot of luxuries, such as even teachers sucking up to you. With my signature charming smile, I tell the guy, "Nope, Elia has been absolutely wonderful. I'm just running to grab a cup of coffee."

The teacher's nose wrinkles. "No food or drink is allowed in classrooms, so please finish it before returning."

With a two-finger salute to the teacher and a wink at Elia, I exit the classroom and make my way out of the building. I take the back exit, as I suspect Seth wouldn't want to have our showdown out front where anyone could see. The area behind the dance headquarters is a little more secluded.

As expected, Seth's waiting for me right outside the door, leaning with his back against the brick wall of the building, one leg kicked up, foot resting flat on the wall, and eyes narrowed on me. The early morning sun makes him look even paler than usual, almost demonic as he watches my approach.

I stop in front of him and cross my arms over my chest, ready to get this bullshit done with.

Seth says, "Depending on how this conversation goes, you might earn yourself a hospital trip."

I feel a grim smile pull on my lips. "Funny, I was just thinking the same about you."

Chapter Ten

Carson

Seth nods once, accepting my threat. He's someone who's very accustomed to navigating high-stakes and dangerous situations; it's why he's gotten as far as he has in life as fast as he has. Working under pressure is a specialty of his, which is why I'm not keen on getting in a competition over the first thing I've been interested in for quite some time. Seth will not make an easy opponent, and I know just how dirty he fights because we've spent years on the same side of the battlefield. Having him on your team guarantees a win. Going against him guarantees a bloodbath.

The issue is, I'm the same way. I don't wear my darkness on my sleeve like Seth does, but I also don't pull punches when I'm going after something I want. I can fight just as low and dirty as him; it just isn't my preferred method of conduct. I always try the diplomatic path, but like Seth, I'm willing to do what needs to be done.

"You want her. I've also decided I want her—not just my muse, but *Eliana*. We're both going to go after her. For the sake of not destroying our friendship and ending up with one or both of us dead, I have an offer for you," Seth tells me.

Interest piqued, I give him a nod. "Go on."

Seth offers me a smile that's so dark it has the effect of raising the hairs on the back of my neck. I've seen him wear that look when going into whichever proverbial battle he's engaged in; it's the *I'm closing in on the kill* smile. The *I've already won, you just don't know it yet* smile.

Seth offers, "We both pursue her in whichever manner we see fit. Eventually, she'll choose one of us or neither. When that time comes, we respect her choice. If she makes the wrong choice with you, I'll back off."

I think for a while before responding, because everything Seth does is calculated. If he's making me this offer, that means he already believes he has a path to win. Otherwise, we'd be fighting right now instead of talking. In addition to being calculated, Seth is also as meticulous as it gets; he wouldn't be here if he hadn't thought everything through. If I agree, there's a decent chance I'll be walking into a trap.

The upside is that Seth is not the only cunning motherfucker in this friendship. If he wants to make this a race for her hand a-la-medieval competition style, I'll play, but it'll be by *my* rules. I'm already insinuated in her life; if he pulls something similar, that means I'll just need to work twice as hard.

For a reason that's beyond me, knowing that I'm about to expend a great deal of time, effort and probably money to the cause of getting the first girl I've taken interest in to return my interest makes me smile. It's refreshing to actually have to work for something and there's nothing wrong with a little friendly competition.

"What made you change your mind?" I ask Seth. "Two nights ago, you were adamant she was your muse and nothing more."

A rare smile curls the corners of his lips, startling me. Not because Seth's incapable of smiling—he has facial expressions down to a science, says it's part of blending in—but because along with this smile comes a look of fondness in his eyes that tells me I'm in trouble. If he were intent on Elia that would be one thing, but I have never seen him be fond of anything that's not of his own creation. Not even me. He might *like* me enough to tolerate me, but he's certainly not fond of me; that would connote affection I'm quite sure he's incapable of feeling.

"She's... singular. In the course of two conversations over as many hours in which I spent most of the time being ignored, she managed to capture me. It'd only be fair to return the favor." He pauses, and is that *excitement* in his expression? Seth doesn't *do* excitement—he gets too bored by things too quickly. He adds on, "And she knows the Renaissance. Truly knows it."

Ah. So that's why Seth has an almost manic glint in his eye that tells me our friendly little competition will end up being anything but friendly. Passion would not be a strong enough word to describe his sentiments on the historical art periods; it's more of an obsession. If Little E managed to demonstrate that she's knowledgeable when it comes to the subject of his passions, on top of him already being convinced she's his muse... yeah, this isn't gonna be a clean fight.

"What's your game plan?" I ask him.

His smile turns into a smirk. "Wouldn't you like to know? I'll tell you this; I took inspiration from you managing to wriggle your way into her campus life."

Fuck. I give him a flat look. "Which classes did you transfer into for her?"

When I was at the admissions office yesterday, figuring out how to carve a spot in Elia's life for myself, I also got a copy of her schedule. In addition to spending most of her waking hours dancing, she's also decided to torture herself with an art history degree, which requires a whole slew of its own courses. Art history is one of Seth's passions—it isn't difficult to draw the conclusion that he's also done his research and started finding a way into her life. The question is, which specific classes? If I know, I can try to put a stop to it.

Seth's smirk grows and his eyes gleam with pleasure as he watches the realization dawn on me that this is going to be an uphill battle every step of the way. Previously, I only had to work against Elia's own drawbacks; if I'm also having to work against Seth's bullshit, this is going to turn into quite the ordeal.

For a moment, I contemplate the merits of the other option: backing off. I don't want to destroy my most valued friendship over this. Despite being one sick fuck, Seth and I have weathered some shitty life storms together. He's had my back when I needed it most, just like I've had his. Do I really want to risk that over a *girl*? Sure, she's unique and fascinating, but she can't be the only one in the world with those qualities. It's not like I intend to marry her—although I don't think I'll be through with her any time soon, permanence is not a word in my dictionary—so what would the harm be in stepping aside this once?

Her crystalline eyes—sometimes blue, sometimes grey, always *stunning*—flash across my mind. She's mainly gazed at me with contempt, but earlier in the stairwell I felt something I hadn't felt for her yet. *Burning* desire. I'm very familiar with giving into desires, but usually my desire is for release. With her, my desire wasn't about release, it was about *her*. Back in the stairwell, I *know* she felt something too. Otherwise, she wouldn't have stumbled back and held me at bay. I saw reciprocated desire in her eyes, and I absolutely refuse to back down until I've pulled that desire to the surface and exploited it for all its worth. I don't know what will happen between me and Elia, but I do know that I'm sticking around to find out.

Seth and I have been friends for years. We've had friendly bets and competitions before and survived it. It's never been over a woman previously, but even so, I need to trust that our bond is strong enough to survive us both being interested in the same girl. What I trust a little less is that Seth will play fair by any stretch of the imagination; I know he'll be sabotaging me at every given opportunity, which means I need to be prepared to sabotage him right back.

"I'll throw you a bone; I transferred into her art history classes. Funny enough, we took a very similar AP schedule in high school, both with a special interest in art," Seth informs me with the beginnings of a smirk. "In fact, it seems she and I have quite a bit in common for me to work off of."

I say flatly, "I didn't know she was a psychopath."

Seth gives me a shark's smile; all teeth, no humor. It's the same smile he gives opponents before going in for the kill. "I wouldn't be attracted to someone who's the same as me, Carson. Put me in a room with the female version of myself, and only I would walk out of there with my limbs intact."

I scoff. "So, what is it, then? You're not interested in anyone; why her?"

Seth lifts a shoulder. "She might not be as limitless as I am, but she's as passionate as I am."

That makes me laugh. "You're not passionate, Seth, you're calculated as fuck."

He inclines his head. "When it comes to my passions, there is little I won't do. Life has taught me that being calculated and methodical often yields the desired effect. Why does one cancel out the other? Passion and calculation can coexist just fine."

"Okay, Machiavelli," I mutter sarcastically.

The thing is, Seth is not the only calculated fucker in our friendship. There's a reason we get along so well; we both have a good mind for business and strategy. The difference between us—short of me having the capacity to feel empathy—is that Seth makes no effort to hide how calculated and manipulative he is, whereas I smother my darker side with heaps of charm.

Something's telling me that I may have agreed to his offer a little too quickly; this is bound to turn ugly fast.

"Ground rules," Seth says, as though reading my mind. "Elia's safety comes first. I heard about the possibility that she's on a killer's radar; if she gets hurt or killed on your watch, odds are I'll hurt or kill you in the same way."

The threat is a little far, but I see where Seth's coming from. How he already knows what I just found out about Elia's evening last night, I'm not sure, but Seth's wealthy enough to have his sources. The idea that a killer might've seen her is not comforting, especially considering her propensity for catching people's eyes.

I don't think Elia knows it, but when she walks into a room, heads turn. It's not just her beauty, though that is astounding; it's her presence. Her energy is impossible to ignore, it's like a physical force. If the killer saw her, I can't discount the idea that he *noticed* her, too.

To distract myself from that rabbit hole, I comment, "You seem surprisingly serious here. What's the endgame?"

Seth lifts a shoulder. "At the very least, she's my muse. I'll be needing her for my art. Beyond that? You'll see. But I'll tell you this; I'm not playing around here. If you are, that's going to present a problem."

I shake my head. Just a minute ago, I tried to convince myself to walk away; it didn't work. Which means that, whatever this is and whatever I'm feeling for Elia, it's not a joke.

"I'm serious about this. Which is why I'm adding another ground rule; whatever sabotage we do to each other, it can't end in expulsion, prison, or death." If I'm making a deal with Seth, I need to clarify the fine print to protect my ass. Friendly competition or not, nobody sane gets on the opposite side of Seth. It's fortunate that I've never been entirely sane.

Seth inclines his head, pushing off the wall and holding out his hand. "Then may the best man win."

I know my grin is calculated as I take his hand in mine and give it a shake, not wincing at his bone-crushing grip. Instead, I squeeze his hand harder, gratified when I feel one of his knuckles pop and his left eye twitches. In response, he doubles down, squeezing so tight that three of my knuckles pop. I keep my face clear of emotions, though; I'm not stupid enough to give Seth a reaction. He lives for those.

Instead, I say in the most casual tone I can manage, "May the best man win."

Chapter Eleven

Elia

C arson doesn't return to class for an hour, and when he does, it's with a sly expression that makes me suspect he's up to something. I have to force myself to focus on dance once he's back in his seat in the corner of the room, because his presence naturally draws my gaze to him repeatedly, distracting me and necessitating the teacher to correct my technique twice. Both times, Scarlett flashes me a smug smile, as if to say *you won't be getting any more roles with that.* Instead of being offended or irritated, I take the queen bitch's glare as motivation. We've already had our skirmishes this year; I haven't let her get to me so far, I certainly won't start now.

Inhaling a deep breath, I clear my mind of anything unrelated to dancing—the same way I had to learn to do while getting tormented by my neurotic mother—and get my head back in the game.

After that, class goes off without a hitch. At the end, the teacher—the same man who directed Sleeping Beauty, Mr.

Sanders—pulls me into the hall for a word. Nervous as hell that I'll get a verbal smackdown for messing up in the middle of class and lose my shot at any more lead roles, I have to clasp my hands together to keep them from trembling.

Mr. Sanders, a surprisingly gentle man in his late forties, offers me a reassuring smile upon seeing my tenseness. He leads me to a hallway with no foot traffic so we can speak in private, but I'm still nervous someone might overhear him lecturing me on technique and presume my solid spot as one of the freshmen stars is up for grabs. It's not; I killed myself to dance the best I could, and I won't let anyone take that from me.

"Take a breath, Elia, you're not in trouble. Other than those two corrections, you were fantastic during class. Besides, I assume the corrections were only necessary because of that Ajax boy. That's actually what I'd like to discuss with you."

I glance at the time on my phone, saying nervously, "Okay, but I have bar class in two minutes."

Sanders waves a dismissive hand. "I'll walk you there and let the teacher know I held you back, but this won't take long. Mr. Ajax—Father, not son—is actually funding a new production this year. A ballet written and choreographed by me. It's a retelling of the Greek myth of Pandora's Box, and you can probably imagine how excited I am to get started." He gives me a moment to take this in, and I try to reign in a premature expression of excitement, because I'm 90% sure where this conversation is going and *holy fuck* if I'm right.

Sanders goes on, "I'd like you to know that you popped into administration's mind for the role of Pandora—after seeing you dance Aurora, I'm confident you're the ideal company member for the role. However, I understand you have a very challenging schedule this year, so I wanted to ask in advance whether it'd be wise to assume you'll have time for added rehearsal hours. Since I'll be choreographing as we go, it *will* take up many hours for every member of the cast, even more so for principals and leads. I'd need you to be able to commit to three hours of evening choreography and rehearsal three times a week, to start with. Is this achievable?"

Several emotions pass through me at once. Excitement, joy, pleasure at being picked out of the masses and recognized so soon, along with an overwhelming terror that I've bitten off more than I can chew this year. If I do evening rehearsals, odds are I won't have the time or energy to work on top of that. I was *really* looking forward to taking one of the jobs teaching dance to young girls, not just for the extra income, but because I love making dance more accessible to those who want to pursue it. I'll probably be giving that up if I take this offer, and I'll be giving up any spare drops of free time I might've had, but this is something that could make my career before I'm even done with college.

If the show is successful when it opens, there's a chance it'll go on tour over the summer. If I'm cast as lead and the audience likes me as much as they did when I played Aurora, that means I'll most likely get invited to the tour. That alone would garner international notice—not just getting noticed in the states, as I've spent years working towards—and would set me on a principal dancer path for the rest of my career. This opportunity is unprecedented, and impossible to turn down.

Before I can talk myself out of it or consider the personal toll it'll likely end up taking, I say, "Mr. Sanders, I would be *honored* to be a part of your creation. I have classes every weekday until four, and twice a week I'll be volunteering during evenings at a museum for my art history degree. If that won't interrupt the schedule, please, count me in."

Sanders smiles at me, and I can feel his excitement. If I'm not mistaken, this would be the first full-length show he'll choreograph and direct single handedly, which means it'll be as big a deal to him as it is to me, and I have yet *another* opportunity in this situation to make a connection with a well-known and very well-connected director turned choreographer. While Sanders is tough and pitiless during class—as all the teachers need to be—otherwise the dancers wouldn't improve and grow—the little I've seen of him outside of it makes me think he'd be a great person to learn from. He knows the dance industry; he was a ballet dancer for close to twenty years before moving on to teaching and directing.

"I'm thrilled to hear that. If something changes, I'd ask you to let me know this week, because auditions start soon and cast list will be going up in a few weeks."

There is quite literally nothing that could rip me away from this opportunity, but I don't say that aloud in case I sound over eager. Instead, I say firmly, "I'll give you my word now that, so long as you're willing to keep me, I'm committed to this show. I can't wait to learn as much as I can from the experience."

Sanders nods, reaching out to give my shoulder a friendly squeeze. "I'm glad. Let's get you to class before Moira bites my head off for holding dancers back from their courses."

As we walk, I realize that there's someone else who certainly deserves a spot in the cast. Before I think it through, I say, "If you'll allow me, might I recommend another dancer for the cast?"

My teacher looks mildly curious and slightly skeptical as he nods, permitting me to dare and offer suggestion. In the world of dance—ballet especially, which Sanders was trained in and danced for two decades—ballerina's do not ask questions or give input; they follow direction. The masters, directors, and choreographers are the brains; the ballerinas are just the puppets. I know I need to be careful about my wording here.

April has already been so kind to me, and I haven't really had the *time* to give anything back to her other than thanks and company. Just an hour ago, while Carson was out supposedly getting coffee, Scarlett tried to trip me while Sanders wasn't looking; April spilled water in the spot where Scarlett was dancing when *she* wasn't looking, and Scarlett ended up flat on her ass while Sanders was correcting her.

So, I'm pretty much ready to do anything to help April out and strengthen our new friendship. Something tells me she'll be integral if I'm going to get through the next four years, and beyond that, I genuinely like her.

Since I haven't practiced what I'd say to Sanders and don't have a meticulous script to stick to, I just blurt the truth. "April danced the evil queen *very* well. She's driven, hardworking, and has excellent training. I've spent the last month working on technique with her on a daily basis, and hers is as good as mine. If you think I'd be good for the show, I believe she'd be an ideal candidate, as well."

Sanders looks surprised at my words, skepticism cleared from his expression. More, he looks interested, which bodes well.

He inclines his head ever so slightly. "April's performance in Sleeping Beauty already bumped her to round two of auditions for my show. Your pitch just got her into round three."

Auditions here go round by round; the initial cuts take three rounds, and the fourth round—or final—is when the group that's been kept gets cast into roles. If I got April into round three, that means she's already in the show, it's just up to her audition on which role she'll dance.

Sanders doesn't say anything else, but he doesn't need to. I'm exhilarated and extremely pleased with myself for giving April a leg up, as she's been doing for me since we met. As a bonus, hearing him take suggestions gives me a lot of hope for the show. Many choreographers make the mistake of not listening to input from the very people who make up the heart and soul of their shows, which I always think is a mistake because the dancers are the ones who can *feel* the story. Perhaps Sander's background in ballet makes him more conscientious than most.

I also can't *wait* to tell April. She should still have time to teach classes, so this wouldn't impede any of her other pursuits.

As promised, my director walks with me to my following class. Carson is standing outside of the classroom, arms crossed over his chest, looking annoyed. As soon as he sees me with Sanders, his look of irritation deepens and his gaze flicks between us.

He calls out, "I was starting to think you'd abandoned me. That wouldn't be a nice thing to do to the person who'll decide whether or not this department sees a six-figure-plus check by winter break."

I have to hold back a gasp, mortified at his directness and the way he looks right into Sanders eyes as he says it, as if he wants to intimidate a man twenty years his senior. Since I don't want to get grouped in with Carson's disrespect, I say to Sanders quickly, "I'm *so* sorry."

Sanders gives me a reassuring smile. "That's alright, not everyone's brought up with manners. Mr. Ajax, I hope the department meets your standards, as a bonus would be incredibly useful and help us put on more productions for the public to enjoy." My teacher speaks the words like he's reading them from an advertising script, his voice a little rough, as if he's forcing himself to say it.

Considering Carson's outrageous rudeness, I don't blame him. I have to wonder what brought this on, though, since Carson has yet to shove it in my face that he's wealthy. His general appearance, clothing, and mannerisms do the talking without him needing to. To see him be so tactless doesn't make sense. He certainly hasn't brought his money up, possibly because it's painfully clear I am on the exact opposite end of the spectrum to him; a flat broke scholarship kid whose only possibility of wealth requires back-breaking hard work. I didn't get *anything* handed to me, I've had to fight tooth and nail for everything I have, which admittedly isn't much.

Hearing a plain reminder of Carson being the exact opposite to me serves the purpose of pissing me the hell off. I already know the game we're playing; as long as I play nice, my department gets rewarded. I'm fine with that so long as it remains an unspoken agreement and doesn't get shoved in my face, I still have my damn pride. Now he's gone and shoved it in my face.

Fuck this. I was okay with being shadowed by Carson because I thought his interest in me would be enough to keep his manners in check. Obviously, I was wrong to assume that. My temper flares, and as I always do when that happens, I get rude.

"For someone whose only achievement in life is breaking the world record for condoms bought in a month, you've got a lot of nerve," I snap.

Now it's Sanders turn to hold back a gasp. He actually muffles it with his hand, and then something adjacent to a snort escapes him, probably to cover his laugh. Carson, on the other hand, doesn't look amused whatsoever. His eyes narrow on me in consideration, and the corners of his lips tilt down with displeasure. His gaze sharpens and a chill skitters up my spine, telling me to tread *very* carefully.

Unfortunately, when I'm pissed, I'm far less prone to adhering to common sense, so I don't backtrack or apologize. Instead I hold his gaze boldly, *daring* him to say something in return.

After several infinitely long moments, Carson lets out a puff of laughter. "You really are something else, Princess, you know that? The only problem is that other people keep noticing, too."

His latter words make it click in my mind; he got rude because he was *jealous*. That alone is so surprising I almost burst out laughing. Now the way he looked between Sanders and I, all judgmental and speculative, makes sense—as does his comment. It certainly doesn't excuse what he said, but it explains it. Nevertheless, I won't let him talk down to me or the teacher who's giving me the greatest opportunity of my life. I also won't tolerate his bullshit.

I might not have nearly as many zeroes in my bank account as Carson, but I do have one hell of a work ethic, motivation, ambition, and a reasonably quick mind. Many also say I have talent. That makes me formidable and powerful in my own right, something I've learned again and again through the repeated trials by fire that life has thrown at me. If I let Carson think he can get away with shit like this, this situation will get intolerable, quick.

I turn to Sanders with a smile. "Can I have a moment with Carson?"

Sanders nods and walks away, deciding I can handle Carson and my next teacher's wrath on my own.

I walk right up to Carson, going as far as to press my index finger to his chest. "We're done for the day. Get the fuck out of my sight. If you don't want me to spend the term ignoring you, *never* lord your wealth over me again. It's disgusting."

Not waiting for a response, I push past him and head into my class.

Chapter Twelve

Carson doesn't follow me into the classroom, and I don't see him around headquarters for the rest of the day, so I think it's safe to assume he's decided to take my warning and back off for now. That's probably for the best, considering I was ready to throat-punch him for pulling the money card. I won't deny that I have a chip on my shoulder when it comes to wealth.

I'll tolerate a lot of shit from people, but I have *years* of memories of having to save up to buy my own clothes and essentially supporting myself while money that was *meant* for me was instead being spent on my mom's vanity. She took special pleasure in setting ridiculous standards I had to meet in order to get an allowance, one of the main standards being maintaining a certain weight—a number she'd drop whenever she felt like it, often far below what was healthy. Naturally, I was working by the time I was fourteen, because I understood I'd never get consistent support from her and if I wanted to succeed, I'd have to do it working against the curveballs she'd throw at me.

While she didn't mind spending money on making me appear as the perfect daughter, especially when it came to performances, I was on my own for everything else. I've been budgeting since I learned arithmetic; I have literally had issues with money since I could comprehend what issues with money are. That's not to mention the filthy rich ex I had to put up with, who I managed to safely get away from just a few months ago. So, Carson's little stunt does *not* sit well with me. The fact that he respected my wishes and left barely puts a dent in my irritation, because I know I'm stuck with him for the rest of term. I could spend it ignoring him, and I'm sorely tempted to do so, but I also suspect how I treat him will affect the dollar figure on the check the department will receive, which means playing nice is in my own best interest as well as everyone's here.

I also know that an endorsement from the Ajax name would do good things for me. The thing is, I don't need Carson's money or power—I'm doing just fine on my own. My talent and hard work have gotten me far, and seeing those things diminished in the face of money is infuriating.

I contemplate how to handle my Carson situation—whether or not I should try to figure a way out of it—as I'm showering and preparing to sprint to my art classes. Eventually, I decide that for the sake of getting a good rep in the department, I will be perfectly cordial, and that is *all* I'll be. I'm done with any hints of attraction I might've potentially felt for him—he gave me a solid reminder why I don't *get* attracted to guys like him.

April wishes me luck with my first day of art history classes as I'm speedwalking past her through the halls of headquarters. Even though it might make me late, I stop and pull her into the nearest empty studio space.

She says in a purr, "Not that I wouldn't mind getting ravaged by you in a dark classroom, but I'm pretty sure you're straight. What are we doing here?"

A burst of laughter escapes me. April's so quirky and genuine, it's impossible not to adore her.

"It would be getting ravished, not ravaged," I correct her.

She shrugs. "Same difference. Anyway, I know you have to be a mile away in approximately," she pauses to check her watch, "fifteen minutes. What's up?"

I rush out excitedly, "Don't tell anyone—I'm not even supposed to know this yet—but Sanders is choreographing a new show. A retelling of Pandora's Box. He pulled me aside to ask if I'd have time in my schedule for it, and I also recommended you for the cast. Your performance in Sleeping Beauty had you in round two of auditions, now you're in round three."

April's silent after I speak, for so long that I start to grow nervous and fidget. Could I have been wrong in assuming she's okay with me giving her a leg up? It's possible my intervention could be perceived as a hit to her pride, as though I don't think she's capable of making the cast herself. I get so nervous I almost start apologizing prematurely, worried that I angered her somehow. April's the only friend I've made, and the only other *real* girl in the company—I'll crucify myself if I manage to fuck up the friendship this early on.

Before I can let out a stream of barely intelligible apologies, April pulls me into her arms in one of the most smothering hugs I've ever experienced. She holds me so tightly I actually fear she might break something, and when she pulls back, it's with a look of such appreciation I'm touched nearly to tears.

She squeezes my hands. "Thank you, Elia. Seriously."

I wave a hand. "You'd have gotten yourself cast anyway, I'm sure, I just helped move your name up the list—just like you did when you got me the studio job, which I'll barely have any time for. Sanders is choreographing as he goes, so rehearsal hours will be long."

"I don't care if I'm in rehearsal every waking hour," April tells me, voice ringing with sincerity. "We get to be part of an excellent dancer's and possibly up-and-coming choreographers first production. That's worth every hour in the day."

I can't disagree, so instead I give her one last quick hug before swinging my backpack over my shoulder and sprinting my way to the first class of my art history degree.

The arts department is its own conglomeration of buildings, and all of my classes are held in the same building, meaning I won't have to sprint between them as well as to them. I rush into my Early to Pre-Middle Ages Art History course just as the professor's setting up behind a wooden desk at the front of the generic large classroom, complete with four dozen or so desks, most of which are already taken. I grimace when I see the front row is already full, meaning I won't get a first-row seat to my studies. Usually, I like to be front and center—it's the best spot to see the board, establish friendly contact with the professor, and try to get noticed as a particularly hard worker.

Resigned to getting lost in the masses, I trudge my way through the rows of desks until I find an open one. I'm dismayed to see the last one available is in the back row, but absolutely shocked when I see who's sitting next to it, staring at me like a predator locked onto prey: Seth Balor.

No. *No.* Having Carson infiltrate my life is enough; there is no way Seth is here on accident, and there is no fucking way I am putting up with another rich douchebag today. I've fulfilled my quota for several lifetimes already. Sadly, there is nothing I can do in this situation. I don't know how Seth found out I'm in art history, but then again, if Carson can get himself a spot shadowing me then Seth can transfer into my art courses.

Since I took so many AP and college classes geared towards my art history degree while in high school, I'm technically already in the second year of classes. The Greywood ID I glimpsed when we were at the museum told me that Seth's a junior, and I know he's not an art history major, so there's literally no reason Seth would be sitting here if it wasn't for me.

I dug around on social media last night in my mountains of research while trying to figure out what the hell's going on here and ended up stumbling onto Greywood's Instagram page. Over the summer they did a *profile* on Seth—the same way news stations and magazines do on major public figures. I, of course, read it, and it revealed that his specialty lies in science and engineering, with art being more of a passion. A passion he's already won awards for, but not something he's formally studying here or elsewhere.

Did I really dance Aurora *that* well? I know I'm talented—I've spent my whole life honing and perfecting my talent—but I'm not a fucking deity. Getting stalked as a result of a good performance... well, that's not a complication I expected or foresaw, but it looks like it's a complication I'm going to consistently be dealing with, to the extent of having strangers insinuate themselves into my daily life.

It feels faintly like I'm getting pranked as I sulk my way to the last available seat in the class, drop into the chair, and busy myself pulling my school supplies out of my bag, neatly organizing them on my desk to distract myself from the gaze currently burning a hole in the side of my head. If Seth thinks showing up is going to get a visible reaction from me, he's dead wrong.

"Hello again," he finally says after realizing I won't be the one to break the silence.

I don't bother looking at him when I shoot back, "Don't talk to me."

Voice saturated in amusement, he asks, "Why?"

Is he joking? I glance at his expression, trying to gauge if he's serious. His face is blank, but his eyes are practically lit up with interest as he stares at me. So, he's serious in not understanding why I don't want to talk to him, which means he's either delusional or a psychopath. Which, I'm not sure yet, but what I am sure of is that I have zero interest in sticking around to find out. My life is plenty hectic as is, I don't need to add two rich stalkers to the roster, regardless of how they look.

Out of all the endless reasons I could list, I go with, "Because I'm all out of fuel when it comes to dealing with stalkers today, so you'll have to wait until Wednesday if you want a reaction."

Seth lets out a deep, rumbly chuckle that I feel reverberate through me even though he's seated a few feet away. "It's not called stalking if I'm doing it. I'm far too attractive to be deemed a stalker. How about suitor?"

I snap, "This isn't the fucking bachelorette! And with a body just having dropped on campus last night, it *really* isn't the time to be seen as a stalker."

"Suitor," he corrects.

Instead of stabbing my pen into his neck, which is becoming an increasingly difficult urge to ignore, I inhale a deep breath and straighten my spine.

"I'm not having this argument with you. In fact, I'm not even having this conversation with you. So, let's go back to the part where I told you not to talk to me and pretend that you listened."

He opens his mouth to respond, only to get cut off by the professor as he starts to do roll call. I appreciate the excuse to totally ignore Seth, as I've been wishing to do since I walked in and saw him sitting here. While the question as to why the fuck he's here is taking up most of the space in my mind, I already know there can only be one answer; as absolutely crazy as it is, he's here for me. Seems he's not the only one who left a lasting impression on the other at the museum. I'm tempted to call him out, but he could just say he took a special interest in art this year.

To be fair, when I was reading over the profile of him on Instagram, it did mention that several of his paintings and sculptures are on display in both domestic and international museums, so it wouldn't be *that* much of a stretch to think he'd take some interest in art history. But *now*? As a junior who's already double majoring in science and engineering, he should have a schedule as packed as mine. He certainly shouldn't be able to switch around classes last minute.

That gives me pause, because there is a chance I'm just being paranoid. I'm sleep deprived, just got done with six hours of dancing, and already on edge due to last night's events.

As the professor starts going over the syllabus, Seth leans closer to me, until there's barely a foot of space separating us. "In case there's any doubt, I'm here for you, Eliana. You should've taken me up on my offer for lunch."

CHAPTER THIRTEEN

Seth

I watch her spine snap ramrod straight and shoulders stiffen as my words sink in. I've been watching my Little Muse as she snuck glances at me out of the corner of her eye, wondering if she'd have the balls to ask me outright the question I know must be bouncing around in that pretty head of hers. Since twenty minutes have passed and she still hasn't posed any questions, I decided to answer it for her.

Her head slowly swivels in my direction, and I'm mesmerized by the way her eyes appear more grey than blue in this moment. Her eyes vary in color from an arctic blue reminiscent of a frozen lake to a dark grey that speaks of a coming storm. Right now, everything about her is like an incoming storm; wild, beautiful, barely restrained.

She opens her mouth, probably intending to say something to the effects of telling me to fuck off—which would only amuse me—but seems to think better of it, sealing her lips and pointedly turning her attention back to the professor. I'm fine if she wants to ignore me for now, because I've already planned to ensure it doesn't last forever.

In the time since I last saw her, I've done some digging on my Little Muse. I keep a private investigator on retainer for any time I need to do a deep dive into someone—potential business partners, prospective opportunities, and some of the more dangerous individuals I'm acquainted with—and I instructed him to gather *everything* there is to find about Eliana Pierce.

Turns out, there was quite a bit to find. Social services reports talking about the instability of her mother, hospital stays as a result of malnutrition or the occasional injury inflicted by said mother's boyfriends—I got the file on her yesterday and spent quite some time consumed with the story of my muse. And there *is* quite a story to her. Elia, at eighteen, has overcome and moved past the sort of adversity that would keep most people at rock bottom for life. Honestly, just watching her now while knowing what I know about her brings a sense of awe.

There's something regal about her. She doesn't appear to put any great amount of effort into blending with the masses, nor does she try to distinguish herself as above them, which is precisely why it's so easy to see that she *is* above them. Her talent, intelligence, and fortitude are the reasons she actually survived to tell the tale of her childhood, and yet, she doesn't flaunt any of her admirable qualities. She doesn't hide them either, she just seems content to exist as is and allow her work to speak for her.

It most certainly does. Other than reading the file my PI put together on her, I did some research of my own. There are viral videos all over every major internet and social media platform showcasing the sheer, raw power of her dancing. Some are excerpts from ballets or shows she's done, others are solo videos she made and posted herself, probably for the sake of getting visibility.

I watched every single one, as entranced as when I saw her on stage, and I came to understand exactly what captivated me about her; she is an artist of the highest order. It's clear to see that dancing isn't just physical exercise or passion or even storytelling to her, it comes from the soul. That is something I understand better than most—art is the one way I allow myself to unleash the full weight of my soul.

Elia glances at me from the corner of her eye, rolls her eyes when she sees that, yes, I'm still staring at her, and actually goes as far as to give me her back, shifting sideways in her seat. It was clear to me from the minute she hurried through the door, flustered and flushed from what was probably a sprint from dance headquarters, that she was not in a good mood. From the way she's made a show of ignoring me, even though I am not the only person in the room watching her—several boys and girls in vicinity give her either lustful, interested, or jealous glances regularly, the girl draws attention everywhere she goes—I suspect Carson's done something to piss her off. That's a win for me in the long run, since it'd mean he's already digging his own grave, but while she appears to see me and him as connected it'll be a barrier.

Only one thing to do in this situation: make it obvious that I am certainly *not* him and she'd do well to remember it. She told me at the museum that we were both unnervingly forward; while I can't change my intensity, I can change my tactics and refocus on things I do not share in common with my idiotic friend but do with my muse—such as art. Though I'm unable to negate who I fundamentally am—intense, diabolical, and some would say psychopathic—I can be tactful about how I present those traits. Especially to the most fascinating creature I've stumbled upon in my life, and one who fascinates me more and more by the minute.

I need to lock down Eliana while Carson's still figuring out what exactly he wants. I'm not someone who takes action before considering endgame, unlike my friend who vacillates between desire and reason and therefore ends up fucking himself over before he's even set a gameplan. I read from him earlier that while he was set on pursuing her, he didn't know what he was after; that'll be his fatal flaw. I knew as soon as my muse left me standing and staring after her like a fool in the museum lobby exactly what I wanted from her: everything there is to have.

I don't know how long I'll want that for, but the more I learn about her, the more I suspect my muse might turn into an addiction that I won't want to drop.

I don't make any effort to hide that I watch her for the rest of class, though she eventually switches from pretending to ignore me to *actually* ignoring me in favor of taking notes on her laptop. Luckily, I don't need to waste time on such menial things; I'll remember the professor's lecture and any reading word for word.

When the class ends, Elia gathers her things and stands to leave so quickly, one would be forgiven for thinking the building's on fire. Before she can rush through the aisle, I stand from my seat to block her path. She arches an imperious eyebrow at me, crossing her arms over her chest.

Even though I already know the answer, I ask, "What class do you have next?"

She snips, "None of your business," and then physically shoulders past me. I allow it, content to watch her as I did in the museum. Her mannerisms are bewitching, from the way she carries herself—head held high, shoulders squared—to the way she smiles selectively at passerby's, and seems totally at ease in any given environment.

I catch up to her in the hall, saying conversationally, "I have Renaissance through Modernism up next, which I'm very much looking forward to. I have a feeling I'll be in good company."

Elia's fists clench by her sides, and her nostrils flare with irritation, but she doesn't say anything. In fact, other than subconscious nonverbal responses, she doesn't acknowledge me in any way. I can't have ignoring me become a habit for her, and I have to curb the urge to grab her arm, pull her into the nearest empty space, and show her that it isn't wise to ignore someone like me in a way that ends up with her screams in my ear.

I know I need to build at least somewhat of a connection with her before allowing myself to have her, or I risk getting shut down. I hope for her sake that she doesn't make me wait long, because I don't know how long I'll be able to hold myself in check around her. I've never felt the depth of desire I do for her with anyone else, and uncharted territory like this is inherently dangerous.

I try a different tactic, not anywhere near ready to concede and let her go on pretending I'm not here. "Who's your favorite Renaissance artist?"

She mutters, "Brunelleschi."

"Why's that? He's widely considered to have been an architect and engineer more so than artist."

She stops in front of the classroom where our next class is held, stepping in through the open door and walking to a seat in the first row, dumping her bag on the desk. There are people seated on either side of the desk, but if she thinks that's enough to keep me at bay, she's sorely mistaken.

I drop into the seat behind hers, leaning forward until I'm close enough she'll hear me and feel my breath on the side of her neck. "It's rude not to answer a question."

She glances at me over her shoulder, eyes shuttered. "It's also rude to stalk someone."

I lean my elbow on the desk and prop my chin on my palm, once again making no move to hide that I'm openly staring at her. Frankly, the more people who know that I'm interested, the better; not many are crazy enough to get in my way, Carson being a rare exception. "We agreed I'm a suitor, not stalker. So, I think in my case, it's called courting."

She lets out a delicate snort. "Have you been reading regency romance novels?"

I raise my eyebrows. "Have *you*?" When she doesn't respond, I decide to push a step further. "Do you prefer the gentlemanly, man-child heroes or the ones that are assertive enough to push the heroine against the nearest surface and take what they're both aching for?"

Her cheeks flame, her lips part, and her pupils dilate, confirming that while my intensity tinged with sexuality might make her uncomfortable, it also arouses her. Which means she just might be able to survive me intact. *Very interesting.*

My eyes flick to her lips as they seal up, and then her lovely neck as she swallows. She opens her mouth again, but appears lost for words.

"The Florence Cathedral," she says, somewhat breathlessly.

I blink. "What?"

"Brunelleschi was an architect, engineer, sculptor, and genius, but I consider him an artist above all because of his construction of the Florence Duomo's roof. The Santa Maria del Fiore Cathedral was left unfinished for nearly a century because nobody could figure out how to construct a dome ceiling on a structure of such size. The last civilizations to boast of such an achievement were—"

"Ancient Rome, the eye of the Pantheon," I finish for her, growing more and more enthralled as she speaks. "There's also the Hagia Sophia, principal church in the Byzantine Empire, built five hundred years after the Pantheon and eight hundred years before the Florence Cathedral."

She nods. "Right. Brunelleschi's designs were ingenious, but when I look at the dome roof I don't see the technical genius. I don't even see the cleverness of using a herringbone pattern and lighter materials on the higher parts of the dome over a heavier base—the concept of which was likely inspired by complex mathematics—I see art. So, he's my favorite renaissance *artist*. Followed closely by DaVinci." At the end of her explanation she casts a nervous glance around us, cheeks flaming even brighter to see that, no, I'm not the only fucker who got enthralled by listening to her talk, and then quickly spins around to face the board.

I take the moment to give a dark glare to every male in proximity who's exhibited signs of interest—which is most of them—gratified when most go back to minding their own damn business.

I already knew what I wanted from Elia, and I thought I was patient enough to wait and play the long game. Now, two interactions in, I'm starting to think I either overestimated my self-control or underestimated her ability to affect me. Probably both. Now, I'm starting to wonder just how long I'll be able to keep my desires and intentions on a leash.

For the rest of the class, I think on how I can speed along the process of making Elia mine. Once class wraps up and she, again, scrambles out the door like the room's on fire, I remain in my desk for several minutes. Two times have been enough for her to capture me completely; on the third, I'll be returning the favor.

Unbeknownst to my muse, tonight we happen to share an evening volunteer slot at the very same museum where we first formally met. It'll be dark, mostly deserted, and surrounded by something that I suspect is an aphrodisiac to both of us: age-old art pieces. I intend to show Elia why I'm the right choice before Carson has the chance to fix whatever fuckup he made.

CHAPTER FOURTEEN

Elia

Upon arriving at the museum later that day, I'm unsurprised to see Seth along with the rest of the students standing in the lobby, gathered like loyal soldiers prepared to receive orders. I recognize several other people from my art history classes, and I make a point of smiling at them while ignoring Seth as I join the crowd. A no-reaction policy seems to be my best defense against him. When I don't have the urge to stab a writing tool into his eye, I become so flustered I start to ramble. That hasn't happened to me in a while, and I thought I was past the babbling-schoolgirl phase.

The museum is the same one I visited over the weekend, and despite the complication of Seth's presence, I'm excited to get a new perspective on all of the pieces and collections here. A behind the scenes look into the archives would also be *most* welcome. Which is why, when one of the museum managers that'll serve as our instructor comes out of her office and starts dishing out orders, I volunteer to sift through the archives in search of a sketch she requires. Seth also manages to get a spot in the search party, and we end up being the only two heading to the basement, isolated from the rest of the museum's activity.

The archives are filled with paintings stacked against walls, along with wooden crates probably housing a wealth of unseen valuables. To be allowed back here feels like a privilege I don't deserve, but to be allowed back here with *Seth* is a complication I don't need. I'm already feeling flustered from our conversation earlier—smart and sexy are synonymous in my dictionary, and he's proved to be both drop dead gorgeous *and* insanely intelligent, upping his appeal even more—and being trapped with him in a dim space filled with art that on its own serves as an aphrodisiac does not feel like the wisest move.

Still, his presence doesn't stop me from admiring the art pieces on display, grimy though some of them might be. I also don't miss the dusty couch pushed up against one of the walls, or how Seth also notices it, casting it a contemplative glance as if considering what we might get up to on it.

"We're looking for the Fabergé egg design sketch—Jessica said it would be in one of the wooden boxes," I say aloud, though neither one of us needs the reminder. I want to stay task-oriented, because I suspect that if I let my mind wander it would turn down a dirty path. Six-feet-plus of unbelievably sexy masculinity, gorgeousness, intensity, and jarring intelligence all aimed in my direction is a lot to handle, even with my willpower.

The thing is, the more time I spend with Seth, the less I actually *want* to resist him, even though there's a slew of very obvious reasons I should. Aside from both of us being too busy to date, he is a walking red flag who I suspect doesn't have much regard for other people. That's a shitstorm waiting to happen, and not one I want to get caught up in.

"She also said we weren't permitted to leave until we found it," Seth says, pointedly looking around the room stacked with what must be more than two hundred crates, none of them labeled. "Seems we'll be here for a while."

I point out, "If we stay focused, we should be able to find it within an hour or two."

Seth closes the distance between us in several fluid steps. "I don't want to stay focused. I want to get *very* distracted with you. You want the same thing, yet you fight it. Why?"

I take a nervous step back. Most of the time, I have no problem holding my ground, regardless of how intimidating the person across from me is. I don't have difficulty standing up to Carson or any of the bitchy girls in my company, but Seth is a different story. It's not just that he's intimidating, it's the primal knowledge that I'm completely outmatched. My wit is often enough to get me through tough situations. Seth's too smart for me to outmaneuver, though, and I don't like the sense of vulnerability that creates.

Seth takes a step forward to make up the distance between us, prompting me to take another step back, and for him to take another one closer. I get so caught up in our little dance that I don't realize I've literally cornered myself until I feel the cool wall against my back.

Seth braces an arm over my head, staring down at me with a faint smirk curling his lips. "You really shouldn't back away from someone like me. It kicks in the hunting instinct."

In this moment he is every bit the hunter, and it strikes me just how unsafe this situation is. I didn't think that my physical safety was actually at risk with him at any point, but staring up at him and seeing the dark look in his eyes, I suspect I might've been too quick to assume.

I think Seth is dangerous enough to hurt other people; is it really smart to assume I'm safe just because people saw us go into a room together? I recall what he said to me during our first conversation, about Carson being rich enough to get away with hurting me. What he said probably extends to himself, and now I wonder if that hadn't been a hidden warning.

"What do you want from me?" I whisper.

"Everything."

Everything? I knew he was interested in me—if I'm honest, I'm interested in him as well, despite my best efforts—but to want *everything* from a relative stranger? Does he know the definition of the word? "How could you say that? We barely know each other."

He gets a strange, knowing glint in his eyes. "I know enough."

I shake my head slowly, bracing one hand on his chest to keep at least some distance between us and using my free hand to gesture from him to me. "This can't happen. *We* can't happen. No amount of you or Carson invading my life will change the fact that I'm *not available.*"

Maybe if I say that enough times, it'll fully cement into my brain. Because while I know nothing serious could ever come of me and Seth, staring up at him here, surrounded by art and history, I start to wonder if maybe I can't make a single exception. I've felt a warped attraction to him since the moment I met him, and maybe the solution would be to simply fuck him out of my system.

I don't usually go for casual sex—there needs to be a preexisting interest and connection for me to feel comfortable giving my body to someone else—but this situation has proven to be special. And special circumstances require special solutions.

No. *No.* One time could give Seth the impression that there's potential for something here, which there isn't. It'd end up leading him on and setting me up for bigger problems later.

"Your lips tell a different story from your eyes," he murmurs, gaze flicking between my eyes and lips. "Words can lie. Eyes always tell the truth." With that statement, he leans down and seals his lips over mine.

I've only kissed a handful of times in my life. Before my ex, I hadn't really dated much, and my ex was such a terrible kisser I mostly preferred to avoid it. My ex was a terrible everything—the relationship was more one of convenience than anything else. Each time he'd lean in, I'd turn my head away and give him my cheek just to avoid the gag-reflex that accompanied having someone's tongue shoved down your throat.

This kiss, however, is nothing short of intoxicating. Seth's lips are silky soft and smooth as butter, his tongue is velvet seduction that I can't help but want to feel in other places a little further south, and his entire body is so warm and *hard* it's impossible not to melt into the kiss, if only a little. The dizzying intensity he always exudes multiplies ten-fold until my head is actually spinning, and I tear my mouth away from his, panting and clutching his shoulders. *When did I go from holding him off to just holding him?*

I manage to mutter, "Just... wait, we should talk about this first."

"I don't think so. You'll just convince yourself of what a bad idea this is, forcing me to resort to more drastic methods." He shocks the hell out of me by dropping to his knees, right here on the dirty floor, probably ruining his *far* too expensive pants.

Despite him no longer looming over me, I still feel somewhat trapped, which prompts me to try to wriggle out from between him and the wall. "Are you *threatening* me?"

His hands grip my waist and flatten my back against the wall, the gesture telling me in no uncertain terms that I won't be going anywhere until he's decided to let me. His eyes lock with mine, and the intensity they hold makes my breath catch. "Not threatening, forewarning." After giving my hips a cautioning squeeze, his hands move up, fingers nimbly unbuttoning the front of my blouse. He goes on, "Usually, I'd have more patience, but circumstances are different here. Not only in the irregularity that a living being has managed to catch my interest on a level beyond superficial, but also in that I'm not the only interested party here, which makes speeding along the timeline more pertinent."

I'm so stunned by the fast progression of events that he's already finished unbuttoning my shirt by the time I reach up my hands to swat his away. He catches both of my wrists in one of his massive hands, arching an eyebrow at me. "Do I need to tie these together?"

I consider fighting him in earnest instead of the half-hearted protests I've given so far. I might not want the perpetual storm that I suspect is associated with Seth, but I can admit to myself that in this moment I do want him. Still, letting go could have long term consequences, and I'm not keen to pay when the bill comes due for one night of stupid fun. So, regardless of how much my body might want to say yes, my brain is smarter.

I shake my head. "No, you don't, because nothing is going to happen here."

Seth tilts his head to the side, looking me over. He uses his free hand to part my blouse until my bra is visible, and I gasp when he abruptly yanks on it, freeing one of my breasts to the cool air. "Hard nipples, flushed cheeks, glazed eyes. I bet if I reached between these pretty thighs, I'd find a puddle I'd want to clean up with my tongue. Little Muse, everything about you is saying *more* except your lips. Since you won't use them to tell me why, I don't think I want to hear any more words from you."

Holy mother of fuck, that's hot. It shouldn't be, and while *most* of me is indignant at his presumptuousness, there's a tiny part that's enchanted. Dominance seeps from him at all times, but right now it's so overpowering I'm not sure I want to fight it. But whether or not I want to doesn't change that it's the right thing to do for my own sake. Also, did he just call me *Little Muse?* As in, an artist's muse?

I open my mouth to argue; my words turn into a gasp when he leans forward and his lips close around my nipple. His mouth is hot, wet, and deliciously seductive. He sucks so hard his cheeks hollow and my back arches off the wall as waves of sensation and pleasure shoot through my body, gathering in my core. His teeth scrape across my nipple, adding a bite of pain and drawing a whimper from my lips.

Seth breathes against my flesh, "Yes, just like that. The only noises I want from you are whimpers, moans, and screams." Before my scrambled mind can come up with a reply, he distracts me even further by trailing wet kisses down my stomach, the soft brush of his lips occasionally followed up with a nip.

Almost a year with my ex, and I didn't come a single time, during all the sex and fooling around. Five minutes in with Seth and I'm ready to explode from need.

And still, my mind can't help partially wandering down the path that this is a terrible idea, despite the cloud of lust currently fogging up my brain. When he unzips my skirt and tugs at the fabric so it pools around my ankles, I manage to get my head on straight long enough to say, "We shouldn't. We can't."

Seth splays his hand low on my stomach, so low that his palm covers the front of my panties and I can feel the heel of his hand in the apex between my thighs. He leans forward, biting my hip so sharply I yelp and try to jerk away, to no avail. The pain quickly blooms into pleasure that makes my pussy pulse with need.

Seth says ever so gently, "You don't have a say here, Little Muse. I'm going to do whatever I please, and all you get to do is take it."

Once again, something that absolutely should not be arousing ends up striking me as smoking hot. It's probably because I'm used to sex being a chore where I have to do all the work to get off whoever I'm fucking while receiving nothing in return, so the idea of not having to do anything but take what I'm given—especially when it's pleasure—makes my entire body hum with need.

His fingers start tracing along the edge of my panties, and my already-labored breathing speeds up even further until I feel like I've just run a twenty-mile marathon. The anticipation and desire wars with common sense and a strong feeling that I'm in *way* over my head here, which somehow only manages to further my arousal.

That frightens me enough to jerk my hands so abruptly I actually manage to free them from Seth's grip, which admittedly loosened as he was paying more attention to other parts of my body. I use my newfound freedom to right my bra strap and twirl away from my spot trapped against the wall. Seth appears more surprised than anything, looking from me to the wall in front of him where I just was and back at me. I use his moment of distraction to swoop my clothes off the ground, tugging on my skirt haphazardly and shrugging on my blouse while somehow speedwalking to the entrance of the room. Only once I'm at the door with a half-buttoned shirt and half-zipped skirt do I risk looking back to Seth.

He's risen from his kneeling position but hasn't moved more than that. His eyes are locked on me, as intense as they were earlier, but now there's excitement layered on top of interest. His entire body is tense as a bow, ready to launch, and I know I need to get out of here *yesterday* if I want to avoid making a ridiculously stupid decision, because holy *shit* is the guy dark seduction personified.

I say hurriedly, "I'm going to tell Jessica I wasn't feeling well and hope she doesn't put me on some permanent blacklist; have fun looking for the sketch."

Chapter Fifteen

C arson's suspiciously absent the following day, meaning I get a break from the insanity that he and Seth bring to the table. Considering their friendship and somewhat strange connection, I've started to view them as a unit, especially since they're currently acting as the heralds of chaos in my life. I also don't see Seth—Tuesdays and Thursdays are for my English and writing courses, and not even he's psychotic enough to change an entire schedule for the sake of pursuing a dancer.

I'm glad to be stalker-free on Tuesday, as the second day of the school year marks the start of auditions for Sanders's version of Pandora's Box. Auditions are done throughout the day, with groups of 6 dancers at a time being pulled from class to face a panel of teachers. At noon, which marks the end of the dance day for most of us, the callback list is posted in the entryway hall. I'm pleased to see April's name along with mine on the page, less pleased to note that Scarlett also made it into the running.

On Wednesday morning, I know my luck of being left alone by the universe has run out when I open my dorm room door to find Carson waiting for me. He's holding a carrier tray with two takeout coffee cups in one hand, using his free hand to scroll through his phone. When he looks up at me, his eyes are guarded, and his expression is contrite. He pockets his phone and holds one of the cups out to me.

I hesitantly accept the offering, mainly because it's too-fucking-early o'clock in the morning. When I take a sip, I find the coffee to be exactly how I like it, with cream and sugar.

"Did you know King threw away the beginning of his Carrie manuscript? His wife fished it out of the garbage and told him to keep writing," Carson says.

There's one way to break the ice. Carson seems relatively subdued this morning, and he brought good coffee, so I decide to go with the flow. "Carrie also wasn't an overnight sensation. It didn't *really* sell until the books were changed from hardcover to softcover."

Carson grins. "A girl after my heart."

I snort. "Definitely not." Then, more out of curiosity than anything, I ask, "Where were you yesterday?"

His grin grows until it's showcasing pearly white teeth. "Why? Did you miss me, Princess?" When I give him an incredulous look, he chuckles. "Unfortunately, I'll only be your shadow Mondays, Wednesdays, and some Fridays. Tuesday and Thursday mornings I'm booked with either classes or work."

Standing here, having a reasonably civil interaction, I can't stop my mind from wandering to Monday night, when my interaction with Seth was markedly *un*civilized. It was a twisted game, animalistic and rudimentary in nature, which is ironic because it didn't even get very far—I came to my senses and got out of there. Thinking back to it, I start to feel oddly guilty, as I'm here with Carson not two days later. Does he know what happened with Seth? Are they close enough to share intimate details about their so-called conquests?

I know it's a guy thing to compare and contrast various sexual activities, but I wouldn't be okay knowing I was being talked about in *that* way. Something tells me if Carson knew, he'd be in a much worse mood, which means I won't have to deal with a tantrum for now. I'm still too mortified over the whole endeavor to spend much time even thinking about it, so *I* certainly don't have any intention of telling Carson anything. Nevertheless, it feels a little wrong not to.

April comes breezing out of her dorm room as I'm locking mine and pauses in front of Carson to shoot him a dirty look. "You have the balls to sully my hallway at 6am and neglected to bring me a coffee?"

Carson gives her an easy, charming smile. "I'll bring you one if you say please and agree to occasionally pass on information about our lovely Elia here."

I let out a groan. "Are you seriously hiring my own friend to spy on me *in front of my face?*"

April shushes me. "Of course he isn't. He just wants to be able to pester me for your phone number and about your favorite color and other girly shit, right, Carson?"

Carson nods easily, going with it instead of denying. "You know it. I've already filled three notebooks with Mrs. Eliana Ajax surrounded by hearts."

April laughs, seeming surprised. I'm pleasantly surprised, too, because most men would shut down and turn prickly at being teased like that, but Carson seems content to play along rather than risk his masculine pride. I like that more than I'm willing to admit, as it's genuine and funny instead of polished and pampered.

April shrugs. "Coffee for info sounds good, but I'm not saying please, Ajax. I'm also not divulging anything more than I want about my friend, so my offer is whatever crumbs I feel like throwing you about her. Take it or leave it."

I hide a laugh behind my hand. April doesn't have quite as much of a chip on her shoulder as I do when it comes to wealth, but from what she's told me, she's also had to put up with her fair share of shit from overprivileged classmates who didn't like her solely because she belonged to a family of immigrants who didn't have a collective income that was upwards of ten figures.

"Done," Carson says easily. Then, as further enticement, he hands April the last remaining coffee. "If you like black with sugar, consider this a downpayment."

I'm taken aback at the sliver of generosity, even if it's wrapped in manufactured charm. Carson does not strike me as the sort of person to be magnanimous unless it served his own ends. That could be my dislike of people as wealthy as him coming out, though. I'm sure not *all* of them are the selfish, spoiled, pampered assholes I had to suffer through high school with.

Not all of them are my ex, who had more money in his trust fund than he could burn in three lifetimes, and never let me forget it for a moment. I was only with him because he thought I fit his narrative—he was the most popular boy in football, and he wanted a popular and talented girl in the dance company on his arm who could make him look and sound smarter, even if she was on the opposite side of the socioeconomic spectrum. Even among the 1%, money isn't everything, and my ex needed me to make him look better and sound smarter for his family. The only reason I stayed with him as long as I did is because I knew breaking up before the end of the school year would prompt him into starting a smear campaign against me around the school, and I didn't want to go through the hassle.

So, I suffered through eight months with him, and at the end I promised myself to *never* put myself at the mercy of the wealthy again, because I spent the better part of nine months as a puppet my boyfriend felt he had the right to control simply because of the cosmic difference between our bank accounts.

Carson, however, is yet to come across as controlling or one of the people who pushes his wealth into your face, the incident yesterday aside. That makes him even more interesting, because oftentimes great wealth leads to great entitlement, but he doesn't seem like the entitled manchild I generally expect from his kind.

April takes a sip of her coffee, makes a noise of approval, and nods at Carson. "You've got yourself a bona fide spy, rich boy. Just keep in mind I won't pass on anything truly incriminating, and I'll probably take advantage of my position to become a double agent and inform on you to Elia. Is that gonna be a problem?"

Carson remarks, "Nope," at the same time that I say, "April, I think I'm in love with you."

April flashes me a brilliant smile. "Who can blame you? I'm fucking fantastic. Anyway, see you two at headquarters—I'm gonna sprint so I don't freeze into an ice block." With that, she jogs down the hall and disappears into the stairwell.

While I admire April's ability to be perfectly awake at fuck-knows-o'clock in the morning, I am *not* quite so eager to be up before the sun. I've never been a morning person, and just because I have to get up early to accommodate an absolutely insane schedule does not, in any way shape or form, mean that I enjoy it. Most of the time I feel like a zombie before 9am, especially if I haven't had coffee.

So, despite the cloud of sheer irritation that seems to travel with Carson wherever he goes, I'm glad his presence means I got a coffee. And I also can't deny that my curiosity about him is progressively unfurling each time I interact with him. He seems to be a walking paradox; while being the very characterization of the terrible 1%, he doesn't act like it. Granted, my ex didn't act like it either until we'd been together long enough that I couldn't get away from him without causing problems, but frankly, I'd seen that coming a mile away and had just been too entangled for an easy escape. I don't see Carson lording his status over me, save for moments when his temper might flare.

Appearance aside, he doesn't really act obscenely rich. Most people with an impressive bank account have a certain swagger about them—as if they believe the world should bow to their feet simply because they're overprivileged. It's exhibited in the way they walk, speak, and generally conduct themselves. I'm yet to see that cocky swagger come out with Carson, though I keep expecting it.

Like yesterday, Carson follows me to the elevator as I press the call button.

"I heard you got stuck in archives with Seth on Monday," he comments casually.

My cheeks instantly flame as I whip around to face him, mortified that Carson knows what I did with Seth on Monday. Or, more accurately, what Seth did *to* me as I leaned against the wall, breathless and too turned on to stop him. The elevator arrives, and I use it as a distraction to ignore Carson and ignore the embarrassment overtaking every inch of my being.

Carson goes on, "Your blush tells me the encounter wasn't purely intellectual or artistic. Good to know."

I nervously tuck my hair behind my ear, unsure of what to say or how to react. It sounds like Seth hadn't told Carson everything, and my reaction is what gave it away, which pisses me off. What pisses me off more is the misplaced guilt I feel, which I know is born of being stuck between two predators, both of whom are dead set on their hunt for me. The realization that I have very little control here is disconcerting, but the realization that the lack of control was almost *exciting* to me Monday night is even more concerning.

What surprises me is that Carson doesn't seem shocked or even mildly put off by the news—instead, he seems extremely focused and serious. His eyebrows are drawn as he follows me out of the building and walks with me towards the dance headquarters, his entire body tense. He's not reacting in the way I would've expected, with anger, instead he looks to be lost in thought as we enter headquarters and I jog up the stairwell.

The tension is so poignant I can't stop myself from saying, "Why aren't you saying anything?"

Carson responds, "What do you expect me to say? I'm jealous as fuck, sure, but it's not like you're mine yet. Until I finally manage to get you to agree to give us a shot, you're free game."

I frown. "Yet? And free game? I don't foresee me ever being yours in any capacity, and I'm not a game."

Carson opens the stairwell door for me. "I suppose I'm more optimistic, and I'm not implying that you're a game. Only that day one with you taught me to keep a lid on my jealousy, and I'm trying to exercise some self-control. That sucks, because how I *want* to respond to Seth's making a move is to one-up him—which I know I could in a heartbeat."

There's a bit of insight and personal growth I didn't foresee. I can sense the tension from Carson, but he *isn't* doing anything about it, such as making a comment about the size of the check my department will get from him. He's keeping himself leashed, aside from the one-up comment, which means he isn't the typical privileged trust fund brat. At the very least, he's capable of holding control over himself for the sake of achieving a goal. That might come if he's as business minded as being in the business program and working in his father's company might demand. Or it could stem from him having a sliver of character under the money.

With a reluctant smile and eye roll, I tell him, "Self-control is proving difficult, hmm? Poor you, slumming it with the rest of us plebians."

"I'm hesitant to say this around you, but the truth is this is probably the hardest I've worked to get what I want in... ever," he admits.

That tidbit of honesty both endears and irritates me. Endears, because he has the balls to say it out loud to me even though it might not be what I want to hear. Irritates, because that statement is the *definition* of being overprivileged.

"It's good for you to have to work for something unattainable. We all need to experience failure now and again to keep us humble," I say, my tone faintly teasing.

Carson nods grimly. "Suffering builds character."

His latter statement doesn't sound *entirely* like a joke, which kicks my curiosity into gear. Could Carson know something about suffering? Before I can do something as stupid as ask, we arrive at class, and I submit myself to another day of rigorous training while my shadow watches me from spots in the corner, gaze never faltering.

Chapter Sixteen

My first half of the day goes surprisingly smoothly—Carson is relatively subdued and seems content in his position as a silent shadow. At the end, he once *again* asks me to go out with him, and I once again shoot him down—though I must admit, it's with a little more reluctance this time. I think if I spent time with him I could actually like him, but that's the thing; I don't *want* to get caught up in liking anyone this year. My freshman year isn't for school crushes or relationships, it's for my career.

I was already stupid enough to let Seth get as far as he did Monday night, and at this point there's no denying I feel a warped attraction to him—to *both* of them—which is mind-muddling and fucked and something I'd like to extricate myself out of *yesterday*. What's even weirder is that they both seem to be in a competition with each other, and neither of them mind it. I basically admitted without words that Seth and I did more than just talk Monday night, and Carson's reaction was one of such ease there's no way he *didn't* expect something like that to happen.

I feel like I'm steadily getting trapped between two very dangerous men, and I don't know how to slow the roll, stop, or go back to before they saw me dancing and decided to do *whatever* it is that's happening. To compete for me?

I'm in a haze as I walk into my first art history class for the day, a fog of embarrassment, mortification, and anger that I did what I did with Seth. I haven't exactly set a no-sex rule for myself this year, in case nights become too lonely and I need to blow off steam, but I *did* set a no-relationships rule so I could focus on dance and my studies. I've already met two figures who are working to tear down that rule, and I don't like the lack of control in this situation.

Seth's once again seated in the very back of the classroom and, once again, the last seat available is the one right beside him. Somehow, I doubt that's by accident. I didn't expect to get prime seating choice in this class because even making it on time is tricky, but Seth is obviously a popular figure, whether or not he enjoys that popularity; there's no *way* girls wouldn't try to surround him from all sides. In fact, on every seat around him except the one right beside him, there *are* girls, all of whom look readily interested in him. His attention doesn't go to them, though, not even for a moment. From the second I enter the classroom, his eyes are glued to me.

I drop into the desk beside his, trying and failing to prevent my cheeks and neck from heating as memories from Monday night decide to take up residence in the forefront of my brain. His voice, dark seduction. His touch, measured and alluring and totally dominating. His lips, like a pillowy cloud traveling over me. *His mouth...*

"Good afternoon," he greets.

Really? Good afternoon? After what happened the last time I saw him?

I glance at Seth from the corner of my eye, taking a second to really study him. He wears a white button up and black slacks, his clothing expensive and well-made but not overstated. Everything about him is polished, but I'm starting to realize that it's less *polished* and more *measured* and *calculated*. I get the feeling that there is nothing Seth does without a reason, though I doubt he shares those reasons with anyone. Which bears the question, what exactly is his reason for being interested in me?

I've learned from experience that ignoring him only gets him to push harder, so I say, "Hey," and then pull my laptop out of my bag and give it my full attention.

My plan of politely distancing myself from him goes out the window when he leans close—so close his breath tickles my ear—and says, "I was very disappointed when you ran out on me the other night. I didn't get to find out what you taste like."

I physically jerk away at that, casting a glance around to see if any of our classmates caught that crude statement. They didn't; he spoke the words softly so only I could hear, and the effect it has on me is disproportionate. While my brain screams at me to ignore this person who seems to have no sense of how social interactions generally go—namely, don't start out with talking about *tasting someone*—the part of me farther south starts to pulse the same way it did that night, as if in remembrance of how close I got to finding out what *that* sexual act feels like.

From the reviews I heard, when a guy isn't clueless—which most are—oral sex is *mind blowing*. I wouldn't know; I was only ever on the giving end of oral, and while Seth's words startle the shit out of me, they also kind of turn me on and kick my curiosity into overdrive. What if I'd stayed just a few more minutes in that dark museum archive? What sort of pleasure could I have been in for?

I give my head a shake, blinking several times. That right there is the danger of people like Seth; their intensity is so overwhelming they can control those around them with minimal effort. I *like* to think I'm smarter than the fly that gets trapped in a spider's web, but I'm also smart enough not to underestimate the capabilities of someone like Seth. I could be tangled up in his web long before realizing it.

I learned from my first experience with him in the museum during daytime that the only way to keep up with him is to be just as sporadic, dizzying, and discombobulating. So, instead of telling him how patently inappropriate his comment is—which he already knows—I decide to switch topics.

"I'm assuming you found the Fabergé egg design sketch?"

One of his eyebrows twitches slightly, telling me that my question surprised him. He probably expected me to squirm in my seat; while I very much *want* to, giving him the reactions he's seeking won't get me anywhere but screwed. Literally and figuratively.

"I did," he tells me. Then, in a soft voice only for me, "I would've preferred to do it *after* I made you come a few times, but I made do."

Okay, enough. There's only one weapon in my arsenal that seemed to get a reaction out of him; he *really* doesn't like it when I ignore him. Granted, it takes a good deal of emotional energy to do so as he's rather persistent, but perhaps the threat will make him ease up.

"If you don't quit trying to seduce me, I'll go back to ignoring you."

Surprisingly, *it works*. Seth's eyes gleam as he holds his hands up in mock surrender. "We can table that discussion for the next time we're alone together."

"Something that won't be happening again," I inform him.

He raises one eyebrow, intentionally this time, and his gaze turns more grey than hazel—those small specks of steel expanding until they swallow the iris. "You sure?"

I'd like to say that I'm abso-fucking-lutely certain, but I also know in my bones that, somehow, we will end up alone together again. I can already tell from our numbered interactions that Seth is as cunning as a person can be, and he is *very* skilled in getting what he wants. If he wants to get me alone again, I'll probably have very little say in the matter. And, considering his magnetic seductiveness, I'll need a chastity belt to get through that encounter intact.

"If I had it my way," I tell him, just as the professor gets the class in order and starts the lecture.

Seth doesn't try to talk to me for the rest of the class. He also doesn't take any notes or even appear to actually be listening to the teacher. I struggle to concentrate at first, but once the professor really starts to dig into the topic, my attention gets fixed on one of my favorite things: art history. At the end of class, before I'm done packing up, Seth is out of his seat and hovering by my desk, towering over me.

"Do you have any concept of personal space?" I ask him conversationally as I gather my laptop and textbook into my bag.

"Most of the time, yes. In fact, I very much dislike when people violate my personal space without permission. You're an exception—I can't seem to get close enough to you," he replies.

I stand from my seat at the same time that he takes a small step forward, leaving us chest-to-chest. The heat of his rock-solid body against mine throws me right back to the archives, once again sending a blush scorching up my skin. I put a hand flat on his chest and use it to push him back.

Then, without another word, I walk out of the classroom, knowing that he's following close behind.

"Have you considered that *I* might not like having my personal space invaded?" I ask when he falls into stride beside me in the crowded hallway.

He nods. "Of course. I always consider other people's desires, dislikes, and reactions. You might not *want* to like it when I get close, but you do."

I give him an irritated look, because I do *not* like getting read like a book. I don't like being around people as intuitive as Seth is.

"Are you done with your analysis of me, Dr. Freud?" I ask sarcastically, growing irritated.

Seth lets out a laugh that startles me. I've heard him chuckle before, which was its own experience, but his laugh is infused with a darkness that I suspect stems from his soul. It's edgy and enthralling, a gritty, smoky sound that feels like it reaches out and wraps around my chest.

"Nowhere near," he tells me as I enter my next classroom, taking a desk at the front. He drops onto the seat behind me, then leans forward to tell me, "In fact, I believe I'm just getting started."

I don't know how to respond to that—telling him that I'm not available hasn't been doing the trick—so I don't. I sit quietly through the class, letting myself get lost in the beauty and intricacy of Renaissance art.

It's only after class, when I check my messages, that my mood *really* plummets. I always have my phone turned off during classes, so I missed the several texts April's sent me.

> **April:** *Are you okay?*

The first text is strange considering we just spoke before I left for my afternoon classes. The text she sent a few minutes later is more concerning.

> **April:** *Ignore anything you've seen on social media.*

Then, there's the alarming one.

It can't be more than ten seconds before she sends me a link to Instagram. Heart pounding, already knowing that whatever it is, it can't possibly be good if there are vindictive girls in the dance company involved, I click the link.

I'm unprepared for the image—*images*—that assault my eyes. The post is from an anonymous account, and it's made up of three separate pictures. The first is a screenshot from a porno, where a woman's on her hands and knees, with one guy in front of her with his dick in her mouth, and another guy behind her fucking her. *Carson's* face is pasted onto the guy in front, and *Seth's* is pasted to the one taking her from behind. *My face* is photoshopped onto her body—the photoshop job is shitty and subpar, but the message is quite clear.

My stomach flips over and nausea creeps up my throat as I stare in disbelief, unable to wrap my head around what I'm seeing because *what in the actual fuck?*

Horrified, I scroll to the next photo, seeing that it's a shot of Carson and I at dance headquarters: it must've been taken earlier between classes. In the photo, we're both in the hallway, surrounded by people—he's leaned down to murmur something in my ear, and there's a reluctant smile playing on my lips. It was taken when I shot down his offer of a date earlier.

I scroll again to the next picture, seeing that this must've been taken by a student in my very last class period, because it's of the moment where Seth was murmuring some very inappropriate things in my ear, and I'm beet-red, looking startled and embarrassed and very flushed.

My eyes flick down to the caption: *looks like our dance co's newest star pupil has already started making her rounds with campus royalty. #fuckingyourwaytothetop #thatslow #ElianatheSwinger #horizontaltango*

"Oh my god," I murmur numbly, feeling like all the strength's been siphoned out of me.

Chapter Seventeen

A full-body chill settles over me as I stare at the post on my phone. I knew that getting a lead role would invite competition, but I didn't think *anyone* would go as far as to do something as disgusting as this. Not only is it an obvious lie, this is something that could *wreck my dance career*. All it takes is one wrong rumor, and I'm blacklisted for life, *just* when I've gotten a principal spot in a debut production.

If dance administration sees this, they could argue that I'm in violation of the morality clause in the contract that each company member signs and is expected to uphold. Of course, the porn shot is so fake it would take an idiot to believe it, but... the dance department has no reason to protect me if I'm bringing unnecessary heat on them, *or if* I'm making them look bad.

The post already has *thousands* of likes, and when I click on the account tag, I see that it's an anonymous account with few followers that only has the single post about me, meaning someone actually *created an Instagram account* to fuck with me.

Have I... have I left myself open to this form of attack in some way? Could it be on me that people managed to get two shots while I was in a position that could be viewed as compromising? I'm in no way a fan of victim-blaming culture, but it's an unfortunate truth that there are steps women can take to shield themselves from this sort of shit. Obviously, I have not been careful enough.

"What's wrong?" Seth asks.

I startle, having been so distracted by the insane Instagram post that I forgot all about his presence. Since the class ended minutes ago, the professor has left and the room is clear, leaving only us. Still, I can't help chancing a nervous glance around, as I don't want there to be more people with phone cameras at the ready.

When I don't respond, Seth takes the liberty of plucking my phone from my stiff hands. I don't even have the presence of mind to snatch it back; I'm too shocked, too numb, and absolutely *terrified* that one awful post is all it'll take to stop my dancing dead in its tracks.

"What the fuck?" Seth mutters.

That snaps me out of my shock, at least partially, and I realize just what a bad idea being here, alone with him, is. It's now glaringly obvious that I have a target on my back, most likely courtesy of some of the mean girls in the dance program, which means I have to watch my step *extra* carefully. That means not ever getting photographed with Seth or Carson again, which means never being close enough to get photographed with them again.

The fact that they've both insinuated themselves into my campus life won't make that easy, but I don't have another choice. I stand so abruptly my knees bang my desk, nearly sending my laptop falling to the floor. I manage to catch it before it hits the ground, shove it into my bag, and snatch my phone from Seth's hands before hurrying to the door.

Seth catches my arm before I can make it. "Elia, wait—"

"*No,*" I snap, jerking my arm away. "Whatever was happening here, it's over. My career comes first. I'm not at Greywood to fuck around and get stalked by *campus royalty,* I'm here to earn two degrees that'll set me up for life. Don't talk to me again. Don't come near me again. And if you have a single drop of mercy in your body, tell Carson to back the hell off, too."

My words cause Seth's demeanor to shift. He's always intimidating, but the change that comes over him... he's no longer just intimidating, now every bit of him is *threatening.* His eyes darken until the irises look black, and when he takes hold of my arm again, his grip is so steel-like I know there's no way I'll escape unless he chooses to let me. That causes everything inside me to freeze, because I have a feeling my words just unlocked a side of Seth that I don't want to see.

He walks me backwards until my back hits a wall and leans down until we're eye to eye. Caught in the path of his dangerous stare, I find it difficult to breathe as goosebumps rise along my arms.

Seth takes my phone back from me, holds it up directly in front of my face, and says, "Whoever did this, I'll take care of them. They have no bearing and no say in what happens between you and me. Don't let them interfere, or we're going to have problems."

His words ignite an anger in me that overpowers the fear. I snap, "There *is* no we! There never fucking was! I have known you and Carson for less than a week, during which time I've dedicated ample effort to *trying to make you go away.* Now, some shit like *this* happens, and frankly, it feels like a much-needed wakeup call. I get that you're a campus king—something like this will probably somehow get you even more positive attention—but it could *ruin my life*! If you have *any* regard for me, you'll fuck off—"

He reaches up to press his thumb over my lips, sealing them, and every instinct tells me that I've sent this hunter into turbo mode with my words, and I may not like the result. His neck is corded, the veins and arteries bulging beneath the skin, his entire body is tense—not the way it was in the archives, it's somehow more threatening. For the first time, my instincts tell me that I might actually be in danger here. Not in danger of him physically hurting me, I don't think, but some sort of danger.

"Stop," he tells me shortly, the word harsh and clipped. "I'll let you in on a little something: I don't like people often. It's even rarer for someone to catch my interest. Now, put those two together and add a spark of connection like there is here, between us? Unheard of. If you think I'm going to walk away because some petty campus rat thought it'd be funny to tear down the star of the dance company, you are very, *very* mistaken. I'm not done with you, Little Muse, nowhere near. In fact, I'm starting to suspect I never will be. So *this* shit?" he says, shaking my phone, "it's not going to stop me. It's not going to slow me. It's not even a blip on my fucking radar, other than adding some revenge to my to-do list."

He inhales a deep breath and seems to gain some composure with the gesture. The feral, threatening energy emanating from him reels back in, smoothing his facial expression and leaving his usual calculating mask, but now that I've seen the other side, I don't think I can forget it. I don't think it'd be wise to forget—in fact, I suspect that forgetting just how much of a predator Seth truly is very well may have cost people their lives in the past.

I don't sense that anything I say or do right now will get through to him or change his mind. I'm also still too shocked and horrified to put a solid argument together, so I take the only viable option; I pluck my phone back from him, pick up my bag, and run out the door.

***

April finds me in my dorm room a few hours later, curled up on my bed and doing homework on my laptop. Thankfully, there are a few more hours left before I have to go to the museum, where I'll inevitably face ridicule from my peers and whatever bullshit from Seth.

I let April into my dorm room after hearing her knocks, and she takes one look at me—folded in on myself, hugging my waist, ready to crawl into a hole of obscurity and stay there for the rest of my life—and pulls me into her arms for a hug.

"Babe," she sighs, stroking a hand through my hair soothingly. "Don't let it get to you. Bitches will be bitches, don't let them drag you down."

I don't know why, but being offered comfort is the thing that finally bursts the dam and makes me cry. I don't cry often—after growing up the way I did, it takes a *lot* to get under my skin—but seeing the post and understanding the absolute *hatred* of me that must have fueled it... I just feel a little depleted. I haven't been cruel to anyone or singled them out. I haven't deliberately crossed anyone in the dance program. I haven't done *anything* to deserve this, and yet it's *my* face pasted onto that fucking picture.

"Who could've done this? *Why* would they do it?" I ask April in a wobbly voice. April just about always radiates strength and confidence, and right now I wish I could borrow some of it.

"My best guess is that the post is Scarlett's handywork," April tells me, leading me over to my bed and taking a seat on it beside me. "She has minions all over campus—if she put out word for people to snap photos of you, they'd do it. She's got a lot of social power at Greywood, as she's been the dance program's star pupil going on three years, got cast as Aurora for the last two years, but now she's been upstaged by a freshman. Carson snubbing her Monday couldn't have helped."

That brings on a fresh round of tears. "Why does being a good dancer automatically make me the enemy? I have *nothing* against her. I've done *nothing* to her."

"Of course you haven't," April says calmly, using the voice one might with a psychiatric patient. "But the only instigation some people need is talent and success, which threatens them. You're the best in the company, that makes you a natural enemy to every other girl and the dancer that every boy wants to be on stage with. Do you even know how much you helped Sean just through your pas-de-deux's? He had scouts calling him from around the country, offering him spots at other schools."

Sean, my not-quite-prince-charming in the Sleeping Beauty production, was an excellent stage partner. He was much taller than me, which got a bit tricky at times, but in the end we pushed through rehearsals and I think we did marvelously together on stage. I'm pleased to hear April thinks the same, and happy that Sean got recognition—he's a fantastic dancer and definitely deserves to be seen for it. As great as that is, it's beside the point.

"What am I supposed to do tomorrow?" I ask April. "How do I face all of those *awful* girls?"

April puts her arm around me and pulls me close, somehow sensing how badly I need to be held right now.

I've never actually received much physical comfort in my life—my mom was a non-starter and did not have one single maternal bone in her body, so I learned to be my own comforter and supporter, but that often left me wanting for at least *one* person who was on my side. It feels amazing to finally have an actual friend—not someone who attaches themselves to me so they get some of the spotlight, but someone who actually *cares*.

"With your shoulders back and head held high," April tells me. "This will all blow over soon; the dance co will only talk about it until the next piece of gossip is out, which won't take more than a few days."

I'm not so confident, but I nod, accepting that what'll happen will happen, and I'll just have to deal with the blows as they come.

CHAPTER EIGHTEEN

I arrive to the museum in a daze, half-expecting my classmates to all be shooting me dirty looks or whispering about me. Instead, I get lucky with my chosen company; if anyone saw the disgusting photo, they don't mention it or treat me any differently. Seth stands at the edge of the gathered group, darkness radiating off of him and eyes fixed on me, as I suspect they'll continue to be each time we're in proximity.

Somehow, I get sent back to the archives once again, with just Seth as company, once again. I try to ask Jessica, our manager, for a different assignment; the eyebrow-arch she gives me in response tells me that a student is in *no* position to request anything from her. So, I head to the archives once again, this time with *far* more determination to keep my distance from Seth.

At least there's no one else here to snap pictures when I'm not looking. That serves as a cold consolation.

This time, our assignment is much more complex; we're meant to start digging through and cataloguing the horribly disorganized archives, a task that Jessica rather gleefully informed me will probably take the rest of term. Which means I'll be down here with Seth, alone, twice a week, for the rest of term. Not the safest or smartest scenario, but also not something I can wriggle my way out of.

As soon as we're in the archives, Seth drops his cross-body bag onto the floor, and then pulls out a manilla folder, using it to motion to me. I was ready to tell him that we need to work on opposite sides of the room, but something about the swath of papers he's holding catches my interest.

Seth closes the distance between us and holds the folder up in front of my face. "In here is enough incriminating information about the person who posted that picture to get them suspended, possibly expelled. Add my testimony against them on top of it, and I can guarantee nobody will be stupid enough to come after you again."

It takes a moment for my foggy brain, depleted from the stress of today, to catch up with what he's saying. Once I do, my only thought is *holy shit*. Basically, Seth is currently holding the keys to my reprieve, the best way to take down whoever put up that awful picture—probably Scarlett.

I eye Seth warily, knowing that the file will not come for free. I don't know how he managed to get such information in the few hours since I ran out on him, but I do know that I'm desperate enough for absolution to do just about anything he asks to get it. I have a strong sense that Scarlett was the one to do the dirty work, and I am *aching* to be absolved of this bullshit and have the spotlight shine on someone else—someone who's actually at fault.

That means that there's little I won't do to get my hands on the information, something that Seth knows, and something he'll probably exploit to the fullest.

I ask jadedly, "I'm assuming I won't be getting that file for free?"

The corner of his lips kick up as he shakes his head. "No, you will not. I have conditions."

As expected. Seth's going to extort whatever he can from me, since he has something I desperately need, and I otherwise wouldn't give him the time of day. To call him Machiavellian would be an understatement; I'm pretty sure he could outmaneuver Machiavelli himself.

I feel my shoulders droop. "What do you want for it?"

Seth reaches forward and twists a lock of my hair around his finger. "Two things. First of all, you let me finish what I started the other night. No objections, no takebacks, no stopping until I've had my fill. Second of all, you pose for my art a few times a week."

So, he's going to use the information to get concessions I otherwise never would've given him. His manipulation game is a little frightening, but also... I wanted to finish what we started the other night, too, I just didn't feel like I could say yes. Not of my own volition, not knowing it could potentially set me on a dark path. Now, though, I'm not in a position to say no, and surprisingly, that makes me feel kind of liberated. I'm no longer liable if shit goes wrong, because I don't *really* have a choice. I need something that he has. Besides, my curiosity has had me thinking about what we *almost* did the other night on a loop, and to be honest, it was probably only a matter of time before that curiosity came to a head.

That takes care of his first request. His second request, though, is more problematic. Not just because I know it's dangerous to end up alone with him several times a week, but also because I don't have the spare time to pose for art for hours on end. My schedule is packed as is, and I planned on using the occasional pocket of free space to work at one of the youth dance studios. I probably would only have had time for it once or twice a week, especially with Pandora's Box, but still... that's money that I need.

I inhale a deep breath and force myself to be clever about this. I'm not the only one here who wants something from the other; it's also obvious that Seth is willing to go to great lengths to get *me,* which I can take advantage of. I'm no stranger to negotiations, and rule number one is to never take the first offer on the table. If Seth wants me to pose for him, taking time that I could be using to earn some much-needed extra income, he'll have to make it worth my while.

The file is enough for me to let go of my inhibitions tonight and allow him to do what he wishes to me—especially since I suspect I'll be in for some mind-bending pleasure—but information isn't enough for him to commandeer my free time for who knows how long.

I say, "I'll agree to your first condition in exchange for the file. If you want me to take time out of my life that I could otherwise use to make money, though, I'm going to request reimbursement."

Surprise briefly flickers over Seth's expression. He probably thought I was emotional and frightened enough to agree to whatever he asked; while I *am* afraid of rumors about me spreading unchecked, I also understand that he wants me a great deal—enough for me to wrangle more from him. I might not be at Greywood for a business degree, but I know a bit about negotiations and strategic thinking.

If I can view this as a business arrangement—one I could stand to financially benefit from—it would take care of my guilt for giving in. If my posing for him becomes a job, especially a well-paying one, then it'll be nothing more than a work agreement that I could view as a clever investment. My time in return for his money. *I'm sure he has plenty to spare.* While I'd *never* accept a handout, this wouldn't be a handout.

"What were you planning to do for work?" he asks me.

I respond, "Teaching some ballet classes to young dancers in the area, Wednesdays and Saturdays." After painstakingly going through each minute of my class and dance schedule, I managed to find two open timeslots that I could put to use.

He nods his head slowly. "And what would be the hourly pay?"

I pause, considering if I should lie and tell him I'd be making more than I really would, so that he'd be inclined to offer a higher rate. *Probably not the best idea.* It'd only be a matter of time before he found out, and then he could hold that over my head.

So, I say with a bland smile, "Dismal, but I'd have loved the work enough to do it for free. If you want me to tolerate your presence instead of fill my heart with the joy of teaching youngsters how to tell stories with their bodies, you'll need to make it worth my while."

A gleam of excitement creeps into his eyes, and I realize just how much he's enjoying this back-and-forth. Maybe that's one of the reasons he's interested in me; I'm not a push over, and even though he frightens me, I'm not afraid to stand up to him if it means getting what I need out of the situation. I very much doubt many people in Seth's life have the spine to stand up to him and negotiate with him, but I've already survived much worse in life than a Machiavellian suitor, especially since he doesn't seem to have any interest in hurting me or fucking me over. Fucking me, yes, but that I can handle. *I think.*

"Every time I think I have you figured out, you surprise me," he says softly, almost fondly. "I like that more than you could know. Fine, how about this for a starting rate: 100$ per hour. We'll set hours to work around your schedule."

I have to physically stop my eyes from bulging at the figure he casually throws out, because I'd have made one tenth of that working at a studio. Instead of letting excitement at the money I could very much use overwhelm me, I force my brain to stay in negotiation mode. If he's starting the bid for my time at 100$, that means he *really* wants me to pose for him, which tells me I have plenty of space to drive the price up.

I say, "150, and I get to do homework while posing. Also, no nudity. My clothes stay on."

Seth rumbles, "Fine. I'll draw up a fucking contract. Tonight, if you want the file, you'll get on that couch and let me enjoy you. We can iron out the job details later."

I say, "One more thing. You tell me what's going on between you and Carson. You're both pursuing me, you're both aware that the other is pursuing me, and yet you continue. Why?"

Seth works his jaw for a little bit, seeming to consider his response carefully. After several moments, he says, "We both saw you, liked you, and wanted you. In the interest of not ending up in a scenario where I feel compelled to employ potentially deadly sabotage, we made a deal: we both court you how we see fit, and when you make your choice, the other respects it. Call it a gentlemen's agreement."

I blink several times while processing that. So, I was right; they are in some sort of competition for me, one with pre-arranged terms and agreements. I've gotta say, that is *beyond* strange, but also weirdly civilized. I think back to my ex; jealous was not a strong enough word to describe him.

One time, a nice boy in my AP English class passed me a note to ask me out, despite knowing I was dating. When my ex found out, he went after the kid so hard the poor boy eventually had to transfer schools. This isn't like that whatsoever, which brings me a measure of comfort. At least I know my actions, conscious or subconscious, won't end up getting anyone hurt.

"One last question," I say.

His eyes flick to my lips, and he licks his as an expression of hunger overtakes his handsome features, making his eyes glow. "Ask."

"Your nickname for me. Muse, Little Muse, whatever it is. Why do you call me that?"

He growls, "Because from the moment I saw you, I knew you were my muse."

That's a little disconcerting, and the intensity with which he says it is overwhelming, but at the same time I have to admit that it's hot. His desire for me, the intensity behind that desire... it's beyond anything I could've fathomed.

I nod once. "Okay, Balor. You've got yourself a deal. The contents of that file better be fucking *golden*."

His lips kick up into a small, smug smirk. "Oh, I assure you, they are. Get on the couch."

Chapter Nineteen

Well, looks like we're getting straight to business. Now that he's actually given me an order, the nerves are starting to set in. Butterflies take up flight in my stomach, and I have to wonder if it was the best idea to agree to this as quickly as I did. Do I want to see where Seth was going Monday night? As much as I wish I didn't, yes. But even though this no longer feels like me deliberately making a bad decision, and there's clearly something in it for me, I'm still hesitant.

To stall, I say, "Is it the best idea to do anything down here? Jessica could walk in at any moment, and then she'd have both our heads."

Seth licks his lips, the gesture reminiscent of a hungry lion. "I locked the door when we came in. Regardless, nobody has any reason to come here; we're literally saddled with the worst job out of all of the students. Jessica will be too busy in her office to spare us a thought, and the others are too scared of getting put on archive duty to come down here." He pauses to run his eyes over me again, more slowly, more thoroughly, in a way that makes the butterflies in my stomach travel further south. "I have you all to myself."

I can't stop myself from saying, "For now. If you're in a competition for me, who's to say the opposition won't win? Or that I won't do the smart thing and choose myself instead of either of you?"

Seth drops the file on top of his bag, closes the distance between us, and snakes an arm around my waist—as he seems prone to doing—to pull me closer to him. The breath shutters out of me as he gazes down at me, the green in his eyes becoming more pronounced until they're more emerald than anything else.

"You're too intrigued to walk away," he assures me, as though he can see inside my thoughts.

The thing is, he's right. I am too intrigued to walk away from him; even standing here now, I can't stop thinking about how his mouth felt on my breasts, stomach, and navel. I can't stop imagining what other tricks he might have up his sleeve.

"You also feel like you can't morally say yes to me, for whatever reason," Seth goes on, using his free hand to tug at the material of my shirt, rubbing the cotton between his fingers. "So, I've realized I need to be more creative." He bends down until his head is right by my ear. "This is me being creative. Now, take off your shirt and jeans like a good girl so I don't rip them, and get on the fucking couch. I haven't slept the last two days, imagining your taste, scent, the sound of your moans in my ear... tonight, I'm getting my fill."

He releases me abruptly, and I feel like I'm left with no option but to follow his instructions. The way he spoke is so intense, so authoritative, so deliciously *dominant*. Seth is a person who could easily take my will from my hands and mold it into his own, and right now, I'm inclined to let him. I want to see where it goes. Crazy as it is, he wasn't wrong in the classroom earlier; there *is* a connection between us. The connection is twisted and a little scary, but there's no use in denying that it exists.

I trail my way through the stacks and towards the couch, giving the surface an assessing once-over. I don't know what other people might've gotten up to on this couch, so I'm not ecstatic to use it. Seth rectifies that by withdrawing a folded blanket from his bag, walking over to me, and spreading the material over the cushions.

As he does so, he says, "I believe I gave you very clear instructions, and for a good reason. If your shirt and pants aren't off in the next thirty seconds, I'm going to rip them off, and then you'll have earned yourself a punishment."

His words spring me into motion. I pull my shirt over my head, leaving my upper half clad in a bra, and then unbutton and unzip my jeans, stepping out of them. Seth watches me do so with the stark focus of a predator closing in on its next meal. He takes a moment to run his eyes over every inch of my body, which is now only covered in a bra and thin pair of panties. He reaches out with his hand, smoothing it over my stomach, causing me to startle. I'm so wound up, both with anxiety and anticipation that I'm ready to explode.

"You're so fucking beautiful," he murmurs, bringing up his other hand to span my waist. Both hands then travel to my back, unclipping my bra so nimbly I don't realize what he's doing until he's already pulling the straps down my shoulders. Out of instinct, I clamp my arms together over my breasts to trap my bra in place, not used to having my body studied so intensely or intimately.

Seth clicks his tongue. "Ah-ah. None of that, Little Muse. You agreed to pay the price for the file, and I'm collecting payment now." He tilts his head to the side, assessing me. "Maybe I should tie these pretty hands together. Then they won't be able to get in my way."

My pussy clenches at that, convulsing around air, and I'm startled to realize how much his words turn me on. The idea of being bound and helpless is not something I ever expected to be up my alley—the one time my ex suggested it, I calmly told him that I'd fucking report him if he tried some shit like that—but with Seth, it seems my true desire is to yield control to him. Twisted, and not something I should feel towards someone who I suspect sits firmly on the anti-social spectrum—a man who certainly exhibits some psychopathic traits—but here I am. Here *we* are.

"You like the idea," Seth says, sounding titillated at the prospect.

"I dislike how well you can read me," I admit, still not lowering my arms.

That causes his eyes to gleam even brighter. "Would you like to know a secret, Little Muse?"

I nod, feeling like I'm in some sort of trance.

"I don't like how well you can read me either. It unnerves me how quickly your mind works to put puzzle pieces together, and at the same time, it enthralls me." With that, he pulls my arms down and yanks my bra off. In the next second, he does some weird Houdini trick that ends up with my hands bound, by my own bra. His actions are so quick and blurring I don't actually realize I'm bound until he pushes me down onto the couch, and I can't use my hands to brace myself, instead bouncing on the cushions and falling against the spine of the couch.

I stare up at him with wide doe-eyes, equal parts frightened and entranced by him.

Just like he did Monday, he drops to his knees in front of me, and reaches his hands towards the waistband of my panties. With my hands bound tightly together, I don't bother trying to stop him. Even if I wanted to, which I don't—I'm already too turned on—I couldn't. He pulls the flimsy material of my underwear down my legs, tosses them over his shoulder, and then places his palms flat on my knees, using his hands to spread my thighs open until I'm totally exposed to him.

"Little Muse, you're already glistening," he murmurs, staring at my pussy so intently I start to squirm.

Suddenly, I feel like this was a *terrible* idea. I could've bargained for something other than *this* in return for that file—why did I have to agree to his first term? Nerves travel from my stomach to my chest, turning my breathing harsh, and I try to sit up.

"Wait, Seth," I say, using my bound hands to cover myself. "I don't think we should—"

Seth grabs my hands and uses them to yank me towards him so abruptly I gasp, leaving an inch of space between our faces. "We have an agreement, Eliana. I wouldn't recommend trying to renege. You won't like what I do in response."

That sounds vaguely like a threat. His tone is soft but his eyes are hard and cool, boring into mine and telling me silently that there is fuckall I can do to stop him.

Seth hooks his hands under my knees, using them to jerk my lower body forward, until his face is level with my pussy. Before I can open my mouth to protest again, he reaches forward and strokes a finger along my slit. I'm so sensitive and wound up from nerves, I jerk and moan as his finger brushes my clit.

"For the last two nights, all I've thought of—*dreamed* of—is finding out what you taste like," Seth tells me, before dipping his finger into my channel. I squeeze around it, unsure if I want to pull him further in or push him out, but he doesn't seem to care. He withdraws his finger, and I'm treated to the ridiculously erotic sight of him sucking it into his mouth. His eyes blaze, turning an even *brighter* green, and he mutters a curse. "Too fucking good."

Then, his mouth is on the most intimate part of me, and my eyes roll into the back of my head as he laps at my slit, slowly and leisurely, as if he's savoring a ten-course meal. His fingers dig into my thighs so hard I'm pretty sure I'll have bruises tomorrow, but the pleasure of his hot, wet, and *very* skilled mouth takes up all of my attention. I don't think how I'll berate myself about this tomorrow. I don't think about how screwed up it is that we're doing this *here*, with students and faculty milling about above us. I'm not capable of thinking, *period*, all I'm capable of right now is feeling.

And *god* does this feel good. Seth uses his thumbs to spread my pussy open wider, then dives in like a starved man, thrusting his tongue into my channel and drawing a series of noises I didn't know I was capable of making from me. He alternates between where he licks, sucks, and nibbles, watching my reactions carefully. When he does something that draws a particularly loud moan or makes me squirm, he repeats the gestures until I'm shaking, wound so tight I'm ready to explode at any second.

His lips close over my clit, suckling gently at the same time that two fingers slide inside of me, and I can't help myself—I moan and writhe and quite possibly beg him to keep going. He curves the fingers inside me upward, hitting a spot that makes stars explode across my vision, and when his teeth scrape over my clit, adding a touch of pain to the tsunami of pleasure, the dam within me bursts. I orgasm with full-body convulsions and a shout that makes me glad we're underground, far out of earshot of anyone. Seth keeps eating me through my orgasm, like he's determined to lap up every drop I give him, only stopping when I've fallen still with just the occasional tremor passing through me.

His eyes flick up to meet mine, and my breath catches when he licks his lips, humming with satisfaction. He almost seems as sated as I am, which doesn't make sense. My experience with sex is pretty limited, but I've had enough girlfriends to know that rarely does a guy actually *enjoy* giving oral—from my understanding, they only give so they get.

Seth, though, doesn't seem to be in this for any reason other than wanting to taste me, which just makes him hotter.

The fingers still seated deep inside of me scissor and thrust, pulling a whimper from me. His lips kick up at the corners before he leans forward and sucks my nipple deep into his mouth, making my back arch. I'm so worn out from the one orgasm, I don't think it's possible for me to start building to another, but his hot mouth around my nipple combined with his fingers teasing all sorts of places inside me I didn't even know existed causes a coil to form low in my belly again. Seth switches his attention to my other breast at the same time he brings his thumb up to rub small, oh-so-precise circles on my clit.

I mewl, "Wait, I can't—"

He cuts off my words by *biting* my nipple. Not a small scrape of the teeth but a full on nip that sends pain coursing through my entire breast. That pain seems to travel downwards, joining the tension in my core that *just keeps building*. The movement of his thumb over my clit speeds up, until I can't hold back—I come again, this time with a scream that bounces across the archives. Only when I'm done does Seth release my nipple with a pop, before giving me a grin that's so boyish and handsome it catches me off guard.

My entire body feels languid and sapped of strength as I fall against the back of the couch, trying to catch my breath, reaching up with my bound hands to wipe the sheen of sweat off my forehead. Then, I extend my hands to Seth, awkwardly murmuring, "Will you?"

With a little smirk that practically reeks of smug masculinity, he reaches up and undoes the knot with a single yank. Then, he plants a kiss on each of my wrists, the gesture surprisingly gentle, before seating himself on the couch and pulling me into his side. I let him, too depleted to protest, and not really wanting to anyways. He's warm and he smells like a delicious spicy cologne, and as his arms close around me, I exhale a deep breath, letting my eyes flutter shut.

So *that's* what a real orgasm's supposed to be like.

Chapter Twenty

Despite feeling so languid I could fall asleep cuddled right up to Seth, I have to tell him, "This doesn't mean anything."

He strokes a few strands of hair off my forehead, looking contemplative. "Whatever you say." Then, he leans down and seals his lips over mine. I let him kiss me, feeling weirdly treasured and cherished even while he basically fucks my mouth with his tongue, dominating and taking. I taste myself on his lips, which is a little weird but also *scorching* hot. Once he's practically sucked the soul out of my body, he releases my lips, closing me in the circle of his arms. It's a little strange being naked while he's still fully clothed, but I don't *not* like it. I'm just not used to it—I'm totally unfamiliar with all of what's happened since I agreed to the deal.

I say, "I should get dressed. We need to get to work. You might not need this degree, but I do."

Seth replies, "In a minute," stroking his hand down my spine. After a moment, he says, "You have the softest skin."

I give him a wary glance. "Don't go all Hannibal Lecter on me."

His lips quirk. "Quid pro quo, Clarice."

I can't stop my smile as I say, "Quid pro quo, doctor."

For the first time since I've met him, a genuine smile breaks out on Seth's lips. Not a dark smirk or half-grin or any of the carefully constructed expressions he usually displays, but a full-blown smile that shows off gleaming white teeth. His eyes soften, too, and he strokes his thumb over my cheek.

"You keep making me like you more and more," he murmurs. "I don't think you know how dangerous that is."

Because I'm not ready to unpack that, I ask him, "Who's your favorite Renaissance artist?" He asked me on Monday, but I was too irritated to return the question. Maybe it's the post-orgasm buzz, but right now, I'm feeling particularly cuddly and talkative.

He tilts his head to the side, studying me with those bottomless eyes. "Same as your second-favorite. Davinci."

That interests me. "Why?"

He reaches a hand over to test the weight of my breast, running his thumb over my nipple as he answers. "I relate to him. He was one of the brightest minds to ever live, and the side effect of genius is often madness. He was also a polymath with specialty in art, engineering, and some would say strategy. What's not to like?"

I smile a little. "You're like the lovechild of Davinci and Machiavelli." My smile fades. "That makes you dangerous."

He squeezes my nipple, making me gasp. "I am dangerous," he admits. His eyes flick up to meet mine. "But not to you, not in the way you might fear. I don't think I could hurt you even if I wanted to. I want to protect you." His brows furrow as he speaks, hinting that having a protective instinct towards someone might be new territory to him. He doesn't seem to know how to handle it.

I don't know how to handle it, either. His intensity, his attention, is a little frightening—there's no denying it—but it's also a turn on. The fact that this man, who I suspect has seen and done some scary shit in his life, has interest in protecting me is also strangely comforting.

To change topics before my mind travels too far down a rabbit hole, I ask, "So, what's in the file?"

Seth's lips quirk. "I tracked down the IP address of the Instagram account, which led me to a computer belonging to an individual who made the post."

My brows furrow. "You know how to track IP addresses? Isn't that a hacker thing?"

Seth strokes a hand through my hair. "I've picked up on some useful skills in life."

My frown deepens. Deciding to ignore the fact that he has skills that aren't just useful, they're also *illegal*, I ask, "Isn't presenting information that was gained through illegal means incriminating? What's to say I won't get in trouble right along with whoever made the post?"

Seth taps my nose. "Because *I'll* be the one presenting the information. Trust me, they wouldn't dare dispute it or press how I got it. If they do, they'll just risk the university losing one of its shining stars." Before I can comment on how stuck-up that sounds, he says, "The person you're looking for is Scarlett Adams, who I believe you already suspected."

I nod slowly, because he's right; I did expect her to be the one. April made a convincing case earlier, and besides that, I already know that Scarlett despises me. Her hatred sparked the day I got Aurora and has strengthened each time I succeed in the company. Considering that she's the very definition of the bitchy queen bee stereotype, I guess it was only a matter of time before she came for me. I suspect that stems from her seeing me as a threat to her status as the best and most adored member of the dance company.

The thing is, I don't *want* to be a threat to her or anyone in the company. I'm someone who genuinely believes that talent accelerates talent—the more great dancers there are on stage, *the better the production will be.* I don't want to get the talented girls out of my way; I want to work with them. But if Scarlett's going to try to impede that and go as far as creating social media accounts just to fuck with me, I can't let that slide.

I'm not usually a snitch. I take no pleasure in going to teachers to complain about students—it's not necessarily that I hate conflict, more so that I've seen just how much resentment conflict can breed. While I know that telling on Scarlett is in my best interest, I don't feel good about it.

"Why do you look so conflicted?" Seth asks, watching every nuance of my expression intently.

I sigh. "I'm not in love with the idea of being a tattletale."

Seth raises his eyebrows, his expression incredulous. "Why the fuck not? She deserves it. She deliberately targeted you in the grossest way possible, simply because you're more talented than her. Why wouldn't you want to see her pay for it?"

I recognize that this is one of the cardinal differences between Seth and I; he'd be happy to burn someone's life to the ground if they cross him, while I'd much rather find a peaceful solution. Not necessarily because I'm a pacifist, but because I don't like starting vendettas. Those things get ugly, *fast*, and there's also the matter that I don't have the resources to protect myself from the fallout.

"I'm not a vengeful person," I tell him honestly. "I don't feel the need to see others fall so I can rise. I honestly wish Scarlett hadn't done that, because I don't *want* to create a stir. That's not the nature of being part of a team or in a company. We should be aiding each other, not trying to get rid of the competition."

Seth appears incredulous, disbelieving. "You're telling me you've never wanted to get revenge on someone?"

No, I can't honestly say that. There have been times in my life where I was all too happy to see someone's failure—my mother, for example. Although egg-donor would be a better description of her. She was so selfish, so cruel, and *awful* that when I got the news that her prescription medication addiction had ended up with her death, I breathed a sigh of relief and sent a prayer of thanks to whatever higher power exists. I would have never done anything to actively hurt her, that would've been stooping to her level which I trained myself to be above from a young age, but having her gone from my life took away a good deal of the barriers I faced.

It was only at the beginning of last summer—when I'd just turned eighteen and moved out of her house to stay with a friend and get the hell away from her toxicity—that I got the call from the local hospital. The person calling asked me what I'd like to do for funeral arrangements; I told them to take the cheapest possible route, which ended up being cremation. I didn't give a shit what happened to her body, if it wouldn't have raised red flags I'd have told them they could dissect and study her corpse if they wished to. That way, she could've had more usefulness in death than she did in life.

I guess that was my greatest act of revenge thus far. My mother lived for attention, thrived off of it. She wanted to be revered, respected, and coveted. Of course, that's hard to achieve as a college dropout with no measurable success in life, so she often settled for negative attention over positive. To her, attention was attention. The cruelest thing I could do to her in death is deprive her of what she lived for in life, and that's exactly what I did.

There was no funeral service. No burial, headstone, not even a named spot in a columbarium. I allowed her to be forgotten, discredited, and ignored. That wasn't even hard to do; she didn't have anybody in her life who would've wanted to attend her funeral. She was estranged from her parents for years before they passed away, and she'd been incapable of keeping a friend, let alone a boyfriend, for more than a few months.

It wasn't a straightforward method of revenge, but it was effective. I got far more satisfaction knowing she'd die a nobody than I would've from actively ruining her life or going to the police with tales of her incompetence. She perversely got a kick out of it when social services would come to check on my welfare, so I had no desire to feed into her twisted need for attention.

"My methods of revenge are generally subtle," I finally respond.

That appears to interest Seth. He raises his eyebrows and asks, "Oh yeah?"

I know he's waiting for more information, but I'm not going to give it to him. Just because he went down on me—and, I'll admit, blew my mind—doesn't suddenly make me an open book.

I nod slowly, not offering any words.

He presses, "Like what?"

I arch an eyebrow at him. "What are *your* methods of revenge?"

"Whatever will hurt the person I'm taking revenge on most. Humiliation, discrediting, loss of what they care for, lighting the match that sets their world on fire—it differs on a case-to-case basis. Generally, if I'm really aching to satisfy a personal vendetta, I'll aim for something draconian," he answers immediately.

I ask warily, "Do I want to know?"

He shakes his head. "No, Little Muse, I don't think you do. That would send you running, and then I'd chase and catch you, which you might not like very much."

My brows furrow as I contemplate his words, a cold sliver of fear traveling through me. Seth may not be inclined to unleash the more sadistic part of himself on me—a sadistic side that I knew existed from our first meeting—but that doesn't mean that it isn't there. I suspect there are demons within him that *would* send me running away, because I have a keen sense of self-preservation. One that developed over years of neglect and, occasionally, abuse.

"What if I did something to anger you?" I ask him, needing to know. "Would you get... draconian on me?"

He doesn't pause before saying, "I'd never treat you like I would an enemy or adversary. You don't need to fear that from me."

"Do I need to fear you at all?" I push. I need clarity on the exact level of danger I'm in here. I don't think being around him would ever be *safe*, but there's a difference between being perfectly safe and being in harmful, perhaps deadly territory.

"That depends," he tells me. "Do you plan on trying to run away from me? From *us*?"

"What if I did?" I question, not ready to let up until I know the worst-case scenario.

He tilts his head to the side, stroking over my bottom lip with his thumb. "If you run, it'll kick my hunting instinct into overdrive. I'll chase you, capture you, and probably keep you to myself until you've come around. Or forever, take your pick."

A cold sliver of fear wraps around my chest, speeding up my heartrate. "What about Carson?" I ask. "Aren't you willing to concede to him?"

Seth pushes his thumb into my mouth, silencing me. "I was. Now that I know you better, I'm not so sure I can honor our agreement. You're fast becoming an addiction."

CHAPTER TWENTY-ONE

The next morning, I'm summoned to dance HQ's administrative offices to speak to Moira. I already know what it's about, and I walk into the office with my head held high, shoulders back, ready to inform her that if admins try to take any action against me I'll sue them so fucking fast their heads will spin. I don't actually have the means to make that happen, but I do have rage and morality on my side.

My thoughts come to a screeching halt when I open the door to see who's already in Moira's office: Seth *and* Carson. They're both seated across from the program director at her desk.

Oh, fuck. Looks like they teamed up. I guess it makes sense—after all, the post targeted both of them as well as me—but I didn't expect *this*. From what Seth told me last night, the two are in a very strange, almost medieval competition for me, so seeing them sharing a space... I'm not sure how to handle it or what to say.

I remain frozen in the doorway, looking from Seth, to Carson, to Moira, and back again, unsure of where to focus my attention or how to approach. There's a third chair set between Carson and Seth, a chair

I assume I'm meant to take, but I'm not exactly keen on the idea of *literally* being between them. Figuratively is already enough for me.

Even the air in the room feels a little stifling, as if both of their presence intermixed sucks out most of the oxygen and replaces it with pheromones.

Moira clears her throat when I linger in the doorway too long. "Ah, Eliana. Come in, have a seat. We were just discussing the unfortunate social media post that circulated around campus yesterday."

Unable to do anything but follow instruction—probably courtesy of my ballet training, it's very difficult for me to ignore direction from my superiors even if I want to—I slowly walk into the room. Seth turns to look at me over his shoulder, his eyes shining a particularly light hue of grey this morning. Those eyes travel up and down my body, before settling on my face, and a small, secretive smile pulls on the corner of his lips. I try and fail to hide a blush, because I think we're both remembering the same thing.

Carson also fixes his blue gaze on me, giving me a full-blown smile that shows off straight white teeth. "Princess," he greets, causing me to blush even more because calling me that endearment in front of Moira *really* doesn't set the right tone here.

I sink into the remaining chair, crossing my legs and folding my hands on my lap to prevent from squirming. I'm no stranger to uncomfortable situations—as a dancer, it's kind of inevitable—but being seated between two suitors, one of whom is probably something approaching a psychopath and the other a golden boy with a hidden darkness is unnerving.

This close, their presence is like a physical force. Even though they're no longer staring at me, which hopefully means they have some sense of general politeness, I can still feel their gazes on me, like a hundred phantom hands crawling over my skin.

I murmur a quiet, "Good morning," my gaze fixed on Moira.

She nods. "Yes, I suppose it is a surprisingly fortuitous morning, following the difficult afternoon you must've had yesterday. Imagine my surprise when, first thing, I'm approached both by our greatest benefactor's son, who happens to be your shadow for the term, and also one of Greywood's brightest science and engineering students. Mr. Balor presented me with some damning evidence he received from his private investigator, regarding the person who made the inappropriate post yesterday."

So that's the story Seth's going with; that he wasn't the one who broke the law to track down our huckleberry. He assured me that he wouldn't incriminate himself in the process last night, but I didn't expect him to pass off his work as someone else's.

"Oh?" I try to sound shocked.

My eyes flick down to Moira's desk, where the very same file Seth presented me with last night rests. On it are copies of the horrible pictures, along with what looks like some legal paperwork and some other loose pages containing numbers and symbols I don't recognize but are probably some sort of digital language serving as evidence.

Moira nods, her eyes darkening and lips pinching with displeasure as she says, "Indeed. I'm sorry to tell you, it looks like Scarlett Adams was the one who made the post. Seth and Carson are both here to ensure administration takes proper action, so that neither of them feels compelled to press defamation charges against her."

Well, there's a surefire way to demand action. I study Moira closely, trying to gauge her stance on the situation. I don't think she'd be pleased that one of her company dancers went rogue and tried to smear the name of another, coincidentally bringing two very powerful students into it, but I also don't think she's happy to have students' decades younger than her threatening action against one of her star pupils.

From the sense I've gotten so far, nobody here—teachers and faculty included—particularly *like* Scarlett, but there is no denying she's one of the best dancers in the program. Her shitty personality isn't fun to deal with, but she has talent and ambition, which is as good as gold in our industry.

I let my gaze flick down to my hands, trying to muster up more surprise. "I see," I say, furrowing my brows. "Well, that's distressing to hear. I'd hoped whoever made the post wasn't affiliated with the company at all." I meet Moira's eyes, leaving the ball in her court.

Moira gives a tense nod. "We will be taking swift action now that we know the source of the post. Scarlett will be suspended from classes and shows pending a *formal* investigation." Her eyes flick to look at Seth's as she says the last part, silently transmitting that while she can't ignore what he's presented to her, she doesn't need to wholly abide by it, either.

Seth gives her a smile of such sincerity and contriteness that I almost fall over in my chair. His entire face morphs, turning from the usual blank mask with only micro-expressions to something that looks misleadingly human. "When I saw the post, I was quite upset. Elia and I share a collection of art courses, and I've enjoyed spending time with her. To see our relationship characterized in such a grotesque way that defamed *both* of us... well, I felt compelled to do something."

Moira *eats that shit right up.* Her eyes soften, as does her posture, and I can practically see the moment she gets it in her head that I potentially have two suitors to vie for my hand; she looks from Seth to Carson with a glimmer of excitement in her eyes, before fixing her gaze back on me.

"How *kind*," she practically gushes.

I remember how, the night I found the body, she compared my situation with Carson to a ballet. Her words were something like, *damsel meets prince, sparks fly*. Well, now she has *two* princes after her company's glowing damsel in distress, and she couldn't look more pleased with the situation.

Carson decides to jump in. "I've only had a few chances to shadow Elia, but she's a fantastic dancer and tour guide. It was deeply distressing to see *our* relationship misrepresented, too." The way he puts emphasis on the word *our* and flicks a glance at Seth as he says it, tells me that he's basically trying to piss all over me in front of his rival.

Seth is trying to do the same, albeit more subtly and manipulatively. He's more inclined to take the calculated route—last night and this morning are prime examples of that. I was set to never speak to him again, until he managed to track down the person who made the post and used the information as leverage to get exactly what he wanted from me. Granted, I twisted the situation at least somewhat to work in my favor—after all, my posing for whatever art he makes is now a well-paying job instead of a condition for the file on Scarlett—but I still can't ignore the level of deliberation that must fuel his every move.

Moira lets out a small squeak of excitement. "I'm so glad our star student is getting attention from all corners of campus."

In other words, she's excited about the extra attention I'll bring to the department. If Seth and Carson flock over, it stands to reason a good deal of their wealthy peers might also take a sudden interest in the dance program and company.

I startle when Carson actually reaches over and puts his hand on my thigh, nearly jumping out of my skin at the contact. He says, "Eliana is difficult not to pay attention to. I'm happy we could work out an agreement where I get more of her time—she has so little of it between classes and rehearsals."

Moira says on a dreamy sigh, "Well, we're always happy to work with our most generous patrons."

Seth, obviously displeased with Carson, barks, "When are you planning on taking action against Ms. Adams ridiculous display of character inferiority?"

Moira gives her head a shake, as if to clear it. A woman who's *decades* my senior seems to be as susceptible to the spells Carson and Seth weave wherever they go as I am—as everyone is. I'd have thought her years of working with young adults would've taught her how to navigate through bullshit, but evidently not.

Moira stands from her desk and says, "I'll have one of our security guards aid me in helping Scarlett gather her items from her locker and then escort her out. Eliana, you're welcome to join your first class. Grab one of my signed late slips before you go to avoid any reprimands." She gestures to the corner of her desk, where a stack of papers, presumably late slips, sit. With that, she stands and flutters out of the room, seeming all too happy to leave me alone with my two insane self-proclaimed suitors.

As soon as she's gone, I pluck Carson's hand off my thigh and give him a glare. He returns my ire with his usual, charming golden-boy smile. "Don't like it when I touch you, Princess?"

Seth rumbles, "Perhaps your touch isn't as skilled as mine. Bow out now while you have the chance, Carson, before you've made an utter fool of yourself."

I stand from my seat and whip around to glare at Seth, because his statement reveals that I've experienced his touch and implies that I found it more pleasing than Carson's. I do *not* want whatever strange rivalry is going on between them to devolve into sharing those kinds of stories. I'm also deeply uncomfortable being stuck between them.

Seth's lips quirk as he stares up at me. Not a smile, but a distant approximation of one. "You don't want him to know just how much you liked my touch last night? How much both of us enjoyed your nectar on my tongue?"

I growl, "*No!*"

At the same time, Carson says in an interested voice, "Do go on. When it's my turn, I'll be sure to cover whichever bases you inevitably missed."

Ready to rip my hair out, I point my finger between the two of them. "Whatever competition you're in, leave me out of it. This school year is stressful enough, I'm not going to let your pissing contest over me—which I don't even condone in the first place—stress me out even more." With that, I grab my bag and rush out of the room.

Chapter Twenty-Two

Scarlett storms into my bar class not fifteen minutes after I've joined, her face flaming red with anger. Moira and a security guard rush in after her, pausing in the doorway. I'd guess that Scarlett was getting escorted off premises when she decided to take a segue to fuck with me some more. Everyone in the class pauses in their dancing as she pushes people aside to get to me; the teacher falls silent mid-instruction, watching with wide eyes. I straighten my spine and face Scarlett head on as she storms up to me.

She presses a finger to my chest and hisses, "You frigid *cunt*. You got your boyfriends to snitch on me? *Really*? Fucking campus royalty to get a leg up isn't enough, you have to use them to make up bullshit about me?"

You could hear a pin drop in the silence that echoes after her statement; it's like the very world around us has gone still to make space for this show-down. Even Moira and the security guard remain frozen in the doorway, watching the confrontation along with everyone else.

I take my time pushing Scarlett's manicured finger out of my chest, keeping my facial expression blank as I stare into her eyes.

"I didn't ask Seth or Carson to do anything. You defamed them with that nasty post, and there are consequences. If you'd just come for me it would've been one thing; instead you had to make the idiotic move of pulling very powerful families into it. Did you really *not* expect to get blowback for a stunt like that?"

Scarlett lets out an enraged growl. "You're a goddamn liar! I didn't do *anything!*"

She's so obviously lying, I only credit her denial with a snort. "Say what you wish, Scar, but IP addresses don't lie."

"You had them plant evidence on me, because you can't *stand* that I'm a better dancer than you. That's stooping pretty fucking low to get rid of the competition, Eliana."

This time, she actually goes as far as to try to *shove me*, which would have sent me tumbling into the bar behind me and crashing to the floor, if I wasn't already expecting it. As is, I catch her hands in a steel grip. She tries to jerk them away, but I hold firm, absolutely fed up with her bullshit. She's patently projecting her own faults onto me, and I'm not in the mood to tolerate it.

"You want to know something, Scarlett?" I ask her softly. "I have—*had*—nothing against you. I do think you're one of the best dancers in the company, which is why *I wanted to work with you.* I'd have loved to share a stage with you, because the more talent there is in a show, *the better it does with the public.* Remember how I asked you if you wanted to work on our technique together after hours during Sleeping Beauty rehearsals?"

Her face gets a bit pale, because she deliberately embarrassed me my second week here, when I dared approach her with an offer of friendship and kindness. It was in front of most of the company, and she laughed in my face before telling me she didn't waste time on novices. Just about every person in this room witnessed that.

"You wanted to leech off my stardom!" she snaps, growing desperate.

I shake my head slowly. "You're wrong. I wanted your advice because you'd played Aurora for two years, quite brilliantly from what I'd heard. I had a very deep respect for that, because it is not easy to land such a big role in the first production of the year, as we all know. I came to you, hat in hand, and you threw it in my face. Tried to make a mockery of my spirit of teamwork in front of everyone."

As I say the last part, I let my gaze settle on the few dancers spread across the room who'd joined Scarlett in laughing at me that day. Now, all of them appear nervous and uncomfortable, shifting their weight and pointedly avoiding my gaze. *So, this is how the social order works.* The queen bee gets an escort out of headquarters, all her once-loyal minions that would have previously jumped to her defense now stay dead silent.

I go on, "That was what it was—I understood we'd never get along, so I gave you space. But then, you escalated with a post that could've gotten me in serious shit were anyone stupid enough to credit it. If you'd have left me alone the way I left you alone, we wouldn't be here. Instead, you felt compelled to cut down a dancer who threatened your position rather than taking her under your wing for the betterment of the company. Now, here we are. Spread your bullshit about not being the one to make the post if you want, but I'm quite sure there's no doubt among everyone here that only you are vindictive, cruel, and tacky enough to pull something like that."

I release her hands abruptly, and she stumbles back, wide-eyed and starting to look slightly nervous. I don't blame her; I'm angrier than I've been in some time, because I can see from her expression just how much she craves hurting me, and that is *not* what being a member of a dance company entails. It pisses me off even more that all the members of this class that previously flocked to her, some of whom I *know* liked and commented on that post, are now conspicuously silent.

Scarlett straightens her shoulders and tosses her hair, fixing me with a cool gaze, trying and failing to look confident. "Whatever. Even if I did make that post, who can blame me? You're such an easy target. A weakling. Seriously, who the hell tries to work *with* the competition rather than tearing them down?"

Wow. Her logic is so warped and skewed I don't even feel like trying to untangle it.

I say, "Someone who's committed to the program and company, as every member should be. It's quite sad to see such horrible examples of teamwork set by our most senior and accomplished dancers. It's even more disheartening to see the pack mindset that had so many people supporting you when they should've called you out for your cruelty."

Scarlett rolls her eyes. "Being a righteous bitch won't get you anywhere."

I nod slowly. "Interesting take on the situation. See, what I learned is that being a bully will eventually end with consequences. I hope everyone else here's smart enough to take the moral—aside from you, of course. If this farce has taught me *anything*, it's that women like you are lost causes." I feel myself smile a little, but the smile is cold. "You know, you remind me so much of my mother." My smile fades, replaced by a stark blankness that looks like it startles Scarlett. "Her vanity eventually led to her death. Hopefully you smarten up quicker than she did."

Scarlett's jaw slackens for a moment before she shouts, "You *cunt!*" and lunges at me. I step out of the way, and in her blind rage, she ends up crashing straight into the bar, sending it tumbling to the ground and gets pulled down along with it, ending up in a heap on the floor.

Moira says, "That's enough. Scarlett, if you don't let the officer escort you off premise, I'm afraid I'll be compelled to take further legal action."

April, from her spot at the bar alongside the left wall of the class, whistles loud enough for everyone to hear. "Oh, how the mighty have fallen."

She catches my eye and gives me a bright smile of encouragement, mouthing *you're a badass*. I honestly didn't rant at Scarlett to better my own social standing or feel like a badass, I did it because girls like Scarlett need to be chastised publicly so that the people who once flocked to them understand their own faults and stupidity.

Scarlett's power came from the illusion of power more than any-thing. She is—*was*, now that she'll probably get kicked out—one of the best dancers in the company, but that wasn't what made up the majority of her power. What gave her power was the borderline-un-hinged reverence she received from other dancers who wanted to share some of her spotlight. She perpetuated a culture of competition, meanness, and cruelty that created a vicious cycle—dancers would tear each other down on their way to the top, rather than supporting and giving each other a leg up.

My friendship with April is prime proof that the exact opposite works. In terms of freshmen, there's no denying we're the two top female dancers—many will say we're two of the best dancers in the company *period*, but I try not to get ahead of myself by believing that. April and I could've gotten into a competition and tried to knock each other down; instead, in the five weeks we've been here we've worked very closely together, and both of us have benefited from it *majorly*. One of the main reasons I danced Aurora as well as I did is from my daily sessions after hours with April, and the reason she got a premature spot on the Pandora retelling cast list, before anyone else even knew about it, is because I was repaying her kindness in turn.

If that spirit could spread to the rest of the company, I have little doubt we'll be one of the most formidable in the states.

"Alright, let's focus back on our bar work," the class instructor calls, clapping his hands together.

I help the others who were sharing my bar pick it back up and right it as Scarlett awkwardly scrambles to her feet and trails out of the room, led by the officer and followed by Moira. Once they're out of the doorway, I spot Seth and Carson lingering in the hall. I don't know how much of my exchange with Scarlett they heard, but judging from their expressions as they blatantly stare at me, they must've caught quite a bit.

Seth is looking at me like he wants to strip me down and turn me into a ten-course meal, *again*. Carson has raised eyebrows with a look of faint surprise, and a glint of what also might be pride lights up both of their eyes.

Although the scene Scarlett just made would've served to discredit the last of anyone who believed the post, Seth and Carson watching me could put more fuel on the flames. I don't think anyone will have the nerve to accuse me of fucking my way to the top again, but there's a chance people will start speculating that Seth and Carson might both be pursuing me, which they are. That would cause a scandal of its own; one of our headline dancers being sought after by the two campus kings. I don't want that to be the underline of my career, so I turn away from my two suitors-slash-stalkers and get back to work.

Chapter Twenty-Three

Even though it's supposed to be one of my stalker-free days, I cross paths with Carson after I've finished my last class of the day, as I'm walking back to my dorms from French. Like the dance program, the art history track requires completion of at least one language course, with recommendations being either French or Italian. I plan to take French my first two years, then switch over to Italian for the last two.

Naturally, I'm dog-tired from the long day and seemingly endless week, so when Carson falls into step beside me on the stone pathway, I don't even bother commenting or telling him to go away. Aside from the fact that I don't detest him, he did me a favor today—Carson had no obligation to go to Moira's office and demand action, but he did. I had a deal with Seth that got him to intervene on my behalf; Carson did so just because.

I'm not thrilled by the way I was bickered over like a piece of meat, but then again, I understand that men are strange creatures with even stranger ways.

Carson breaks the silence by saying, "I'll admit, you knocking Scarlett off her pedestal was the hottest thing I've seen in... ever. My hard on *still* hasn't gone away."

Since I'm slowly getting used to the innuendo he throws out at regular intervals, I don't bother admonishing him. In a way, there's a sort of twisted charm to it. He isn't asking or demanding anything of me, just letting me know the effect I have on him. In crude terms, sure, but there's nothing forceful about it.

I say, "That sounds painful. You know what they say about erections that last more than four hours—there might be a hospital trip in your future."

He replies, "Nah, I'll just rub one out later while picturing you. I'll admit, I'm pretty sad that Seth's already gotten a taste of you, whereas I haven't even managed to wrangle a kiss or agreement for a date."

And that's all it takes for my blush to return full force. I cast a glance around to make sure nobody's close enough to hear, before responding, "You really have no shame, do you?"

"When it comes to you? Apparently not," he volleys back.

I feel a reluctant smile tug on my lips. "For your information, I did what I did with Seth as part of a mutually beneficial exchange."

Carson nods. "Ah. Right. He mentioned that there was a little persuasion involved—a specialty of his." After a pause, he goes on, "I'm starting to think that might be the best path to take with you. So, what's your greatest desire, Elia? I'll do my upmost to make it come true in return for a date."

I let out a long sigh. I might be getting used to having Carson and Seth in my life, competing for me, but I'm still not comfortable with it. *Rich people certainly live life differently from us mortals.* Instead of playing into Carson's hands, I ask him the question that's been bouncing around in my head for some time.

"Why are you so set on going out with me? I promise you, I'm not all that interesting, and the date will not end with sex."

In the stairwell the other day, he told me his interest in me wasn't purely sexual, and that he felt chemistry between us that he hasn't felt with anyone else. I didn't entirely believe him, I've learned through April's gossip his reputation on campus precedes him, but if he was just after sex, why would he have been in the office this morning? Why would he continue seeking me out despite my shooting him down every time?

"You fascinate me. When I find out why, I'll let you know. Until then, I'll keep annoying you and showing up randomly until you give me a shot," Carson tells me.

I slow my walk before stopping altogether, turning to look at him. Carson is an anomaly of sorts that interests me, too. He doesn't act like I'd expect him to, like I've learned to expect from overly wealthy trust fund brats. In fact, his pursual of me alone tells me that he doesn't mind putting in hard work to get what he wants. I've only known him for a number of days, but that's been enough to teach me how relentless he is.

Maybe it wouldn't be the worst thing in the world to give some leeway to my own curiosity about him. I've made it patently clear that sex is off the table, but what harm would going out with him do? It might explain the conundrum of Carson Ajax once and for all.

"So, what annoyance do you intend to bring to the table today?" I ask him.

He responds, "The usual. There's a great burger joint in the city, not too far from here. Fifteen minute drive. I'll have you back well before your bedtime. Interested?"

Although I have homework I could be doing and a job to negotiate with Seth, I consider going out with Carson just this once, simply to see where it goes. It would be pushing against my no-dating rule, but not crossing it because it's just one time. Besides, I'm *starving*, and my university food card only offers a rather subpar selection in the cafeteria. I haven't eaten out in what feels like forever, and I can't remember the last time I had a good burger.

I tell Carson, "Alright, Ajax, but you're buying. And I reserve the right to end the meal whenever I feel like, especially if you piss me off, at which point you'll drive me back to campus without complaint or bullshit."

His head actually jerks back. "Alright? Just like that?" he asks.

I shrug. "Unless, of course, you've changed your mind or can't agree to my terms. In which case, I have a boatload of homework to do—"

"Nope, terms are agreed upon." He grins. "You're sexy when you get bossy, you know that?"

I wrinkle my nose with feigned distaste. "Lock it up, Carson. I'm already starting to regret this."

"Too late," he says, his grin widening. "I have you to myself for the next... however long it takes for me to irritate you into leaving. I promise to be on my best behavior. Mostly."

I arch an unimpressed eyebrow at him, and he responds by slipping an arm around my waist and starting to steer me in the direction of one of the student parking lots. I let him, although I have a sneaking suspicion that I just might be making a mistake here. Then again, I did something that's likely a much bigger mistake last night, so this is pretty mild in comparison.

Once we're situated in his car, Carson asks me, "What made you start dancing?"

I hesitate, unsure how I feel about the whole getting to know each other more thing. Mainly because if I answer questions, I'll be compelled to ask him some, and I don't think I want to find out if

I genuinely like him. That's a distraction. Then again, I did agree to this, so it wouldn't be fair to shut him down. I resolve to be relatively open-minded, just this one time. Call it an experiment of sorts.

I respond, "My mom signed me up for ballet classes when I was four. I loved them. By the time I was six, my ballet master was singling me out in smaller groups taken from the larger pool of my classmates to perform in shows, and it became clear I was pretty good at that art form. I also loved it—the music, the movement, the feeling of expressing myself without words." I don't add in that I had a few developmental issues with speaking when I was young, which were probably the result of my mother continuing to abuse prescription medications and alcohol *while she was pregnant with me*. That's a bit too personal.

Carson nods, turning the car onto the highway that leads straight to the city. "Were you close with your mom?"

His usage of past tense reminds me that he was listening earlier when I compared Scarlett to my mother.

I answer honestly, "Not at all." My voice comes out with more firmness than I intend, and I internally wince at myself. My mother's not a topic I like broaching often.

He arches an eyebrow, casting me a sidelong glance. Because I don't want to further that line of inquiry, I ask, "What made you become a business major? If you got into the Greywood's business program, you have to be half-decent at what you do." The programs at our university are notoriously selective and extremely difficult to get into.

Carson gives a half-smile. "That, or your parents need to be rich enough to pay your way in. I think I inherited the business mind from my father." He pauses. "I'm not close with him either. He's a piece of shit, to be honest. Flagrantly cheats on my mother, was never home while I was growing up. But he's one hell of a businessman, as his worldwide empire can attest to.

"When I was in high school, I saved up my allowance for the year and ended up buying a restaurant I really liked, one that was going to close down because the foot traffic was declining. It was family-owned, and the owners were old and not technologically adept. I took over the marketing and branding, put a few strategies in place, shifted around the menu a bit to fit seasons, and within a year, the place was flush with customers and regulars, which brought solid cashflow. The next summer another location opened up, and then another a few months after that. I led with that on my application for the business program, and I guess Greywood liked it enough that Dad didn't even have to bribe my way in here."

I listen with deepening interest. Carson really *isn't* just a pretty face. The fact that he had an allowance generous enough to allow him to buy a *restaurant* after just a year is a bit galling, but at the same time, that tells me he has good money-management skills and a knack for the sort of strategy it takes to survive in American businesses. That he took a small, failing business and turned it into a flourishing chain while *still in high school* is certainly impressive.

Both of us having strained relationships with parents also makes me feel like there's a sort of kinship here. My mother was the definition of a terrible, narcissistic waste of air, and it sounds like his father is a terrible, cheating asshole.

"Why does your mom stay with your dad?" I blurt before I can think better of it.

Carson takes a moment to respond, and I sense he's deciding how much to tell me. Finally, he says, "Divorcing from a narcissist, especially a rich one, is asking for a battle you can't possibly win. At this point, they barely see each other, so they're married only in name.

He has a string of younger mistresses, and she's been seeing a guy who makes her smile. The arrangement isn't the best, but it's the least-bloody outcome possible." Then, he asks, "How did your mom pass? What happened?"

He pulls into the parking lot of a small strip mall, finding a spot in the back row of cars to park. On the far side of a line of stores is an outdated-looking spot with a sign over the door reading M's Diner, and another sign advertising the best burgers in the city with a neon glow in the window. It has a line of people waiting outside, which tells me the advertisement might actually be on par with quality of food.

As I unbuckle my seatbelt, I glance at Carson as I respond, "Karma."

Then, I get out of the car. Carson follows suit, not asking any more questions, even though I can tell he wants to push. I appreciate his self-restraint, because I've told him as much as I'm going to today about that part of my life. I prefer to leave my mother dead in the past, instead of letting her invade my present.

She did her level best to ruin me as a person, trying to make me into an insecure, broken adult with no will or voice of my own. Her efforts inadvertently caused me to become the exact opposite; completely self-reliant, someone who can survive just fine on their own without the aid of others. Living in a house with her meant getting drowned in her bullshit on a daily basis, and the fact that I survived that relatively intact taught me that there's very little I *wouldn't* be able to get through in this world. In a supremely twisted way, she gave me the gift of independence from an early age, because I knew I could never be dependent on her. I could never trust her; she'd fuck me over at the earliest opportunity.

When we walk up to the restaurant, I understand why there's a line of people waiting; it's a relatively small place with only a handful of tables where someone can sit to eat. It looks like it would be better for takeout or ordering, which is why I'm surprised when Carson bypasses the line of people and walks straight inside. Those waiting in line cast us dirty looks, and I return them with a somewhat apologetic smile as I follow Carson inside.

The interior is set up kind of like a retro fifty's diner, with linoleum floors, checkered tables scattered around, accompanied by red chairs, and black-and-white framed pictures of old cars on the walls. A jukebox sits proudly in the corner by the window, playing a Bob Dylan song. Carson walks straight up to the hostess stand, and the woman standing behind the counter pauses in speaking to a customer to beam at him. She looks to be somewhere in her fifties and is clearly familiar with Carson—she leaves the customer mid-sentence, walks around the counter, and pulls Carson into a hug. I watch the strange exchange with growing interest, wondering just what the hell is going on here. This is one of the hole-in-the-wall diners where most rich people wouldn't be caught dead, and yet Carson knows the staff.

"I was wondering when I'd see you back around here! Place hasn't been the same with your annoying ass sullying the back table," she says, pulling back and reaching up to ruffle Carson's hair.

Her eyes shift to me where I stand slightly behind Carson, and widen with excitement as she looks back and forward between us. "And you brought a girl!" The way she says *girl* is similar to how some might say *alien*.

Before I can respond or even breathe, I'm pulled into a crushing hug as well, finding myself nearly smothered in her arms. When she pulls back, it's to pat my hair and cheeks, saying, "Carson's been coming here regularly for the last two years, but he's never brought a gal around! And such a pretty one, too. I'm Miranda, and you are?"

I'm so baffled by this whole situation—the restaurant, the grand-motherly hostess who's on a first name basis with Carson, the fact that I'm evidently the first girl he brought here—that I can't find any words. I look to Carson with wide eyes, only to find him smiling somewhat... *sheepishly?* He's always struck me as so confident, so in charge, but right now he seems unsure of himself, which is surprisingly endearing.

Carson tells Miranda, "This is my friend Eliana, and I think she'd like food more than smothering. You got any open tables?"

Miranda looks between the two of us with raised eyebrows before saying, "*Friend*, huh? Well then, y'all go on and take the table in the back, the waiter will be with you in a jiff."

CHAPTER TWENTY-FOUR

"This is definitely unexpected," I admit to Carson once we're seated.

When he said a great burger joint, I half-expected him to end up taking me to some ridiculously upscale restaurant with tiny burgers and disproportionate costs, where I'd feel terribly underdressed and out of place. M's diner came straight out of left field, which I *really* like. The unexpectedness of it—seeing that despite his wealth, Carson is down-to-earth, makes me soften a bit.

Carson leans back in his seat and slides a laminated menu across the table to me. "Yeah? Where did you think I'd take you?"

"Somewhere I'd stick out like a sore thumb," I reply.

Eyes scanning over his own menu, he says, "You *do* draw attention wherever you go, but not in a bad way."

I feel my eyebrows furrow a little. "What do you mean?"

I know my *dancing* gets attention, and I'm a fairly sociable person, but I'm not terribly popular—nor do I want to be. I experienced intense popularity in my senior year of high school with my ex and found that I did not like it all that much. It was just too *fake*. People were nice to each other not because they liked their friends but because they wanted to sit higher on the social food chain. It struck me as disingenuous and not altogether beneficial, because there were no true friends amongst the popular kids. Only people who pretended to be friends in attempts to heighten their own status.

"Heads turn when you walk into a room, Princess," Carson tells me, looking up from his menu.

I shake my head. "That's not true."

He arches an eyebrow. "It is, you just don't care enough to notice it. If you don't believe me, take a look around."

Feeling my frown deepen, I glance around the dining area, where about a dozen other tables are scattered. To my profound shock, several people avert their gaze from my table as I run my eyes over them, both men and women.

I look back at Carson. "They're staring at you, not me. I believe you're referred to as Greywood's royalty, and it looks like most of the people here are students."

He lets out a low chuckle. "Some of them are looking at me, yes. I'm pretty used to it—that's something that naturally comes with my last name, and spectacular looks." He gives me a playful wink with the latter. "But trust me when I say, most are looking at you. Also, the both of us. If I do say so myself, we make quite a stunning pair. Wanna make it official? *Really* give them something to stare at?"

I can't suppress an eyeroll at that, even though it makes me smile. "I thought you were going to be on your best behavior?"

He holds up his hands in a mock placatory gesture. "Fair enough, Little E. I did promise that. You can't blame me for trying, though."

A female waitress who I'd guess is a student from Greywood waltzes up to the table. She's dressed in a 1950's waitress uniform, with a short black skirt and red shirt that's halfway unbuttoned, showcasing generous cleavage. She gives Carson a sultry smile while barely sparing me a glance.

She purrs, "What can I get you, handsome?"

A small sigh escapes me. First, Scarlett came onto him on day one of class and now this girl. It seems that everywhere he goes, Carson will attract female attention, which is a bit irritating—even though I can't blame girls for looking or flirting. He is, after all, *very* attractive, even though I try to ignore that for the sake of my sanity.

Carson gives her a cursory glance, then looks back to his menu as he orders, "I'll get M's burger, extra fries, and a sprite."

Since I was so engrossed in conversation with him, strange though it is, I didn't actually get a chance to peruse the menu. I briefly scan over the items before settling on, "Cheeseburger and a water, please."

In the past, if my mom caught wind of me eating such calorie-heavy food, I'd have been on a diet of kale and arugula for a month. So, despite knowing I have a decent metabolism—mostly due to the fact that I've been dancing several hours every day for the last many years—a niggle of guilt starts up in my chest.

For just about my entire life, my issue was being *under*weight. At almost every doctor's appointment I've ever been to, I've been told I need to gain some weight to stay healthy, even though I wouldn't actually be permitted to do so under the watchful eye of my mother. It was just over this last summer, once I was out from under Mom's thumb, that I was able to get myself back in a healthy range—a task that proved to be far more difficult than I presumed, primarily because I've been undereating my whole life. I managed to get with a nutritionist who put me on a meal plan that got me where I needed to be, but it was a struggle.

Even still, that's one of the few things that haunt me from my mother; guilt over food. The guilt is totally misplaced, which I know *logically*, but combine my upbringing with the uber-skinny mindset of most dancers, and it's hard to enjoy something like a hamburger without overthinking it.

The waitress adjusts her cleavage, making it pop out even more, and tells Carson, "Let me know if there's *anything* else I can do for you."

Irritated from my train of thought combined with the waitress's patent flirting even though Carson is here *with another girl*, I ask, "Does the same offer extend to me? Or is it just hot guys who get the special treatment?"

The waitress's expression morphs into a scowl as she turns a glare on me. Since I'm very used to handling mean girls, I lean back in my seat and arch an eyebrow at her. She tosses her blonde hair over her shoulder with a little huff, before turning and striding away.

Carson says with amusement, "*Hot* guy? I think that's the first compliment I've gotten from you, and it wasn't even directed at me."

I give him my most unamused look. "Let's not pretend you're oblivious to your appearance and the effect it has on the female population."

He nods mildly. "I'm certainly more aware of it than you are of the way you affect the male population. If our waiter was a guy, I can guarantee roles would be reversed, and I'd be the one warning him off."

That makes me bristle. "I wasn't warning her off, I was just pointing out it's rude to flirt with a man who's obviously on a date."

I realize my mistake when Carson's eyebrows practically hit his hairline, and his lips turn into a cheshire cat like grin, dripping with smugness. *Crap.* I didn't mean to call this a date; it *isn't*, it's just me deciding to see if his presence will be bearable for however long he shadows and stalks me.

"A *date*?" Carson questions, his voice lilting.

"I imagine that's how it would appear to passerby's," I say quickly. "I mean..." feeling tongue tied, I open and close my mouth several times. Carson watches with endless amusement, relishing seeing me twisted up in knots. "It's not a date. It's just... two people eating together. In a totally platonic way."

He makes me sweat it out for a while longer before murmuring, "Whatever you say, Princess." Then, he leans forward, bracing his elbows on the table. "Anytime you want to go out in a *totally platonic way*, you just let me know. I'll clear my schedule."

"You're insufferable," I say primly.

"And you're starting to succumb to my charms," he returns.

That gives me pause, because he's not wrong, and that is *not* part of my plan for the year. Maybe I shouldn't have agreed to this—no, I *definitely* shouldn't have agreed to this, but it's too late now. Much as I hate to admit it, I am enjoying spending time with Carson. My interest in him is deepening, just like my interest in Seth deepens each time I spend time with him.

I feel somewhat like I'm digging myself into a grave that I'll regret quite soon. I briefly contemplate asking Carson to take me home, but I don't want to. It's more my fear of getting in too deep that drives it.

Sensing my discomfort, Carson switches topics. "I've heard through the grapevine that Sanders is planning another production. A *new* ballet, that he'll be choreographing single handedly. How's that going?"

Grateful for the switch in conversation, I tell Carson about the retelling of Pandora's Box, the casting process, and the fact that next week will be round three of auditions, and then the cast list will be posted. I tell him I'm *really* excited to be a part of it, even though it means that what little free time I might've had will disappear altogether.

After twenty minutes, our food arrives; both of us dig in, and I'm grateful to find that no guilt assails me over the tremendous caloric intake. We eat, sip at our drinks, and talk about various things. Carson tells me a little more about the restaurant chain he owns, mentioning that he'd be happy to take me to one of the locations, which is just a two-hour drive from school. I tell him not to push his luck, even though I am curious enough that I might agree, if I didn't have an overly packed schedule as is.

Overall, I realize that spending time with him is surprisingly enjoyable. *Too* enjoyable, because his presence is so lighthearted and easy-going it's effortless to be around him. Lunch passes in a breeze as we talk and exchange stories and jokes, and before I know it, nearly two hours have gone by.

After driving me back to school, Carson insists on walking with me up to my dorms. When I tell him it's not necessary, he informs me that he takes his role as my shadow and protector very seriously. I can't tell if he's kidding or not, but considering the recent nefarious activities on campus, I don't mind.

When we get to my hallway, I see April standing outside of her dorm room, her face unusually pale, looking somewhat stricken. Worried, I quicken my stride until I'm in front of her and ask, "What's wrong? Is everything okay?"

She opens and closes her mouth several times, appearing to be lost for words. Carson catches up, standing behind me, but I don't look back at him—I'm too focused on April. I can tell that whatever she's about to say, it's going to be *bad*. The energy radiating from her is nervous and frantic, and her expression appears *lost*, for lack of a better word. I haven't known April terribly long, but in the time since we got to campus and became friends, she's never once seemed wobbly or off kilter, which makes my chest feel heavy with anxiety.

Finally, she says, "It's Scarlett. Sometime during the school day, she went missing."

Carson says behind me, "The bitch probably cut and run after getting caught for her bullshit."

April shakes her head. "I don't think so. Her dorm room was broken into, and..."

Oh god. "And what?" I press.

April meets my eyes. "And there's was blood found in it. Hers, presumably. And I mean a good amount of blood, Elia. There were also signs of a struggle. The police are up on the fifth floor now, investigating, but I think she's been taken."

Cold settles over every inch of me, and flashes of the body I discovered by dance HQ less than a week ago run through my mind. I swallow hard, my throat feeling dry and scratchy as my mind starts to devolve into worst case scenarios. Except, the scenarios I'm imagining don't seem very far out there. The scary thing is that they seem *plausible*.

The policewoman who escorted me home on the night I discovered the body told me that preliminary suspicion was that they were dealing with a male perpetrator who was experienced with this sort of thing. For Scarlett to go missing in the *middle of the school day* in *broad daylight* seems at once sloppy and clever in a twisted way. Clever, because most or all the students who live here were out in classes, leaving the coast somewhat clear. Sloppy, because it was daytime, where anyone could've seen.

I ask through numb lips, "Were there any witnesses? Did anyone see what happened?"

April shakes her head jerkily. "No. I overheard two cops talking about it when I snuck onto the fifth floor to see what the commotion was about, and the cops were saying nobody has come forward with anything. Then again, this only happened in the last three hours, but something's telling me this was coordinated."

I stare at her with bafflement. "But why *Scarlett?* She's popular, has a lot of friends—"

"She's a social queen but total jerk," April cuts me off. "Word on the street is that the dead arts student was a mean girl, too. She'd pulled some nasty pranks around campus last year. Nobody dares speak badly about her out in the open now, but it doesn't sound like she was a nice person. Scarlett certainly wasn't, either. She was a total asshole, as evidenced by your showdown in class."

A debilitating sense of shame gets a grip on me. I was mean to Scarlett earlier. In fact, I deliberately humiliated her, both because she tried to do the same to me and to make sure nobody else in dance tried to follow her footsteps and work to turn our company members against me. Now, she's missing, probably in the hands of the same psychopath who got to the arts student.

"Jesus Christ," I whisper. "Do the cops have any leads? Anywhere to look? I've read that the first twelve hours are the most important in abduction cases."

April shakes her head again. "Not that I heard. She's just gone."

She's just gone. Those words echo in my head again and again, as I start to imagine pictures of Scarlett ending up like that arts student—tortured to death and then dumped somewhere for an innocent passerby to find. *Dear god.* Feeling like all of the strength's been sapped from my body, I stumble backwards until I'm leaning against my dorm room door, sagging against it.

There's *nowhere safe* on Greywood campus. If the psycho got to Scarlett in broad daylight with no witnesses, it stands to reason that he could get to anyone anywhere. My heart pounds in my chest so hard I'm almost worried it might actually explode, and I feel a sheen of sweat start to form on my brow.

Carson steps up in front of me, his features solemn, his eyes glinting with concern. "Are you okay?" he asks me.

I shake my head from side to side, because there is no fucking way to be okay in a circumstance like this. If I thought I felt terribly unsafe after finding the first body, knowing that a second victim was snatched right from the same dorms *I live in* is incomprehensibly worse. I can't seem to move, in fact I can barely breathe.

April straightens her back and says, "I'm gonna go see if I can find out anything else. I'll keep you updated." Her eyes shift to Carson. "You gonna stay here?"

Carson looks at me. "Do you want me to stay?"

I nod quickly and continuously, because there is no fucking way I want to be alone now. In fact, I don't even want to be *here* right now, but where else could I go? The dorm is my home for the next four years. I can't exactly find a hotel to stay in, because I'm here on scholarship and lucky that the scholarship came with boarding and a meal plan. I don't have a dime to spare, which leaves me trapped.

April nods, then turns and speedwalks down the hallway, disappearing out of sight. I turn around to face my dorm room but feel too frozen to actually draw out my key to open it. My entire body feels stiff, as if it's encased in plaster.

Carson steps up beside me and puts a hand on my shoulder, startling me so much I jump.

He asks me calmly, "Where's your key?"

I manage to fish it out of my pocket with stiff fingers, but my hands are so shaky I can't actually fit it into the keyhole. Carson gently pushes me aside, takes the key from my grip, and unlocks my door. He takes my hand and leads me over to my bed. I sink down on it, a sense of numbness washing over me. Dimly, I think I might be in shock, but my scrambled thoughts don't leave enough room for me to actually process the thought. Feeling like I'm on autopilot, I lay down on my side and curl up into a ball, shivering. It's pretty warm in my room, the radiator by the window is doing its job, but that can't penetrate the chill that seems like it's taken up residence in my very bones.

I feel the mattress dip and shift at my back, but don't have the presence of mind to look over my shoulder. After a moment, a strong arm wraps around my middle and pulls me back into a hard, warm chest. In any other circumstance, Carson laying with me might make me panic, but right now I need it. I need his warmth and solid presence, because I feel like I'm a step away from crumbling.

Carson murmurs in my ear, "I won't let anything happen to you."

"Promise?" I ask shakily.

"I swear," he confirms.

That actually works in calming me down, if only minutely. I'm very used to dealing with life all on my own—growing up the way I did, there really wasn't another choice. But *this?* This I can't get through on my own. I like to think I'm a strong, relatively brave person, but strength and bravery aren't enough to protect me from whatever psycho took Scarlett. As much as I hate to admit it, I need Carson's strength because I can't seem to find enough of my own.

Carson doesn't attempt to get frisky with me, probably sensing that I can't handle his endless innuendo or relentless flirting right now. Instead, he simply lays with me, allowing me to absorb his strength and warmth until my shivering's receded and my breathing has somewhat evened out.

He strokes a hand up and down my arm, the gesture soothing and calming, until my eyes are fluttering closed. The adrenaline crash brings with it a wave of exhaustion, as if my mind and body can't handle the weight of my anxiety without shutting down to process.

Feeling at once like I'm spinning out of control and yet strangely content in the circle of Carson's arms, I let darkness pull me into a restless sleep.

CHAPTER TWENTY-FIVE

W hen I wake up, it's to a fog that feels like it weighs heavily on me. There's a weight on my waist, surrounding my body, which is all it takes for recent events to come crashing back to the forefront of my mind. Then, my eyes snap open, and I find myself staring at the strong arm curled around my waist, the large hand resting on my belly, and I feel the pleasant heat of *Carson Ajax* snuggled up against my back. I turn over slowly and come face-to-face, chest-to-chest with Carson. He's staring at me with an intense focus. His eyes are unblinking as they travel over my face, and one glance at the clock on my nightstand tells me he's stayed here with me like this for hours.

Feeling strangely shy and immensely awkward, I murmur, "Hi."

"Hello," Carson returns with a small smile.

I blink a couple times, wanting to thank him but feeling embarrassed that I freaked out and had a panic attack. He's now seen me at my worst, a state that I don't like *anyone* seeing me in. Usually when I get too anxious, I'll isolate myself and wait out the nerves until I calm down because hysterics are not a good look on me. Granted, the fact that someone I know got abducted from the building I live in might get me some leeway, but still.

"How are you feeling?" Carson asks.

I consider that before responding. Even despite the insanity of recent events, I feel strangely safe wrapped up in his arms. Certainly calmer than I should, like his presence alone can protect me. Nevertheless, I can't help but feel like this is somewhat wrong, like I'm leading Carson on. he stayed and watched over me like a boyfriend would, promised to protect me like a boyfriend would, while I refuse to acknowledge that going out with him earlier was anything more than two people platonically getting food together.

"Okay," I settle on.

He arches an eyebrow. "Is that why it took you so long to answer?"

That makes me frown a little. "I feel like this shouldn't be happening. We're not together in any capacity, and yet here you are. Holding me like... you know."

Carson strokes his hand up and down my arm soothingly. "This doesn't have to mean anything, Elia. If you want, we can label it as a friend looking out for you in a time of need."

But the thing is, it *does* mean something. The tenderness Carson's capable of showing makes me like him even more, which is dangerous. I say, "But you like me."

Carson smiles. "And you like me, but we can pretend that isn't the case. For now, at least. Right now, my priority is your safety." He pauses to glance around the room. "I gotta say, I don't like the idea of you staying here. The dorms haven't exactly proven to be impenetrable."

I look down at his chest. He's right, but there's absolutely nothing I can do to rectify that fact. "I don't have anywhere else to go."

"You could stay with me. I have an apartment in the city, with impeccable security and a guest room."

I feel my head jerk back at that. We barely know each other and he's offering for me to *move in with him*? If I thought Seth's only setting was full steam ahead, Carson's setting is a NASCAR driver.

I open my mouth to tell him he's ridiculous; he puts his pointer finger to my lips, preventing me from speaking.

"Before you shoot me down, take a second to think. I won't pressure you into anything, this will be a temporary solution until the school makes some serious security upgrades to program dormitories. I've been on the phone with some administrators in the last few hours while you slept, they're going to put a security system in the dorms that requires ID verification to unlock doors and windows. In the interim, there'll be campus officers stationed around, but that doesn't make me feel any better, and I don't think it'd make you feel better either. I saw you earlier, Elia, you were *terrified*. I would be, too, in your position. Let me help you until things get figured out. It doesn't have to mean anything beyond my vested interest in your safety."

Let me help you. I don't often hear those words. It's always been me versus the world, me helping myself against all odds. Then again, these aren't odds I can beat alone—I'm in a pretty abstract situation with a psycho on the loose who has a predilection for snatching up girls in broad daylight. I simply don't have the tools to protect myself from that. But to accept Carson's offer feels like giving in, regardless of his assurances that it doesn't mean anything.

Sharing an apartment with him also sounds like a recipe for disaster. I find it difficult to resist his charms when we're surrounded by people; how will I keep myself in check if we're *alone* at night together? The answer is, I probably won't.

I've already given into Seth *way* more than I intended to, and his charm is wrapped up in a somewhat psychopathic darkness that frightens me. Carson's charm is much lighter, easier, and more tender, all things that call to me as much as Seth's darkness.

Regardless, my leaving here wouldn't make much of a difference; there are still hundreds of students housed in these dorms, all of whom will still be in danger. April, who lives across the hall from me, would be in danger. I can't just leave her.

"I can't," I murmur.

Carson looks equal parts dejected and unaccepting. He grips my shoulders and says, "You can't just stay here, Elia."

"April's here," I respond. "I won't leave her behind. Besides, I don't know that us together in an apartment would be the best idea."

"It's a better idea than you getting dangled in front of a killer," Carson snaps.

"If I'm being dangled in front of the killer, so is she," I say, sitting up and scooting to the end of the bed, letting Carson's arm fall off of me. Without it, I feel strangely cold, almost bereft, but I also don't feel like staying cuddled up to him is in my best interest. I stand from the bed and walk over to my dresser, opening one of the drawers and grabbing a sweater. As I pull it on, I turn back to face Carson.

"I appreciate you staying with me. It's probably one of the nicest things anyone's ever done for me." That last part slips out by accident, and I feel my cheeks redden in embarrassment and realization that what Carson did actually *is* the nicest thing anyone's done for me in distant memory. "I also thank you for the offer, but I can't accept it."

Carson stands from my bed, his expression frustrated. "I can't just let you stay here where you could get *taken*."

I don't want to stay here either, but I *really* don't feel like I have another choice. I won't abandon April, because she's also one of the few people in my life to ever be kind to me. She's the first *real* friend I've had in a long time—even the friends from my high school dance days were mostly superficial. Not as bad as the company girls here, but not great, either.

I look at the floor. "I don't think I will. If what April said earlier is right, the killer has a thing for mean girls. I won't profess to be the kindest person in the world, but I'm not outwardly a bitch. I certainly don't have a habit of tearing other people down to make myself feel better."

We both know I'm grasping at straws. Just because the killer took two campus jerks doesn't mean that's his MO, but as of now, that's all us civilians have to go on. I don't think *any* female on campus is totally safe right now, I certainly doubt that any of us *feel* safe, but the situation is what it is. I just have to hope that the police will do their job and track down whoever did this.

Once again, the policewoman's words come back to me: *someone who's done this before.* It's possible—no, *probable*—that the killer has taken more lives elsewhere and Greywood campus just happens to be the current hunting ground.

Carson runs a hand through his hair, looking genuinely disheveled. That he cares so deeply for my safety is touching and a little worrying. Worrying, because the fact of the matter is that we barely know each other. We've only really hung out once, today—that shouldn't be enough to make him so invested in my wellbeing.

Then again, dancing a role well shouldn't have been enough to attract the attention of both him *and* Seth, and yet it did. It seems like a lot of shit is playing out weirdly these days.

Finally, Carson walks up to the door. He turns to tell me over his shoulder, "This conversation isn't over. There'll be police crawling outside tonight, which should be enough for your safety, but we'll be finishing our talk tomorrow." With that, he opens the door and steps out, shutting it behind him. I hug my waist, feeling strangely lonely without him even though I've fared well enough on my own in this dorm for the last month.

*****

It can't be more than an hour after Carson leaves when I hear the boom of April's knocks on my door. At this point, I'm familiar enough with the thunderous noise to place it as belonging to her, so I slip off of where I've been doing homework on my bed and let her in. She's holding two cups of instant noodles in her hands—a scholarship student's bread and butter. Even though I ate a heavy lunch, I take one of the cups and join her in sitting on my floor, our backs up against the bed.

"This is getting to be a thing," she says, slurping her noodles while watching me from the corner of her eye. "The killer strikes, we end up on your floor to speculate."

I lift my cup in salute. "What did you find out?"

"Not as much as I wanted to," April replies. "Eavesdropping only gets you so far with cops. I was able to glean that they have jack shit to go on. We do live in a time where it's far easier to get rumors from the internet and social media, which have proven most useful in the past. Not in this scenario, though. I searched through all the socials, and it doesn't look like *anyone* saw anything."

"How can that be?" I ask with disbelief. "There's an entire campus full of students. How could *no one* have seen a *killer* abducting one of the most popular girls on campus?"

April lifts her shoulder, slurping more noodles before responding. "No idea. Whoever did this had to be *good* to get away with it in the middle of the day. The whole living in a murder mystery is starting to feel more and more real, and a lot less entertaining. On the plus side, our dormitories are going to be getting a serious security upgrade."

I nod. "Carson mentioned that."

April's eyes sharpen on me and she lowers her steaming cup to stare at me, expectation in her eyes. "So what's up with Carson? You two came in together... were you coming back from a date?"

I frown. "You really want to talk about that with everything else that's going on right now?"

April nods. "Yes. Yes, I do. I need a distraction, and your love life seems like prime entertainment. I didn't grill you about the photos of you with Carson *and* Seth Balor yesterday because they were attached to that horrible *other* picture and you were on the verge of a breakdown, but now, I'd very much like to know what's going on."

I pause before responding, because I don't know how to explain to her what's going on when I still haven't been able to fully grasp it. It's still weird to think that I have two wealthy suitors who are in a literal competition over me, and it's even more disconcerting to slowly realize that I like *both* of them. Seth's dark magnetism calls to me on a level I didn't know existed, and Carson's surprising depth of character and light-heartedness—which I suspect hides some darkness of his own—is equally intriguing to me.

April nudges my shoulder with hers when I take too long, saying, "Spill, bitch."

With a sigh, I do. I tell her about my run-ins with them—the PG version, because I have no interest in hearing what she'd say if I admitted Seth went down on me last night. I tell her about my classes with Seth and my times getting stuck in the archives with him, glossing over the details, and about my late lunch with Carson earlier today. At the end of my explanation, April's grinning like a loon.

"So, to recap, you have two hot, rich guys who have enough interest in you to *fight each other* over it? That's fucking *awesome*. With them around, I doubt the killer would even be able to get close to you." Her smile falters, and her expression turns contemplative. "Do you think they have any friends who are into Asian girls? Maybe I could also get myself a suitor to scare away the boogeyman."

Unable to help myself, I laugh. "I'll be sure to ask."

She gives me a decisive nod. "You do that. I'll be expecting an answer shortly." She cranes her neck to look at the clock on my bedside stand, then sighs. "Well, there are enough cops crawling the place that I'm not afraid of getting murdered in my sleep tonight, so I'm heading to bed. I'm also going to join you on your walk to dance dorms with Carson tomorrow; I'm sure that wall of muscle can serve as a nice deterrent for both of us."

I smile at that. "I'm sure he won't mind. Shit's getting scary around here."

"That it is," she agrees. She stands, stretches her arms above her head, and strides to my door. Before leaving, she tosses over her shoulder, "Good night, sleep tight, have hot wet dreams about your two non-lethal stalkers."

Chapter Twenty-Six

I spend the night tossing and turning, my mind tormenting me with worry over what might be happening to Scarlett. I have absolutely no affection for that girl, but at the same time, I feel terrible. I gave her the verbal smackdown of the century, and then she got *kidnapped*. I can't stop picturing *her* face on the body of the arts student I discovered the day before start of school, which makes getting sleep nearly impossible.

When Carson shows up with *three* coffees in the morning—one for me, one for him, and one for April—I'm surprisingly grateful to see him, and almost wish that he stayed. Maybe then I'd have actually gotten some rest. As promised, April joins us in walking to dance HQ.

There, I lose myself in the motions of my body for the next six hours, grateful to get a break from my thoughts. Carson shadows me for the first half of the day, as per usual. What's *un*usual is that he goes as far as to take me all the way to my art history classes, saying that he doesn't want me alone on campus at any time, even when I'm sprinting from class to class. He doesn't bring up the idea of me staying with him again, though I have a feeling he wants to push until I give in.

When I get to my art class, I don't even bother to complain or roll my eyes upon seeing Seth in his usual seat in the back row, with the seat right next to him being the last available one. Instead, growing used to his antics, I drop into the chair and start organizing my things on my desk.

That comes to a pause when Seth drops a packet of papers on my desk, right on top of my laptop. Before even looking them over, I toss him a questioning frown. "What's this?"

He smiles a special sort of smile that does strange things to me. It isn't a kind or friendly smile, it's one dripping with darkness. It's a smile that makes me suspect he plans on eating me alive, which makes me think back to the other night when he was doing just that. It was almost a little frightening in its intensity, but also the single hottest thing I have ever experienced. The skill this man has with his mouth alone is deadly. Desire heats my body from the inside out as I stare at the sensual curve of his lips.

"This is the contract we discussed, before moving onto more enjoyable activities," Seth responds.

I ignore the latter part of his sentence and focus on the former, turning my attention to the pages in front of me and scanning them. I'm reasonably familiar with contracts as I've already signed many through the course of my career as a dancer. Companies and productions both generally have contracts for each dancer that lay out expectation for each member.

Aside from those contracts, I started working when I was just fourteen, which also taught me about basic contracts. It was the earliest age I could legally get a job, and by then I knew damn well that financial responsibility would fall solely to me, because my mother couldn't be trusted with money—she'd spend it all on herself. For the first two years, I worked customer service jobs in retail to save money for ballet supplies that my mother wouldn't cover. Then, I started working summer jobs at dance camps as a student instructor, which turned into switching out retail for teaching those classes even during the school year.

The contract Seth drew up, as he promised he would, is pretty standard for freelance work—which I guess posing for art falls under. It's loosely worded when it comes to expectations regarding time, laying out that we'll settle on verbal agreements for hours that will be adhered to, but requiring a minimum of ten hours a month. *A month*, which means Seth expects for us to continue on with this for some time. I guess he wasn't kidding when he called me his muse.

It also lays out the startling rate of 150$ per hour of sitting for him, and even clarifies no-nudity, along with the fact that I'm permitted to engage in school related activities during work hours. I'm a little surprised that he went into such depth and added in every demand I made, but I shouldn't be. At this point, I understand that Seth is as meticulous as it gets, and he's probably someone who looks at situations from every possible angle before choosing a course of action.

"This looks fine," I tell Seth. "The one thing I can't guarantee is the ten hours a month; I don't know if I'll have ten free hours a month. Rehearsals for a new production are starting soon."

Seth lifts a shoulder. "I'll add a penalty section."

I feel my eyebrows furrow at that. "What sort of penalties? If it's to try to lower the pay rate or fine me, we're going to have problems."

The corners of his lips twitch. "It won't affect the pay, and it'll be nothing you won't enjoy. You'll see when I write it in. Now, shh. The professor's about to start his lecture."

Before I can say something along the lines of, *you're one to shush me*, the professor starts speaking, so I toss an eye roll at Seth before dropping the contract into my backpack, settling back into my seat, and starting on notes.

***

Later in the afternoon, after I've finished all of my classes, I return to my dormitories to find an unexpected sight. Carson is standing in front of the dorm room right next to mine, *unlocking it with a key.* I stop mid-stride, blinking several times as I watch him. *Has my shitty sleep schedule started causing hallucinations?*

Carson turns his head towards me as if sensing my presence, and gives me a bright smile. "Hey, Princess," he greets.

I take slow steps towards him, casting a glance around to see if anyone else is witnessing whatever is going on here. Carson shouldn't magically have a key to the dorm room next to mine; the guy who has the room next to me is in one of the fine arts programs. I've exchanged pleasantries and greetings with him a few times in passing, so I can't quite reconcile what's going on here.

"Um..." I trail off, coming to a stop beside Carson. He opens the door to the room, revealing a single cardboard box in the center of the now-barren space. There's nothing in this room to indicate that, just earlier this morning, a different student was living here; it's been stripped bare. Even the mattress is clear of blankets and pillows.

I look back to Carson with wide eyes. He watches my astonishment with an amused grin curling his lips, appearing perfectly at ease with whatever the hell is happening here.

"What's going on?" I question slowly.

Carson's grin grows. "Well, you turned down my offer last night rather immovably, so I decided that instead of you coming to me, I'd come to you. I told you when I gave you a ride home after Sleeping Beauty I had a designated room; all the program students get one. Nice that we don't have to put up with roommates, even if the rooms are the size of a closet."

I open and close my mouth several times, before finally saying, "Okay, I know I've had a stressful time of it recently, but I'm positive I did not hallucinate a different student living here just this morning."

Carson nods easily. "Yeah, there was another kid here. He was happy to switch dorms with me after some incentive."

When Carson says incentive, I assume it means something along the lines of handing the dude a wad of cash. That'd be plenty to make most students in these dorms very agreeable and amenable to a change of scene. After all, people with money don't end up in cramped matchbox rooms.

"Why?" I ask aimlessly. Why would Carson do that *for me?*

At this point there's no denying that a good deal of chemistry exists between us, but that chemistry shouldn't be enough for him to uproot his life simply because I—along with everyone else who lives in these dorms or goes to Greywood—am in a certain amount of danger until the psycho killer/ kidnapper has been caught. Part of me wants to assume that Carson's sudden moving in has nothing to do with me, but I know that's simply stupidity and shock. There's literally no reason for him to be here if it weren't for me, especially after our conversation last night.

"If I'm here, I can make sure you're safe," Carson explains, seeming far too nonchalant. "I heard you last night about not wanting to leave April on her own. I can see you two are good friends. I don't want to put my only source of intel about you at risk, either." The latter is said teasingly, topped off with a wink.

I continue staring at Carson wide-eyed, trying to make sense of this. Is he really *that* into me? Enough to literally uproot his life and move out of his apartment, which is probably much nicer than the shabby dorms?

"This is deeply strange," I tell him.

He shrugs. "So is the spark I feel between us, because like I've told you before, I'm yet to feel it with anyone else. I'm not eager to risk losing it. So, I'll be spending my nights not far from you, ready to intervene should anything go wrong. I don't actually think it will, the security upgrade here will be done soon and it'll be a good one, but it pays to be safe." He steps forward, picks up a lock of my hair, and twirls it around his finger. "You can't be *that* surprised. You already know I'm willing to take extreme measures to get closer to you."

"Yes," I say slowly, "though I still don't understand why. I'm not the most interesting girl in the world."

"You are to me," he responds simply, and that response does something to me.

I'm accustomed to being unwanted in my life; my mother was sure to tell me on a near daily basis that I was the greatest mistake of her life, that she wished she'd aborted me as soon as she found out she was pregnant. She blamed me for my father leaving, blamed me for everything that was wrong in her life.

Even in dance, I've always known that I'm only wanted because of my talent and work ethic, not because of who I am as a person. My ex only wanted me for his image. My friends in high school were only really my friends because I had de-facto popularity due to my dance abilities. Nobody's ever actually wanted me for who I am, only for what I represented.

So, the fact that Carson wants me enough to uproot his life for my sake, while I've spent most of our time together shooting him down… it makes something warm and fuzzy take up residence in my chest. He wants me, me as a *person*, not just me as a dancer. Maybe that's part of why I've been so set on keeping him at a distance; previously, he was just a man who wanted sex from me, at least in my eyes. This right here fully cements that that's not the case whatsoever. Yesterday went to prove it, too. He laid beside me in my bed for hours while I slept off the crash that followed my anxiety attack, and when I woke up, he didn't try anything sexual. In fact, what he did try was to get me to *move in with him* for the sake of my safety. When I said no, *he* came to *me.*

Carson's eyes flick over my face, taking in every detail of my expression as I stare at him, and then a sly, playful smile curls his lips. "You just fell in love with me, didn't you?"

That snaps me out of my thoughts, at least partially, because if he keeps making moves like this there's a chance I actually might. "No."

Carson nods. "You totally did. That's okay—you'll be happy to know you're in the company of masses. You call me a stalker, but you don't know what real stalking is; the number of girls I've had to fend off with a metal pole after a single night together isn't even funny."

I scowl. "Now you're being irritating."

"And you're trying to deny the truth," he says, his smile growing.

I push a finger into his chest. "If anything, *you're* the one who's in love with *me.* Moving into the room next to mine after already getting yourself a spot as my campus shadow is the very *definition* of stalking."

"Now she's deflecting," Carson taunts. "Listen, Princess, there's really nothing to be ashamed of. You're one of hundreds. You should let me know if you'll be breaking down my door to get to me, though;

I'll have to install another lock if you turn out to be anything like the rest."

Alright, now he really is starting to piss me off, which happens to be a welcome shift from the warmth he was causing within me; warmth that I'm frightened could be the stirrings of something. Not love, but some form of attachment. Generally speaking, I avoid getting attached to people, because my life has shown me that everyone leaves eventually. Usually, that leaving is devastatingly painful because there's little that hurts as much as the abrupt severing of an attachment.

I was deeply attached to my mother as a child. It was only during my early teenage years that I understood how horrible that attachment was, how much pain it brought me, so I resolved to *de*tach from her, at least emotionally. It took time, especially since I still lived with her; in fact, it took *years* for me to feel nothing but apathy when it came to her, but that's ultimately something that freed me.

Carson nudges my shoulder with his, pulling me out of my thoughts. "Since I've decided to move across the city to defend your safety and honor, maybe you'd like to help me unpack?"

I lightly slap his shoulder. "Nice try, loverboy. You get to deal with the effects of your craziness on your own; I'll be doing homework in my room."

Carson pouts, and I hate how much I like that pout. I hate how I stare at the curve of his lips longer than I should. Being alone in his new room with him would not be in my best interest; I honestly don't know if I'll be able to keep a leash on myself. I walk the seven steps from his room to my own, and give him a two finger salute after unlocking my door and pushing it open.

"Have fun with that single cardboard box, Ajax," I say as I step in.

Just before the door closes behind me, I hear Carson call out, "You know where to find me if you change your mind, Princess."

Chapter Twenty-Seven

T he next weeks pass in something of a haze. I attend my classes at school and volunteer times at the museum, while spending almost all of my time either in the company of Seth or Carson, both of whom have insinuated themselves into my daily life so well I start to grow used to them.

Now that he lives right next to me, Carson walks me and April to dance HQ every morning, though he only stays to shadow me on the allotted Mondays, Wednesdays, and Fridays. Seth continues attending art classes and volunteer times at the local museum with me and continues taking every opportunity to try to seduce me. I hold firm against his efforts because I know just how dangerous his seduction can be.

I spend my nights doing homework and scouring the internet for any sign of Scarlett popping up but find nothing. Three days after she disappears, a new security system is installed in the program dorms. It's coded to each student's ID badge, requiring them to swipe it if they want to enter the building. Then there's another scanner and keycode required for the elevator. Additionally, there are now cameras with motion sensors in the entryway, most halls, and elevator. I'm surprised that Greywood is willing to pour money into such an advanced system but considering what's been going on around campus since the start of the year, I really shouldn't be. There's one student dead and another missing; if Greywood was the U.S. government, it'd be on defcon 2.

I spend my Saturdays with April, exploring the city. We take a walk in the city's park, buy popsicles for a dollar from an ice cream stand, visit various monuments and hot spots, and talk more about our lives. I really enjoy spending time with her, because she's so genuine and true to herself it's refreshing.

Then, the first Sunday of October rolls around, which is meant to be my first evening posing for Seth. I signed the contract last week after he edited it, even though I was quite wary of the elusive penalty section he added. The section states that penalties are up to him to determine on a case-to-case basis but clarifies that they won't be financial or physically harmful. The man certainly likes to cover his bases while somehow still leaving me in suspense.

I'm not sure what he expects me to wear or do, so I throw on a casual getup of jeans and a warm sweater and stuff my backpack full of homework while waiting for his text. He programmed his number into my phone during one of our evenings in the museum archives when we were deciding a start date and time for my posing job and told me he'd pick me up to take me to his place.

Like Carson, he has an apartment in the city. People as rich as them don't need to be confined to dormitories with the rest of us plebians. The fact that Carson's still here even after the security system was installed is a little boggling to me—I thought he'd have been out of here at the first opportunity. Instead, he's stayed and continued in his attempts to get me to go out with him.

Last night he went as far as to bring takeout Chinese food to *me*; I didn't refuse because like any scholarship student, I'm not one to turn down a free meal. We ate together in his dorm room while doing homework—it was so pleasant and *normal* that I didn't quite know what to make of it. I also found out that my physical attraction to him has been deepening, because there were several moments when I was sorely tempted to kiss him. I restrained myself, but it was touch and go for a while.

He found out that I'll be posing for Seth's art while we were talking, and seemed rather displeased about the fact, though he didn't try to stop me from doing so. That just served to make me see him as even farther removed from people like my ex; he doesn't try to control me, instead he just wants to spend time with me.

What's dangerous is that I want to spend time with him, too. I also want to spend time with Seth, and the fact that I'm becoming equally attracted to both of them—albeit for different reasons—is frightening. Seth's dark magnetism, intensity, and generalized lack of sanity speaks to me as much as Carson's easy-going, fun, friendly yet deeply understanding demeanor does. In many ways, they're like night and day, and I like both of those things. I love standing under the beams of moonlight as much as I enjoy basking in the warm rays of sun, and that translates to enjoying spending time with them equally, which makes me feel very guilty. I shouldn't be giving so much focus to them; this year was supposed to be about focusing on myself.

I'm grateful that they're not intrusive enough that my studies and grades suffer, but they're intrusive enough that every free moment I have, I'm thinking about them.

My phone goes off with a vibration, and I check the screen to see Seth texting that he's waiting for me outside dorms. I sling my backpack over my shoulder, slip on my sneakers, and head out, feeling deeply nervous yet also somewhat excited. I'm resolved to not get physical with Seth tonight—no touching, no anything that will inevitably weaken me and end up with us in some particularly compromising positions. Even despite my resolve, I know Seth well enough at this point to understand he's capable of crumbling that resolve if he so chooses to.

I find him exactly where he said he'd be; waiting for me on the steps leading up to the building. As soon as I open the front door, his eyes—which were previously scanning the outside surroundings with something resembling boredom—sharpen with interest. Those eyes slowly travel down my body, taking in my casual clothing, before settling back on my face.

"Ready?" he asks with a secretive smile.

I lift a shoulder. "Considering you're yet to tell me exactly what posing for you entails, how could I be?"

He slides an arm around my waist as if we're a couple and uses it to steer me towards the program dorm parking lot, leading me up to a sleek black Mercedes. I can't help the snort of amusement that escapes me; the car seems perfectly suited to him. Black like his soul, fast like his only setting—full steam ahead—and luxurious like I assume his bank account is.

He opens the passenger side door for me, the gesture surprisingly chivalrous, and closes it after I've climbed in. He rounds the car with a few strides, gets into the driver's side, and turns it on before peeling out of the parking lot.

We don't speak much during the drive, and with each mile we pass I feel myself growing more and more nervous, fidgeting in my seat. Seth pulls into an underground parking garage beneath a high-rise building, parks the car, and then escorts me to a bank of elevators.

Once inside, he presses the button for the *top floor*, and the elevator begins its startlingly fast ascent.

"Exactly how rich are you?" I ask him, unable to help myself even though I know it's a rude question.

Seth's lips curl. "I don't think you really want the answer to that, Little Muse."

He's probably right; if I associate a dollar figure in a bank account with him, there are decent odds my opinion of him will drop significantly. I can't exactly help how averse I am to people with too much money, but I can stay blissfully ignorant when it comes to certain individuals. At least, for now.

Still, my curiosity doesn't allow me to leave the topic alone. "You've never spoken about your parents..."

"You've never asked about them," he returns calmly.

Touche. I say, "I'm assuming you're a trust fund kid—"

"You assume wrong," Seth interrupts smoothly. The elevator arrives with a ding, and he leads me into a hallway decorated with cream and golden tones. Golden wall lamps mount the cream walls of the hallway on either side, and the noise of our footsteps is absorbed by the red, lush carpet.

Seth goes on, "My parents are both dead. My mother died when I was a toddler, and my father died a few years ago. Until his death, I hadn't seen a penny of his money—he had no interest in caring for a child."

That tidbit of knowledge is fascinating. Seems like I have some very pointed things in common with him; abandonment of one parent, and neglect by another. I want to question him more, find out what his life was like growing up, but just barely manage to restrain myself from doing so as he unlocks the door to the very last apartment of the hallway, and opens it. I follow him inside, my step somewhat hesitant, getting startled when lights that must be motion-activated flick on with our arrival, revealing a modest entryway along with what appears to be a living room beyond it. To the right of us is a hall, but it's the view in front that really interests me.

The open floorplan allows a view directly into the living room, which is decorated in a minimalistic fashion with shades of grey and black. The back wall is comprised of floor to ceiling windows, showing off a gorgeous view of the city with mountains in the distance. The wall to the right of it is covered in bookshelves, each alcove stuffed with books. In the center of the bookshelves is a doorway that I assume leads into a bedroom. The wall opposite to it is a smooth grey color, boasting of a stone fireplace and a black three-piece furniture set in front of it. In the middle of the room, the dark wood flooring is covered in plastic tarp, on top of which stands an easel, propping up a blank white canvas. There's a small black table beside the easel that has several jars of paints, brushes, and a palette haphazardly scattered on it. Beside it sits a single wooden chair, splattered with paint and what looks like remnants of dried clay.

Feeling inexplicably nervous, I ask, "What now?"

Seth lets out a dark chuckle. "Now, you let me position you how I want, and stay as still as possible while I paint."

I arch an eyebrow at him. "I thought I could do homework?"

Seth kicks off his shoes on a carpet beside the doorway, drops his keys onto a small white table next to it, and pads his way into the main room.

He throws over his shoulder, "You can, but not for the first little bit while I get an outline. It shouldn't take more than an hour to get it right."

I toe off my shoes, then watch as he turns the sofa in front of the fireplace around, so that it's facing the easel. He rolls up the sleeves of his black dress shirt, exposing thick, veiny forearms that my eyes linger on for just a touch too long, before coming back my way. Once in front of me, he takes my hand in his, which startles me more than it should. Seth does not strike me as a person to lead someone by their hand—more herald them where he wants under threat—but lead me by my hand he does, pushing me down onto the couch.

CHAPTER TWENTY-EIGHT

I drop my backpack onto the floor beside me and then stare up at Seth as I sink onto the cushions, feeling my heart pound in my chest because the last time we were in such a position, things turned sexual very quickly, and while my body would *love* a repeat of that, my brain is not quite so accommodating to the thought.

"Lay on your side, facing me," Seth tells me.

I move to follow his instructions, laying on my left side, feeling more and more awkward with each passing second. Then, Seth kneels beside me, which makes my breath catch.

He smirks at me. "Lost in memories?"

Yes, but there's no way I'm admitting it out loud and giving into his taunts. I say, "You know it. Getting covered in dust while cataloguing every item in the museum archives has been pretty riveting."

His smirk drops as he arches an eyebrow at me, but he doesn't press any further. "Put your left arm under your head to support it." When I do as he asks, he inclines his head. "Very good." He proceeds to give me a series of instructions along with praise each time I follow through to his satisfaction. "Now draw your right leg up so your knee's almost at your abdomen. Yes, just like that. Your left leg, bend it just a little bit so it doesn't cramp—good. Finally, your free arm, drape it over the curve of your hip so it rests on your thigh... excellent."

With each bit of praise, I feel myself start to inadvertently relax, drawn into a trance by him—the same trance he seems versed at putting people around him in. The difference with me is that I'm very aware of what he's doing, the way he's lulling and almost hypnotizing me with softly spoken instructions topped off with honeyed approval, and I'm allowing it to happen rather than falling victim to him like a mortal might to a god.

Seth reaches forward to arrange my hair, letting it spill over down my chest. He curls the ends of it a bit, right over my breasts, and his fingers brush against the material of my bra and then collarbone in a way that I'm positive is not accidental.

I give him a censuring look. "Behave."

He responds with a little smirk, before brushing his thumb over my bottom lip. "Little Muse, you should know better than to expect a monster to be on its best behavior."

Despite his words, he relents, standing and walking over to the easel, sinking into the chair behind it. My view of him isn't obstructed because of the way he angled the couch, so I watch as he picks up a pencil from the table, sharpens the tip of it manually with a folding pocket knife, and then starts drawing on the canvas, eyes flicking to me periodically.

"This would go quite a bit quicker if you didn't make me put in that no-nudity clause," he comments. "I have to put my imagination to use."

I say with a sigh, "You've already seen me naked once, Seth, and I think that's more than enough. Don't get greedy."

He pauses in drawing, and his eyes lock with mine. "That's not a reasonable thing to ask, Elia. I'm beyond greedy for you—I'm fucking *ravenous*. You have no idea the things I'd like to do to you, but instead, I'm settling for painting you. I hope you know that's an impressive amount of restraint for me. If I had it my way, I'd have eaten your pussy until you came so many times you were limp, then fucked you until the worst of my obsession about finding out what you'd feel like falling apart around my cock was abated, then positioned you how I want while you were too tired to protest, and *then* gotten to work with the taste of you still on my tongue and sound of your screams still in my ear."

I gape at him—the only response I seem capable of for upwards of a minute. Meanwhile, Seth's hand resumes guiding his pencil across the canvas as if he *didn't* just lay out one of the strangest yet most erotic scenarios one could possibly think of in a situation like this. Times like this, I wonder if there's *anything* normal about the way he thinks, speaks, or behaves.

"How can you just say something like that, all nonchalant?" I finally manage to ask, forcing the words past stunned lips.

He replies, "I don't find myself constrained by the same social rules most others do. If I want to tell you what I'm really thinking, I'll do it. Mainly because I don't particularly care if it makes you uncomfortable or brings that pretty blush to your cheeks—in fact, I like inciting that reaction. I like knowing I can get in your head, because you sure as fuck live rent-free in mine."

That's equal parts interesting and worrying. The more time I spend with Seth, the surer I am that his brain doesn't function the way most others do. Whatever way it does function gives him the sort of latitude that most people would feel uncomfortable or guilty about, but the thing is I don't know that Seth is familiar with emotions such as discomfort or guilt.

After half an hour or so has passed in silence, Seth lifts his pencil from the canvas and leans closer to the drawing, taking a good look at whatever he's created. He glances between me and the canvas before shaking his head with an expression of disapproval.

He pushes his chair back, then holds his hand out to me. "Come here, Little Muse."

Mainly because I'm too comfortable to move, I say, "I think I'm good here."

Seth's eyes cut back to me with a soul-penetrating stare, one that raises the hairs on the back of my neck. "Come here, Eliana. Your time is mine while you're posing for me. I need a close visual to get the delicate features of that beautiful face just right."

Beautiful face. He's practically drowning me with praise I'm unused to, and the funny thing is, he doesn't even seem to realize it. Instead, he's just saying whatever's on his mind with minimal filtration.

I stand from the couch, stretching my arms above my head, and walk over to him with light, hesitant steps. Being too close to Seth feels like a gamble, considering his lack of boundaries and the fact that his lack of boundaries is something of a turn on for me.

He watches me approach, eyes morphing into a stormy grey, and gives me the smile of a shark once I'm directly in front of him. Then he leans back in his chair and pats his thigh.

I feel my eyes bulge. "You want me to... sit on your lap?"

That seems like a rather peculiar position for an artist and subject. Far more intimate than what I expected, but then again, with Seth it seems prudent to simply expect the unexpected—he never quite behaves the way I anticipate.

He inclines his head once. "You signed the contract, Elia. I get to pose you however I wish, so long as your clothes stay on."

I narrow my eyes. "You're a sneaky motherfucker."

That brings his smirk back. "Since the day I was born."

Then, unimpressed with my lack of action, he drops the pencil on the table and takes hold of my arm, pulling me down on top of him. I land on one of his legs, sitting sideways, my legs bracketed by his. He takes the opportunity to run his hands through my hair, rearranging it to his liking while I gawk at him. Bold isn't a strong enough word for him; Seth does whatever he wants, whenever he wants, and is a master at trapping other people in situations where he holds all of the control.

He uses two fingers to tilt my chin up, then tells me, "Stay still."

Picking up his pencil, he leans forward to resume sketching. I try to glance over my shoulder to glimpse his progress, only to have him take hold of my chin with his free hand to redirect my attention back to him.

"No peeking, Little Muse. You'll see my creation when I'm ready for you to, not before."

I blink up at him. Even with the height advantage of being seated on his lap, I have to tilt my head back to meet his eyes—he's still a good head taller than me like this. His hand loosens on my chin, then strokes over my neck before creeping down to my lower back, using his hold to move me even closer to him until one of my arms is pressed against him. I fold my hands in my lap, feeling nervous and off-kilter.

"That won't do," he says with a sigh.

Not asking for my permission, he uses both hands to lift one of my legs and shift it over his so that I'm straddling his leg and facing him head on. I let out a gasp as my pussy grinds against his thigh with the gesture, creating a delicious pressure, which makes his eyes flare in turn.

"Feel good?" he asks, a little smugly.

I'm quick to shake my head in denial, which only appears to irritate him. He returns one hand to my back, this time using it to move my hips forward, grinding me against him again.

I shift my hips back and glare at him. "Am I here to sit for your art or get tortured?"

He tilts his head to the side. "Why not both?"

"Because you promised me I could do homework once you're done with the sketching part, and I have a lot on my plate. So, either stick to your word or let me out of the contract."

He says with a sigh, "Fine. I'm sure there'll be time to play with you later."

I shake my head. "No, there won't be. I'm here for two and a half or three hours, and I expect to not waste the entire time. Your games will only get you so far with me, Seth."

He lifts a shoulder nonchalantly, but returns to sketching, the hand resting on my lower back staying motionless. "I can assure you this isn't a waste of time. My paintings sell for a pretty penny, and now that I've found my muse, I believe I'll be able to create my best content to date."

I give him an unamused look. "You get ten hours of my time a month, do with it what you will. Beyond that, my time is my own."

Still staring at the canvas and focusing on the motions of his pencil, he says, "I will own you, Elia. All of your time, down to every second. I'll tame you."

I shake my head. "I can't be owned or tamed."

He arches an eyebrow. "You sure? Because the way I see it, I'm already most of the way there."

That pisses me off, and I stiffen, any traces of building arousal leaving me. I'm not a chattel or a piece of meat that can be owned;

I have *far* more value than that. All my life, people have tried to own me. First my mother, then companies and studios, then my ex. None of them have succeeded, I've remained independent despite the best efforts of the people around me.

Seth is deeply mistaken if he thinks he'll ever own *or* tame me. I might agree to some quid pro quo situations with him, especially when they offer benefits to me, but that doesn't give him absolute power over me; the only power he'll have is the power *I* afford him.

I want to splash paint on him, stand, and leave, but with several deep breaths I manage to remind myself that reacting rashly wouldn't be helpful for me. I'm here for a good purpose; my time in return for his money. That I can live with, and that is *all* I intend to give him.

For the next two hours he sketches me, then eventually sends me back to the couch and starts on the painting, allowing me to read from a textbook and write out one of my assignments. I keep my mind firmly in check, not allowing my thoughts to wander to him in any sexual way again.

He wants to *own* me? It'll be my pleasure to show him that while he'll be one of many to try, he'll also join all of them in failure.

Chapter Twenty-Nine

I'm still seething when Seth drives me home. He either senses that or is too caught up in thinking about his art, because conversation between us is the bare minimum. He insists on walking me from the car to my dorm, which I don't mind, purely because it's difficult to feel safe with all the recent chaos on campus. Without saying goodbye, I use my student ID card to get into the building, and then head up to my floor.

Seth obviously thinks he already has me in the bag, that I'm a sure thing for him, which makes me beyond determined to prove him wrong. So, instead of going to my dorm room, I knock on the one right next to it—Carson's room. It's late, probably after eleven, but the light streaming from under the door tells me that he's not yet asleep. Even if he was, I'd knock until he woke up, because unlike what Seth seems to think, I do not belong to him. I belong solely to myself. And, if I'm being honest with myself, I want both of these men with equal vigor, albeit for different reasons.

Seth has an intensity and disdain for the normal within him that calls to me; his neurodivergent nature is fascinating. He's like a puzzle that I feel compelled to figure out, for some reason that's beyond my understanding. His soul is as twisted as it gets, which can make him too much. Frightening in his intensity, and so self-assured it can get very frustrating, as tonight has proven.

Carson is different. His nature is lighter, brighter, and easier to be around. He's also not at all what appearances dictate, with a personality that might seem superficial on the surface, but the layers beneath prove it's anything but. He's someone who will stalk me relentlessly, yes, but not in a way that's intimidating. I think he's just genuinely never been in a situation where he wants someone enough to pursue them, so the way he goes about it is a little strange.

Realistically, there's nothing to stop me from having both of them—at least in a physical way—other than myself. Frankly, I'm tired of standing in the way of my desires. I won't commit to anything with either of them, but that doesn't mean I can't still find some enjoyment. I've sampled what Seth has to offer, now it looks like the right time to see what I'd get with Carson.

The door handle turns and the door swings inward, revealing a tired-looking Carson. He's wearing a plain white shirt and grey sweatpants, which is the most casual I've ever seen him dressed. While I very much enjoy the sight of him in one of his tailored suits, he even looks hot like *this*; dressed down and probably preparing to go to sleep. The shirt stretches over his muscles, highlighting the broadness of his shoulders along with his corded biceps.

Before he can say anything, I push him into his dorm room with a hand on his hard chest, shut the door behind me, and then grab a fistful of his shirt to yank him down so I can fuse my lips with his. Carson stiffens, and to my great consternation, pulls his head back.

"Elia, what the fuck?" he breathes, blue eyes flicking over me. Those eyes showcase surprise rather than the desire I was hoping for.

As incentive to get his ass in gear, I pull my shirt over my head and let it drop to the floor, leaving the upper half of my body clad in only a bra. Carson doesn't even drop his eyes to ogle my breasts like any man in his right mind would; instead, he keeps them firmly on mine. That fact alone is deeply surprising, I'd have thought he'd enjoy whatever show I was willing to put on for him.

"Where is this coming from?" he asks.

I lift my shoulders in a half shrug. "Does it matter?"

Carson nods. "Yes, it does. You were just with Seth, and now here you are offering yourself up to me after holding firm. I'm gonna need you to fill me in on what prompted this before I do anything."

At that, I start feeling uncertain. Did I make the wrong call coming here? Is Carson not interested in me anymore? That thought seems absurd, he's living in dorms just to be closer to me, but it would explain why after pestering and pestering me he's suddenly... not turning me down, but not accepting my clear offer, either.

I don't feel like lying right now and making up bullshit that will get Carson's questions to stop—he doesn't deserve that, even though it might make things more simple. But if simplicity equals deceit, then I want no part in it.

So, I decide to go with honesty.

"Seth seems to be under the impression that he owns me," I blurt.

Carson's eyes shutter as he takes in my words, and his shoulders droop a little. "So, you're just here to prove him wrong." His words aren't a question, more so of a statement.

I sense an undercurrent of pain in his words that seriously bothers me—I don't want to hurt him. I'm a little startled that I'm capable of eliciting a response such as pain from him, because that indicates that he cares. You can't get hurt by people you don't give a shit about, it's the people dear to you that have the power to do damage.

"Not just because of that," I say quickly, which is the truth. "I'm here because I want to be. Because I want you. I've wanted you for a while now. Seth's words might've given me another reason, but they aren't the only reason."

Carson stares at me for several infinitely long moments, seeming to gauge the sincerity of my statement. The flicker of pain in his expression is wiped away, replaced with consideration as we watch each other, like he's deciding on how to proceed.

He's quiet for so long that I grow nervous, which prompts me into saying, "Look, you have two options here. Fuck me or send me away."

If he sends me away, it'll be quite the blow to my ego—one it might take a while to recover from—but I'll leave, with embarrassment and dejection to keep me company. I don't know if I'd ever have the nerve to try this again in that scenario, which is a risk I'm now wondering if it was worth it to take.

When I think I might explode from nerves, Carson says, "I'm not going to fuck you if it's an act of vengeance for you, Elia. I want you so much sometimes I think I'm losing my mind, but I'm not taking you unless I'm certain you want me just as badly."

I can work with that. Fucking him right now isn't an act of vengeance, it's more so exploring my options. Seth pissed me off, yes, but I wouldn't be here if I didn't want to be here regardless of Seth's bullshit.

I let out a groan of irritation. "I want you, Carson. I'd have ended up here sooner or later; Seth just made sure it was *sooner* rather than *later*."

Carson takes my hand in his, entwining our fingers. His hand is big and warm, dwarfing mine and making me feel strangely safe. "What does this mean, Elia? Is it just sex, or is it you saying you're finally ready to actually explore this thing between us?"

I hesitate. I'm not willing to commit to anyone; not Carson, not Seth. This wouldn't be anything beyond a physical act for me, satiating curiosity that's been progressively building and proving a point. Not just to Seth, but to myself; that I *can't* be owned.

I don't want to hurt Carson, but he seems so sincere I also don't want to lie to him. "It would just be sex."

After several seconds of silence, he chuckles. "From my understanding, relationships usually lead to sex—not the other way around."

That makes me laugh. "How would you know? Have you ever been in a relationship?"

He shakes his head slowly. "Before now, I've never wanted to share my life with someone."

Because I don't want to explore the stirring of emotions his words cause, I say, "There's nothing usual about this situation, or about either of us. I don't want a relationship; I don't really have *time* for a relationship. But I do want you, here and now."

"I want you, too," Carson says lowly. "I'll give you a fair heads up; if you get in my bed, it'll make my pursuit of you triple."

That's a worry for another time. "Warning received. Now, are we going to fuck or am I going to have to go to bed like this, wound up and unsatisfied?"

Carson tugs me to him, then lifts me into his arms so abruptly I squeal. My legs wrap around his waist and my arms wind around his shoulder. I stare into his eyes, which are no longer questioning or uncertain; they're resolute and brimming with desire. "I'd *never* leave you unsatisfied, Princess."

With that, he cups the back of my head with one hand, threading his fingers through my hair, and slowly directs my mouth to his. His lips are soft, like two pillows made of clouds, and so *tender* and *gentle* it catches me off guard. The way he cherishes my mouth; kissing, nibbling, softly probing my lips with his tongue until I part them to allow him entry, catches me off guard. It's not that the kiss isn't passionate; it certainly is. His tongue twines with mine, his grip on my waist and in my hair tightens, and I feel the bulge of his erection slowly growing against me, pressing right into my center, the longer we kiss. It's that I didn't expect such softness from him, such adoration. It feels like he's worshipping my mouth with his rather than conquering it, and that makes a fuzzy warmth take up residence in my chest, joining the heat that travels further south.

He tastes sweet and minty, he feels safe and warm, and his gentleness is a drug I could easily get hooked on. He pulls his mouth away to kiss a trail down my neck, at the same time that he walks me over to the bed and slowly lowers me down to it, climbing on top of me. His lips break away from my skin and he stares down at me with such reverence I don't know what to do with it or how to react.

What I know without a doubt is that I want more of him and more of this, with a desperation I hadn't known I was capable of.

CHAPTER THIRTY

He leans back long enough to pull his shirt over his head, tossing it on the carpeted floor behind him, then slides his hands under my back to run his fingers along my bra until he finds the clip, undoing it. He takes his time sliding my bra off of me, his eyes traveling over my arms, across my neck and collarbones, and then finally down to my chest as he pulls the straps off.

For some reason, I start to feel a tad insecure. Carson's reputation around campus is legendary; he's slept with supermodels and socialites, and has his pick of the litter when it comes to women. I know I'm not *ugly*, but I do have small breasts, right on the border between an A and B-cup. He's probably been with women who have tits the size of melons, and I don't know if mine are enough to be attractive to him.

"Stop worrying your lip," he tells me, eyes flicking back to mine. "Don't be shy with me."

How he can read my flash of insecurity, I have no idea, but it just serves to make me feel even more shy under his penetrating stare.

I glance down at my chest and say almost apologetically, "They're small."

He reaches up with a hand to press his thumb against my lips, silencing me. This time, he goes as far as to push the digit into my mouth. Caught in the heat of his gaze, I let him.

"Listen to me: you're perfect. Everything about you is perfect." His free hand travels down to cup my breast. "These are perfect, just enough to fill my palms. Natural, beautiful, *exactly* right."

His words have the dual effect of chasing away any insecurity and emboldening me, because they're spoken with a reverence that feels like it reaches into my soul and soothes it, fills it with affection. I suck on his thumb, then nip the tip of it lightly with my teeth, which makes him suck his bottom lip into his mouth as his eyes turn even brighter and his pupils dilate.

"Naughty girl," he tells me. "I like that a *lot*. You look so sweet, but you have a bite to you. A softness, too."

He takes his thumb out of my mouth before shifting his hips back. He unbuttons and unzips my jeans nimbly, then moves to the side of me to slowly peel them off my legs, eyes following every inch of skin as it's exposed. It's like he wants to commit every bit of me to memory, savor this moment.

Once my jeans are out of the way, his focus shifts to my panties, which are plain beige cotton—nothing special, not what I would've put on if I expected to end up here tonight. He doesn't seem to mind as he strokes his fingers over the material before hooking his thumbs underneath the waistband and also dragging them off my legs. He spreads my thighs, then settles himself between them, taking several beats to drink in every inch of my naked body before turning his gaze to my pussy.

His eyes flick up to meet mine as two fingers boldly reach to stroke against my slit. He curls them, finding my clit and rubbing over it gently, drawing a gasp from me. One hand travels back to my breast, this time rolling my nipple between two fingers as he finds rhythm with his fingers down below, slowly rubbing his thumb over my clit while his index finger slides inside me. He curves the finger upwards at the same time he presses down on my clit, hard, pulling a moan from my lips.

He mutters a curse under his breath in response, speeding up the motions on my clit as he leans down to suck my neglected nipple into his mouth, running his tongue over it. The double stimulation on my breasts and pussy winds me tight, speeding my breaths into pants and causing my heart to race.

He kisses a wet path down my chest, stomach, and navel, spreading my thighs wider with his shoulders before taking his thumb off my clit and latching onto it with his mouth, rolling it between his lips before laving it with his tongue. My back arches as I whimper, his attention on my pussy causing a knot of tension to form low in my belly. When I think I can't take any more, he scoops up some of the wetness that's been leaking out of me with his thumb and uses it to rim the bud of my ass, while the finger inside me and his lips on my clit continue turning me into a languid, moldable puddle. The taboo of feeling his thumb *there*, where nobody has ventured before, makes me tense up but it also pushes me even closer to an orgasm.

His thumb increases its pressure insistently, and I glance down to watch him, head buried between my legs, totally concentrated on me and doing things to me I previously hadn't dreamt of. When he penetrates my ass with the tip of his finger, it sends my orgasm hurtling into me with such intensity I use a hand to cover my mouth in an attempt to muffle my cries. His fingers pull out of me and his tongue thrusts inside my convulsing pussy, prolonging my orgasm, practically drinking up the rush of wetness that escapes. He continues eating me out until my legs are shaking and I'm whimpering, until I reach down to thread my fingers through his hair and pull him away from my sensitive flesh.

With a low curse, Carson rises above me and stares down at my body, which is now glistening with a fine sheen of sweat. "You taste as sweet as I thought you would, Princess."

I can't help but breathe, "You're depraved."

He responds with a grin, "You loved it. Came so hard you nearly broke my finger off. Next, I'm gonna feel that around my cock. Any objections?"

I shake my head side to side so quickly it sends my hair flying, which draws an amused chuckle from him. He makes quick work of stripping his pants and boxers, and I barely get a glimpse of his cock—engorged and swollen, the tip glistening with a pearl of pre-cum, so big a flicker of fear travels through me—before he presses the thick head against my entrance with one hand, bracing the other beside my head.

A low groan escapes me as he starts to push his way inside of me. I'm dripping wet, but there's still a fair bit of resistance from his size and the fact that my inner muscles are still clenching from my orgasm. I revel in the burn as he works his way deeper, breathing harshly, sweat glistening over his chest.

"*Fuck,* you're tight," he says. "So damn good."

I hook a leg over his waist to pull him deeper as he braces his other hand beside my head, the cords in his neck bulging. "I could get fucking addicted to this pussy," he tells me, forcing his way in further which pulls a whine from me. The intrusion hurts, but the pain isn't bad, in fact it just helps the mounting pleasure inside me. My first orgasm hasn't ebbed, yet I can already feel myself building my way to another.

After Carson's impaled me on what feels like a foot of his cock, he's finally fully seated inside of me with our bodies connected. I gasp and blink, trying and failing to get accustomed to the intrusion, to his size. The rumors about him weren't wrong; he's packing a goddamn monster down below.

Carson drops his forehead down to mine, breathing harshly, seeming like he's trying to adjust to the sensation of being inside me as much as I am. Beyond the bite of pain it feels really, *really* good, his cock stretching me tight and stroking over places I hadn't even known existed until this moment.

More than that, there's a sense of connection here that I've never experienced during sex. Probably because I never *really* wanted to have it before now—I just didn't feel like finding out what would happen if I said no to my ex. This, though, is a new and almost enlightening experience. I stroke my hands through Carson's hair, run my nails lightly over his neck, drawing a shudder from him. It feels like there are hairline cracks forming along my chest, and he's sneaking his way into them, filling me not only physically but emotionally too.

Startled, I realize just how much I *like* this. Not the physical pleasure, which is pretty amazing, but also the emotional pleasure, which sends all kinds of feel-good hormones through my brain.

Carson seems to mirror my sentiment because he says softly in my ear, "You feel like home."

That's almost too much; the gentleness and earnestness in his voice sneaks under my skin and burrows in there, carving out a spot uniquely for him.

"Don't make me beg," I murmur in his ear, mainly because the emotions he's causing are too overwhelming. "Get moving."

He lets out a breath of laughter that tickles my cheek, presses a tender kiss against my lips, and then raises himself up over me. My back arches as he slowly slides his length out of me, only halfway, before smoothly sinking back in. He repeats the languid gesture until my inner muscles adjust and I feel myself relax around him. He feels it, too, and picks up his pace. I slide my hands up his arms, smoothing my fingers over his biceps, before winding them behind his neck and pulling him down for a kiss.

Our lips connect with a frenzy of passion, tongues twining, and I start feeling like I'm getting drunk on just his taste and the feeling of his thrusts, which send starbursts of pleasure up my spine. He rears back, appearing almost animalistic with passion, and hooks a hand under one of my thighs, using it to lift my leg and stretch it upwards until my thigh is pinned down right next to my head. The position opens me further; getting manhandled to Carson's liking is *insanely* hot.

His free hand travels down to my clit, which is already sensitive from the attention he's given it, and when I feel his fingers rub over it my eyes widen and I give my head a shake. The pleasure mounts until it's too much, too overwhelming, and the fact that I can do nothing to stop it is as erotic as the sex itself.

Carson's gaze locks on mine, watching every nuance of my expression as his thrusts speed up until his pace is almost feral and will definitely leave me sore.

He pinches my clit with two fingers and tugs on it, at the same time that he commands, *"Come."*

My body obeys as if he's my master. A scream gets caught in my throat as my orgasm slams into me like a train, blinding and shattering in its intensity. I feel him thrust jerkily three more times before he stills, and my convulsing muscles make me feel every twitch of his cock as he spills inside of me.

He collapses on top of me, before flipping us over so that I'm laying partially draped over him. My head rests on his chest, which is rising and falling rapidly, my arm is around his waist and one of my legs is tangled with his.

Because I really don't know how to react to my emotions, I ask him dryly, "Do I need to get tested?"

He stiffens under me for a moment before relaxing. "No. I've never fucked without a condom before, but I still get tested regularly just to make sure. I'm clean." He pauses. "Are you on birth control?"

I nod against his chest, marveling at how fast his heart is beating and the fact that I can hear it. "Yup. I take the pill." Then, when his words really register, my head lifts from his chest as I stare down at him in shock. "You've *never* had sex without a condom before now?"

His eyes half-lidded, he shakes his head.

I blink. "Then why didn't you use one with me?"

He uses a hand on the small of my back to pull me down against him. "For the very reason I've been telling you all along, though you haven't been listening; you're different. I don't know why, but you are. I've never acted like a stalker or moved into a prison-sized dorm room for a girl before. In fact, the most effort I've gone through is sending a text. So, when you offered yourself up to me, I didn't exactly have the focus to think of something like a condom."

For the first time since we've started our little dance, I think I believe him. Thus far, all of his actions have gone to prove his words; he's gone out of his way repeatedly to spend time with me, actually going as far as to move out of whatever swanky apartment he must live in and into the shabby dorms just to be near me, all while I've been shooting him down and denying that there is or ever could be anything between us.

Even with the sex we just had… he was focused on me the entire time. My pleasure, my enjoyment—he just spent the better part of an hour worshipping my body. It seems pretty pointless to deny that there is something here.

The only problem is, as much as I'm pissed at him right now, there's also proven to be something between me and Seth. I don't feel right leading them both on, but I'm also starting to hesitate in letting either of them go. I want to explore whatever there is on both ends, even though it's twisted and fucked up and so unconventional the mere thought makes me nervous.

Then again, didn't they both agree to compete for me? I'd just be going along with what they've already set in motion if I continue on. There's also the issue of me having a packed schedule, but both have already proven crafty enough to get around that.

"I like you, Little E, a lot. I don't think that's going anywhere, so I'm not going anywhere, either."

I nuzzle closer to his chest, enjoying the warmth he radiates. "Even though the building's technically safe now?"

Carson lets out a faint scoff. "ID badges can get stolen, just as key-codes can be shared. The killer managed to take Scarlett from dorms in *broad daylight*, so I don't know that keycards are going to make much of a difference. Even if the building had pentagon-level security, I'd still stay, because you're here."

I let out a sigh. "You make it really hard not to like you."

I can hear the smile in Carson's voice when he says, "So my charm's finally starting to get to you."

I roll my eyes. "Ah, the infamous charm that had you proposition-ing me within ten minutes of us meeting. After you took my book and refused to leave me alone."

Carson responds, a little smugly, "Well, you're here, aren't you? I must be doing *something* right."

Unfortunately for me, he is. Carson's different from what I assumed he would be; he has more depth and more intellect than I thought. And that sex... well, if I'm not careful, I might end up catching an addiction. It's a little unnerving; I had sex dozens, even hundreds of times with my ex, and before that, there was a fumbling boy who took my virginity—none of those experiences were anything to write home about. My first time was out of curiosity and not wanting to be the last girl on the dance team to get her V-card punched, and with my ex, I knew saying no wouldn't go over well for me, so I let him use me to get off for the sake of not making things worse.

In the short time since I've been at Greywood, I've had two mind-bending experiences, with two different men that are both competing for me. The pleasure alone is enough to get me hooked, and I'm afraid if I keep indulging, I just might.

I push myself into a sitting position, casting a glance around my room in search of my clothes. Carson takes my wrist, turning my attention back to him. "What are you doing?"

"Grabbing my stuff so I can take a shower and then go to sleep," I respond.

He frowns. "You should just stay. I'm a pro cuddler."

I arch an eyebrow at him. "I'm sure you are, what with all the practice. Rumor has it half the girls on campus know about your *cuddling* abilities, as do a good portion of the supermodels and socialites in America. Some of them married, if whispers are to be believed."

Carson's frown morphs into a smile. "I like the hint of jealousy in your tone. For your information, I don't cuddle with hookups, which is what all the others were. You're not."

Pushing off the bed and retrieving my clothes that are scattered across the carpet, I start to dress. "Then how would you know you're a *pro* cuddler? Seems like you need to have some credentials for that title."

Carson watches me tug on my clothes with a look of disappointment. "If you must know, I learned most of the cuddling from animals. My father wasn't home enough to pay attention to the fact that I had a propensity for bringing home strays and rescues; my house was always full of dogs and cats. Pets are very big on cuddles and affection."

I pause in pulling on my jeans, nearly tripping over them, because that's surprisingly adorable.

"Your mom was okay with it?" I ask.

Carson nods. "She was a vet before marrying my dad and losing her right to be anything but a housewife. We'd volunteer at animal shelters together on weekends, and she always welcomed new additions to the house."

I smile at that, imagining a young Carson, walking into whatever McMansion he must've lived in, clutching his newest found friend to his chest and asking his mom if he could add another member to their furry family.

I say, "Pictures or it didn't happen."

Carson chuckles. "I'll dig through the archives and find some. Are you sure you want to leave?"

Want to? No. Surprisingly, I very much want to stay, but I know I need to leave, for my own sake as well as his.

"The mattresses here are too small to fit both of us, and I don't feel like getting caught by April doing the walk of shame first thing, so yes. I'll see you in the A.M."

Chapter Thirty-One

I'm on edge throughout Monday morning. Carson greets me with the usual cup of coffee—one he must run out *very* early to get for me—walks me and April to HQ, then shadows me until noon as usual. Being with him is as easy as it's ever been—he continues cracking jokes, both of the dirty and funny nature, then runs with me to the art buildings so I won't be late, before watching me go inside. He doesn't showcase a hint of awkwardness.

It's seeing Seth that I'm worried about. I don't have a good poker face, and I'm not a particularly good liar; it's very possible that I'll just end up blurting the fact that I had sex with Carson last night. While that's *mainly* a bad thing, there's a small part of me that wants to rub it in his face. Although I didn't just do what I did because Seth pissed me off, he did prompt me into satiating a craving that's been building, because his ego and arrogance made him state his intention to *own* me.

I take my usual seat behind him in the back of class. As always, he's sitting at his desk without a notebook or pen, looking to all the world like he couldn't be more bored.

I don't greet him; surprisingly, he doesn't greet me either, just goes through his usual routine of staring at me intently.

"You're coming with me to an art exhibition tonight," he says out of the blue.

I startle, glancing at him. "I'm *what*?"

"I have an event I need to attend tonight; you're going to be my date."

After the way he pissed me off last night, this is the route he's deciding to go? *Telling* me I'm doing something with him rather than *asking* me if I will?

"No, I'm not," I say flatly.

Seth shifts in his seat, leaning across the aisle until his lips are right at my ear. It takes all my focus to stay in place rather than shift around nervously. "Last night I stayed in front of the dormitories for a while. See, I wanted to make sure you got to your room safely—I was planning on waiting until I saw your dorm light click on through the window. *Instead,* I saw something far more interesting; the silhouettes of two people in the room right by yours. The one where Carson's decided to quarantine himself."

My heartbeat triples in pace, and my breath stutters out of my chest. Carson and I both have windows in our rooms that face the front of the dormitories, ones that could be seen through by someone loitering in front. Thinking back, I realize that Carson's window shades weren't drawn; anyone who was looking could've glimpsed us kissing... and more. Evidently, Seth did. Mortification washes over me as I slowly turn my head to the side to gaze at him, searching his expression for a hint as to how he might be feeling and what reaction I should expect.

He gives away nothing. "You gave Carson an in—not long after that lunch date you two shared—now it's my turn. I'll pick you up at seven."

I gawk at him. Lowering my voice to a whisper so no eavesdroppers can overhear, I say, "I'm not going with you tonight after you *watched* me sleep with Carson."

A muscle in Seth's jaw ticks. "I assure you, I didn't stay for the whole show. Only long enough to understand where things were going. If I'd stayed, there's no telling what I'd have done, or whether or not Carson would've survived it."

His tone is menacing, which makes me even more nervous at the prospect of going with him somewhere tonight. "And that right there is why I *won't* be going with you to your event."

Seth lets out a dark chuckle. "I won't hurt you, Little Muse. I might be enraged that Carson got to have you before me, but I suppose I shouldn't be surprised. I pushed you, you pushed back. I like that very much, even though I don't like *how* you pushed back."

The shocks just keep rolling in. Seth *likes* the fact that I fucked Carson because he pushed me? After a moment, the twisted logic of it hits me. In a way, my actions proved that I'm not someone he'll be able to jerk around or manipulate to extreme extents, which appears to invigorate Seth rather than put him off. There's a weird sense to it; if he's gone through life knowing how to turn the people around him into puppets on strings, being presented with someone who that doesn't work on must be intriguing. Add in the fact that he's convinced I'm his muse, and I suppose in a very strange and uniquely Seth way, it makes sense.

That still doesn't mean I'll be going out with him.

I say, "I'm not going. Even if I wanted to, I imagine any art event you frequent will be classy, and I'm all out of black-tie attire."

Seth's lips twitch. "I'd like to see you in any state of dress or undress, but alas, I don't want you cold during winter. I'll take you shopping, be ready at five thirty."

"I can't afford an impromptu shopping trip," I snark.

"It'll be on my dime," Seth replies.

I inhale a deep breath, trying to think what reason I could list for not going that might stick. "We have the museum volunteer hours tonight, neither of us can skip without risking Jessica's wrath. And her wrath might mean having to retake the credit."

Seth shakes his head. "I've already spoken to her, we're permitted to miss our volunteer hours tonight."

God, he thought of everything, didn't he? Even as the thought passes through my mind, it's followed by *of course he did*, he's Seth. I haven't known him for all that long, but it doesn't take a genius to see that thinking ten steps ahead is a specialty of his. What I did last night only motivated him further.

"I have homework—"

Seth's sigh cuts me off. "No, you don't. I've watched you, Little Muse; you do all of your assignments on the day they're assigned in anticipation of upcoming dance rehearsals that'll start eating up most of your evening hours."

He's right, I am proficient with homework because I know that very soon rehearsals for Pandora's Box will begin, and I want to be in the habit of getting things done in advance. How *he* knows that, I'm not sure, but Seth seems to know a great deal about many things that interest him; right now I'm something of interest to him, so it stands to reason that he'd do everything in his considerable power to know *me*.

"Is there anything I could say to get out of this that you wouldn't immediately refute?" I ask irritably.

Seth's lips stretch into a calculated smile. "No, there is not. You're going with me tonight, come hell or highwater. To clarify, I'd be the hell *and* the high water, so you might as well resign yourself to your fate." He pauses. "I actually think you'll quite enjoy it, or I wouldn't be so insistent."

I snort. "Yes, you would."

He gives a single nod. "Yes, I probably would, but only because I plan things in advance. I was going to ask you to come with me either way today—you're already on the guest list as my plus-one—but now I'm simply more motivated to get your agreement. If you don't like it, we can leave."

I give my head a shake. "You know you're annoying as hell, right?"

He tilts his head to the side. "I think you're the first person, possibly ever, to call me annoying. Most are too afraid to."

That makes my lips quirk. "I won't tolerate your bullshit, Seth. Yes, you're intimidating, but I've dealt with my fair share of intimidating people, none of whom had the same level of control over themselves as you do. If I could handle them, I can handle you."

Seth reaches out to stroke his hand through my hair, the gesture surprisingly intimate. "Your fortitude is probably one of the things I like most about you."

The sincerity and thoughtfulness of the compliment softens me, because my fortitude is a point of pride for me. Life has thrown a *lot* of shit my way already, and I've survived it all; that gives me the confidence that there isn't much I won't be able to survive.

After a long beat of silence, I say, "I don't like shopping."

He lets out a soft puff of laughter. "First woman who's said that to me, and not entirely surprising. You'll like it when you're shopping with me. Now, pay attention to the lecture, and be ready for me at five thirty."

***

As soon as I'm back to my dorms after my class of the day, April's familiar bangs sound on my door. I open it and let her in, startled when she throws her arms around me and lets out a shriek that can probably be heard by everyone in the building.

"The cast list went up right after you left for your afternoon classes!" she squeals, pulling back to look at me. She's practically vibrating with excitement.

I close the door and pull her in. "Give me all the details!"

We both take a seat cross-legged on my bed, and April's so exulted she bounces up and down. "Okay, so first, Sanders gave a little speech about the structure of the cast; he's done a bunch of gender reversals because he's fucking *awesome* like that. A lot of male gods will be made into women, vice versa. The production is split into three acts: Creation, Gift Bestowal, and The Box. Zeus is a woman, so are Hephaestus and Hermes—Sanders said that's because women are far cleverer than mythology credits them for. Likewise, Athena, Aphrodite, and Hera are male. Pretty much the only people who stayed the gender mythology assigned them are Pandora, Epimetheus, and Prometheus."

I take April's hands in mine. "Stop holding back and spill the important stuff!"

April beams. "There are three leads: Zeus, Epimetheus, and Pandora. *I* got cast as Zeus, Sean's Epimetheus, and you're Pandora!"

She ends her statement in another shriek; this time, I can't help but join her. I already knew my odds of getting cast as Pandora were good, but after the auditions I was a bit nervous—everyone who made it to the third round was *so good* it was insane. But to know that I still managed to snag one of the leads and that *April* got the other is so exhilarating, I can't keep quiet.

"That's *so exciting!*" I practically shout. "When do rehearsals start? Tell me everything!"

April spends the next ten minutes giving me a breakdown of the technicalities of the production. The show will begin in early December; the first three weeks of rehearsal are for blocking and choreography, the rest are for the rigorous rehearsal period that'll lead up to the show, which will be running once during weeknights, then twice on weekends until winter break, an insanely long run-time for a college production.

A lot of the choreography and rehearsal time has been worked into our class schedules; the leads and other important characters will get pulled from regular classes for two hours every school day to work with Sanders. In addition, we'll be expected to put in extra time on Tuesday, Thursday, and Saturday nights—anywhere from two to three hours, depending on how things go. The schedule will be crazy, but *totally* worth it.

I sigh happily when she's done, feeling pure elation course through my veins, along with a healthy dose of adrenaline. "April, we're gonna be stars if we do well here."

"I *know!* It'll set us on a principal dance path for life."

I glance over at the clock on my nightstand, startled when I see it's already five. Seth will be back for me in a half hour to take me shopping before some mysterious art event.

April asks, "Why did you just stiffen while glancing at the time? You have plans tonight?"

I pause. "Actually... yeah. Seth's, um, taking me to some sort of art event tonight. When I tried to get out of it by saying I didn't have anything to wear, he told me he'd take me *shopping*. He'll be here in half an hour."

April's eyes brighten with interest. "So, he and Carson are still competing for your hand? I maintain that you're one lucky bitch. Who are you leaning towards?"

That I can't answer, because I don't know. I like both of them with increasing intensity when we spend time together. If asked to pick, I might say Carson, because he's easier to be around. But Seth's also magnetic, so I could just as easily choose him. I let out a groan.

"That bad?" April asks.

I respond, "You have *no* idea. They're both good and bad in their own ways."

April nods slowly. "Have you found out if they have any hot rich friends who might be interested in me?"

I say honestly, "April, half the boys and girls on campus are interested in you. You're hot as fuck, sharp as a tack, and so quick it's a race to keep up with you."

She blinks. "Wow. I should put that as my bio on some dating apps."

I laugh. "You do that. In the meantime, I'm gonna try to shore myself up for whatever it is Seth's bringing me to tonight."

She play-punches my shoulder. "Good luck. Let me know all the dirty deets in the morning."

Chapter Thirty-Two

Seth texts me that he's outside at five thirty on the dot. Dressed in my usual afternoon getup of jeans and a sweater, I head out of my room, pausing when I see that Carson's heading into his. He stops in unlocking the door to his dorm room to smile at me.

"Hey, Princess. Going somewhere?"

Instantly, guilt flashes through me. I slept with him last night, and now I'm heading out on a... well, *date* with Seth. I don't want to outright tell him that, because the thought of hurting his feelings makes me queasy, but at the same time I also don't want to lie to him.

He reads my indecision before I can answer. "Out with Seth?"

I nod slowly, bracing myself for his reaction. Carson's silent for a moment, before saying, "Well, I did sign myself up for this torture. I'd tell you to have fun, but I hope he blows it and you end up coming back early. He won't, of course, Seth's too calculated for that, but a guy can hope."

"Are you mad?" I ask.

He's quick to answer, "Not at you, no. I'm pissed at Balor for pulling me into our agreement, and for the clause I stupidly added

about not sabotaging each other to the point of prison or expulsion."
A sardonic smile curls his lips as he takes in my expression of disbelief.
"At the time, I thought I was protecting myself from his insanity, but
it seems you've cost me a good deal of the sanity I had, because right
now I either want to kill him or tie you to my bed and make you come
so many times you're too tired to go anywhere."

Woah. His words cause a rush of heat to gather between my legs,
and I shift as I feel my panties grow damp. My experience with both of
my suitors is showing me parts of myself that I hadn't known existed.
I find his words so titillating that I'm curious to find out what the
scenario he described would be like. Before meeting Carson and Seth,
the only pleasure I ever got was orchestrated by my fingers and some
fantasies of my favorite actors. I knew, in theory, that it was possible
to orgasm at the hands of a man, but now I know in practice how
explosive it actually is, and as much as it shames me to admit it, I want
more.

Carson's smile morphs into a secretive, seductive one. "Do you like
that idea?"

I say too quickly, "No."

He chuckles. "Is that why your cheeks and neck are the color of a
fire engine?"

Saving me from further embarrassment, my phone starts ringing in
my hand, and I glance at the screen to see that Seth's calling. Carson
sees, too, and lets out a snort of amusement. "We'll table this discussion for a later time, Princess. I'll see you later."

He unlocks his dorm room and steps inside without further ado,
and I pick up Seth's call to tell him I'm on my way down.

***

Shopping with Seth ends up being different from what I expected. He takes us to a mall in the city, where he's already *called ahead* to several stores and had dresses he thought would suit me put on hold. All in all, the shopping trip itself takes a measly half hour, because he's planned in advance. He also insists on seeing me model each dress, but he doesn't try to tell me which one to choose. It looks like he enjoys taking in my reactions and indecision before I finally settle on a floor-length, navy-blue dress made of gorgeous, flowing silk. It molds to my body like a second skin from the sweetheart's neckline to my knees, where it flares out into a skirt that makes it look like rushing water each time I move. It has off-the-shoulder straps that are studded with jewels, and a built-in sash at my waist also encrusted with jewels.

It's probably the most beautiful dress I've ever seen, let alone worn. When I try to ask Seth what the price is—we shop at stores that don't even have price tags, which tells me that the items for sale are *very* expensive—he tells me not to worry about it, before presenting me with a gorgeous pair of black heels that are made of smooth velvet, also with crystal detailing.

Since we're going straight to the art event from the mall, I end up wearing the purchases out of the stores.

Now, forty minutes into our drive, I'm starting to grow nervous with the air of mystique around tonight. We're both dressed in black-tie attire—Seth is wearing a tailored tuxedo that makes him look *sinfully* hot, so I know the *art event* we're going to is probably very exclusive and fancy, but I don't know much beyond that, other than it taking place at a large, esteemed museum about an hour's drive from campus in a neighboring city.

"What's the exhibition going to be like?" I ask him.

Seth's lips quirk, and he takes his eyes off the road for the briefest moment to slide me a glance. "You'll see."

I sulk at that. "Who makes up the body of the guest list? It can't all be college students if we're dressed like this."

Seth lets out a breath of laughter. "Admirers of the arts, mostly. Several of the patrons have museum wings around the world named after them. There are a couple businessmen from foreign countries—it's a mix of people, really, but the one thing they have in common is reverence for the art that'll be shown tonight."

"Who's the artist?" I ask curiously.

Seth bites his bottom lip. "You have a lot of questions, Little Muse. Need something to take your mind off talking?" One of his hands leaves the wheel and lands on my thigh, making my breath catch. Our skin is only separated by a thin layer of silk, and I can feel the heat of his hand like a brand on my leg.

"In case you don't recall, this dress has no side-slits for any funny business, Balor. You won't be getting underneath it easily."

Seth's hand rubs up and down my thigh, slowly. He says, "Pity. I'll be sure to insist on one with easy-access next time."

"You're quick to assume there'll be a next time," I observe. "What if tonight is all it takes to cure me of any desire to spend more time with you?"

His lips curl into an approximation of a smile. "Good thing I have you under contract to pose for me ten hours each month. Even if you don't end up enjoying tonight—which, I assure you, will not be the case—I have a guarantee of more of your time. Aside from the posing, we also happen to share classes and volunteer hours together. You'll find it isn't quite so easy to get away from me, Elia."

To change the subject, I ask, "How did you swing that? Getting a spot in my classes, I mean. You couldn't have had more than a day to figure that out."

"I don't need more than an hour to put my resourcefulness to good use," Seth replies smoothly. "It was quite simple, actually. I went to the administration office and informed them that I'd like to add some formal education to my art resume." He pauses for a quick laugh. "As if my critically acclaimed work doesn't speak for itself. Anyway, since Greywood delights in taking partial credit for all of my work—art, engineering, biochemistry—they were more than happy to accommodate my wishes."

"Careful there with the arrogance, you're getting back into the asshole-y territory that didn't serve you well yesterday," I warn him. "Critically acclaimed work or no, you're still just a college student."

Seth replies, "Calling me *just a college student* is like calling you *just a dancer*. Entirely missing the point, and a devaluation neither of us deserve. I know the worth of my work, not because of arrogance, but because of the reaction it provokes from others. Just like you should know yours for the same reasons. We're both exceptional, albeit in different fields."

I fall silent at that, stunned from one of the greatest compliments I've received in some time, especially because Seth didn't say it in a praising tone—no, he sounded much more matter of fact, as if he's stating the obvious. The first time I met him, he called me the best contemporary dance has to offer, which I didn't pay all that much attention to because I was distracted by his strangeness. Now, his words spark a warmth in my chest, which is not a feeling I expected to associate with him.

The car turns off the highway and onto city streets, and my attention shifts from him to our surroundings as we cruise through a well-lit city that boasts of a strange mixture of skyscrapers and cottage-like buildings that hint at its historical value.

Seth pulls us into a parking lot in front of a large building that could be likened to an old monastery or temple in structure, although the materials it's made with appear to be primarily glass and steel, a very modern twist on a base with ancient inspiration.

Seth comments, "Fashionably late, just how I like it." When I move to open the car door, he says with a frown, "Don't. I'll get it."

Before I can respond, he steps out of the car, pulling on a thick wool jacket while striding to my side and opening the door for me. He offers me his hand, which I awkwardly take.

"What's with the gentleman routine?" I ask him.

He retrieves my coat from my seat and helps me put it on. "It's not a routine, it's how one behaves on a date—especially to a formal event like this. Even if we were going to eat at a fast-food restaurant, I'd still behave with chivalry. I'm not a nomad, and you deserve the best."

He offers me his arm, which I take, letting him escort me through the snow-dusted parking lot and up the granite steps leading to the arched entrance of the museum.

"I'll give you one heads up about tonight, some of the guests have darker dealings, both in the domestic and international markets."

I stiffen. "If you're about to bring me into a place where there are mob associates with no morals and your art is used to launder money, that's gonna be a problem."

Seth lets out one of his rare genuine laughs, amused. "There may be some mob associates in attendance, though I can assure you their moral codes are quite impressive."

I don't mind rubbing elbows with people who have under the table dealings, after all I understand quite well that just donating to the arts is a form of a tax write off, but I won't share a space with mafia men who think sex slavery is a good profit-turner.

"I only need to know if they deal in the skin trade," I tell Seth.

He glances down at me, appearing slightly surprised at my bluntness. "No, Little Muse, they do not. In fact, they make points of killing those who do. The reason I'm telling you this is you might hear some incriminating things tonight, do not repeat them."

That reassures me, and I feel my shoulders relax. I'm well-versed at keeping my mouth shut; as long as the discussion topic isn't human trafficking, I don't particularly care.

At the door there are several security guards posted; not all of them appear to be museum security, who are dressed in specific blue uniforms. Several of them are dressed in black, surveying the area with suspicious gazes. A guard stationed in front of an entrance booth, holding an iPad, asks for our names—when Seth gives them, the guard visibly straightens.

"Mr. Balor," he says, looking Seth up and down with curiosity. "Go right in."

He doesn't acknowledge me, which I don't mind—I'd be more than happy to go unnoticed here. I've recently found myself as the center of *far* too much attention. Seth leads me into the museum, pausing briefly at coat check to give over our jackets, before taking me by the hand as we walk deeper into the museum. The walls are made of tan, cracked marble, the roof is a large dome made of gorgeous stained glass, and the entrance area appears to have been converted into its own exhibit room, with a flow of well-dressed people walking around, interacting, and admiring the several beautiful sculptures stationed on plinths around the room.

Seth tells me, "This room is for the sculptures—four all in all. The wing to the left is for the paintings. There are four of those on display, too."

"You still haven't told me whose work is being showcased," I remind him, even as I walk up to the nearest plinth displaying a sculpture of a magnificent stallion that appears to have been welded from charred metal.

The sculpture is large, sitting atop a low marble stand, and the top of the horse's head—which is upturned towards the ceiling—is my height. From the horse's opened mouth comes a stream of intertwined metal strands that take the shape of fire, giving the almost gothic horse a mythical twist. It's beautiful, masterfully crafted, and so visceral it's hard to look away from it.

Seth's arm slips around my waist as he pulls me closer, before whispering in my ear, "Me. The work on display tonight is mine."

CHAPTER THIRTY-THREE

I gape at Seth, looking between him and the sculpture in front of us, feeling a little awe-struck. *He* created this? I step closer to the sculpture, taking a more thorough look at it. It's gothic, intense, and a little frightening, so although I'm astounded by his talent, I can also see how it fits him and his personality.

I wave a hand at the sculpture, dumbstruck. "This is…" I trail off, unable to find the right description. No adjective is strong enough to characterize just how *incredible* the work is. Seth watches me with an amused glimmer in his eyes, patiently waiting for me to finish my sentence. "*Breathtaking.*"

Seth inclines his head. "I'm glad you think so. Of all the sculptures here, this one took the longest; I was working on this for three weeks straight over the summer. I barely slept."

"How?" I blurt, still finding it hard to speak in full sentences.

Seth says, "Metal, welding, a fuck ton of scrapes and burns. The fire was the tricky part since I decided to go with metal strands rather than the sheet metal used for the rest of the hell horse."

I knew Seth was talented—the profile I read on him had a few pictures of his works, but I didn't know he was *this* good. I couldn't have guessed—this looks like it was made by someone with decades of experience, someone twice Seth's age at least.

I ask, "What was the inspiration behind it?"

He replies, "Power. That's the theme of the exhibition. It's showcasing my works from the last year—my agent insisted on throwing something together and inviting a premier list of guests so the art would sell well. Come on, I want to show you the rest."

Before he can lead me deeper into the museum, we're surrounded by several people, all of them a good deal older than us, and all of them heaping praise on Seth. He doesn't look like he particularly cares about the admiration, though he does spend about twenty minutes exchanging pleasantries and small talk with the passerby's, answering questions and even handing out business cards from his pocket.

The spectators seem as curious about me as they are about him—Seth introduces me as both his date for tonight *and* his muse for his upcoming collection. Instead of leaving it at that, he also begins talking about my dancing in Greywood's company, pretty much running a marketing campaign for me and getting agreement from several of the people to come and watch Greywood's upcoming dance productions. I expected him to make tonight all about him, which would've been fair; after all, people are here to applaud his art and talent, not to hear about his date. Instead, he keeps me front and center in conversations, talking me up.

I try not to fidget or give away too much of my discomfort, because this situation is new territory for me. I don't know how to respond to it, just like I'm not sure how to feel about it. Flattered, of course, but also confused and uncomfortable. The way Seth's talking about me, the way his arm stays around my waist, hand occasionally flexing on my hip—one would be forgiven for assuming that I'm his girlfriend, not just his date for the night.

He's opening up a door of connections with wealthy patrons for me, something I didn't even ask for and he does without prompting. It's surprisingly touching.

Eventually, he says, "Please excuse my rudeness, but I'm eager to show Eliana around the other art on display tonight."

He gets a few winks and backslaps before the crowd around us disperses. Then, he leads me around all four sculptures—all of them wildly different from each other in both material and style, but equally extraordinary. There's a bouquet of flowers sculpted from clay, painted with meticulous detail that depicts blood dripping down the stems, a sculpture made of granite that shows a miniature man hefting a larger-than-life heart on his shoulders—not the cartoon heart, but an actual human heart with all the veins, arteries, and valves—and a clay sculpture of a face; one half of it smiling evilly, the other half devoid of expression.

After that, we head into the wing showcasing Seth's paintings, where I'm even more awed. He's talented with sculptures and figures, but his paintings are masterful. There are landscapes filled with blood, images of men and women in battle, abstracts so colorful they make my eyes hurt. Once I've seen everything, I turn back to Seth and say, "Calling you talented wouldn't be giving you enough credit."

He smiles a rare genuine smile that glints with pleasure. "Thank you. If you like these, though, I think you'll be floored by my upcoming creations. Now that I've found my muse, I expect my artistry will significantly improve."

"That implies there's more room for improvement," I say, baffled.

Seth shrugs, slipping his other arm around my waist and pulling me closer until we're chest to chest, with me staring up at him. "There's always room for improvement in the arts, Little Muse. You should know that better than most."

I *do* know that. As a spectator, it's easy to call something perfection—as the artist, perfection is an abstract concept that's unachievable. There are always methods to improve artistry, whether it be painting or dancing.

"Thank you for bringing me here," I tell him sincerely.

He leans down to brush his lips over mine, a gesture so gentle it surprises me. I'm not accustomed to gentleness from Seth, I'm used to the stark ferocity he displays when going after something he wants. His tongue runs over my bottom lip, then he sucks it into his mouth before biting down on it, hard enough that I startle and nearly yelp. *There's* the real Seth. He laves his tongue over the sore spot on my lip, before pulling back.

He says, "Now you'll have an imprint of my teeth on your lip for the rest of the night. Maybe it'll stop me from getting jealous enough to rip the throat out of every man who checks you out. They're all at least twice your age, for fuck's sake."

I'm about to respond when a new voice interrupts, "Seth Balor, the man of the hour."

The voice carries a heavy Russian accent, and I pull away from Seth to look in the direction of it, spotting an elegant, well-dressed couple a few feet away from us. The man who greeted Seth is a *giant*; somewhere in the vicinity of six and a half feet tall, he has short dark hair, intense teal eyes, and a jaw covered in dark stubble. Beside him is a petite, *gorgeous* woman who looks to be around my height; she has raven black hair that's swept up into an elegant twist, showing off a neck that's covered in diamonds, high cheekbones, and the most vivid green eyes I've ever seen.

"Sergei Novikov, I wasn't sure you'd be able to make it," Seth says, letting go of me and reaching out to clasp hands with the giant. Then, he looks to the woman. "And you must be Kira, Sergei's lovely bride." Seth takes her hand and brushes a kiss across her knuckles, before pulling me closer. "This is my date, Eliana."

Kira says, "It's lovely to meet you both. Mr. Balor, the two sculptures you created for our estate's garden are my favorites; when Sergei told me they were made by a college student, I was compelled to see more." Her accent is American—east-coast, if I were to take a guess, which piques my curiosity.

Sergei adds, "Compelled enough to wrangle me into stepping foot back into this godforsaken country." He glances at me and says lightly, "Last time I was here, it ended with incarceration. Fortunately, it also brought me to my magnificent wife."

I'm a little shocked at how casually he talks about getting thrown in jail last time he was in the states. Seth did say there were going to be some people with darker dealings here tonight.

Seth says, "That's why I wasn't sure you'd accept my invitation. Last I heard you were still on the FBI's most-wanted list."

Kira's green eyes flit to me and she says pleasantly, "Is it the wisest to be discussing such matters here and now?"

I respond calmly, "I'm familiar with the concept of discretion, and wouldn't deign to repeat anything I hear in these parts." I mean my words; if Seth's trusting me enough to speak freely with these *friends* of his, I won't betray that trust. It's comforting to know that he won't lie to me.

Sergei lets out a laugh, looking me up and down curiously. "Good." Then back to Seth, "You'd be amazed the leeway your government will give in return for some information on their opposition."

Huh. Seems Seth really does have a colorful group of friends.

Seth's phone chimes in his pocket and he says pleasantly, "Excuse me," before pulling it out and glancing at the notification. Unable to help myself, I glance at it too, only to stiffen when a link takes him to a news website local to Greywood, which announces: *Missing dance student's body discovered on college campus.*

My chest constricts as I sway, feeling like all the strength's been siphoned from me. That can only mean one thing: Scarlett's been killed and dumped. A slew of emotions overwhelm me; guilt, fear, anger. Guilt that my last exchange with Scarlett was to put her down in front of the company, fear that the killer really has struck again, and anger that I couldn't even have *one* pleasant night without the problems in my life deciding to make an appearance.

Maybe that's my fault. Should I really be out, enjoying myself with Seth, while heinous crimes have been taking place on and around campus? It almost feels like I'm tempting fate, trying to get away from everything, and this is her way of punishing me; reminding me that a pretty dress, lovely event, and darkly magnetic date won't be able to get me away from the difficulties she's determined to present.

Sergei clears his throat. "Is everything alright?"

Seth pockets his phone and turns to look at me. Whatever he sees in my expression makes him take my hand and tug me closer to him. To Kira and Sergei, he says, "Our campus has recently been plagued by what's starting to look like a serial killer with dark methods. The first body was discovered the day before school started, by Eliana. A few days later another girl disappeared from dorms during broad daylight, her body's just been dumped on campus as well."

Kira's eyes brighten with interest at Seth's words, surprising me. She asks, "Have any details of the killings been released? Pictures or causes of death?"

Her questions shock me, as does the new excitement in her voice, as if she enjoys the thought of there being a killer on the loose.

Kira notices my discomfort and tells me, "I was a forensic psychologist before meeting Sergei, with my specialty being criminal profiling. If you have enough information, I could put together a profile of the killer for you. It could help you know what to be on the lookout for."

"You were the best of your kind, Kirachka. Still are," Sergei tells Kira affectionately.

Seth says, "There's a true crime website that managed to get details on the last killing, pictures of the body along with cause of death—I can check to see if they've caught up with the newest one yet." He looks to me and asks, "Are you okay with this?"

I'm not okay with the situation at *all,* but I won't turn down help from an expert. I say to Kira, "If you could help, I'd appreciate it. Being a woman on campus has recently turned into a dangerous game."

If I wasn't constantly being accosted by Seth or Carson, I'd probably be in much worse shape. The realization dawns on me that, despite the craziness they've brought into my life, both Seth and Carson have also brought a sense of safety and a very welcome distraction from the horrors on campus. I feel bad even thinking it, but their presence in my life—while turning it upside down in many ways—has also brought stability.

Without them, I don't think I'd be faring half as well as I am. I'd be experiencing far more panic attacks, and probably spiraling into a pit of despair.

Kira pulls out her phone, recites her phone number to Seth, then says, "Send me whatever information you can get. I'll put together a generalized profile to the best of my ability and send it back to you."

I tell her, "So far, the killer seems to have a penchant for young female arts students. First one to die was a painter, and the most recent one was a girl in my dance company, Scarlett. There's been some speculation around campus that they were not nice girls. I can say from personal experience that Scarlett had a propensity for tearing people down to her own betterment, and the whispers say that the painter had a similar personality."

Kira nods. "In that case, the murders are probably revenge killings of some kind, most likely tied into childhood trauma regarding the mother figure or another female in the familial circle."

Nausea starts to crawl up my throat as a sense of coldness settles over me. I try to mask it, but it's difficult not to outwardly shake under the force of my terror. Seth wraps an arm around my shoulder, then says to Kira and Sergei, "It was a pleasure seeing you again. Please, enjoy the exhibit. If you decide on another purchase, I'll be happy to know my art is in good hands."

He walks us away from the well-matched, though admittedly strange, couple, and into a wing of the museum that's been roped off. I don't care that we're stepping into a restricted area; right now, getting away from people is a top priority so that I don't have a public breakdown and embarrass Seth.

Seth leads me over to a small recamier propped beneath a painting, then takes a seat and pulls me onto his lap, fitting my back against his chest and wrapping his arms around my waist. He murmurs in my ear, "You don't need to be afraid. Whatever happens, I promise I'll protect you."

His words make me aware of just how fast my heart is pounding and how quickly my breaths are coming; I'm close to hyperventilating, as if I just ran a marathon. The warmth from Seth's chest against my back barely helps stave off the cold that's now so pronounced I can't stop myself from shivering.

"The killer took her from my dorm," I say faintly. "What's to say I won't be next? Or April? Or any other unsuspecting student?"

Seth says firmly, "You won't be next because I won't fucking allow it, Eliana."

My anxiety only serves to heighten my temper. "You're only saying that because you think I'm your muse and are caught up in a competition for me!" I snap. "What happens if I put a stop to our little game, stop giving into you and Carson? What happens if I choose *myself* instead of either of you? Or if you get bored of me? What happens when you really get to know me and decide I'm damaged goods?"

Only once I've said the words do I realize the very real fear that fuels them. I'm undoubtedly scared of the killer, but that's not the only fear that's plaguing me. There's also the fear that Carson and Seth are half-assed in their desire for me, that once they really get to know me, know that I come from a broken home with no family connections and a shitty ex who fucked with my sense of self, they'll move on to the next object of interest and desire. I'll be left in the rearview mirror as I always have been.

I've never been a priority to anyone; for a time, I wasn't even a priority for myself. I can't continue whatever's going on with either man pursuing me unless I know I'm a priority for them, which is an unreasonable thing to demand. Even if they were to declare me as a priority, *that* has its own complications; I want both of them. They both satisfy different sides of me. Seth has an allure and complexity that draws me in, and his single-minded focus and intensity is drugging. Carson has a light, a kindness and affection within him that acts as a soothing balm on the dark, scarred edges of my soul, and brings out the lighter parts of me that have stayed dormant in the face of adversity for far too long.

Last night with Carson was amazing, the sense of connection, light-heartedness, and freedom from complication was exactly what I needed. Yet tonight, before the news of Scarlett's death broke, I've been enjoying myself just as much with Seth, enthralled by his creations and the glimpses they offer into his mind. I like the fact that he's a puzzle, an enigma that takes focus and concentration to figure out—I like that he's so calculated and pathological it's somewhat unnerving, and that he channels all of that twistedness into his desire for me.

I think I might be starting to fall for *both* of them, while unsure what the endgame is. I can't choose one without scorning and hurting the other, which I don't want to do.

Seth turns me sideways so that I'm cradled to his chest like a child and uses a hand on my chin to direct my gaze towards his burning one. "I won't lose interest in you. This isn't just a passing fancy or temporary infatuation for me; it's already proven to be much, *much* more. What I feel for you grows in intensity by the day, by the fucking *minute*. When I'm not around you, you plague my thoughts. When I sleep, my dreams are about you. You aren't just my muse; you're *mine*. I'll let you in on a little secret, Eliana, I don't feel emotions often. I feel things towards people even less. Yet with you... every time I look at you, I feel *so much*. Respect, interest, even affection, which is new for me. That won't change if you choose Carson or decide to do away with both of us. Nothing you could do would change that."

His words ease my fear, but only in part. What if I end up wanting both of them, as I'm already starting to? I don't think that Seth would be on board with that, I don't even know how the mechanics of that would work. I can't think about that right now; it'll just make my head spin. I inhale several deep breaths, trying to calm myself, reminding myself that I don't have to make any decisions today, tomorrow, or even this month. Right now, I'm just along for the ride that Seth and Carson are taking me on—having them around also offers the added bonus of protection, which I could very much use right now.

I murmur, "I'm sorry. I didn't mean to snap at you. I'm just..." I trail off, trying to find the right word.

"Confused? Scared? Wound up?" Seth supplies.

I nod. "Yes, all of those things. I'm not used to any of this, so I don't know how to react to it."

Part of me is surprised by his ability to read my emotions and sentiments so well when he seems to be lacking in those departments, but in a way it makes sense. From what I've seen of him, Seth is skilled at handling people and understanding them, which probably comes from the fact that he isn't *like* most of them and has studied those around him to learn how to be a functional member of society.

He told me that his father didn't care for him last night, now I start to wonder if that accounts for just how different he is. I know better than most just how a shitty parent can shape their child, either for better or for worse.

Seth tucks my head into his chest, stroking a hand through my hair. "It's okay, Elia. You don't have to make any decisions right now, I wanted to take you away from Greywood to give you a night you could enjoy without worries." He releases a sigh. "The pesky campus killer decided to get in the way of that." After a pause, he goes on, "I've done all the required mingling for the evening already. My agent had another event tonight, so I don't need to speak with him; if you want, we can leave. Grab dinner before heading back to campus."

I stiffen. "I don't want to go back to campus tonight." Even with Carson in the dorm room beside me, I think stepping foot on Grey-wood grounds right now—considering how anxious I am—will lead straight to a meltdown.

Seth continues running his fingers through my hair soothingly. "You're welcome to stay at my apartment, I could drive you back in time for morning classes." Before I can protest, he adds, "I'll sleep on the couch, Little Muse. I'm not going to take advantage of you when your thoughts and feelings are a spiral of turmoil. I might not be a good man, but I'm not *that* sort of man."

I settle deeper into his arms, inhaling his scent—fresh cotton and a spicy cologne. It soothes me.

"I feel bad making you leave your own show, especially since I can honestly tell you I'll probably be really shitty company tonight. I'm not in a good headspace," I murmur.

Seth says, "You're not making me do anything, I'm offering. Being in your company could never be shitty, even if you're more sullen than usual. Trust me to take care of you, just for tonight, Elia. I won't let you down."

The fact that he actually wants to take care of me, with no measurable benefit to himself, makes a fuzzy feeling take up residence in my chest. Before he and Carson infiltrated my life, there was nobody who ever wanted to take care of me.

"Okay."

Chapter Thirty-Four

I opt out of getting dinner locally, because one of the unfortunate leftovers from my childhood is I can't eat when I'm anxious; if I try to force it, I'll throw up. The drive back to Seth's apartment is silent. Once we're in his apartment, I start to question my decision of coming here tonight; question the impression it might give him.

Then, I remind myself that he pretty much saw me have sex with his friend last night, and his response was to lightly blackmail me into attending his own art show as his date. That indicates that Seth's aware of my position and indecision, and is proceeding how he wishes to nonetheless.

Seth leads me by my hand through his living room and into his bedroom. Automatic lights flick on with our entry, and I cast a glance around, taking in the white walls, dark flooring, and large bed propped up against a wall with the grey bedspread neatly made. Above the bed hangs a large portrait that draws my attention. It appears to be a remake of Da Vinci's Vitruvian Man, except the man is a demon instead of a human. There are still four arms and four legs connected to one torso, but the body is painted in tones of dark red, and from the head of this creature stems sharp, gleaming black horns. Its fingers are tipped by dark claws, and its toes are hooves.

I say faintly, "Woah."

Seth moves until he's standing beside me, gazing at the painting along with me. A glance at him shows that his perusal of the art appears more critical, while mine is simply stunned.

He says, "I made this a few months after my father died. At the time, I was going through a dark biblical phase. I wanted to capture the correct proportions of a presumedly perfect demon, and I used da Vinci's sketch as a base. It's not my best work."

I turn to him with a dropped jaw. "*You* made that?"

I shouldn't be surprised; the exhibit tonight proved just how talented Seth is, but this is eerie and almost frightening in its beauty.

Seth nods. "I did. Pulled an image from a recurring nightmare, then built on it." He walks over to a wardrobe stationed against the opposite wall, then pulls out a large grey shirt. "Since you don't have any pajamas, and I assume you don't want to wear the jeans and sweater you had on before we went shopping to bed, hopefully this'll suffice."

I might be uncomfortable taking it with a different person, but Seth's already seen me naked and done things to me that still make my cheeks flame when I think about them, so I take the shirt from him. He points me towards the bathroom, which is made of all white marble with a silver sink and clear glass shower. I change, do my business, and use his toothpaste on my finger to freshen my teeth at least somewhat before emerging again, only to find an empty bedroom.

Seth calls out, "In the living room."

I follow his voice, stopping in the entryway of the living room and watching as he pulls a fresh set of sheets and blankets over the couch.

I say, "I can take the couch."

Seth replies, "Absolutely not. The bed's yours." He takes a seat on the edge of the couch, and his eyes run over me with a glint. "I like seeing you in my shirt. I might want to paint you that way one of these days."

I respond lightly, "You're in charge of the wardrobe and posing, Seth. Though I would like to see what that first painting's shaping up to look like." After seeing his art tonight, I have a good idea that it'll be stunning, but likely with a dark twist of some sort.

He says, "You'll see it when I'm further along. Are you sure you don't want to eat anything before bed? It's nearly midnight, and I suspect you haven't eaten since lunch."

I sigh. "I can't eat when I'm wound up. Believe me, I want to; I know I should just for the sake of having enough energy to dance tomorrow, but..." I give a hapless shrug.

Seth tilts his head to the side as he considers me. After a long silence, he says, "I have a feeling there's something more to that story. If you want to tell me, I'll be happy to listen."

Not now, and probably not any time soon. That would take discussing my mother, which I really prefer to avoid. I hate the fact that she was able to leave any sort of mark on me, because I know that was always her intent. To break me so that I'd need her, so that I'd be willing to tolerate her abuse and neglect because I'd be too weak to turn to anything else.

"Maybe another time," I say noncommittally.

Seth nods. "Very well. Goodnight, Little Muse. I'll drive you to campus at five thirty. Let me know if you need anything."

"Goodnight, Seth. Thank you for this, and for tonight. I'm sorry if I ruined it."

He gives me a small smile that almost appears amused. "You didn't ruin my night, you made it just by being there. Sleep well."

***

The unfortunate thing is, I can't actually fall asleep, no matter how hard I try. My mind keeps wandering to Scarlett, the fact that there's a very real possibility that one of her last conversations on this earth consisted of me tearing her down. Then, she was taken and *killed*. I can't imagine the killing was clean, either—if the same person who killed the painter also took her, Scarlett's death was probably painfully prolonged and extremely gory and bloody.

Along with guilt over Scarlett, my stomach churns with the idea that the victim could've easily been me, or April, or any one of the other students who live at program dorms. It feels like there's nowhere safe to turn to.

After hours of tossing around in Seth's bedding, trying and failing to calm myself, I give up. I'm a productive person by nature; if I can't fall asleep, then there's no point in lying around. When insomnia decides to torture me, I've learned to take it in stride. My mind will give out eventually and I'll fall asleep; if that isn't tonight or even tomorrow night, it just means I'll sleep all the better when I do finally pass out.

I stand from the bed, blinking when the bedroom lights automatically turn on, blinding me. Recalling the bookshelf in the living room, I tiptoe out, praying that the automatic lights don't turn on there and wake Seth. Unfortunately for me, the moment I step a toe into the large living room, they do. Seth isn't sleeping soundly on the couch, though. When the lights flick on, they reveal him, sitting in the center of the room. He has a similar setup going on to last night, when I was posing for him; he's seated on a wooden chair with an easel and canvas in front of him and a table of supplies beside him. He's dressed only in sweatpants, no shirt, so I get a glimpse of his back muscles flexing as he glides a paintbrush across the canvas.

At my entrance, he glances over his shoulder, looking me up and down. He has a lit cigarette between his lips, which he takes in his free hand before blowing a cloud of smoke upwards. Usually I find smoking disgusting; with Seth, it only adds to his dark artist vibe, making him even hotter.

"Couldn't sleep?" he asks, setting the paintbrush on the side table.

I shake my head. "No, I couldn't."

He inclines his head. "Not surprising. In your shoes, I don't know if I'd be able to sleep, either."

"Why couldn't you?" I ask curiously.

I doubt Seth being awake right now is due to distress; I don't know if he's even capable of feeling something like that. From what I've seen, his emotional repertoire is *very* modest. He's capable of amusement, lust, probably anger. Beyond that, I don't know.

He lifts a shoulder. "I don't usually sleep very well. I go through a cycle—I'll stay awake for a few days, then crash and sleep for ten hours. It's been that way since I was a kid."

Curiously, I ask, "Is that what it's like to have the mind of a genius?"

He lets out a chuckle. "You think I'm a genius?"

I nod slowly. "That's not a compliment. All historical records indicate that genius often walks hand in hand with madness. You obviously don't think the way other people do—otherwise you wouldn't already be an engineer *and* scientist *and* acclaimed artist. Your way of manipulating people around you, pulling their strings like a puppet master, is also a pretty strong indicator. I think you have a brilliant mind, but I don't think that's as pleasant as people make it out to be." My voice quiets. "I think your brain tortures you more than most. Otherwise, how would you have so many achievements at such a young age?"

Seth's eyes take on a glimmer of something undefinable. Not any of his usual basic emotions that I've observed, this is something else. If I didn't know better, I might call it fondness or affection.

"Have you been reading up on me, Little Muse? Maybe I'm not the only stalker in this relationship."

That brings a reluctant smile to my lips. "Finding information on your achievements isn't hard; all it took was typing your name into google, and article after article popped up. I don't know if that's stalking so much as curiosity. After all, I'm not the one who got my school schedule changed in order to get closer to the other."

Seth takes another drag from the cigarette, motioning for me to come closer with his hand. I walk up to him, taking a curious look at the canvas. Before I can see more than dark, blended colors of midnight blue, forest green, and royal purple, Seth takes my hand and spins me around to face him, looking up at me with his mesmerizing hazel eyes.

"Remember when I told you your perceptiveness unnerves me?" he questions quietly. "This is one of those times. Not a lot of people can read me, and I prefer it that way. In the past, people who got close to me didn't exactly survive it intact. You, though... your quiet strength and way of seeing things for exactly what they are draws me to you more and more." He pauses, reaching up to stroke a hand through my hair. "Is it any wonder I can't stay away from you?"

"Your intensity is what unnerves me," I admit. "I don't know how to handle it. I also like it, despite myself. I like you, but I like Carson too. A lot. I like the way both of you make me feel, even though it can be a little frightening." My brows draw together. "Despite the insanity going on around us, when I'm with either of you, I feel safe."

Seth considers my words for several long moments in silence. Finally, he says, "We both fulfill different needs for you. With me, it's the darkness, the complexity. With him, it's the light and simplicity."

Once again, he's proving himself *very* good at reading people. There's no point in denying it, so I admit quietly, "Yes. I don't think I'll be able to choose between you. If anything, I'd have to choose neither of you."

Seth's hand travels down to my arm, and he takes hold of my wrist to gently pull me onto his lap. "You don't have to, not now."

I shake my head. "I don't want to, period. Regardless of timing. Now's especially bad, sure, because there's a lot on my plate. But my sentiments towards you won't change later. If anything, the complications will drive me away. I've lived my whole life with problem after problem, Seth, I don't want to deal with any more that I don't have to."

He slides an arm around my waist, his brows drawing together. "Are you calling me a complication?" He doesn't sound particularly pleased at the prospect.

"Yes," I respond frankly. "You are. All on your own, you are a complication, because I think you know better than anyone that you are not an easy man to be around. You're tiring; exhausting, even, but that on its own wouldn't bother me, because I really do like you. The real problem is that I like Carson just as much as I like you, and both of you are in pursuit of me with the expectation that I'll choose. I won't, Seth. The more I get to know you both, the more time I spend with you, the more I wish I'd just met one of you. Because now I'm getting pushed towards an impossible choice that I can't make."

It doesn't help that both of them are accepting of their competition to the extent of not even being upset when I get sexual with the other. Carson wasn't mad when he figured that something occurred between me and Seth in the archives, and Seth wasn't mad when he basically watched me fuck Carson. Maybe they were upset with each other, but not at me. If one of them directed any anger at me, that would've made it easy to choose the other. That's what I keep expecting, but it doesn't happen.

"I hear you, and your concerns," Seth tells me, his hand rubbing circles on my back. "I'll need to think on them, on how to find a resolution that works. For now, though, I want you to let go of your concerns, and trust that I'll do my best to see to them. Can you do that for me?"

Chapter Thirty-Five

I let out a long breath, considering my answer. I can't stop all my underlying worries, but so far, Seth hasn't led me wrong. Still, I'm not a person who trusts easily, and I'm anxious by nature. Seth's cunning personality makes me want to distrust him on principle, but he hasn't given me any reason to think he poses a threat to me. For now, there's no reason I can't relax and just enjoy the time with him. While I'm with him, in this apartment with excellent security that'll be even more difficult to break into than the dorms, I'm safe. Besides that, I like spending time with Seth, even though he sometimes says things that piss me off.

I wind my arms around his neck and say, "So long as you don't spew more bullshit about owning me, yes."

His lips quirk as he pulls me tighter against him. "It's hard not to want to own you, Little Muse. I won't deny that I have a deep-seated need to possess you, body and soul. You're so unique, so clever, so quick; who wouldn't want you all for themselves? For the sake of your comfort, though, I'll refrain." He trails his lips up the side of my neck. "You haven't eaten anything for some time. Will you?"

My stomach's still twisted up in knots from lingering stress, and I don't want to risk throwing up in Seth's bathroom after a failed attempt at eating. I know myself well enough to know that if I can't eat, trying to force it will only result in vomiting.

I say with a sigh, "I wish."

He pulls back to look into my eyes. "I want you to tell me about that. I won't force you, but I'd like to know."

I chew on my lip for a moment, contemplating whether I want to let Seth in by opening myself up to him, before finally deciding there's no harm in sharing *some* of my struggles.

"My mom was not a good person, and certainly not a good mother. Throughout my entire childhood, but especially after I started ballet, she'd keep me on impossibly strict diets. It got bad a few times. As in, I ended up in the hospital getting treated for malnutrition bad. Food was one of her prime ways to control me, and she exerted her power over me like that often. I've spent most of my life underweight. After I turned eighteen and moved out, I started seeing a nutritionist who helped me get to where I need to be, but there are some leftovers from childhood that I can't shake. One of them is that I literally can't eat when I'm anxious; if I do, my body won't accept it and I'll almost always end up vomiting."

Seth doesn't look remotely surprised by what I'm telling him, but he does look angry. No, not just angry, *furious*. He could make a serial killer look like a cuddly teddy bear in comparison. His breathing becomes harsher, like a panting bull before it charges at the red flag, all the veins and tendons in his neck bulge, and his upper lip curls with menace.

"It's not a big deal," I say quickly. "She's gone now, and I do my best to not let her affect me in death like she worked to so relentlessly in life."

Seth sets his cigarette in the ash tray on the side table, then uses his free hand to cup the back of my neck, pulling me forward until our foreheads are touching. The moment feels intense, deeply intimate, and the sense of connection it creates almost startles me.

After what could be a minute or an hour of us sitting like that, Seth pulls his head back, moving his second hand down to the small of my back. He doesn't say anything about my mother like I expect him to. Instead, he tells me, "I told you that my father had no interest in taking care of children, but that was the very least of my problems with him. He was a violent man. Rich enough to bury police reports made by my teachers at school after they'd glimpse the bruises on me, so I had nowhere to turn. When I was younger, I believed him when he said I'd earned the beatings and pain, even for the most minor infractions. Then I grew up a bit, and started realizing that what I was going through at home wasn't normal—mainly because other kids at school would tell all these great stories about spending time with their parents, but all I had was pain. I understood that I didn't deserve it, I just got really unlucky with my parent." He pauses to inhale a deep breath. "I was a smart kid. By fourth grade I was winning state awards for science projects and such. But no amount of intelligence could let me prevail over Dad's connections in high places and unique way of worming himself out of getting caught. He was a cunning, manipulative motherfucker. By the time I was sixteen, I was already getting scholarship offers to go to college, but Dad wouldn't let me leave. I lived with him until I was eighteen and got accepted to Greywood on a full ride scholarship—a godsend, since I knew my father wouldn't pay for a college education. A year later, he died. It was the best thing that ever happened to me."

Jesus Christ. I had a feeling when Seth mentioned his dad last night that he might've had a difficult childhood, but I didn't expect *this*.

At least my mom never hit me—she knew that'd get her sent to prison—but she did starve me and emotionally abuse me from the time I could remember. I celebrated her death just like Seth must've celebrated his father's.

"Thank you for telling me that," I murmur.

Seth nods slowly, searching my eyes. "I want you to understand that I think we have a lot more in common than initial impressions might indicate, Little Muse."

I feel a small smile curl my lips. "My first impression when we met was that you might be a killer."

Seth doesn't blink. "What if I am?" Something about his words, followed by the insight into his childhood, makes it click in my mind. He was a smart kid, but never smart enough to take on the connections and reach of his father, who I assume had some measure of power among the upper class. Then, Seth left home, and a year later his father dies.

I know why my mother died; I was no longer around to fill her need for attention, and she went through yet another breakup around the time I moved out, which left her with nothing to live for. The child support checks stopped arriving the moment I turned 18, and the bank was threatening to take her house to clear her copious debts. She was a goner either way, but she wanted to go on her own terms. Whether she knew she'd die or not, she took far too many pills, and that was it.

Seth's father was obviously wealthy, he likely had a well-paying job or a trust fund, and from the sense I'm getting, he was not the type to do something stupid that would result in his own death. In fact, Seth described him as cunning and manipulative. Seth clearly wanted revenge for a childhood full of pain, and away from his fathers control, he could've found the means to get it.

I swallow hard but take care not to stiffen. I can sense from the way Seth's searching my expression with his eyes that he's waiting for a reaction, for condemnation. While I myself would never commit murder, I won't deny that there were many times when I wished my mother would drop dead. I just couldn't ever fathom being the cause of that. Seth, though, raised with violence... he might've wanted to end his father. And, even if he did have something to do with his father's death, I don't know that I'd blame him. If his father was above the justice system, that meant he needed to be served justice in a different way.

I exhale a deep breath. "I'm going to ask you a question, and I'd like you to answer honestly. Whatever you say won't leave this room."

Seth nods slowly, once, and his hold on me tightens as if he's preparing for me to run. I move my hands to his shoulders and smooth my palms down his arms, rubbing my thumbs over his biceps. I knew from the first that Seth was capable of hurting and possibly killing someone, this will just give me confirmation.

"Did you..." I pause to clear my throat, as the words seem stuck in it. "Did you kill your father?"

"Yes," Seth says plainly. "I had professional help, but yes, the death was orchestrated by me."

At least he's honest. I wouldn't expect anything less of him. Seth has been painfully honest with me from the get-go. Our second night in the archives, he outright admitted that he was dangerous, but he also told me that he wouldn't hurt me.

I don't think I'm a naïve person; I understand that death is part of life, and sometimes, death is what's necessary to keep people safe. There are some people who *deserve* to die, even our justice system agrees with that, though the system can't always deliver the necessary justice. More than anyone, I believe that people who hurt children deserve to die, as they taint lives before those lives can really even start. My mother tainted me from the time I could remember, and she never actually laid a cruel hand on me. Seth's father didn't just taint him, he twisted Seth—quite possibly made him into the dark person he is today.

I can picture a young, perhaps more idealistic version of Seth, too smart for his own good, going home from school every day only to experience abuse. His childhood was effectively robbed from him; it's only fair that he retaliated.

"Okay," I say with a nod.

Surprise travels through Seth's expression. "Okay?"

I nod again. "He hurt a child. You prevented him from doing that ever again. The justice system failed, so you took matters into your own hands. I can't criticize that."

Seth's features harden. "Don't romanticize me, Eliana. My father might be the first person I killed, but he isn't the last. He also isn't the only person whose reputation I've destroyed, life I've upended. I'm not a good man."

With each of his words, his arms tighten around me. Even while he's verbally pushing me away, maybe trying to scare me, he's physically making sure I stay where I am, with him. The hardness in his tone tips me off that this is a test of sorts, even if he doesn't know it is. He's pushing me to see how I react, to see if I'll run. This is a precarious situation where I have to choose my moves wisely.

I lean closer to him. "Do you make a habit of raping and pillaging?"

He stiffens. "What? No."

"Are you a cannibal?"

His voice dripping with disgust, he snaps, "*No.*"

"Do you hurt women or children?"

He gives his head a shake, as if he can't comprehend my line of inquiry. "*No!* Where the hell is this coming from?"

I shrug. "A girl's gotta cover her most important bases. You tell me you're a bad man? Okay. As long as you don't engage in the listed activities, I think I can live with that."

He's shocked to silence for several moments. Finally, he says, "I make sport out of lighting the match that sets someone's world on fire. People's lives are like Jenga puzzles to me; I like drawing out the two or three blocks it takes to tumble the entire tower."

"What kind of people do you do that to?" I ask.

He blinks. "What?"

I reply, "It's a simple question. I already knew you were pathological, sociopathic in some ways, but I don't think you're indiscriminate. You're not a rapist, pillager, cannibal, or someone who targets innocents. So, if I were to take a guess, I'd say you go after bad people. Those like your father, maybe, or worse. Am I wrong?"

He shakes his head slowly. "You're not wrong, but you are missing the picture. I once followed a man for three days, stalking him, just to get photographic evidence of him with his mistress. I then sent those photographs to his wife, who passed them on to others. He got fired from a very prestigious job a few days later. Since that wasn't enough to completely destroy him, I found evidence that he'd betrayed a criminal organization he had ties to and sent it to the top men of that organization; a month later, they made him disappear."

I ask, "What did he do?"

Seth works his jaw before responding, "His wife had a miscarriage after he pushed her down the stairs. Apparently, he didn't want another kid. He also had connections in high places, so the courts wouldn't have gotten him."

"You took it upon yourself to light his life on fire. Sounds well deserved," I respond.

Seth snaps, "I would've killed him if he wasn't so high-profile."

I let out a sigh. "Look, Seth, I knew you weren't a good person from the first time we met, but you aren't an indiscriminate killer, either, which makes you better than some of the men I've known. If you're going to keep trying to scare me with tales of your twisted valor, it'll only bore me."

Seth spends several minutes staring at me, brows creased and expression fluctuating from irritated to confused. I get the sense that he's trying to figure me out at this moment, because he didn't expect my acceptance of his darkest parts. Admittedly, those parts are a little frightening, but they're nothing I can't handle. His grip on me loosens and tightens repeatedly, a hint of his inner turmoil.

Finally, he says, "I hope you know, you've just sealed your fate."

I tilt my head to the side. "What do you mean?"

He uses one hand to tuck an errant lock of hair behind my ear. "Whatever happens from here on out, Elia, you're mine."

Chapter Thirty-Six

In the morning, Seth drives me back to campus at 5:30. After our conversation last night, we moved to the couch together and talked Renaissance art until I eventually fell asleep, somewhere around 3 or 4 A.M. I woke up in his arms, to find him staring down at me with his usual steady, unblinking gaze. Before starting the trek back to dorms, Seth whipped me up a delicious omelet, then gave me a kiss on the lips and promised to see me later.

In my room, I quickly change into dance clothes and gather my school supplies for the day, finishing just in time for Carson's usual knocks to sound at the door. This time, when I open it, he doesn't seem to be in the best of moods; in fact, a slight frown mars his features as he hands me a cup of coffee.

"You didn't come back last night," he says.

Right. I shift awkwardly from foot to foot before saying, "News of Scarlett's body being found broke while I was out with Seth. I was too rattled to come back, I didn't want to run into a similar crowd of police, students, and teachers that were present when I discovered the first body."

Carson takes a sip from his coffee, his eyes flitting over me. "You stayed at Seth's apartment?"

It feels like there's no right answer to that. I really, *really* don't want to hurt Carson, as my connection with him has been deepening, but so has my connection with Seth. The turmoil I managed to push aside just hours ago returns full force.

Trying to keep guilt from my expression, I slowly nod. I brace myself for a negative reaction, some reprimand, but aside from the brief flash of pain that crosses Carson's features, nothing else comes.

He tells me, "That's for the best. Campus was not a good place to be last night, it got pretty hectic. If I hadn't been waiting for you to make sure you got back safe, I might've headed back to my apartment for the evening."

"I'm sorry," I murmur.

April's door opens and she steps out, looking bleary-eyed and exhausted with undereye circles and her hair sticking up in every direction. Carson turns to look at her as she says, "Dance classes got cancelled today, as the department's in a bit of a clusterfuck over Scarlett. Thought you should know, Elia, in case you didn't see the email they sent out. I don't know about either of you, but I'm going back to bed."

With that, she goes back into her room and closes the door. Carson turns back to me, and we spend several long moments staring at each other, a million unspoken things passed between our gazes. Carson's eyes are filled with longing and a hint of dejection that makes me feel horrible.

I can't just leave things like this between us, so I open my door wider and say, "Come in. We should talk."

His gaze hardens at my words, and he says, "You're not ending whatever we have. This thing between us, it's real. I'm not letting go of it. I don't care if I have to fucking *share* you with my psychopath of a friend—"

I reach out to take his free hand, threading our fingers together and cutting him off mid-rant. "I'm not ending anything with you. I like you too much, just like I like Seth too much to end it with him. Right now, I don't have an answer as to which one of you I'll choose, I don't even *want* to make a choice. Seth invigorates me, but you... you stabilize me and brighten my day." I blink several times as my eyes start to sting with tears.

That's what makes me realize that I'm already in too deep, with both of them. I've only known them for a couple of weeks, but in that time they've managed to worm their way under my defenses, and make a home for themselves in the soft, malleable part of my heart. I don't want to lose either of them by choosing the other, I don't know that I can. If anything, like I told Seth last night, I'd end up choosing neither to spare all of us the heartache. I can't do that now, though.

For now, all I can do is treasure the time I spend with both of them, because they've managed to abate the loneliness that's plagued me for most of my life. Loneliness so poignant and intense, so consuming that it had become a standard for me; I didn't know any other way. I didn't even realize how bad it was until the two men came along and chased it away.

"Don't cry," Carson says, stepping into my room. His face registers a mixture of panic and fear. "Please, Little E, don't cry. We'll figure it out together. We'll figure everything out, I promise." He steps into my room; I shuffle back, releasing his hand to swipe at the tears that are starting to fall.

He closes the door behind him, sets his coffee on my chest of drawers, doing the same with mine, and then pulls me into his arms.

"I'm sorry," I repeat, starting to feel a little pathetic. "I'm not usually a crier, but two bodies have dropped now, and the most recent one is a girl I made minced meat out of hours before she went missing. Then, there's you and Seth—fuck both of you, by the way, for making me like you so much. *And* I just got cast as a lead in the dance program's newest production." My tears start to flow more freely, staining Carson's shirt. "I'm just overwhelmed, and scared, and so irritated with you for making me like you this much. I wasn't supposed to like you. You represent everything I've come to despise in this world, *except you don't.* How is that fair?"

Carson shushes me and holds me even tighter. Slowly, I wrap my arms around him and accept the warmth and comfort he's providing, even though I know this will only make me like him more and make it harder when I eventually have to turn my back on both him and Seth. I understand that's the direction this is heading in; I'm not cruel enough to make a choice between them, I'd rather break my own heart by choosing neither.

"You don't have to do anything now, Little E. No choices, no anything." He lets out a deep sigh, resting his chin on my forehead. "Your tears are killing me. I can't stand the thought of making you sad. I want to make you happy."

That makes me cry even harder, because one of my problems is the fact that he does make me happy. "I'm just overwhelmed," I say between hiccups, feeling pathetic. "And I hate you *so much* for turning out to be a genuinely good person. Why couldn't you have been a pushy, asshole trust fund brat like my ex?"

Carson stiffens at my words, and I realize I might've revealed too much, but right now I don't care. I can't. I'm exhausted, emotionally and physically. After a few seconds the tension leeches from Carson and his hands start rubbing up and down my spine soothingly.

"What can I do to help?" he asks.

I say emphatically, "Stop being so good to me."

He lets out a soft chuckle that tickles the crown of my head. "I can't do that, Princess. What else?"

I sniffle. "Just... stay with me."

"I will," he tells me.

He holds me while I cry into his chest, staining his shirt with tears and snot. I don't just cry because of my turmoil in this moment, the tears relieve stress that's been building and building within me since I got to campus. First, I had to deal with Scarlett's bullshit while in rehearsals. Then, I was the one to find the first body of the female painter. After that, it was dealing with Seth and Carson's relentless stalking, only to have them actually manage to worm their ways into my life, all while school and dance continued rising in intensity. Last night, *Scarlett's* body dropped.

After a while, my tears slow down, before eventually stopping. On the heels of my breakdown comes a wave of embarrassment. I pull away from Carson, wiping my eyes on the sleeves of my sweater.

Carson takes my shoulders and asks, "Better?"

I nod. "I'm not usually like that. I don't want you to think I'm weak."

He lets out a soft chuckle. "Elia, there isn't anything you could do that would make me think you're weak. Tears are not a sign of weakness, they're just a sign of pent-up emotions. Everything I've seen and learned about you makes me believe you're one of the strongest people I've ever met."

I exhale a deep breath, trying to gather my thoughts. I feel my brows crease as I look up at Carson. "Hold on, it's Tuesday. Don't you have morning classes Tuesdays and Thursday's?"

Carson shakes his head. "No, Little E, I work for one of my father's companies in town on Tuesday and Thursday mornings as part of my credits. I called in sick today, though. I wouldn't have been of any use there anyways, since my thoughts would have been of you. I needed to make sure you got back okay."

It takes concentrated effort not to start crying at that—I don't think I can handle Carson's kindness. Very few people in my life have been genuinely kind to me without underlying, self-serving reasons, so I don't know how to properly respond.

We stare at each other for a while, before I finally say, "I'm going to go take a shower. You can go in to work, tell them you magically got better. I don't want to hold you back."

"You're not holding me back," he replies instantly. "I like spending time with you. I already took the day off, and my afternoon classes were cancelled in lieu of the situation last night. I think most students are off today." He pauses, thinking for a moment, before saying, "Since we're both free for the day, I propose we spend it together, away from Greywood. It could help get your mind off the shit that's been going on around you."

I shift from foot to foot. Do I want to get away from Greywood? Yes. But I don't want to give Carson an even greater opportunity to worm his way into my heart.

He seems to sense this, because he adds, "There's no pressure, Princess. No right or wrong, no choices. Just a break from everything for today."

That does sound enticing. "What do you have in mind?" I ask.

A grin spreads on his lips. "There's a national park about a forty-minute drive away. A beautiful mountain with plenty of hiking trails. I heard a good amount of snow has dropped there recently, so it should be like a winter wonderland. We could drive up, take a hike, maybe have a picnic."

I perk up a little at his idea. I know Vermont has some beautiful nature in-state, and I love spending time outdoors, *especially* in the winter when there are no mosquitos or spiders to plague me. I even brought my old hiking gear with me to campus, items that I bought over the years for camping trips with friends, including snow pants and a warm jacket.

"That sounds lovely, actually," I say. "Give me half an hour to shower and dress?"

Carson nods. "See you soon."

Chapter Thirty-Seven

About an hour and a half later, Carson parks his blue car at the base of a *gorgeous,* snowy mountain. I get out of the car, gazing excitedly at the sight of a wide trailhead that leads up and into the thick forest. The air tastes fresh and crisp, absent of the stuffiness that comes with living close to a city. It's cold, cold enough that my breath puffs out in front of me, making me glad I'm wearing two sweaters under my jacket, along with the well-insulated winter boots I splurged on before coming to Greywood.

Carson also gets out of the car, watching with an expression of amusement as I take in the vibrant beauty around me. So much snow has fallen in the last week, it's hard to see the evergreen trees underneath the blanket of white.

The parking lot only has a few other cars parked around and there aren't many footprints in the snow, meaning Carson and I will probably get most of the mountain to ourselves. He pulls a backpack out of the back seat before locking the car. "Let's get moving before we freeze."

"It's *so pretty*," I say, barely keeping myself from jogging ahead. I pull warm gloves onto my hands before starting towards the trailhead, which is marked off by a small steel gate to keep cars from entering.

Carson says, "So, you're a snow person, huh?"

I slip around the gate, glancing at him over my shoulder before turning my gaze towards the tall trees that envelope us. Beneath the scent of fresh snow and evergreen there's also the faint smell of burning pine from a campfire somewhere.

"Definitely," I respond. "I'm a nature person in general, I've always loved hiking and exploring forests, but all the more so when there's snow."

Carson hums. "I would've thought you'd be more drawn to beaches and warmth."

I laugh, shaking my head as he catches up with me and we walk side by side. "Beaches mean sand, and sand is like an STD—once you have it, it's very difficult to make it go away. Kind of like glitter; don't get me started on the shows I've done that were glitter heavy. I swear I still sometimes find that sparkly stuff in my clothes."

My mood is brighter simply because of getting away from campus and out into nature, making me more talkative and upbeat. The company helps, too; I relax around Carson, like I don't have to think through every word before speaking.

"I'll take your word for it," Carson says with a chuckle. "What's the draw to snowy forests, though? It's easy to freeze your ass off in places like this if you don't know what you're doing."

I make a *pfft* sound. "As long as you keep moving, you're fine unless it's arctic level temperatures. Although summer hikes are lovely, they also mean bugs. Mosquitos have it out for me, I always return from a warm hike covered in bug bites and spend the next days scratching off the top layer my skin. Winter means no bugs, and I also think it's prettier. More serene, too, as less people are inclined to go hiking in the snow. I've always found it peaceful." I look at the stillness and serenity around me and release a sigh of contentment. "There was a mountain range about three hours' drive from where I grew up; I used to go on a week-long camping trip every winter break, usually with members of whatever dance company or production I was in at the time."

Carson takes my gloved hand in his, using it to pull me close so he can wrap an arm around me. He smiles down at me, and I feel my chest fill up with warmth at the sight of that smile. It's so carefree and light, so filled with pleasure, I can't help but smile back.

I'm finding out more and more that spending time with Carson makes it easy to forget about worries and struggles. He has a way of brightening his surroundings, of helping shed all the extra weight that life heaps onto our shoulders.

A flash of movement from the corner of my eye catches my attention, and I turn my head in time to see a bundle of red fur crossing the pathway ahead of us; a fox. I freeze in place, and grab Carson's arm to stop him, too. The fox isn't alone, it's followed by several of its cubs, all of whom waddle along the pathway, leaving little pawprints in the snow. I count six little ones following their mom, and I barely contain myself from cooing over them.

Once they're back in the forest and out of sight, I turn to Carson and beam. "That was the cutest thing ever. Oh, I wish I'd gotten a picture! Did you see the adorable little babies? God, I just wanted to steal one and keep it for myself."

Carson laughs, and I thread my arm through his as we continue walking forward. "That wouldn't be the best idea, Princess. My mom worked with some fox rescues in her days as a vet; they're not easy creatures to look after. They piss everywhere to mark their territory, including on each other, and they aren't very adept to getting trained by humans."

My curiosity's piqued by the fondness in Carson's voice as he talks about his mother. His expression softens, too, but there's also a hint of melancholy.

"Can you tell me more about her?" I ask. "I wanted to be a vet for a while when I was younger. Then, my mom told me in no uncertain terms that I'd have to end up killing animals, which was the end of that dream."

Carson grimaces in disgust. "Your mom sounds like a real piece of work, Little E, euthanasia is a small part of veterinary work and only ever a last resort. My mom is like a ray of sunlight. Or she was, before my father came along and did his level best to dim it. When he couldn't make her totally conform to his ways, he took off with a line of younger women who could fill his desires." He shakes his head. "Only reason Dad doesn't allow for a divorce is that she had me, and I'm his sole heir; a divorce would be bad publicity and might tarnish his shiny image."

I let out a noise of distaste. "He sounds like a grade-A asshole."

Carson nods. "He is. Good thing for me is, he's content to leave me and Mom to our own devices. As long as I continue to do well in school and in his company, he doesn't care enough to take a closer look at my life, which suits me just fine. My mom, though..." he trails off, and I glance up at him to see a look of deep fondness settled on his features. "She's the fucking best, in every way. Growing up with her, especially when Dad was gone—which was almost always—was a joy. She's really clever, would always be creating games for us to play. She allowed me to bring home as many strays and rescues as I felt like—we even ended up designating a few acres of our property for all the pets. She's where I get my love of nature from; we'd go horseback riding in the mountains every weekend in the summers."

The faintest sliver of jealousy moves through me, causing me to stiffen ever so slightly. Thankfully, under the many layers of clothing, Carson doesn't seem to feel it. I immediately berate myself; it's not fair for me to get jealous of him having what every child should, a strong relationship with a parent. I know he struggles with his dad, but the way he's describing his mom... I hate myself for thinking it, but I envy that. It makes me so blatantly aware of how awful *my* mother was.

I try to push that aside as Carson continues, "I actually brought one of our rescues with me to my apartment near Greywood—"

I let out a gasp. "Carson, you've left a dog all on their own while you were in dorms?"

Carson chuckles. "Relax, Elia, it's a cat. I check in on him daily, and I have a sitter on call in case I can't. He has an electronic water fountain and feeder, plus I have cameras in the apartment to make sure he's not getting in too much trouble. He's actually really sweet, taught me a lot of my pro-cuddling skills."

I grin. "What's his name?"

Carson bites the side of his cheek. "I'm not sure if I want to tell you. You're going to make fun of me."

I bump his arm with mine. "Come on, Carson, I promise I won't laugh."

He squints at me, before finally saying, "Mewlius Caesar."

I have to suck my bottom lip between my teeth to stop myself from bursting out into laughter. Even then, a giggle escapes, which makes Carson glare at me playfully.

Trying to keep my voice steady, I ask, "You named your cat Mewlius Caesar? As in..." I pause as a small snort sneaks through my lips and try to keep myself composed.

Carson sighs. "I was going through an old history phase, my thirteen-year-old self thought that was exceedingly clever."

I try to keep my smile to a minimum as I nod sagely.

Carson says, "It was between that and Cleopawtra."

At that, I can't help myself, I burst out in gales of laughter. Carson frowns at me playfully, then reaches down to toss some snow at me, which only makes me laugh harder. This eventually devolves into a snow-throwing fight, which then progresses into a snowball fight.

Finally, once we're both covered head-to-toe with snow and both laughing, we call it a draw.

Carson says, "Come on, let's go on a bit farther. There's a bridge up ahead where we can do lunch."

I shake my head to get the snow out of my hair, feeling all warm and fuzzy despite the cold. "Why are you so good?"

Carson shrugs, taking my hand. "I think you bring out the best in me, Little E."

Together, we walk to the bridge Carson described, which shows off a gorgeous, scenic view of a frozen waterfall. We end up eating lunch right there, setting up in the snow with some sandwiches and sodas Carson takes out of his backpack. We talk more, about everything from our childhoods to trading funny stories, keeping the conversation light. Carson tells me a little more about his position in his father's company, his current roles in management and how he'll be expected to work his way up the company food chain before taking his father's place. I notice he doesn't sound particularly happy or excited when talking about his future in the company, though, which makes me curious.

I ask, "Why do you sound like someone who's off to the gallows when talking about your dad's company?"

Carson gives me an amused, if somewhat sad, smile. "Because my father is not a good man, Little E, and I don't look forward to the day I'll have to take his position in life."

I scoot closer to him, wanting to offer him comfort. "We don't have to be our parents," I tell him. "Their baggage isn't ours to carry."

Carson sighs. "It's not quite so simple for me, Princess. The company my dad's currently the head of was started by my grandfather decades ago. He had an inheritance from *his* parents that he used to get into oil. He spent thirty years expanding his company, amassing money and power, then passed it down to my dad who's making it even *bigger*. This is the family torch; I can't just leave it behind. If my dad weren't such an asshole, I don't think I would be so averse to it. He just has a tendency to go about things in the worst way possible."

I rub my hand up and down his arm, empathy filling me. I'm really starting to understand that, while he grew up in a life of privilege, Carson also has heavy crosses to bear. I want to take his problems from him somehow, lighten his burden.

I really am getting in too deep here.

I brush that thought aside, because I don't want to ruin this moment. Despite the depth of our conversation, I'm enjoying this time with Carson, especially since it frees me from the worries of campus for at least a little while.

"So go about it the way you think is right," I tell Carson. "Do things *your* way. The world is progressing, change is a constant—you don't have to replicate your father's business models and habits, you can and *should* make your own way. It could help if you try to view it all as an opportunity to do better rather than a ball and chain forcing you to repeat history."

Carson smiles a little, clasping my hand in his. "You have a way of brightening things, Little E. Making them seem more bearable even when they suck."

I lift a shoulder. "Call it a childhood leftover. I grew up learning to force myself to see the silver linings and upside, or I would've been miserable all the time."

That much is true. It was beyond difficult to stay positive and upbeat when I had a mother who was constantly working to bring me down so that I'd be dependent on her. She wanted full control over my life, even though she despised me on principle—I think what she really wanted was the ability to shape and mold me to her whims and specification, to be the reason for my success or failure. It was almost like she felt I belonged to her for the simple fact that she carried me in her body for nine months and grew me.

She'd bring that up to me constantly; the way I ruined her life and her figure. That I was the ball and chain around her ankle. She hated the very sight of me, which in hindsight I think is because I represented everything she wasn't; youth and vibrance. Because of that, she constantly sought to hurt me, destroy me, and simultaneously take credit as the sole reason for my achievements.

Carson says playfully, "You're too wise for such a young, tiny thing."

I frown at him, also playfully. "I'm only a few years younger than you."

Carson nods. "And I'm still as immature as it gets, so my point stands."

I tilt my head at his words. "I don't think you're immature at all," I tell him. "I think you might like being perceived that way because it takes away the fear of failure; if people don't expect much from you, then you can't disappoint them. I think that's the reason why you turn to sex and women and playboy, rakish methods—it's easy to keep things surface-level and light that way, to avoid any depth. It's all a self-defense mechanism to protect you from harm, not to mention a way to avoid your fears."

I realize the truth in my words only as I speak them, and they paint Carson in a whole new light for me. He avoids being serious, avoids any sort of depth because he fears that's a direct path to turn into his father, which is admittedly heart-wrenching. His father, who destroyed his mother and sounds like a grade-A asshole all around.

I don't think Carson realizes that he could never be like his father, because he has a genuinely *good* soul. If I'm of any indication, when he *does* come to care about someone, he cares *very* deeply and with his whole being. It's why he moved into dorms just because I felt unsafe there.

I feel a warmth in my chest as I stare at him, followed by a few fissures that seem like they crawl right along my heart, cracking it open to make more space for him, for this. *God, no.* Not with him. I already like and care about Carson too much, I can't afford to *love* him, too. I know that can only end in pain, because my feelings for Seth are growing, as well.

I need to compartmentalize if I have a prayer of surviving the next few weeks, let alone the rest of the year with them. I doubt my arrangement with Carson will extend past first term, because he seems like a busy guy who's putting parts of his life on hold for me, which can't last forever. Same goes for Seth. While their pursuit of me has been relentless, that's what's happening *now*, I can't presume that it'll extend far into the future, despite their assurances. Since I also can't bring myself to end things with either one of them, I just need to enjoy the time with them I have.

Their infatuation will run its course, and eventually, despite the sweet words I've heard from both of them, I believe they'll move on to bigger, better things. All I can do is bask in the *now*, even if I know it won't extend to the future.

CHAPTER THIRTY-EIGHT

Seth

I stare at the canvas in front of me, twirling my paintbrush in my hand and trying to assess exactly what's missing from it. The painting is a reimagining of Botticelli's Venus and Mars, with my Little Muse as Venus. Of course, there's no Mars just yet, which leaves a glaring blank spot on one side of the canvas, but that's not what's bothering me—I can be patient when it comes to the stages of my paintings. I understood I'd paint Elia first, then find a male model for Mars or just use my imagination. What's bothering me is her facial expression—it's not quite right.

This is the second project I've started featuring Elia, and not one I've had her pose for yet—this one comes from my imagination; I'll have her pose for it later. When I started on this painting, I didn't want an exact replica of the original Mars and Venus; I wanted to take the seed concepts behind the masterpiece, twist them, and make them my own. Thus, my muse's positioning is different from the actual Venus's, and the positioning of whoever I choose as Mars will be adjusted accordingly. The original piece is meant to speak of love conquering strife; the love and fertility goddess Venus is seated across from a sleeping war god, Mars. Mars's weapons are in the hands of Satyrs, hinting at his disarmament, and the whole allegory is that love conquers even war.

My painting will be different; it'll be about how even the darkest creatures can be captured by love. The overall message of the painting will still be love, but it'll be more geared towards the conquest of love rather than what love can conquer. My Mars, when I paint him, won't be sleeping docilely across from my Muse, instead it's far more likely that I'll have him holding Eliana tightly, in a way that speaks to his refusal of letting go of her. Of claiming and possessing her.

I know that this is, of course, a massive self-insertion—it's a reflection of how *I* refuse to let go of Eliana.

The problem I'm coming to understand is that I myself might not be able to keep her. Not alone, anyway. I recall her words from last night: *if anything, I'd have to choose neither of you*. That's unacceptable to me; the very thought of her walking away makes me itchy with the need to do something that'll prevent such an outcome. Elia has proven herself to be a beacon of light to me, a sliver of hope that there's more to this world than pain and cruelty.

Before, I could only take solace and find beauty in my art, and even then everything had such a dark twist that it was difficult to class my work as *beautiful*, more so *revealing* and *dark*. Then, Elia came along and showed me that there is much more beauty to be found in this world. The prospect of losing her does not sit well with me *at all*, and I understand there's very little I wouldn't do to keep her.

My phone rings on my side table, distracting me from my thoughts. I wipe my hands on a paint-stained rag, then check who the caller is: *Sergei Novikov.* A bratva boss that owns half of Eurasia, and an associate I've enjoyed working with on a few occasions.

I pick up the call, setting it on speakerphone so I can multitask. "Sergei. Good to hear from you."

Sergei responds, "And you, Seth. I'm sure you've heard the news by now, your hell horse sculpture caught Kira's eye. She insisted we collect it and add it to our sculpture garden."

I got the call from my agent this morning, after dropping off Elia on campus and finding out that classes were cancelled today. Hopefully that'll give admin an opportunity to get their heads out of their asses and figure out how they'll approach having a murderer using their campus as hunting grounds.

"I have heard, about the sculpture and two paintings you also purchased. All my favorite pieces from the collection, which just reaffirms your excellent taste. I'm glad the works will have homes where they'll be properly appreciated." For all of his underground dealings, one of the first things I understood upon my introduction to Sergei was that he had good taste. Both in business and in art.

Sergei says dryly, "I'm sure the price we settled on with your agent was also a highlight. Your work is in very high demand, I had to outbid several interested parties." He lets out a sigh. "The things we do for love."

That's a statement I never expected to hear from Sergei. I've known him for about three years now, and we've had both business and personal dealings. One of the things I've always respected about him is just how much of a cold fucker he is, down to the bone. Hearing that he'd shacked up with an American forensic psychologist last year was very surprising, and receiving the invite to their wedding over the summer was shocking. I already knew about Kira because Sergei had commissioned me to create sculptures for their new home. I was rather disappointed to miss their wedding because of a scheduling conflict. I made them another sculpture to go along with the first as a present, mainly because Sergei is not the type of man it's wise to offend.

"I'm sure you're not calling to just discuss art," I say.

Sergei responds, "Correct. I'm calling because my wife has taken the liberty of putting together a potential profile on your killer. I had a few sources at the local PD's send over the coronary reports and files on the deceased women to help her; my Kira has been rather consumed by her project in the last day. I suspect she misses forensic work more than she realized."

I let out a snort. "Being the queen of the criminal underworld isn't enough to suit her forensic needs?"

Sergei chuckles. "She's on the exact opposite side of the law from what she's used to. In our world, men like your killer are hunted and tortured to death to make a statement that'll deter any potential copycats. In your world, you have to rely on subpar justice systems to catch and put down the rabid dogs, which gives them far more room to roam free."

Fair point. That's precisely why I, much like Sergei, prefer to do my work in the shadows. If I can find him, I'll kill whoever's been terrorizing Greywood campus and living in Elia's head rent-free before he can cause any more problems, or bodies.

"This is certainly a riveting premise for a morality debate," I say flatly. "Who's in the right? The mob boss who uses his methods to effectively cleanse the world of heinous people, while selling military-grade weapons on the black market, or the police force that relies on the letter of the law to get their work done, often at the pace of molasses? Effectiveness versus legality."

Sergei chuckles. "You should engage Kira in that debate; she took the state championship in her college debate days."

"Which must've been when she was something like fifteen, considering her accomplishments at twenty-five."

"Fourteen, actually," Sergei corrects. "She finished undergrad by the time she was sixteen. Anyway, I'll send you over all the information I have along with Kira's conclusions. Hopefully it'll help."

The pride in his voice as he speaks of his wife doesn't cease to surprise me. For the years I knew him before Kira, I was confident that Sergei, like me, did not have time or energy for women outside of when it came to satisfying a few basic needs. Then a witty American came along and managed to fundamentally change him.

It dawns on me that Sergei might not be a bad person to converse with about my growing fixation on Eliana. He fell in love, and by all appearances that's only made him stronger.

I ask him, "When did you know that Kira was the one for you?"

Sergei responds instantly, "From day one. I knew I wanted her from the moment I laid eyes on her, and it only took a single conversation—during which I was wearing a jumpsuit, handcuffed to a table—for my obsession to unfold. It's only grown in strength since."

I knew from the first time I saw Eliana, dancing her heart out on stage, that she was my muse. It wasn't until we'd spoken in the museum that I actually saw her as not just a muse, but a person I was *fascinated* by. The difference between me and Sergei is that he only had Kira's drawbacks to compete with, while I have both Eliana's wariness and Carson to handle on my journey to make her mine. I also understand that if I want to keep her, that might entail sharing her.

"How far would you go to keep Kira?" I ask him.

Again, without delay, he says, "Any length. I'd move mountains, spill rivers of blood, bend the very threads of fate to my whim in order to have her." After a pause, he goes on, "I'm assuming you're asking because you're having some similar sentiments towards the dancer you had on your arm last night?"

I grunt an affirmative. "It's complicated, though."

"How so?" Sergei questions.

I sigh, putting down my paintbrush on the table and trading it for a cigarette. Once I've lit up, I respond, "She's not like me—not entirely, anyways. She has darkness in her, but she's much more than that darkness. You and Kira are a perfect match from what I've seen and heard; you complete each other. Elia completes me, but I don't think I could ever complete her. Parts of her, maybe, but not all of her. She's too complex for that."

"Ah," Sergei says. "So, there's competition for her hand and heart. You could always kill the competition—it's what I do in business."

As much as the thought once tempted me... "I can't in this scenario. The competition happens to be my closest—" not to mention *only* "—friend. To add to things, he completes the parts of her I can't."

I suck in the smoke from my cigarette, taking a long drag and hoping the nicotine will somehow clear my thoughts and calm my sense of restlessness. It doesn't; in my entire life, the only thing that could calm my restlessness was art. Now, I've found that Eliana has an even greater effect when it comes to centering me.

It infuriates part of me that Carson offers her what I'm unable to, and yet it makes perfect sense. Elia's a multi-faceted creature, something I understood the first time I talked to her. She's a blend of dark and light, of depth so intense it could rival Mariana's Trench and lightness that makes her float into the atmosphere. I can see that neither darkness nor light could satisfy her, only the right mixture of both. That brings me to the startling realization that it's very possible, even probable, that I'll always crave her more than she craves me. I'll need her more than she'll need me.

"A complicated situation, indeed," Sergei agrees mildly. "What do you intend to do about it?"

That, I don't know yet. I ask, "Would you ever share Kira with anyone?"

Sergei barks out a laugh. "Abso*lutely* not. Never. She's mine." After a pause, he goes on, "But that is because we are a perfect fit; two puzzle pieces that almost seem like they were specifically engineered to click together."

Whereas I'm a puzzle piece that only clicks on one side of Elia. She needs another to fit the other side and complete the picture.

"What if that weren't the case? What if Kira needed another to fully complete her?"

"She wouldn't, and I don't work with hypothetical situations," Sergei says bluntly. "Your situation is markedly different than mine. If what you need to keep your woman is to share her with another, then find a way to make peace with it and figure it out. In many cases I put Kira's needs above mine, because meeting them is precisely what meets mine. If you feel the same way, then do whatever it takes."

"Even if it means not being the only man in her life?" I grumble.

"Even then," Sergei confirms. "Besides, polyamory might still be taboo, but it's far from unheard of, especially in the upper circles of society."

"The upper circles of society are precisely where most of the dirty shit goes down. People who are above the law and social norms are exactly those who don't indulge in either. They're just skilled with keeping things behind closed doors." Most of the time. Even when they don't, they have plenty of money to throw at problems to get them to disappear; something I learned from my father.

"You already know what you need to do," Sergei senses. "It sounds as though she's the one for you, Seth. If that's the case, then do what it takes to keep her. One thing love has taught me is the power of giving, how fulfilling it can be. Give her what she needs so that she can continue to give you what you need."

In other words, get to work figuring out the technicality of how a fucking three-way relationship will work, get Carson on board, and then somehow get Elia on board. She might not know it or understand it, but she does need both of us. I don't believe a single man could handle her, with all of her facets and nuances; something that digs at my pride to admit. However, if setting aside my pride is what it takes to have her, then I'll do it.

My eyes return to the painting again, and I feel like I'm looking at it in a new light. I see what it's missing; more, I see that if I want to make it properly, I'm going to have to start from scratch, and I'll need both my Venus and Mars to pose for it.

"Thank you for the call, and please thank your wife for her work," I tell Sergei. "How will she be sending the information?"

He makes a dismissive noise. "I'll email it to you within the hour and pass on your thanks, though it isn't a bother. I see a great deal of myself in you, Seth. If you do ever have interest in stepping further into the underworld, you know where to find me." With that, he hangs up, and I get to work.

CHAPTER THIRTY-NINE

Elia

After we finish up our hike and come down the mountain, Carson declares that he's not ready to release me from our day-date until he's fed me. We make our way back to M's diner, where Miranda hustles us to the same table we sat at last time and takes our orders herself.

Once she's gone, I sigh. "Two burgers in a single year. If my mom were here, she'd probably have a stroke."

As soon as the words are out, I wince, knowing that they open a door to questions in a way I'd usually avoid.

Carson says, "Each time you've mentioned her it's always been with such disdain. Do you ever miss her?"

"Do you miss your father when he's away?" I question in turn.

Carson's lips twitch, and I watch as he unzips his forest-green sweater, revealing the tight white shirt beneath. "No, but he's alive.

I know I'll see him again, though admittedly at times I wish I wouldn't."

"My mom was a bad person all around," I say solemnly. "I don't miss her at all."

Carson's leg nudges mine under the table. "I told you about my daddy problems. Let's hear about your parental grievances."

I thought the prospect of talking about my mom two times in less than a day would make me clam up, but it doesn't. Instead, it's almost like the topic is easier to broach because I already unburdened a lot of myself to Seth last night. Surprisingly, that doesn't feel as ill-advised and dangerous as I thought it would; instead, I feel a little lighter, as if letting people in isn't a vulnerability, but a way to shed weight.

"My mom never grew out of being a petty adolescent," I say. "Living with her was like living with a teenager; attention-seeking and dramatic all the time. She had no positive decision-making skills and would bring around boyfriends of bad varieties. She also had a serious eating disorder in her youth, which made her very restrictive with *my* food habits as well as her own. There were times where she wouldn't feed me for a day or two, saying that fasting is good for the figure, and then I'd end up in Urgent Care after collapsing."

Carson's expression slowly morphs into one of anger as I talk. He asks, "Nobody took you away from her? That's neglect at its finest. No, worse, it's outright abuse."

I shake my head. "She always cleaned her act up when people started asking questions, at least for as long as it took before they moved onto the next case. She never hit me—though a few of her boyfriends did—so there wasn't anything solid that would make the state intervene permanently. I did get taken away from her twice, though, when her neurosis got so bad she'd lose whatever job she was working or have a public episode. She fought like hell to get me back both times. She treated me like she despised me, and at the same time, she wouldn't let go of me."

Carson winces. "Sounds like she was a seriously disturbed individual."

I say, "Please don't pity me. Surviving her made me who I am today."

Carson reaches across the table to take my hand. "I'm not pitying you. I'm *admiring* you. There's a difference, Little E."

My breath hitches as he brushes his thumb back and forth over my knuckles, his touch feather-light and yet somehow soothing. He's silently acknowledging that I'm not alone in my shit, that he's here with me, and the moment feels even more intimate than when we were having sex. I feel like he sees me, *really* sees me, all the more so because he has a neglectful parent, too.

"I was jealous earlier," I blurt, then have to fight the urge to slap my hand over my mouth.

Carson's eyebrows lift and faint amusement crosses his expression. "Of what? I know being rich and having a famous dad doesn't impress you. What do I have that you want? What is there to be jealous about?"

I shrug, sucking in a breath to shore myself up. I already blurted out my feelings, time to explain them. I don't mind being honest with Carson, especially after the day we've spent together. I went from borderline hysterical to enjoying a winter wonderland picturesque hike to getting fed. Still, I'm unused to talking about myself unless it's regarding art or dance.

"Your relationship with your mom," I say. "She sounds so lovely. Pretty much like exactly what I wished *my* mom would be, when I was still young enough to indulge in wishes. I always wanted a pet, some company that didn't yell at me randomly or ignore me when it was mad, but never got it—when I brought a stray kitten into the house, my mom shrieked and had her boyfriend at the time threaten to kill it. So, earlier, I was jealous of you."

I try to withdraw my hand from his, feeling icky for my admission and for experiencing something petty like jealousy when I'm happy that Carson has at least one stable parental figure. He's a great guy, and a big part of that is probably due to his mother, so I shouldn't be envious. Carson's fingers tighten around my hand, not enough to hurt but enough to let me know he doesn't want to let go.

"Considering your mother, I think a touch of jealousy is warranted. I wish I could rewind time and bippity-boppity-boop you a new, better mom, but then again, I don't think you'd be the same person, and I can't be sure if I'd ever meet you. I'm *really* glad I've met you. As for *my* mom, well... I'd like to introduce you to her," Carson says. "I think you two would get along. She's actually the reason Dad donates to the arts as much as he does—aside from the tax write off. She also has a charity she built ground-up that houses stray dogs and cats and finds them new homes." He smiles fondly, and his eyes glimmer as he speaks about her.

This time, jealousy doesn't overcome me—I'm far too focused on the casual bomb he just dropped about me meeting his mother. I'm not against it conceptually, but that feels like something big. Especially when we aren't actually dating, since that would mean I'm dating two guys at once. Which I'm *not*, at least not intentionally.

I clear my throat, pulling my hand from his. "You, uh, want me to *meet your mother?*"

Carson grins. "Yeah, Princess. She'd like you a lot."

"But we're not even dating," I point out dumbly. "I mean, not really. You're still in a match with Seth for my hand, and in case I haven't made it clear, I'm not going to choose one of you. You're both too good to choose between."

Carson's smile falls, replaced with a serious expression that makes my heart beat faster. Is Carson about to give me the ultimatum? I've been expecting it since I found out there was a competition for my affection, the moment when Carson flat out tells me that I need to either choose him or reject him. A sinking feeling settles in my chest and then my gut, like the falling sensation I experienced when I went bungee jumping with an old dance company.

"I don't care, Little E," he says. "This isn't about the competition for me, it's about exploring what I could have with you, which I'm *really* enjoying so far. We'll figure out the difficult shit as we go along, but for now, I like just being with you. Spending time with you makes me happy. So, I really don't give a shit if this is non-exclusive, especially since I know the other party here and have seen his clean STD tests. This situation doesn't make much sense, but it feels good enough that I don't want it to make sense as long as it continues on."

I swallow hard, feeling completely disarmed. My ammunition against Carson is mainly *I can't commit both because of my schedule and because I'm not good at choosing*, which he consistently takes away. The shields I had up because of what I assumed him to be—a shallow trust fund brat—are all but demolished, which leaves me feeling vulnerable. Vulnerable to how much it'll hurt when the other shoe drops, when I understand it's time for me to walk away.

And yet, that isn't enough to make me want to walk away, because this doesn't just feel good for Carson, it feels amazing for me, as well. I don't want to lose the feeling I get when I'm with him.

In a failed attempt to lighten the mood, I quip, "You're pretty casual for talking about Seth that way, implying that we've... or that we will..."

"Fuck?" Carson supplies, making me wince. He laughs at my expression of alarm. "I knew what I was getting myself into. Well, correction, I didn't know how much I'd end up liking you, but I did understand the underlying assumption that I'd be vying for your body as much as your heart."

"How can you be okay with it?" I blurt.

Carson tilts his head to the side, contemplating. "Honestly, it's probably because of who the other person is. Seth. I don't know why, but the idea of you with him repels me much less than the idea of you with anyone else. Which, by the way, is off the table—you're not sleeping with anyone else, are you?"

I could point out the fact that I'm free to sleep with as many people as I want, but I don't ruin the moment by doing that. Instead, I shake my head. "No, I wouldn't even have time for you if you hadn't wormed your way into my life."

Carson nods. "Good. It goes without saying that I haven't fucked anyone since laying eyes on you, too."

I raise my eyebrows. "Does it go without saying? I sort of figured you wouldn't be sleeping around with your relentless pursuit, but that doesn't feel like something to take for granted with you. You know, considering your reputation."

Carson takes my hand in his again. "You were right earlier. Sex was just a convenient and fun way to avoid my feelings, my fears. An excellent pastime, and one I'm quite skilled with, as you can attest." Ignoring my eyeroll, he goes on, "Keeping things light and purely physical is a great way to avoid the pain that inevitably occurs when someone leaves. The thing with you, Little E, is that I think I'd be okay with the pain that would come if you leave, because I'd still have these memories with you to hold onto. That's why I want to eat up all of your time for as long as I can, though I think I'd prefer forever."

Okay, he *really* needs to stop saying things like that if I'm going to survive this at least semi intact.

"You're an asshole," I croak, blinking rapidly to stave off a flood of incoming tears.

I'm not used to having something even half as sweet and thoughtful as that said to me, so hearing it is almost too much. Carson admitting that he'd put himself through heartache if it meant having spent time with me is almost too sweet to bear. I'm torn between the dualistic urge to slap him for making me cry and tear his clothes off so I can screw his brains out.

"And you're starting to fall for me," Carson shoots back with a grin.

Goddamn it, I just might be.

CHAPTER FORTY

Carson

I've fucked a lot of women. Elia's brought up my reputation in passing a couple of times, and I can't honestly say I'm surprised she's heard about my conquests. Most people have—certainly anyone on campus who doesn't live under a rock. Sex is an excellent way to forget whatever worries are weighing on me at the time; my dad being such an absolute douchebag sometimes I think he's a lizard wearing human skin, concern over my mom, fear that my future will turn me into a lizard-monster like my father.

Getting lost in pussy is—*was*—a great way to forget the harsh realities of the world. As long as it came with no strings, no expectations, and no bullshit, it was the perfect escape. Now, though, I find that everything—all of my rules and expectations—have been dropped on their head and remade. Because I'm a thousand percent certain that the only girl who I'll ever want to get lost in again is a petite dancer with sadness in her eyes and a quiet strength that makes her a whole fuck of a lot tougher than most of the people I've had to face off with.

After I finish feeding Little E and slowly worming my way through her steel armor and into her pretty little head—and hopefully heart—I'm not ready to part ways with her. So, I entice her to come to my off-campus apartment and meet Caesar. For the sake of keeping at least some of my masculinity intact, I tell very few people about my cat's full name.

"You live in the same apartment building as Seth?" Elia asks once I've parked the car and ushered her into the elevator, her voice coated with equal parts curiosity and wariness.

I nod. "Sure do, Princess. It's the best building in the city, close to campus, with an excellent view. Mine has a balcony, too, which I think you'll enjoy." I don't mention the fact that my idea of a perfect end to a perfect day would be eating her out on the lounger I have on my balcony, because I've found that Elia is a bit modest, and I don't want to push her too far too fast. I wouldn't expect a girl like her to be so demure, as she oozes sexuality, but I don't think she realizes it.

I also don't mention that I still have every intention of convincing her to move in with me. I know it's too far too fast and our whole situation on its own is complicated as fuck, especially with Seth still being locked onto her like a missile's target system. Above everything—even my desire for her—is a need to keep her safe. It's why I've been torturing myself by staying in the dorms for her ass, because the ID card scanners admin installed wouldn't be enough to deter a seasoned killer.

"I'm here to meet Mewlius, just so you know," Elia says hastily.

I barely contain a snort. "Sure you are, Princess. Just for the cat. I think we both share a fondness for pussies."

She sniffs in a prim way that makes all the blood in my body rush south. "You're incorrigible."

I tug a piece of her hair, like a goddamn school boy. It's a bit too tame for me, and for the thoughts currently running through my mind, so I tangle a hand in her hair, wrapping it around my fist and using it to tug her head back. "And you're not here to pet my cat, you're here to get fucked."

I wouldn't be so forward if I hadn't spent the car ride from the diner to this building teasing Elia with a hand on her thigh, inching it higher with each minute that passed until she was squirming and panting, trying to edge it closer to her center.

Elia's pupils dilate as she sucks in a breath, her eyes dropping to my mouth. I let my eyes wander down to her red-tinted lips, which are plump and full and practically begging to get bitten. Just as the thought passes through my mind, I notice a faint indent on her lower lip, which looks kind of like teeth marks.

Fucking Seth had to mark his territory. I know I'm going to need to figure out what to do about him, where to go from here. I wasn't lying when I told Elia in the diner that I really don't mind the thought of her with Seth as much as I thought I would, though the evidence of his possessiveness on her lip grates at me from a purely competitive standpoint. The few times I've really let my mind wander to the potential of Elia having sex with Seth, I've felt faint stirrings of jealousy but nothing near as intense as when I picture one of the drooling boys in her dance company making a move on her.

With them, I'm ready to commit murder each time I catch one staring at her longingly, but with Seth... I think I just might be able to restrain myself. Mainly because I see that Elia's already starting to care for him, and I don't want to hurt her. Seeing her tears this morning made me feel like something was clawing at my chest, bringing forward some deep, hidden instinct that hadn't reared its head until she came along—the instinct to fix whatever was wrong.

I lean down to claim Elia's lips and leave some of my own marks but am interrupted by the ding of the elevator as it comes to a stop and the doors slide open. Elia glances at the hallway. "At least you're not on the same floor as Seth."

"Why, afraid we'd run into each other?" I ask, tipping her a wink. "I wouldn't mind if he watched."

She arches an imperious eyebrow. "Watched me hang out with Mewlius? Learn how to be a cuddling master from the venerated teacher?"

I pull my bottom lip between my teeth as I stare at her, some strange warmth in my chest making me feel kind of like I'm floating on a cloud. Despite the weight in her eyes, she's so bright. Not just in her intelligence or beauty, but her entire being feels like a ray of sun peeking through the clouds after a terrible storm, lonely yet undaunted. She feels like hope, like warmth, like brightness.

"Watch me fuck you until you're too tired to go back to dorms," I say as I unlock my apartment door and let her in.

My apartment's bigger than Seth's—a point of pride for me—though it's not as technologically advanced. The fuckhead actually created a system he wired into his apartment for all the automatic shit, while the rest of the tenants are stuck with good old fashioned light switches.

I flick on the lights on the wall next to the door, illuminating my apartment. Elia's eyes curiously flit over the entryway and then to my large living room, which has a study nook in the corner with a desk and laptop, along with a sweet furniture set in front of a flatscreen TV. She takes in every shelf, decoration, nook, and cranny, but her eyes really light up when Caesar jumps off of his cat tree in the corner and regally pads over to us.

He's a good-looking little dude, with soot-grey fur, forest-green eyes, and the usual air of *fuck you very much* that all feline creatures possess. I squat down and open my arms, ready to cuddle my way back into his good graces even though I haven't seen him since yesterday when I checked his food, water, and gave him some attention while Elia was out. Instead of coming to me, though, the fucker stops in front of Elia, who kneels in front of him with a wide smile on her face.

She holds out her hand for Caesar to scent. I actually hold my breath, because my man is not the friendliest around strangers—best case scenario he ignores them, worst case scenario he attacks. That's only happened once, though, when Seth threatened me in front of him.

Caesar ducks his head down and nuzzles her hand, purring so loudly the rumbly noise travels through my apartment. I feel my mouth gape slightly; I thought I'd have to coax my furry guy into relaxing around Elia, but instead, the fucker is standing on his hind legs so he can put his front paws on her shoulders and lick her cheek.

She gathers him into her arms and cradles him like a baby, standing and holding him close.

"What the *fuck*," I breathe. "Caesar, you're a goddamn traitor."

"You call him Caesar, hmm?" Elia asks, before murmuring to my cat, "If Brutus went up against you, he'd have fallen on his own knife from how adorable you are." The voice she uses is a cooing baby-voice that makes my cat purr even louder.

Elia wanders into my living room, glancing around the white walls and chestnut flooring. "Cozy. A lot of plants, which I didn't expect from you."

I scratch the back of my neck. "Yeah, most of the decorations are my mom's doing. She was here when I moved in, did all my shopping with me. We ended up stopping by a plant store and she wanted to clear the place out. Settling for a handful was the most I could talk her down."

Eliana walks over to the side table where there's a growing lamp and my... *oh, shit,* I forgot about my pot plant. It's in a glass case not unlike an aquarium, with growing lights above it and a humidity/temperature controller remote on the front panel.

"That's, um..." I trail off trying to come up with an excuse, except I don't have one. What can I say? 'I've never seen that before, officer,' probably wouldn't go over any better than trying to use that excuse on an actual cop. Although I wouldn't mind breaking out some hand-cuffs with Little E, I don't think outright lies will get us anywhere.

"A marijuana plant?" Elia questions, laughter in her voice as she looks over it. "I assume your mom didn't get you this," she tacks on dryly.

I wince. "Yeah, no, she didn't. I have no excuse other than a bad experience with a laced joint when I was in high school. Now I home-grow my shit."

Elia turns around to look at me, and I relax by an approximate fuck-ton when an easy smile pulls on her lips. "Clever. Has it yielded any good harvests?"

Once again, my jaw drops. I expected condemnation from Elia, who I assumed would be strongly anti-weed and alcohol and any form of fun. Instead, she's asking me if I've gotten some good bud from my plant.

I say, "Uh, yeah. I've had it since I came to Greywood. The first har-vest was shit, but I've learned with time. My mom's big on gardening along with animals, so I knew some useful tips."

Elia laughs lightly, eyes sparkling. "I'm sure she wouldn't be happy to know where you're putting those gardening skills to use."

"You're not..." I wave between the plant and myself. "Mad? Worried that I'm a fuckup?"

Elia rolls her eyes with a sigh, still petting Caesar. "It's the twenty first century, Carson. Weed is legal in most states, and even growing it is legal in some states, including this one if I remember correctly. It's not like I've never smoked a joint or had an edible."

I tilt my head to the side, trying to mask my shock. "But you're a dancer."

She nods. "And my body is a temple that I take very careful care of. I rarely drink, I don't smoke cigarettes or vape, I monitor my caffeine intake, but on occasion—no more than once every month or two even during senior year—I'll smoke a joint. Why do you look so surprised?"

"Because you're so perfect," I say. "I expected that you'd be disgusted by..."

"Being a young adult?" Elia asks. "Not in the least. I'd never smoke if I had anything dance wise that day or the next, but sometimes weed helps me chill out. Believe it or not, I need that on occasion."

I feel a grin tug at my lips as I walk up to her, reaching out to pet Caesar as an excuse for eating up all the space between us. That's the thing with Elia; I don't want there to be any space separating us. The more I get to know her, the more desperate I am to keep her. I want all her minutes, all her moments, all her thoughts, because she sure as shit is on my mind just about every minute of every day. She's infected me like a terminal disease, and I'd die a happy death if she were the cause, if it meant I could stay with her forever.

Elia blinks up at me, a blush crawling up her neck to stain her cheeks. Her eyes move from mine to my lips, and it is *so fucking on.*

I'm ready to lean down and devour her when she steps back and says, "Show me your balcony."

On the back wall there's a sliding glass door that leads out to a small balcony with a grill and lounger. I wanted to get a jacuzzi for it, too, but state regulations prevented me from that particular brand of awesome. I mean, who wouldn't want a jacuzzi with a prime city view?

I reluctantly part from Elia to open the door to the balcony, letting in a cool breeze that ruffles Caesar's fur and makes him meow in protest.

"You'll have to leave my little dude inside," I tell Elia. I watch as she presses several kisses to his fur and murmurs to him about being the handsomest kitty in the world, before finally setting him down. As soon as she does he starts rubbing against her legs, winding in and out of them and meowing for her attention.

Elia says, "I'll be back to cuddling you in no time, Mewlius." Then, she lifts her gaze and smiles at me. "Okay, I think I can see where you got your pro-cuddling skills. That one is just the sweetest."

She walks over to me, followed closely by my cat who's trailing at her heels and whining for her attention, not unlike me these last weeks. She steps out onto the balcony. I follow her, sliding the door closed before Caesar can join us and catch a chill or try to jump off again. She looks around the space, eyes settling on the grill before walking to the railing and letting out a sigh of contentment.

I park my ass right next to hers as she leans her elbows on the railing and looks out into the beautiful evening. The sun is setting, casting rays of maroon and red and gold that bounce off her skin, making her look like my personal angel.

"You always surprise me," she says faintly, casting a quick glance at me before returning her gaze to the sunset.

"Oh?" I say. "How so?"

I already know the answer, at least some of it. Eliana looked at me, my clothes, my watch, and dubbed me as a brainless trust fund kid the moment we first met, which makes me wonder if she hasn't run into the worst of my kind in her past. She did mention something about a shitty ex this morning, but I figured it wasn't the time to press. She's done her level best to avoid me while I've done my level best to show her that there's more to me than the numbers in my bank account.

"You're just very unexpected. From what I've observed, rich people have a certain entitlement. They expect the world to land at their feet and get angry and violent when it doesn't. You on the other hand, know how to work for what you want. You *do* work for what you want. You have this big, sensitive heart under all the privilege, and I think you're a genuinely good person. You drive a Tesla luxury car, but also have a cat you rescued. You have a reputation on campus as someone who goes through women like water with little respect or regard, yet I've never felt more cherished or appreciated than when I'm with you."

"I'd like to cherish and appreciate you some more, now," I tell her. "Are you gonna let me?"

She slowly turns her head to face me, this time not for a brief glance but for a good, long look into my eyes. I feel like her grey orbs are penetrating through my skin and searching my soul for something, and I let her see everything. The longing, the affection, the fact that I'm so far gone for her that I don't know if turning back is even in the realm of possibility.

She looks back out to the scenery, appearing like she's searching for something, eyes squinting as they run over the neighboring buildings. Then she pushes off the balcony rail and lifts her shirt over her head, leaving her clad only in a lacey blue bra. I realize she was assessing if anyone would be able to see her if she gets naked here; they won't, my building is tallest in proximity and the few other balconies are empty. I have her all to myself.

Chapter Forty-One

Carson

My breath gets caught in my throat as I look over the expanse of flawless, creamy skin she's offering me. I take my time gazing at her slender, elegant neck, her collarbones, the gentle swell of her breasts, the tiny circumference of her waist and tautness of her stomach with the faint outline of abs. I imagine running my tongue over every inch of her, kissing and sucking and savoring her the way I'm desperate to do.

"Well?" Elia says, almost tauntingly. "Are you just going to stare or are we getting to the fun part?"

Oh, it is *so* on. My hands are clasping her waist before she can blink, hauling her to me and lifting her up. She wraps her legs around my hips and arms around my neck, giggling as I walk her the three feet over to my lounger, which is plenty comfortable and perfect for all the ways I intend to consume her for as long as I possibly can. If I could I'd spend an eternity balls-deep inside this slice of heaven, but she'll tire eventually and I want to get the most I can from her before that point.

I lay her down on the soft cushion, then say, "Lift your hips, Little E. I want to see what color your panties are, if they're as pretty as your bra."

She bats her eyelashes at me and plants her feet, lifting her hips. I slide her pants off her legs, tossing them in the same direction as her shirt, and then spend several moments just staring at her. Her panties match her bra, made of a teal blue material with lace detailing that just about drives me out of my mind. Not because I care all that much about lingerie, but because the color coordination means that she expected our day to end like this and actually dressed up for me.

"I'm going to eat you up, Princess," I tell her, hooking my thumb under the waistband of her panties and ripping one side in my haste to get them off her. Her bra is next, though I'm careful not to rip it.

Then she's laid out in front of me, entirely naked, with stiff nipples and a glistening pussy that makes me lose what faint hold I have on my sanity. She looks like a sacrifice for a hungry god, like an unwrapped present begging to be played with. I want to destroy her pussy as much as I want to cherish her, and the dual urges of the animalistic side of me that wants to fuck and take and the gentler side of me that wants to treat her like a delicate glass figurine heightens my stimulation until my cock starts to pulse painfully.

Elia's eyes drop to the tent in my pants, and she bites her bottom lip. "You, uh, look like you could use some help with that," she says.

I shake my head. "Not yet." Not until I've tasted every inch of her and made her scream so loud it can be heard around the entire city.

I spread her legs with my hands on her thighs, then kneel between them, eyeing the soft blonde curls dusting her pussy in a V-shape on her mound. Everywhere else, she's smooth and bare, which is new. Last time she was neatly trimmed, now it looks like she took a trip to a local salon.

"I got a partial Brazilian a few days ago," she says hesitantly. "The esthetician's department have students who give them for free as part of a practice course."

"You waxed for me?" I say, surprised. "Or for Seth?"

She doesn't respond, pursing her lips. Looks like my girl needs to loosen up a bit—something I'm happy to help her with. I slide one of my palms higher on her thigh, then boldly cup her pussy, grinding the heel of my palm on her clit while nudging her entrance with a finger. She's already *soaking* wet, which makes me draw in a sharp breath.

"Answer me, Little E," I say, my voice a growl. "Who did you do that for?"

She bites her lip, squeezing her eyes shut to avoid responding. I rub my palm over her sensitive nub, trying to get her to loosen up.

After a few moments, it works. "Both of you," she moans. "God, it's so fucked up, but both of you."

I don't love that answer, but I also don't hate it. I'd prefer for Little E to be mine, to only think of me when she does something like get waxed, but... well, I've shared girls with Seth before. I'll be the first to admit, those times were a *lot* of fun. Maybe it wouldn't be the worst idea in the world to share the beautiful creature beneath me. If that's what she's into, I think I'd be into it too. I'm pretty sure I'd be down for anything that she wants, because watching her enjoyment, seeing her pleasure brings *me* pleasure that transcends physical sensation.

I slide a finger deep inside her, watching as the rise and fall of her chest speeds up. "Both of us, hmm?"

She nods emphatically. "Yes. I'm sorry."

I curl the finger inside her, moving my hand so I can search for her G-spot. "Don't apologize, Little E. Never for your desires, not with me." A childlike curiosity overcomes me, mixing with my darker desires and creating the perfect storm of sexual chaos. "I've shared girls with Seth before. They were in for quite the ride." That's an understatement. Seth is an intense motherfucker, in bed and outside of it. He's also suitably sadistic, with pain being his main trade, leaving the pleasuring part to me. I can't imagine what he's like when he fucks solo, but I can imagine he does not give a single fuck about anyone's enjoyment or amusement outside of his own. And the shit that amuses him is generally as dark as his soul.

Elia's pussy clenches tight around my fingers, making my eyebrows raise. Looks like she does, in fact, like the idea, or at least is turned on by it. "Would you like that?" I ask her.

She shakes her head so quickly, I *know* she's lying. Right now, I can tell she's up against her own inhibitions and the taboo of a threesome, which is a lot, especially in our complicated circumstances. I intend to push her past that and get to the truth of the matter, and right now I have the perfect way. Her pussy will be an excellent barometer.

"You sure?" I taunt her, adding a second finger inside her and bringing my thumb up to trap her clit. I don't rub circles or add any stimulation, just keep her sensitive bud pinned down with steady pressure. She bucks her hips, seeking more, which makes me chuckle.

"You don't want to know what it's like having us both playing with you? Pleasuring you? Bringing you to new heights?" Her pussy squeezes so hard around my fingers that it almost hurts, drawing a hiss from me. Oh yeah, Little E's definitely down with that idea.

"He's a lot rougher than I am," I tell her. "He likes to destroy his toys, though I don't think he'd want to destroy you. Wreck your pussy, maybe, but not the rest of you. He's a man obsessed. Then again, so am I."

"Oh my *goddd*," Elia moans out as I start moving my fingers in and out of her, arching her back.

Aaaand that's about all I can take without losing my mind. I pull my fingers out of her, ignoring her whimper of disappointment, and then lean down and latch onto her pussy. I need to taste her; the last time I did got me hooked, now I think I'll need regular hits, preferably several times a day, to keep myself sane. She's a drug I don't want to drop, one I'm happy being addicted to.

Her taste, slightly tangy and sweet, fills my mouth, dances over my tastebuds and turns me into a feral fucking beast. I feast on her pussy, alternating between sucking her clit and thrusting my tongue into her channel, getting as much of her taste as I can, gorging myself on her. When her legs start to shake I slide three fingers inside of her, hooking them upwards at the same time that I suck her clit into my mouth, running my tongue over it. With my free hand, I reach up to find her breast and twist her nipple between my fingers, which is all it takes to set her off. She comes with a loud cry of pleasure, her entire body shaking and trembling, her channel squeezing my fingers so hard they might break right off. If that means they get to stay inside her forever, though, I don't think I'd mind.

"What are you *doing to me*," she breathes out, her eyes glazed and entire body flushed. I like how, when she comes, her blush moves from her neck and cheeks to stain her tits, even her stomach. It's like she comes alive beneath my touch, which is exactly what I want. It's something I'm beginning to crave.

"Tasting you. Fucking you. Ideally, getting you as hooked on me as I am on you," I murmur, kissing my way up her toned body and to her tits. I prop myself up on my elbows on either side of her, then fill my hands with her petal-soft breasts. They fit perfectly in my palms, and I'm struck by the realization that *everything* about this girl is perfect to me. I take my time with her tits, licking a path all the way around them, leaving bite marks on them, sucking her nipple deep into my mouth and trying to get as much of her as I can. All the while, she moans and writhes and begs me to keep going.

Once I part with her breasts, a little reluctantly, I take her mouth—conquer it, really. I'm not in the mood for my usual, sensual, soft routine, I want to goddamn consume her and I'm going to, for as long as she'll let me. If I play my cards right, she won't stop letting me.

"Take off your shirt," she breathes, breaking our kiss.

I feel my lips curve. "Anything for you, Princess."

It takes a millisecond for me to shuck my top, and then I get to work on my pants and briefs, until I'm kneeling between her thighs, naked as the day I was born. Her eyes travel a languid path over my body, followed by her hands. She sits up to touch me everywhere, on my abs, my shoulders, my thighs, my ass, her fingers light and teasing. Then she boldly wraps her hand around my cock, drawing a hiss from me and making my balls tingle.

I'm already prepared to blow like a goddamn rocket, and her small, soft hands are not helping the matter. She starts jerking me off; I only let her get a few pumps in before I lift her by the waist, making her squeal, and plant her right on my lap. Her legs bracket my hips, her *soaking* pussy rubs against my cock, and it's an honest to god struggle not to come right here and now, before I'm even inside of her. I can *feel* the heat of her pussy like a furnace, tantalizing and taunting me.

Her fingers curve into my shoulder blades as I position her so that I'm nudging at her entrance, the crown of my dick getting teased by sheer heaven. Before I can move or start sliding her down on my length, she shocks the hell out of me by slamming herself down on my cock, all in one go, leaving me fully seated inside her. She lets out a cry that's pain mixed with pleasure, nails biting into my skin and head thrown back, while my eyes damn near roll into the back of my head as hot, wet *heaven* encases my dick. Being inside her is always a mind-blowing experience, because nobody has ever fit me so tightly or perfectly—everything about us is right. I flex my hands on her, trying to gain some semblance of control so I don't embarrass myself.

After a moment of shivering, staying still while her body adjusts, she starts to move. Her grey eyes lock on mine as she rides me with so much passion and fervor, I have to grit my teeth and fists to stop from coming prematurely like a fourteen year old. Her pussy squeezes around me so tightly it makes that difficult, scattering my senses until all I can see and feel is her.

I grab her waist, trying to slow and control her movements. "If you don't stop, I'm gonna come," I growl.

She doesn't stop, if anything she *speeds up*, slamming herself down on me repeatedly, her inner muscles clenching me so tight I can't stop a shudder from shooting up my spine. I feel my balls tingle in preparation and let out a low curse.

"Come," she says. "The night's still young."

It's a hit to my reputation, and if Seth knew I blew after five seconds with her like a goddamn novice he'd never let me forget it, but I can't stop myself. My balls tighten, my grip on her becomes steel-like, and I roar as pleasure explodes inside of me, and jet after jet of my come shoots deep inside her. Every bit of me stiffens as I give her a few short, hard thrusts, spilling every drop until I think her pussy might suck out my soul along with my cum. For my entire sexual life I've always been beyond careful to be protected and safe—I even get custom made condoms—but here, with Elia, I can't stand the thought of anything separating us, even a thin layer of latex. *Good thing she's on birth control.*

My orgasm is long and all-consuming, and when I come down from it, my head slumps against Elia's chest. Unable to resist, I pull one of her nipples into my mouth and feel a responding clench of muscles down below.

"Did you…" I pause to catch my breath. "Did you come?" I ask her.

She bites her lip, her eyes sparkling with something that seems far too naughty for my prim and proper girl. "No. This time I wanted to be the one to blow your mind."

"Mission fucking accomplished," I say. "But, for the sake of my pride, I'm gonna need to extract a few more orgasms from you to keep our ratio in check."

Elia laughs, and the noise is like sunlight after a life of darkness, like water after a drought, like hope after years of despair. "What ratio do you have in mind?"

I shrug, laying her down on the cushions and kneeling between her legs, keeping them wrapped around my waist. "I dunno. I think three to one? That sounds like a good goal."

She gasps. "Three to one? Are you crazy? That doesn't sound very realistic *or* fair—"

I cut her off with a kiss. "I promise you I'll make it realistic. My pride wouldn't accept anything else. Now relax and let me get to work."

Chapter Forty-Two

Elia

Several hours later—after round five, or was it seven?—Carson and I sit in his kitchenette area. It's a room to the right of the doorway to his apartment, small with two counters lining the walls, a four-burner stove, and a fridge. He stands at the stove, frying us up an omelet to share. I'm wearing his shirt, seated on the counter beside cutting boards with remnants of bell peppers, onions, and chopped bits of bacon.

"So you can cook," I muse, watching his back muscles ripple as he stands at the stove. "I'd have expected you to have a personal chef or something."

Carson's lips quirk, but he doesn't take his attention off the omelet. "I did have a chef growing up. A couple, actually, as Dad has a habit of firing anyone who Mom likes, but one in particular who taught me. She's a French immigrant, world-class, a goddamn culinary *master*. Dad stole her from one of his competitors after a hostile takeover a few years back, as a final fuck-you to the enemy. Her name's Abigail, she worked for us for about five years. My mom convinced her to give me lessons in cooking starting my junior year of high school, since I was going abroad for the summer. She wanted me to be able to take care of myself."

I lean forward, deeply interested. "What was it like learning from a culinary master?"

He laughs. "Brutal, the first few lessons. She'd yell at me and smack me with wooden spoons and insult my every move. It was irritating as fuck at first, especially to my spoiled ass, but also refreshing. After a few weeks, I stopped being a breathing embarrassment in her kitchen, and a few months in my skills grew to her liking.

"An omelet is something quick to throw together, if you stay over here when you don't have an early morning I'll make you her crepe recipe. I promise it'll result in spontaneous orgasms. If it doesn't, I'll be sure to pick up the slack."

Carson's like an onion; each layer I peel back only reveals another, deeper one below. I find I'm starting to grow pretty interested in what I'll learn about him next. Like I told him earlier, he's just so unexpected.

"Is there anything you aren't good at?" I ask, curiously.

Carson turns off the stove, flips the omelet onto a serving plate, and then expertly slices it up with a few quick strokes of a knife before taking it to the dining table in the corner of the living room. The table's round, just enough to seat four people, and Carson already set placemats and dishes on it while the omelet was frying.

He pulls out my chair for me, takes a seat, and fills both of our glasses from the water jug before serving a large slice of the omelet to both of us and digging in. Between bites, he answers, "I'm not an artsy person. I didn't really get art for a long time—Seth was actually the one who changed that for me. Being his friend came with a crash-course on art and meant getting dragged to museums, so I've begun learning to understand it, but I could never create it. Not like you or him."

I cut into my food thoughtfully, eating quietly and taking my time. I like that he refers to dance as art, as I've met many people who don't. After I've swallowed a bite, I tell Carson, "I couldn't understand art until my preteen years. My mom never took me to museums or anything to try to culture me, but my dance companies would do outings to ballets, operas, museums, and other interesting places regularly, so I'd go with them. It was actually when we did a day trip into New York City to see The MET and also dropped by the Frick Museum that I really grew fascinated with art. I can see it's as impactful, important, and filled with stories as dance, for those who know how to read between the proverbial lines. Once I've saved up enough, probably ten years from now, I want to go on a trip through Europe and go to all the famous museums and historical landmarks."

Carson takes a second, bigger slice of the omelet-pie while remarking, "If you're looking for a travel-buddy, I'd like to put myself forward as a candidate. I can't promise to understand all the cool artsy shit, but I can promise travel on a private plane, many orgasms, excellent lodgings, and good company."

I laugh, a bit awkwardly. My intended trip includes staying at the cheapest hotels and Airbnb's and flying economy on every leg of the journey, which probably doesn't fall in line with the luxury Carson's accustomed to. This is one of those times when I'm reminded just how far on the opposite ends of the wealth spectrum we are.

"I don't think I could afford that," I say, feeling my cheeks heat.

"We can figure out a payment plan," Carson deadpans. "Something along the lines of daily sex. Call it even."

I kick his leg under the table. "That would make me a prostitute."

He makes a face. "Yeah, not the best wording. How about this; I'm pretty sure traveling with you would make everything brighter, more interesting, and make me really happy because you'd be happy. So, don't mention money or worry about it; I have a nine-figure trust fund, and I've done well for myself in the time since I first bought the restaurant I told you about. Which isn't my only source of income. A lot of the time the money comes with a pair of golden handcuffs that I'm not a fan of, Little E. Spending it on you might make it seem at least somewhat worth the hassle."

I'm not sure how to respond to his words, which once again feel like they touch me at my core. I'm starting to realize that people with money aren't free of problems or complications of life, they just have a different, gilded set of difficulties. Carson's making it pretty much impossible to argue with him, but at the same time I don't know what the future holds for us. I like the *now*, but there's no way to be sure what will come after, and I really don't want to think about it today. I just want to enjoy my day away from worries.

"If we're still friends when I go on the trip, I'll consider allowing you to accompany me," I tell Carson, my tone teasing.

Carson blinks slowly. "Considering we'll definitely still be *friends*, I'll start making the plans." The way he emphasizes friends tells me that he knows I'm full of shit and is choosing not to call me on it.

He stands from his seat abruptly and then pulls me from mine, lifting me into his arms and claiming my lips. I hold him tight, letting him kiss me, loving the scent and feel of him and everything about this moment. Carson says, "I'm going to remind you the perks of your *friendship* with me."

***

Too many rounds to count later, I collapse on Carson's bed, too tired to move let alone continue. I called April in between our shower sex and against-the-wall sex to let her know that I wouldn't be back to dorms tonight and to lock her door and stay safe. She told me to have fun getting my brains fucked out of my body, and that she expects every detail when I see her in the morning.

Carson rolls his body sideways, pulling me into the cradle of his arms. At the same time, I feel a small weight leap onto the mattress before soft fur rubs against my leg. I pry my droopy eyes open and glance over my shoulders to find that Mewlius has curled up by my ankles with his cute little head nudging my calves.

Carson mutters, "I think you've kidnapped my cat's affection."

I pull the sheets over our bodies before turning over, leaving my back against his chest. Mewlius takes the opportunity to crawl forward until we're face-to-face, before leaning in to rub his furry cheek against my forehead. I laugh, reaching up with a hand and running my fingers through his soft fur.

Carson says, "Caesar, we're kind of busy right now. Go play on your tree or something." He reaches a hand over me to give the cat a gentle push away from me.

Mewlius hisses at Carson, actually going as far as to swipe a paw out and bat at his arm. Carson lets out an astonished laugh. "Are you kidding me? You're actually going to fight me over her?"

Mewlius responds to that with another hiss, before curling up over the sheet covering my chest and resting his adorable head on my shoulder. His eyes flutter closed, but one cracks open when Carson kisses the back of my shoulder, and he bares a fang at his owner.

"You've gotta be some type of witch, right?" Carson asks me. "I mean, even animals can't resist your charm. Is anyone safe from you? Maybe I should lock you up somewhere and keep you all to myself.

You know, to save countless innocents from falling for you and forming an army."

I chuckle, stroking a hand through Mewlius's fur. "I wouldn't make a very good captive, I'm afraid. If you want to know the truth, I don't try to be charming. I don't try to draw attention to myself, but growing up in dance, I also learned to not resist it. The cards will fall where they will, all I can do is be true to myself. If people like me for that, great, if they don't, I don't need them anyways."

That's an important life lesson I learned, both through my mom and competitive dance. There's no point in trying to shape and mold myself into something I'm not to please others, that's counterproductive. Of course, classical dance is the very art of shaping and molding oneself into the perfect ballerina, the perfect prima, but people who try too hard only set themselves up for failure or end up breaking themselves in the process. I grew up in an environment where my mother made it her mission to try to break me, so I sort of have steel skin when it comes to things like that.

In dance, I listen to instructions, but dance the way I know my body does best—and it works. Outside of dance, I just be myself, and take the hits as they roll in. There's no way to force people to like me, not genuinely, and frankly I don't really want to.

"Tell me something about yourself," Carson says, slipping an arm around my waist and drawing me closer to him. "A secret, deep and dark."

I make a faint humming noise. "That's a big ask."

I feel Carson shrug. "I want to know more about you. Well, in truth, I'd like to know everything there is to know about you and more, but for now I'll settle for one thing. One secret."

That's a bit of a daunting request. I'm not *against* emotional intimacy, per se, but I know that'll muddy the waters between us even more and set me up for a greater heartbreak when it comes time to turn Carson away, because I refuse to hurt him by choosing Seth. Besides, I don't have many great secrets, just painful experiences I keep to myself because talking about them unearths old wounds that are better off left alone.

"What will I get in return?" I ask.

Carson responds, "I'll tell you one of my secrets. Sound fair?"

I nod, albeit a bit hesitantly. Rummaging through my memories, I blurt out the first that comes to mind before I can overthink it. "I have an ex. He was my boyfriend in senior year of high school, and he was not a good guy. He was the definition of a trust fund brat who thought the money in his bank account meant the world should fall at his feet. He asked me out at the start of the year—I think he thought I'd be good for rehabilitating his image with his parents, as he'd spent the previous summer in rehab. I had the best grades in our year and was the school's star dancer, and he was captain of the football team and popular as shit, so the optics were good. I said yes to a date because I didn't really feel like I had the right to turn him down. I didn't like him that much, but I also didn't *dis*like him, and he was nice to me at first, so I let things go on. Then, he became more controlling, and pushy, and just... his privilege peeked through in the ugliest ways." I pause to inhale a deep breath. "Anyways, by the time I knew I wanted out I also knew that he'd run a campaign to ruin my life if I broke up with him, and I didn't have the money or resources to protect myself from that.

"So, I took the path of least resistance, swallowed my pride, and stayed with him. Gritted my teeth every time he touched me and white knuckled my way through it. I knew he'd break up with me at the end of the school year since we were going to colleges in different states; I bided my time and waited. His family was disappointed when we did finally break up, his mom even approached me to ask if I'd be willing to do long-distance with him, but I said I'd be too focused on my studies, which was the truth. I really came to hate him in the time we were together. I think he's one of the few people in my life I've ever truly despised. He used his money as a weapon against anyone weaker than him as well as a conduit to get whatever he wanted, so I came to hate what he represented, too. That's why I wrote you off at the first—I'm only about four months out of my relationship with him, and I was pretty judgy of anyone with enough numbers in their bank account."

Carson's quiet for several minutes after my admission, which makes me a little nervous that I might have overstepped or said too much or erred in some way.

Finally, he says, "I'm sorry you had to deal with that. If you tell me his name, I can ruin his life for you."

A startled burst of laughter escapes me. "I don't think that's necessary. He's in the past, which is where I want to leave him. Now, it's your turn, Ajax. What's you deepest, darkest secret?"

Carson chuckles, and a puff of air tickles the back of my neck, making me shiver. "You'll have to stick around if you want to hear the deepest and darkest, Little E, but I'll give you a secret as promised. When I was seven years old, I came home to hear my dad fucking his secretary in his home office. My mom was right outside the room, tears streaming down her cheeks. He did it on purpose; having an affair right under my mom's nose just to get a reaction out of her. I didn't really understand what was happening at the time, all I could comprehend was my mom's sadness and the sounds of grunting and feminine cries from behind the closed door. She dried her tears and gathered herself when she saw me, then took me out for a hike to get away from the house, but in hindsight I get it. I get how much of a vindictive fucker my dad is to fuck another woman under my mom's nose when he could do it in his actual office, *or* private jet, *or* one of his four homes around this country *or additional five homes around the world*. He chose to do it where my mom lived because he wanted to hurt her for not fitting his mold. I think I started to hate him that day, because I could see even as a child that my father was hurting my mother. That hatred only grew through the years."

Now it's my turn to be silent while processing. I already knew Carson had no love for his father and their relationship was strained at best, but I didn't know that it was *this* bad. His father sounds a lot like my ex, actually, who'd also cheat on me flagrantly just to get a reaction out of me. It didn't work aside from me forcing him to get STD tested on a weekly basis or whenever I heard he'd strayed, which only spurred him into sleeping around even more.

I come to the realization that it isn't wealth that makes people good or bad, it's how they choose to use their resources. A poor man can be as horrible as a rich man, just not as effective with the damage he wreaks. The problem with terrible rich people is that their antics have a lot more reach and power.

"I'm sorry," I murmur.

Carson stiffens, then says, "Don't feel sorry for me, Eliana. I can't handle pity, not from you."

I turn over in his arms, winding mine around his neck and cuddling closer to him, my bare legs getting tangled between his. "I don't pity you at all. When I say I'm sorry, it's not pity, it's empathy—and it's not necessarily empathy for the present version of you, because you turned out fine. I feel for the little boy you once were who got taught all the wrong things in life. It's even worse that your primary positive role model was humiliated and belittled in front of you. I can't fathom how that would've felt, but I assume it wouldn't have been good."

Carson's arms tighten around my waist, and he leans closer to rest his forehead against mine. "It wasn't good. I'm planning a hostile takeover of my dad when it comes time. I want to run him out of his empire with no friends, no support, no allies. Honestly, Little E, I want to make him feel as powerless as he's made Mom over the years."

I stroke the back of his neck with the pads of my fingertips. "Except he didn't make her powerless. He might've tried, but she still got one thing fantastically right: raising you. I can see how deeply she influenced you, that a lot of your good parts stem from her guidance, so I don't think she was powerless at all. In many ways, yes, but not overall. She took the power she had with you and turned it into something beautiful."

Carson brushes his lips against mine. "You think I'm beautiful?"

I nod. "I think you have a beautiful soul beneath all the pomp and glamor. I think you have a depth of character that's unusual for people in your tax bracket." *I think I might be falling in love with you, which is the worst thing I can possibly do because I'm also falling for Seth.* "You also have a smoking hot body. I mean, your abs could've been sculpted by Michelangelo's hand. They're divine."

Carson chuckles. "Divine, huh? You like the way I look, Princess?"

I smack the back of his neck lightly. "You know I do. Otherwise, why would I be here? Your soul isn't enough to get me naked, Ajax, there's gotta be some physical chemistry."

"I think there's plenty of chemistry here," he rumbles. "We should put it to good use while I still have you here, trapped in my lair."

Mewlius leaps off the bed when Carson abruptly rolls on top of me, straddling my waist and looking down at me with something that might be adoration sparkling in his eyes. While I want to get as much of him as I can... "I don't think I'll be much use for another round,

Carson. You've already made me come, like, a bazillion times and I've only gotten to return the favor three times."

Carson arches an eyebrow, running his palms over my waist. "A bazillion times, huh? No, I counted six. Since we've agreed on the three-to-one ratio, we still have a ways to go."

"You were serious about that?" I ask as he scoots down my body until his face is hovering over my pussy. "I thought you were just dirty-talking, or kidding! I'm not superhuman, I can't orgasm *nine times in a row*."

Carson meets my eyes and tips me a wink. "But I am superhuman when it comes to these activities, so I guarantee I'll keep our ratio in check." Then, he spreads my legs and shows me just how serious he is.

Chapter Forty-Three

The next morning, I'm so sore between my legs it hurts to move and when I use the restroom, I feel like I'm peeing fire. Carson notices my obvious discomfort as we have a quick breakfast of coffee and cut fruit before leaving for school and it makes him smug as hell, as if making me sore is an achievement.

Carson parks in front of the program dorms at Greywood so we can grab our school supplies before classes start. I only have fifteen minutes before warmups begin, so I'm in a rush as I hurry up to the door of dormitories. Carson keeps pace with me, but freezes when an unfamiliar voice calls out, "You owe me big time for this, Ajax."

I stop walking as well and whirl around, looking for whoever spoke. It's still dark out, but I make out the cherry glow of a cigarette, alerting me to a person hovering by a broken lamppost not far from the dorm building.

"Don't worry, it's just Ian," Carson murmurs. "I asked him to swing by a few times through the night and make sure nothing looked off, since I knew you'd worry about your friend."

I abruptly swivel my head to stare at Carson, startled. "You did what? Asked a random friend to swing by *in the middle of the night*?" I don't know if that's slightly creepy or incredibly thoughtful. I'm glad there was someone to keep an eye on the building and report any strange activity, but I don't know who Carson assigned to the task.

"He's a night-owl, doesn't sleep much," Carson says. "Kind of like Seth. I'd have asked that bastard if we weren't on shaky footing. Then again, Seth gets bored easily, so he might not have been reliable." Carson turns his head back towards his *friend* and calls out, "I don't think I owe you *big* for this, man, but I'll see about getting you a raise."

Getting him a raise? So, this must be a friend Carson works with. Perhaps another pupil in the business program, who happened to land at Carson's father's company.

The *friend* flicks his cigarette into the bushes, then walks forward until he's at the bottom step leading to dorms. The light from the dimly lit lampposts on either side of the doors illuminate him, and I can't stop the chill that runs over me.

I can see even from here that he's tall, taller than Carson, maybe even a bit taller than Seth. He has green eyes that glimmer like jewels, short chestnut hair that's carelessly tousled, and looks like he drops panties and incinerates hearts for a living. He's attractive, but there's also something profoundly off about him, not unlike the sense I get from Seth. His gaze is flat, his expression is blank, and he looks like he couldn't care less if a nuke went off right in front of him.

"I don't give a fuck about a raise," he tells Carson in a deep baritone that drips with disinterest. "If you want to pay me back, though, a promotion wouldn't be amiss."

Carson snorts. "Earn it."

The man arches a sharply carved eyebrow. "The way you earned everything you have?" His tone drips condescension.

I feel Carson tense beside me. "I started out in the mailroom when I was fourteen, Ian. I have earned my way up, which you know."

A cold smile curves Ian's lips, and he raises his hands in a placatory gesture. "I know, Ajax, I'm just fucking with you." Those green eyes swivel sideways and land on me, giving me a long sweep up and down that raises goosebumps on my arms. Whoever Ian is, I'm pretty sure he's a similar breed to Seth, except something about him just strikes me as more volatile and less measured. Like a volcano waiting to explode.

Ian says, "So this is the girl you've lost your fucking mind over. Moving into the program dorms and missing work. I think I see the appeal."

Suddenly I feel underdressed, even though I'm wearing the thick clothes I went hiking in yesterday.

Carson curves an arm around my waist protectively, drawing me closer to him. "Look all you want, but that's all you get to do."

Ian smirks, a gesture that seems more cruel than mirthful. "Whatever you say."

I clear my throat, growing increasingly uncomfortable, shifting my weight from foot to foot and fighting my instinctual, primal urge to get as far away from Ian as possible. Everything about him drips danger.

Carson looks down at me and says, "Elia, this is Ian Vargas, we're in the business program together and work together, as I'm sure you've surmised. Don't worry, he's all bark and no bite."

"When it comes to your girl, maybe," Ian inserts mildly, his tone uninterested.

Carson ignores that. "His family is actually helping fund your company's upcoming production," Carson tells me, a smile tilting the corner of his lips. "They're the minority contributors, but worth a mention."

"Fuck you, Ajax," Ian says with little rancor. "My dad's writing a check purely for the tax benefits."

I look back at this Ian, taking my time examining him. He meets my gaze, and the hair at the back of my neck stands on end. I know without a doubt I'm currently faced with someone very dangerous, the same way I knew with Seth, except this person is more volatile—I'll bet crueler and more destructive. At a second glance his eyes aren't empty, they house a chaos of sorts. His face looks like it was chiseled by a master artist, almost too perfect in its proportionality. Everything about him, including his black suit under a fashionable overcoat and shiny shoes, is polished to perfection, but it looks *wrong* somehow—almost as if he's a lizard wearing human skin to blend in, and it doesn't quite fit.

A creak sounds as the door to dorms swings open and April saunters out, nose buried in her backpack as she rifles through it for something. When she looks up and sees the three of us standing here, she goes stiff, stopping on the last step leading up to the building's entrance. Her eyes glue themselves to Ian, and the glint of recognition followed by what appears to be sheer disdain in those amber orbs surprises me.

Carson greets, "Hey, April. Perfect timing. Elia told me you've been looking to meet some friends of mine, here's your chance. This is Ian Vargas—"

"I know who that is," April says, her voice flat. She zips her backpack closed, slings it over a shoulder, and straightens, giving Ian a glare that would have another man six feet under. "We went to the same middle school and high school. I'd hoped to never have the displeasure again."

From her tone and overall demeanor, Ian might've been one of the rich assholes she once mentioned who made her feel inadequate for coming from an immigrant family who had to work hard to get by. Instantly, I start to develop a distaste for Ian—if April hates him, I'm honor-bound to hate him, too.

Ian smiles at April. "Good to see you too, Sugarplum. Don't tell me you're still sore about our time in the gallows?"

April tosses her long hair over her shoulder and says, "Don't you have an orphanage to be burning down, or whatever it is that gets your blood rushing?"

Ian tilts his head to the side, his smile dropping as he gets rid of the polite veneer and shows a glimpse of something ugly beneath; something that rears up my protective instincts and makes me *very* worried.

"Don't *you* have a gold-digging scheme to execute somewhere?" Ian turns to Carson. "You said she was looking to meet some friends of yours?" The inquiry is mild, but the implication is clear. He turns back to her and says, "Looks like you're still at your old ways."

April's nostrils flare and her eyes narrow. "Go fuck yourself, Ian. You don't know shit, and with how air-brained you grew up to be, you never will."

With that, she turns onto the path that leads to dance HQ and walks away. Ian watches her go with a hawk's gaze, attentive to detail and deeply interested. It's not unlike the way I've caught Seth staring at me from time to time, except Ian seems more malicious.

Carson looks at his friend. "You hadn't told me you knew April."

"You hadn't asked," Ian replies dismissively. "And I *didn't* know she even went to this school until just now. Not the worst possible development, I suppose." He turns his gaze to me. "You're in the dance company together?"

I frown, nodding. I don't like the idea of telling him anything about April as she clearly wouldn't want me to, but I'm also not prone to being needlessly rude.

Ian nods. "I might start dropping by the shows." He laughs to himself, as if sharing a private joke, then turns and strides away, heading towards the parking lot.

I look at Carson. "Was it just me, or is that one a psychopath?"

Carson chuckles, shuffling sideways and scanning his key card before opening the door. "Very possible, Little E. Let's get our shit and get to class—just know that the entire time you're in that tiny leotard I'll be imagining what I'll do to you next time we're alone."

As I cross the threshold into dorms, I quip, "If my dancing suffers because I'm too sore from last night, I guarantee that won't happen any time soon."

Carson catches my hand and presses a kiss to it. "I think it'd be worth it."

I catch up with April right as we're warming up and preparing to start blocking out Pandora's Box. Between seven and ten we're pulled from regular classes and our credits are being earned by working directly with Sanders in HQ's biggest studio space while he choreographs and prepares his new show. This is one of our first classes with the cast, which only consists of 14 people. Sean, April and I are the principals of the cast; Andrew and another girl, Chloe, are soloists; the rest of the dancers are corps.

Carson takes a seat in a chair by the door, while I take my spot in a corner of the large studio with April, setting up at the bar in front of the mirror and starting to stretch. "What's the deal with Ian?" I ask her. "Seems like there's some bad blood there."

April barks out a short, cruel laugh. "Yeah, you could say that. He's an asshole who made it his mission to make my high school experiences miserable. He succeeded, but thankfully he's a year ahead of me, so at least I got one year in relative peace. When he graduated, I was pretty happy to never have to see him again."

She speaks with such anger and rancor... Ian must've *really* screwed with her and hurt her. That's strange, because April seems to live with impenetrable armor coating her skin that nothing can get past, and she wears that armor *beautifully*.

"You didn't know he went to school here?" I ask, curiously.

April shakes her head. "I didn't exactly keep tabs on him. His goodbye to me came in the form of public humiliation, so I didn't bother following his socials. What the hell was he doing outside our dorm building?"

"Apparently Ian doesn't sleep, so Carson asked him to make a few rounds to dorms through the night and make sure no sketchy shit was going on," I tell her.

April makes a face. "Why?"

I shrug. "Because he knows I worry about your safety in dorms. He tried to get me to move in with him the day Scarlett went missing, and I refused both on the grounds of it being insane and not wanting to leave you behind."

April blinks. "We'll talk about how Carson has already tried to get you to move in with him in a bit. For now, please tell your boyfriend not to send Vargas *anywhere* near me."

"Carson's not my boyfriend, but I'll let him know," I say. "Was Ian that bad?"

April gives a cold, dead laugh. "Worse. Now, circling back to Carson *asking you to move in with him,* what's going on there? Two nights ago, you left with Seth, yesterday morning it was Carson, and you didn't come back until *this* morning..."

I prop my heel on the bar and fold my body over my leg, wrapping my fingers around my foot and stretching out my hamstrings. Turning my head sideways, I tell April, "I have no idea what's going on at this point. I'm just sort of along for this insane ride, but I can admit that shit's getting very deep, fast. I don't really know what to do, April. I like them both a *lot*. I don't want to choose between them, I couldn't stand the thought of hurting them."

April's eyes widen. She says, "*Biiiiiitch*. You went and caught feelings for *both* of your crazy stalkers."

"No I didn't!" I snap. Then, after a wince, "Okay, maybe? I don't know. I'm getting in over my head, I know that, but I also don't want to stop."

I glance over at Carson who, as usual, is staring right at me. His eyes meet mine, and he tips me a cocky little smile that reeks of smug masculinity and pride. I wasn't kidding when I told him that if my soreness thanks to his monster dick and insatiable stamina screws with my dancing, I'm going to be a lot more restrictive about when we have sex. I did pop two Advil before coming to class, and the soreness isn't catastrophic, so I think my body should be fine. My heart is another story.

"Have you thought about just having both of them?" April asks, surprising the hell out of me.

Chapter Forty-Four

I stare at April, wide-eyed, not quite comprehending her suggestion. "What?" I breathe.

She shrugs, stretching one foot above her head. "I just mean that they're both obviously obsessed with you, or they wouldn't be doing such crazy shit to spend time with you. You're now almost a month into the thing you have going on with them, and from what I see neither party is letting up or slowing down. It's not the craziest idea in the world to date both of them. Unless one of them is bad in bed, then just choose the other. Easy-peasy."

I let out a low groan. "Carson is a goddamn sex *god*. As for Seth, we haven't exactly gone all the way, but the stuff we have done... he's kinky. And intense. And very, *very* skillful."

A wide smile stretches April's lips. "I knew it. You've been rocking a post-orgasm glow for a while now. So, to sum up, you have a good time in bed with both, and you're falling for them outside of it. Am I right so far?"

I nod hesitantly. "Unfortunately, yes."

"It's not unfortunate at all," April says. "In fact, I can't tell you how fortunate it is, Elia. You have two very rich men who are moving mountains to be with you, so be with them."

I shake my head. "They're in a *competition* for me, April. I can't choose both of them, the expectation from the start was that I'd eventually choose one or the other, or neither. Trying to have both sounds like a whole lot of complicated, and my life has been complicated enough up until this point."

That's the nature of the problem; the whole situation is so twisted and complex that I'm not really in love with the idea of stepping further into it. I already feel terrible for how far I've allowed myself to fall, getting in deeper would just mean more of a shitstorm that I don't have the time, energy, or inclination to deal with.

"All the best things in life are complicated, messy, and difficult. Trust me on that," April says. "If you want both, go for both, Elia. If they veto the idea, then you'll know to choose yourself instead of either of them."

I let out a noise of irritation. "You're speaking like this is the simplest thing in the world. It's not, April. A three-way relationship would be polyamory. Aside from being very taboo, that's also a lot of moving pieces. I don't know how they'd react to each other or react to sharing me. Having to deal with one of them at a time is already a struggle, I can't imagine what dealing with both at once would entail."

It would probably be very hectic and messy. Last night when Carson told me he'd shared other girls with Seth before, I have to admit, part of me was intrigued. The other part, however, was daunted. They're both very demanding and have a habit of exhausting me when things get sexual, so having them at the same time probably means I'd end up passing out at some point. I also know it would mean a mind-bending amount of pleasure, which is enticing, but I don't know if it's worth the cost.

That's the crux; I don't know if the risk is worth the potential reward, because I don't know exactly what I'd be gaining, other than a lot to deal with on an already-full plate.

"Fair point," April allows. "Okay, answer me this; how has one of them reacted when finding out you got down and dirty with the other?"

I think back to the many times I braced myself for anger or reproach from either of them after just having spent time with the other. When Seth first went down on me, Carson was jealous but contained. When I first had sex with Carson, some of which Seth *witnessed*, his response was to use the information to lightly blackmail me into a date. Then when I came home from a sleepover at Seth's, and started crying in front of Carson, he took me out on one of the best dates of my life. The other spot goes to Seth's gala.

They've both been jealous of the other, but that jealousy has never really struck me as dangerous, more so competitive. If anything, they've been surprisingly subdued and chill about it, even when I had expected anger or drama. I haven't suffered at all from whatever dynamic they have going on.

"They've been pretty mild," I tell April. "Jealous, yes, but mild. Last night when I was, um, you know—"

"Getting your brains fucked out of your body?" April supplies helpfully.

I feel my cheeks burn. "Yeah, that. Carson mentioned something about sharing girls with Seth."

April's eyes sparkle with interest. "Is that so?"

I nod. "Yes."

"And how did you feel about it?" she prods.

"Well, I came harder than I have in my life, which I assume is pretty telling," I admit.

April grins. "Yes, it is. Sounds like the idea's already floating around Carson's head, and I'd be surprised if it hasn't crossed Seth's mind already. That man is cut from the same cloth as Ian, which means he thinks approximately a billion steps ahead. If you're too uncomfortable bringing anything up, wait until they do. I'm pretty sure they will."

"And we're back on the topic of Ian," I observe. "This time with a compliment."

April undergoes a drastic change within a millisecond; her lips twist with disgust and her eyes flare with anger. Her posture becomes tense as a statue, and she pauses in her stretching to give me a jaded glance. "Trust me, Elia, it's not a compliment. Ian is diabolical, pathological, volatile, a bully... in short, the perfect storm of awful. Seth is far more contained and calculated from what I've seen and heard."

"I'm pretty sure Ian's interested in you," I admit. "In some weird, dark way. After you stalked off he stared at you walking away and said something about coming to dance productions. Honestly, the way he looked at you was unnerving. Like predator-stalking-prey."

April scoffs lightly. "I'm nobody's prey, *certainly* not his. If that man were on fire, I'd give him a gasoline shower while singing *Burn Baby Burn*. He made several years of my life nearly intolerable; I will not allow him to do anything like that again. Back then, he was popular and I was the skimpy nerd, so I was easy pickings. Now, I'm a soloist in Greywood's upcoming production with friends and connections in the dance industry and a path forward. If he wants to screw with me, he can try, but that means going to war. And this time, I'll fucking win."

I'm stunned to silence for a moment after her declaration. I look April over, *really* look at her. Her breaths are harsh, angry pants, her cheeks and neck are flushed, her lips are parted, and her amber eyes are blazing with so much intensity they almost look like they're on fire. Whatever she feels towards Ian does seem to be a passionate hatred, but it's the passion that gets me. If there was nothing between them, she'd feel indifference.

"I almost hope you go to war with him, whatever that means," I murmur. "If nothing else, it sounds like that would be supremely interesting to watch."

A dark grin curves her lips as she lowers to the ground, drags her bag closer, and pulls out her pointe shoes, starting to tug them on. I follow suit, joining her on the floor and pulling mine out of my backpack, slipping my feet into them.

April says, "If we go to war, the school might not survive it. We'll see what happens, if he decides to start interfering with my shit."

Right then, Sanders enters the studio and claps his hands together to get all of our attention. Instantly, the room falls dead silent, and everyone present scrambles to stand upright and face him.

"Okay, dancers," he calls out. "Let's get to work. Eliana and Sean, I'd like you front and center please, today we'll be going over the second variation we started working on last time. April, your solo is up next. As for corps, please start on the fifth and sixth variations, for the wedding and then creation of the box."

"We'll talk more later," April whispers to me as we take our places.

I smile at Sean as we walk up to each other at the front of the room. He has short, dirty blonde hair and warm brown eyes that sparkle whenever he dances. I really liked being paired with him in Sleeping Beauty because of how keen he is on working together rather than trying to boss me around. The height difference between us is something to tackle, but with enough work we ended up using it to our advantage.

"Ready for the next show?" Sean asks with a grin.

I smile back. "Yup. Let's give them a star pairing to remember."

Carson coughs into his fist, *loudly*, drawing my attention to where he's seated by the door. He's looking between me and Sean with a *very* displeased expression, one filled with dangerous jealousy that almost borders on rage. He meets my eyes and mouths, *be careful*.

It registers in my mind that he's never been this disgruntled over Seth, but a male I'm paired with in my dance company is a different story. Honestly, it looks like Carson's ready to tear Sean limb from limb, and all he's done is smile at me and talk to me. I roll my eyes at Carson, then pointedly give him my back, turning away from him.

Sanders is speaking to April and the corps dancers right now, giving me and Sean a moment to go through our positions while talking. We start at the beginning of the choreography, slowly moving through it step by step.

"Are you going to Scarlett's funeral this weekend?" Sean asks me as he's spotting my waist while I twirl around in several consecutive pirouettes, turning my mood darker.

While spending time with Carson yesterday, I barely thought about Scarlett and our friendly campus serial killer. That was the whole idea of having a day away from campus, away from the deaths and insanity. Now that I'm back, I almost wish I'd stayed with Carson in the mountains, M's diner, or at his apartment playing with Mewlius and getting so many orgasms I was incoherent by the end of the night. I don't want to deal with all the stress and bullshit that's attached to campus. That's really the beauty of spending time with Carson; he makes me forget about all of the dark shit in my life and stay in the moment with him.

"I didn't receive an invite," I respond to Sean. His hands move to my waist and hoist my body up into an arabesque lift, interrupting conversation as I strive to perfect my form under Sanders's watchful eye.

He sets me back on the floor before saying, "No matter, you're probably better off not going. I don't think it'll be a good time for anyone, considering another Greywood fine arts student just got buried last week."

I wince. "Yeah. Being a female on campus has turned into a dangerous business."

"You're getting along just fine, though, with two of Greywood's most eligible bachelors looking after you," Sean says teasingly, making me fumble in my footwork as I give him a horrified glance.

He says quickly, "I'm not judging, Elia. If your boys weren't straight, I'd probably be going after them myself. Good for you, girl."

I had a niggle that Sean wasn't straight, but now I have confirmation, and on top of that, the comfort of knowing at least my dance partner in the biggest production of my life isn't going to spend our time judging me.

Sean says, "I'm glad you're safe, and a bit jealous of the attention you've been getting. You deserve it, though. Sleeping Beauty with you was the best I've ever danced, so I was happy when we both got leads in Pandora's Box."

He lifts me into his arms and hoists me upward, a moment that in the choreography is meant to look like two lovers embracing. I smile down at him. "I was really glad, too. If you were just three inches shorter, though, I might not feel like I'm dancing with a giant."

After he sets me down we separate, twirling a few feet away from each other. This part of the dance will include contact with the corps, once it's choreographed. When we join again, Sean teases, "Or you could grow a bit, midget. Seriously, you look like you belong in the petite section of the children's store."

I sniff. "I'm five-foot-three, thank you very much."

"My point stands," Sean murmurs, smiling.

We come to the end of our variation, both out of breath. I'm impressed that we managed to hold a conversation through it; the choreography is taxing and precise.

I chide, "Less talking, more working. We need to be perfect or Sanders will start yelling at us instead of the corps dancers."

Sean grins. "Fair enough, Elia. Let's show them how it's done."

CHAPTER FORTY-FIVE

Two weeks pass. I continue getting shadowed by Carson three times a week during morning dance and having afternoon classes along with evening volunteer time with Seth.

During our many hours in the archives, I get to know Seth better. He tells me about his life growing up, his mother who died when he was just a toddler, and more about his interests. He's already gotten himself a reputation in the biochemistry field, having conducted some research during his time as a summer intern that brought him significant accolades. He also has a knack for software engineering, and likes creating smart systems, not unlike the lighting system in his apartment. I get the sense that he's the jack of all trades, capable of any and everything.

When I'm with Carson, we talk about any and everything. He asks a lot about my dream trip to Europe, pulling as many details from me as he can—like the fact that I want to do a castle tour of both Scotland and Germany—and in turn tells me about the places he's travelled. When he was younger, he'd travel with both his parents, but once his father got bored of their family dynamic and stopped joining them,

Carson started doing trips with just his mom, which is when things got interesting. They've scuba dived in the Great Barrier Reef, explored the caves of Slovenia, done inside tours of the greatest pyramids in Egypt… it sounds like his mom loves exploring, and she passed on that love to her son.

Since Greywood does two-term semesters, we're all already studying for our first midterms of the fall semester, so Carson and Seth have less time to whisk me around on extravagant dates and outings. I still end up finding time to make out and fool around with both of them, and each time a part of me feels dirty and wrong. Despite what April suggested, I don't know that either man will be into the idea of a three-way relationship—I don't even think *I'd* be into that. As of now I'm flirting with my no-dating rule, not yet trampling all over it, and I'm not eager for that to change.

I still have to pose for Seth's art as per our contract, and those times are always ridiculously intimate and a tad disturbing. Although I've found myself accepting and even starting to crave the darkness that lives within him, his total disregard towards humanity as a whole occasionally gets a little disconcerting, especially when I compare it to the deep regard he's proven to have for me.

When it comes to me, he fusses over my sleeping and eating habits, and actually goes as far as to sneak takeout into the archives twice a week and feed me any time I pose for him. I have to subscribe to long lectures on a dancer's health needs whenever I say I'm not hungry, which isn't uncommon considering how prone I am to anxiety flashes and the fact that my six-hours-daily exercise actually serves as an appetite blocker.

On the flip side, when discussing world starvation and lack of clean water, Seth criticizes the institutions of government that don't properly feed their people but also says natural selection is bound to pick off the weak and preserve the strong.

Tonight, I'm once again at his apartment, posing for him. I'm laid in the same position on the couch he's had me in for weeks, this time with a textbook in front of me. My eyes scan the page and I jot down notes in the notebook beside it, doing my best to keep my movements minimal so I don't disturb Seth. He's seated in his usual spot, his eyes flickering from me to the canvas as he wields a fine brush with his hand. He's developed a habit of going shirtless whenever we're alone together, possibly because my eyes have a habit of getting glued to his sculpted muscles that speak to the raw power in his body. I occasionally peek up from my textbook to get a glimpse of his biceps flexing as he moves his hand across the canvas. His face is set in a deep mask of concentration, an expression he gets whenever he paints.

"You gonna keep staring at me or actually say something?" Seth asks, breaking the silence.

I quickly look back to my page in the textbook. "Considering I'm getting paid for you to spend time staring at me, I think turnabouts fair play, Balor."

I glance back up to see a sinful smirk curling his lips, one that drips with both calculation and smugness.

"I'm paying you to let me paint you. I spend plenty of time outside our sessions staring at you," Seth responds. "I like that you stare at me too, at least sometimes. I can honestly say, Little Muse, in this world full of boring, dismal people, you're the one eye I seek to attract."

I feel my cheeks heat at his words. He has a propensity for making bold statements like that, ones that few others would make because others care about how they're perceived. Seth is careful about how most of the world perceives him; he shows them the intelligence and calculation and peeks of darkness, but not much else. With me, he's more content to be himself. Somewhat pathological and someone I'm increasingly sure is some variation of a sociopath, which he makes no attempt to hide from me.

He actually appears fascinated with the fact that I see the darkest parts of him, and don't squirm or run away. It's probably because I've already experienced a lot of shit in life, but I can see that while Seth isn't quite *right,* he also has standards he sticks to. Those standards make him better than some of the men I've spent time with, which sort of desensitizes me to Seth.

"You're hard not to look at," I admit. Then, to change the subject, "When are you going to let me see the painting? We've been at this for weeks. Do you usually take this long?"

Seth lets out a faint snort. "No, Little Muse, I do not usually take this long. You can blame yourself for the length of time I'm spending on this, as I don't work on this painting unless you're in front of me. If you want to stay the night any time, I could get the rest done all in one go."

I roll my bottom lip between my teeth. I haven't spent the night with Seth again since his art show, just as we haven't gone all the way yet. We've kissed a *lot,* he's used his fingers and mouth on me and I've jerked him off, but we haven't gone any farther. I'm not opposed to it, I just don't feel like I have the right to make the first move in that direction since I have had sex with Carson. I'll also admit I'm a little unnerved at the idea of having sex with Seth.

What we've done so far has been mind blowing and *very* intense. Seth's always in full control of whatever's happening—often, he'll tie my hands together with a clothing article to ensure he can maneuver me however he wishes. I don't mind that, I'm actually surprisingly drawn to being restrained and yielding all my power to him, especially when he makes it feel so good to not be in control. Still, I worry how much more intense and controlling he'd be if we had sex. Part of me is attracted to the idea, while another part shies away from it.

"I should be done with the parts I need you to sit for after this session," Seth tells me. "Then we'll get started on the next one while I finish the first privately. For the second piece, I'll need another model along with you. A male model. It'll be a reimagining of Venus and Mars, I was thinking I might invite Carson to pose alongside you."

I feel my eyes bulge at how casually he drops that. Thus far, Seth has not offered for us to spend time with Carson once. He's been a little more relaxed about the idea of me being sexual with Carson these last few weeks, but he hasn't tried to get us all together, and I'll admit I didn't expect him to. After all, he's still in competition with Carson, so inviting the competition over shouldn't be on his to-do list.

"You want me to pose with Carson?" I ask slowly. "The guy you're in some weird, medieval race for my hand with?"

Seth lifts a shoulder nonchalantly. "He's a good model. I've used him before, though he always moans about wasting his time sitting still. I have a feeling that if you're in the picture, I won't have to deal with as much complaining from him. That's worth a lot to me."

It feels like he's dodging my question, giving me a bullshit answer to throw me off trail, and I don't know why. Likewise, I don't know the real reason why he'd want to be in a space with both me and Carson. Seth knows I've slept with Carson while I haven't yet with him. For the first little bit, I think that was a point of hurt pride for him, but he's since mellowed out. I still think there must be some ulterior motive here.

I say slowly, "Okay. You're the boss when it comes to my work time with you, so I'll go with whatever you say."

Seth pauses in painting, sets his brush down on the table, and leans back to observe me. "Whatever I say, hmm?"

Okay, maybe that wasn't the best word choice with someone like him. He could take that in a lot of ways that a normal person wouldn't, and I've learned there's nothing normal about Seth. That's part of what makes him so fascinating to me.

"Not *whatever*," I amend, "but you know what I mean."

Seth slowly bobs his head up and down. "So, if I said I want to eat your pussy until your entire body is flushed, would you let me?"

I feel myself tense. During work time we usually stay platonic, though Seth throws out plenty of innuendos to try and succeed in getting my blood rushing. Now he's trying to cross that invisible line, the one that says work hours are for work and not play, and I don't know how to respond. I'm not against the idea of him eating me out since he has that down to a science, but I also feel like that'd be pushing a boundary.

I say, "I don't know. Is it necessary for your art?"

A dark smile decorates Seth's lips, sinful and carnal and oh-so-enticing. "Yes, Little Muse. I've had to imagine the blush that stains your cheeks and neck whenever you come while painting, having the actual thing would be helpful."

"Why do you like doing that so much?" I question curiously. "I'm no expert, but from what I've heard most guys do that as a favor to girls, not because they actually enjoy it."

Seth lets out a light scoff. "I'm not *most guys*, Eliana. I'm me. I don't go down on you as a favor, I do it because you're my favorite dessert and because it turns you nice and moldable beneath my hands. I like the sound of your whimpers, moans, and screams. I like trapping your clit between my teeth, the sound you make when you're a little panicked and a lot turned on. I like seeing how much pain I can add to the pleasure to make it greater, I like learning you the way nobody else has taken the time to. It's their loss, really, and my gain. I do what I do for both my enjoyment and yours. In fact, I think I could say it brings me more enjoyment than you, because it feeds my need for control and turns you into such a lovely masterpiece beneath my touch."

My jaw gapes after his little speech, and I spend several moments staring at him dumbly. His dirty talk game is on another level, and the way he describes the act so carnally and with such detail makes my nipples harden beneath my bra and heat travel south. A low ache starts pulsing between my legs, and my mouth suddenly feels dry.

I say, "Wow. Um, okay. That's a lot."

"I'm a lot," Seth retorts, "as you already know. What I really like is just how well you handle me, Little Muse. How you don't break and only bend as much as you want to. I like that you can take what I dish out without crumbling under the pressure. Very few others are able to, but that's because few others have led your life. Your strength is a huge part of what attracts me to you, but as much as I love seeing it shine through, I also like turning you weak and limp beneath me."

I almost blurt out *just fuck me already*, because hot *damn* he knows how to wind me up. It's almost unfair just how easily he can get into my head and start rearranging my thoughts, switching them seamlessly from business to pleasure.

"Well. If you want to go down on me, I wouldn't exactly object," I say honestly.

Seth tilts his head to the side. "I feel obligated to give you fair warning that I won't be able to hold myself back once your taste is on my tongue. I've dreamt of what you'd feel like squeezing my cock, and my patience is running out."

So he wants to cross *that* line today. On one hand, it's about fucking time, on the other hand, the same niggle of fear that's been present each time I think of going all the way with him returns full force. I don't think it's actually because I'm frightened of having sex with him, more so I'm frightened of what would come after and what it would mean.

Carson's his own deal; I knew from the beginning that, to him, sex is nothing big. He slept his way through most of campus and half the socialites and models in this country, so taking that step with him was one thing. Even with his warning that his pursuit of me would intensify after the first time, I wasn't all that worried.

Seth, on the other hand, doesn't have a history of sexual escapades that can fill up a whole encyclopedia—in fact there are no rumors of his prowess in the sack around campus, which means if he's slept with any student at Greywood, it's been kept on the down low. Even April couldn't find any information on him, and she's an expert when it comes to gossip. That all goes to indicate that this will be a much more significant and meaningful step with him, and I'm not sure I'm ready for it. I don't know if he'll demand exclusivity or what will change, but I have a feeling that this *will* change things.

"What happens after?" I ask.

Seth quirks an eyebrow. "I'll probably use your post-orgasm exhaustion to hold you, as per usual."

Seth does like cuddling after we do anything, but... "That's not what I mean. What happens once we've had sex? What will it change?"

Seth ponders that for several moments before responding, and I hold my breath while waiting for his answer.

After an eternity, he says, "I don't know, Little Muse. If you're worried that I'll start making demands of you, don't. I'd never actively do anything that would push you away. I'll probably be a good deal more possessive, though that won't extend to Carson. If I see another man looking at you in a certain way, though, I can't guarantee that man will have eyes the next day."

I blink. "Your possessiveness wouldn't extend to Carson?"

I think back to April's words, how she rightly pointed out that Seth always thinks many steps ahead and might already have thought on the possibility of sharing me with Carson. Not in a sexual way alone, but in a relationship way.

Seth shakes his head. "No, I wouldn't allow it to. I see that he fulfills the needs in you that I'm unable to, Eliana. I wouldn't deprive you of something or someone important just because I want you all to myself. I thought I would, that I'd be that selfish, but I can't with you. I want to give you the world and more."

"Oh," I say a little dumbly, taken aback by his sincerity. "Okay, then."

That's all the invitation Seth needs. He stands from his chair while I sit upright on the couch, anticipation making the blood in my veins heat up while my heart starts to pound so fast, I'm pretty sure it's about to burst out of my chest. Seth walks up to me slowly, leisurely, taking his time looking me over. Uncomfortable being seated while he towers above me, I come to a stand, which only helps minutely. Our height difference alone is enough to make me feel miniature, whether I'm sitting or standing.

Seth stops directly in front of me with less than a foot separating us, and slowly runs his hands up my bare arms. I'm wearing a tight shirt, and he fingers the hem at my midsection before reaching underneath and running his palm along my waist to settle on the small of my back. My breath hitches as he leans down to hover his lips above mine. He doesn't close the distance between our mouths, instead he just stares at me for several seconds.

"Kiss me," he murmurs.

CHAPTER FORTY-SIX

I comply without hesitation, standing on my tiptoes and gripping his rock-hard shoulders in my hands. I press my body along his as I fuse our mouths, running my tongue along his soft lips and teasingly nipping at them without intruding. Despite the darkness radiating off Seth, the darkness that's always present, I'm feeling playful. I want to see if I can instigate strong reactions out of him through light, teasing touches, driving him out of his mind the way he's always driving me out of mine.

A small voice in my head warns that this is a big step, one I might not have the easiest time coming back from, but the thing is I don't want to come back. Especially with how conscientious Seth is of me and my needs, how he contorts himself to meet them.

After a few minutes of me nibbling and teasing him, the chord of Seth's self-control snaps. He plasters my body more firmly against his with the hand at the small of my back, wraps the other around my chin to angle my head how he wants it, and then basically plunders my mouth—there's no other way to describe it. His tongue explores every millimeter of my lips, my mouth, even my *teeth* get attention, as if he wants to learn me from the inside out. I'm left with nothing to do but clutch his shoulders for dear life and hold on for the ride. His grip on me is steel, his lips and tongue are ravenous, and it lights me up from the inside out.

It doesn't take me long to hook a leg over his waist and start grinding against his erection, which is prominent and thick, nudging at me insistently. Seth lets go of my chin to yank my other leg around his waist, lifting me up in his arms. I hold on tightly as he starts walking us to the bedroom, clutching him and grinding against him and feeling myself reach heights I didn't know existed.

"Tell me you'll stay the night," Seth commands, pulling back. I pry open my eyes, feeling dazed and somewhat oxygen-deprived, which is probably why I nod up at him fuzzily. I'm not sure what he asked me as I'm having a hard time differentiating up from down at the moment, but I'll give him whatever he wants if he keeps kissing me like that.

Seth releases me abruptly, and I yelp as my stomach drops and a falling sensation overcomes me for a second before I feel familiar soft bedding beneath me, cushioning my fall. I crane my neck backwards, spotting Seth's demon painting and confirming that we're now in his bedroom.

"Eyes on me," Seth says, drawing my attention back to him. I feel like I'm a gazelle that the lion's about to devour as I watch him slowly undress, revealing inch after inch of glorious smooth skin stretched over ridiculously well-cut muscles. Once he's fully naked in front of me, I can't help a sigh. He really does look like angels created him with the upmost attention to proportionality and detail. My eyes take their time drinking in his upper body before they travel further south to his cock, which is swollen and engorged and very stiff. I think he might actually be thicker than Carson, which causes a sliver of fear to travel through me, but it only joins my growing arousal.

Seth puts his hands on my thighs, over my jeans, and uses his grip as leverage to yank me closer to him, until my butt is right on the edge of his bed. He unzips and unbuttons my jeans in a businesslike manner, then rips them off me like they've committed a mortal sin against him.

My panties disappear with a harsh tug and a tearing noise, and I make a sound of irritation. "At this rate I'm not going to have any panties left before the semester's over."

I realize my mistake in saying that when Seth's eyes lock with mine, blazing a bright green and laced with enough jealousy to make that uncomfortable falling sensation return to my stomach.

"Is that so? Did Carson also rip a pair?" He drawls.

I don't respond, too afraid to make a peep. Right now, I can see that Seth's firmly in hunter mode, and if I step a toe out of line that could mean trouble for me. Why that thought is so arousing, I really couldn't say.

Seth's lips curl into a smile, but it's a cruel gesture. "I can't say I blame him, Little Muse. You're perfection embodied, of course I'm going to be impatient when finally getting my prize." He reaches for the hem of my shirt, tugging it up and off me before quickly unclipping my bra and discarding it over his shoulder.

Then he places a palm on my chest, right between my breasts, and uses it to push me flat on his bed while standing between my spread thighs. I swallow hard, feeling like there's a lump in my throat, arousal and nerves mixing within me to form a heady concoction of hormones that heightens my anticipation.

"Here's what you should know about me, Eliana," he says while trailing his hand across my chest from one side to the other, pausing to grip my breasts and brush his fingers over my nipples every so often. "It's probably going to hurt with me at times. I'm going to push you, test you, unleash myself on you. That won't be an easy ride. If you need me to stop, your safeword is oxymoron. Unless I hear it, I'm going to play with you the way I've wanted to for *far too fucking long*. Okay?"

The words fall from his lips, both alluring and intimidating. I feel like I'm in a trance once again, as always seems to be the case when it comes to Seth and anything sexual. I want to see exactly what he means when he says play with me, but there's also a flutter of trepidation within me because I've seen just how different Seth is, so his form of playing might not be the safest.

"Oxymoron might be a hard word to say while in the heat of the moment," I point out.

Seth lowers himself to his knees so that his face is level with my pussy, when I try to go up on my elbows, he pushes me back down with the hand still fondling my breasts. I think I hear him mutter *good* but that's lost in translation when his mouth fastens onto my pussy and takes me to new heights. He doesn't tease or take his time, he uses his very talented tongue, lips, and teeth to drive me hard into an orgasm that draws a loud cry from me.

Then he stands, flips me over to my hands and knees with such forcefulness it takes my breath away, and pushes me up the bed to make room for himself before climbing on behind me.

"Grab a pillow," he tells me. "You'll want something to hold onto."

I don't doubt him, because right now, he's a feral beast. I reach up towards the headboard, crawling forward a bit to grab one of the pillows. As soon as I have it under my head Seth flattens a hand between my shoulder blades, pushing my upper body down to the mattress and leaving my ass in the air. I turn my head sideways to avoid suffocation via pillow, and clutch onto the edges of it, panting.

I expect Seth to get right into the fucking part of the evening, which is why I'm shocked when I hear a rustle of the sheets before feeling his teeth sink into one side of my ass. I startle and yelp, instinctively trying to move forward because his bite is nowhere near gentle, and I wasn't expecting *that* sort of pain. Seth snarls and clamps his hands on my hips to keep me still, releasing my ass from his teeth and trailing wet kisses over the sore flesh. I jerk with a whine when he pulls back and spanks the spot he just bit, *hard*. It stings and burns, making me tense, but after a moment the pain turns into a sordid sort of heat and seems to travel straight to my pussy, which only makes me wetter.

He spanks my other cheek before releasing my hip, and then I feel the broad head of his dick prodding insistently against my entrance. His hands slide over my waist, fingers digging into my skin, which is all the warning I get before he *slams* into me with such abruptness that the breath flies out of me, and I release a startled cry.

It hurts in no small way, the pain spreading upward to my womb and down to my thighs, and I realize that's because Seth wanted it to hurt. He wasn't kidding when he warned me earlier. Of course, I could always use my safeword, but then again this pain isn't *bad* per se, just overwhelming and a lot to handle at once. The stretching and burning sensations are strong and insistent, robbing me of breath and my ability to think properly. It prickles and stings as my body instinctually fights the invasion.

He stays still inside me for several moments, but the way his fingers flex on my hips tells me just how much effort that takes. He's holding still to my benefit, and at a personal toll.

Through gritted teeth, he asks me, "You good?"

I'm not capable of speech while impaled with him, but I manage to nod against the pillow. He must not believe me because he continues staying still as my inner muscles clamp and flutter around him and my body tries to accustom itself to an intrusion of that size. When the sharp pain subsides into a dull ache, I let out a shaky sigh and experimentally rock my hips backwards. Seth's hissed breath precedes a harsh grunt as he pulls halfway out of my channel before thrusting back in, just as hard as the first time. This time, however, it no longer feels like I'm being split in half.

He snakes one of his hands around my waist to find my wet folds, and I let a moan out as he circles all of his fingers around the place where we're connected before sliding up to my clit and twirling the pads of his fingertips over it. My inner muscles relax, as does the rest of my body, and a soft sigh escapes me as tension leeches from me. That tension returns when he smacks my ass again with his free hand, and then starts to move in and out of me at a steady, brisk pace. His thrusts are measured yet harsh, and each one draws a small sound from my lips, which only grow in volume when he speeds up the action on my clit.

It feels like he spends an eternity fucking me with that same measured pace, enough to take my breath away, but I can tell he's not unleashing everything, still holding back. I don't like that; I don't want to see what he's like when he's taking it easy, I want all of him. I start rocking my hips back in time to each thrust, trying to encourage him to go faster, do what he wants to me rather than holding himself on such a tight leash. I don't care if it hurts, I'm actually finding out I kind of like the pain.

Seth swears under his breath when I arch my back even more, responding to it by landing several consecutive spanks on my ass, right over the spot where he bit me. "If you don't want me to lose control, you'll stay. Fucking. Still."

"I want you to be you," I respond breathlessly, not ceasing in my movements, trying to entice him further.

Seth's hand flattens on my ass and then his fingers dig into the soft flesh until I feel his nails biting at my skin, just shy of breaking it. "Be careful what you wish for, Little Muse. Once the beast's out, there's no putting him back until he's satisfied."

Feeling emboldened, I shimmy my ass and say, "So let him out. I want to play."

That's all it takes. Seth's thrusts increase with vigor until each one forces me forward on the bed, and the headboard slams loudly against the wall. He slides his hand up my spine before circling it around the front of my neck, using the grip to pull me up until my back is plastered against his chest. His grip on my neck isn't light; each breath I take is met with resistance, and it only takes a minute before random spots of light start swimming in my vision.

I clasp his arm with both of my hands, then let out a squeak as his other hand slaps my aching flesh down below, *hard*. Stinging pain erupts all over my pussy, followed by a knot of tension forming low in my stomach, so intense it feels like it threatens to tear away my existence. I claw at Seth's hand when he smacks my flesh again, then a third time, all while choking me and still thrusting into me like a madman. The stimulation, all of the sensations at once are almost too much to bear, but I wouldn't give this up for anything.

"Are you ready to come?" Seth whispers in my ear with a particularly brutal thrust, circling his fingers over my clit.

I nod as much as his hand on my throat will allow, which admittedly isn't much.

"Good," Seth purrs darkly. "Then beg me for it."

I'm too far gone for pride, so when he eases his grip on my throat, I whine, "Please let me come."

He only allows me two easy breaths of air before tightening his grip again and spanking me, right over my swollen clit. A choked scream escapes me as sharp pain overtakes the pleasure, which morphs into more liquid heat when his fingers return to teasing my clit.

"You'll have to beg prettier than that, Little Muse," Seth growls while continuing to torture me.

His fingers rub up and down and from side to side, pausing every so often to pinch my clit and tug on it. When my pleasure reaches a cresting point, though, he spanks me again—sometimes several times in a row. He continues torturing me while constricting my breathing, and I'm pretty sure I'm about to pass out at any second yet it feels *so damn good* I wouldn't ask him to stop for a million dollars.

"Try again. My advice is to be very nice and *very* convincing," he tells me, before once again easing his hold around my neck.

What escapes me is an incoherent ramble, a recursive variation of *please oh god please let me come,* which actually draws a chuckle of amusement from him. This time I get to breathe freely for the better part of a minute before I'm back to fighting for each inhale and exhale.

He smacks my clit three times in a row, the hardest blows yet, before rubbing it furiously at the same time that he growls, "Come."

I just about *detonate* in his arms, shaking and screaming and begging for him to stop and keep going at the same time. Every inch of my being feels like it's lit on fire, and Seth releases his hold on my throat, allowing a carnal scream to escape my lips. He curses and then pushes my upper half back down on the bed, speeding up his movements until he's basically jackhammering into me, while my orgasm goes on and on for so long I'm nearly incoherent. Two harsh thrusts precede him going completely still, then pumping in and out of me a few times, slower, while I feel warmth bathe my insides.

"Jesus *fuck,*" I think I hear him say behind me as he pulls out. "That was otherworldly."

I happen to agree, but I have neither the voice nor the strength to do more than grunt. Seth falls down beside me, then curls an arm around me and uses it to draw me into his side. My head lands on his shoulder and my bare legs tangle between his.

He rubs a hand up and down my spine and asks me in a voice that's butter-smooth, "Are you tired?"

I nod into his chest with a small whimper that would embarrass me if I had any room for rational thought. As is, though, I'm barely capable of keeping my eyes open, so I let them slide shut. Seth's hand travels from my back to my bare ass, and he starts rubbing his palm over the slightly-sore flesh, right over his bite mark and the spot he spanked repeatedly. The contact feels good, soothing, which makes me nuzzle closer to him.

"Poor Little Muse," Seth says with a chuckle that feels like it vibrates all the way through me. "Exhausted already, even though I've only just gotten started with you."

He slowly shifts his body sideways, using it to roll me over until I'm flat on my back and he's kneeling between my thighs. I crack my eyes open when I feel his cock start to re-harden against my hip, even though he only came a few minutes ago. My eyes widen when he braces one hand by my head while the other travels through my wet folds, leisurely stroking up and down my slit.

I'm sore from the way he's spanked and teased me down there, so I wince a little as his fingers move all around my pussy, pinching my folds and circling over my clit while he watches my facial expression with the attention of a sniper locked on his target. He actually seems to like it when I wince or whine, his eyes flare with interest each time. His quirks will definitely be peeking through in the bedroom—he's obviously a kinky guy, which I expected, though I didn't properly anticipate his vigor or intensity. *No wonder he gave me a safeword.*

Seth's finger probes at my entrance, pausing when I hiss from the sensitivity and pain. He did not take it easy on me, and I'm already feeling the effects of that. Although it was intense, I wouldn't have changed anything, and even though I'm already exhausted, I have no inclination to stop him. I'm finding out that Seth's darkness in the bedroom, while overwhelming, also presses a lot of hot buttons that I didn't even know I had. Having his hand around my throat and hearing him tell me to beg for an orgasm made me come so hard I saw stars. I'm not going to stop him now, especially when I actually like the bite of pain that's coming from our intense sex. I want to see what he does next.

Seth's eyes search mine as his body stays still, not pushing his finger in any further or pulling it out. He's waiting for a cue from me, I realize, and the rush of power that follows my understanding is heady. Seth seems like an all-powerful man, and yet in this moment, *I'm* the one with the power.

I incline my head slightly; he slides his finger fully inside of me, circling it around my sensitive walls while watching my expression carefully. He starts talking to me with a low voice while he plays with my flesh, and each rumbled word only heightens the sensations he's creating within me. "I like this part the most," he murmurs. "The part when I know I should stop and let you rest, but don't. The part where I act like the bastard I am and take more than I'm entitled to. I'm a monster, Eliana, and you've managed to enslave me, so now you get to deal with the monster. The best part is I know I can let him out with you, that you can take it. Do you have any idea how fucking *erotic* that is to me?"

I let out a low moan as his thumb comes to rest on my clit, pressing down with light pressure and moving from side to side. My toes curl as, despite the pain and sensitivity, pleasure also sparks within me.

"You'll come for me again like this," he tells me. "Then again while I'm inside you, at least once. Feeling you fall apart around my cock was better than anything I could've dreamed of. I might let you sleep after that, but I'll probably wake you up in the night to get my fill again. I've had weeks to create fantasy after fantasy with you, Little Muse. I can't get through all of them in one night, but I'm certainly going to make a dent."

Fine by me.

Chapter Forty-Seven

Seth

I let Eliana sleep after I've felt her come in my arms a few more times. I never thought I'd enjoy the act of giving pleasure, but something about her makes the act not only enjoyable, but also addictive. It's the way her eyes light up, the way her breath catches, the sweet sounds she makes, ranging from erotic moans to screams of abandon. Everything draws me deeper into her thrall.

I wake her at around one in the morning, and my wakeup call comes in the form of eating her out until she's pulled from her slumber and comes for me again, this time with a cry that almost sounds a shade panicked. That turns me on more than it should. Once I've fucked her on her side, she falls right back asleep, leaving me to stare at the ceiling while her body's curled around mine, thinking.

I've spent the last weeks contemplating my next steps. My conversation with Sergei left its mark; much of my time, outside of work, is spent on thinking about my future with Eliana, and how I can ensure that there *is* a future. I've occasionally watched her through her dormitory window these last weeks, both when she's alone and when she's with Carson. The purpose of that particular bout of stalking was so that I could understand exactly what her dynamic with him is, and how that'd potentially fit into a three-way dynamic with all of us.

The main thing to contend with is my sense of possessiveness. It's an honest struggle to keep myself on a leash when I glimpse her laughing at something he's said or see one of them lean in for a kiss. In those times, I stop seeing Carson as Carson, and start seeing him as a faceless existential threat to my relationship with Eliana. I know that's partially because what I have with my Little Muse is, as of now, unsolidified. If it were solidified into a labeled relationship, I think some of my possessiveness would ebb, regardless of if Carson is another party in said relationship.

I'm desperate for her to belong to me, even if that means she belongs to him, too. I know myself well enough to know I could handle that. I might not love it, but if I had Eliana, I could cope with it.

That only takes care of one part of the equation, however. I don't know if Carson's had any similar thoughts to mine, the thought of maybe changing the rules of our competition so that we could, theoretically, *both* get her. I need to have a talk with him, lay all the cards and options out on the table and tell him my proposed path forward, one where all parties here could be satisfied.

I've barely spoken to him since the start of the school year. We've bumped into each other a handful of times, both on campus and in our shared apartment building, but those meetings have only yielded taunts and shit-talking. I wouldn't say I exactly *miss* him, but I do resent that I no longer have him readily available when I need a partner in crime or someone to just pass the time with. I also resent that I no longer have a friend I can be myself with, without the mask I have to present to the rest of the world.

I glance back to Eliana, who's partially on top of me as she sleeps, and I must admit, I can't blame Ajax for his growing fascination with her. Elia isn't just beautiful on a physical level, though she does have a stunning figure and breathtaking face—it's her personality where her true beauty shines through. She's quick, witty, and *accepting* in a way I didn't anticipate. So long as something doesn't cross her lines, she can live with it. When I laid some of my darker deeds bare for her to see, fully prepared to chase her ass down after she'd inevitably run from me like I was a house on fire, her acceptance just about floored me. Her insight and way of looking at the world is riveting. Everything about her is like the call of a siren to me, and if she can ensnare me there's no wonder she's ensnared Carson, too.

I flit my eyes over Elia's peaceful, restful features. Her long eyelashes flutter against her cheeks. Her hair, dozens of shades of blonde all thrown together, brushes her high cheekbones and fans down around the elegant slope of her shoulders. Each of her breaths tickle my chest and press her breasts against my ribs, which makes me want to wake her up again by sucking her nipples until they're dark red and covered with the imprints of my teeth.

Instead, I reach for my phone on my nightstand and shoot off a text to Carson.

Seth: *We need to talk.*

I've cooked up all the plans I needed to in my mind, I've done the legwork on my end to prepare for next steps, now it's time to bring Carson onto my side of the playing field. We've always done much better as allies, anyway; having him as a rival recently has been a damper I haven't enjoyed.

Only two minutes pass before he responds.

> **Carson:** *Your place or mine?*

Since there's currently a real-life Sleeping Beauty in my bed...

> **Seth:** *Yours.*

> **Carson:** *What are you waiting for?*

I slowly untangle myself from Eliana, replacing my body with a pillow that she clutches onto as I scoot out of bed. I tug on black sweatpants and a matching T-shirt, all the while barely taking my eyes off my Little Muse because it's impossible to be in a room with her and *not* stare.

I brush my lips over her forehead like a goddamn schoolgirl before heading out of my apartment, locking the front door. It's a short elevator ride down to where Carson resides. Before I can ring the doorbell, the front door swings open, revealing Carson, dressed in sweatpants with no shirt, staring at me with a small smirk. "Here to concede?"

"You'd like that, wouldn't you?" I mutter, shoulder-checking him as I walk inside.

I kick off my shoes by the doorway, then follow Carson as he goes into the kitchen.

Without asking, he pours a few fingers of Blue Label into two ridged crystal glasses, then slides one of them across the counter to me.

I take a sip while we stand across from each other, each a predator in their own right, watching a fellow predator and waiting for them to make a move.

"I'm here about Elia," I say.

Carson nods, taking another sip of his drink. "I figured."

I crack my neck. "Yeah. Here's the deal, Ajax, I'm not giving her up, you're not giving her up, and she's made it clear she'd rather reject both of us than hurt one of us by choosing the other because she's too goddamn good for this world, so as I see it we only have one remaining option."

"That option being?" Carson questions.

Looks like I'll have to spell it out for him plainly. "You. Me. Her. If I need to tolerate you to get her, then I will. And since I can't have her without you, that's exactly what I'm going to fucking do. The question is, will you tolerate me with the same sense of sportsmanship?"

Carson looks at me like I have two heads, which I can't blame him for.

"You're suggesting we *share her?*" he says, sounding stunned. "What do you mean, exactly?"

I shrug. "Polyamory's gained popularity as times have progressed. Granted, it's more common to see multiple women in a relationship with a single man, but the reverse also exists. From what I've seen of Eliana, she's beyond stressed at the idea of turning her back on one of us for the other and would sooner turn her back on both of us. I will not accept that."

"Neither will I," Carson replies, voice filled with steel.

I give him a single nod. I've put a lot of thought into my conundrum with Elia; I've already grown very attached to her, something a traditional man might call falling in love. My form of love, however, is far from traditional. I've never actually felt love for anyone before, so I can only draw on what I've observed with others. Those observations are that people in love are cuddly, warm, and have hearts for eyes, which is not at all what I feel for Eliana. What I feel for her is dark, twisted, a soul-deep possessiveness and need to own her, for her to be mine, even if that means I'll have to share her.

Any time I think of the possibility of her turning her back on me, my body grows uncomfortably hot, my heart races, and I start to sweat. I'll do whatever it takes to prevent that from happening, whatever is necessary to keep her with me.

Carson and I have shared women in the bedroom before, but that was a bit of fun, not anything as serious as a relationship. However, I believe if there's any person in the world I could stomach the thought of sharing Elia with, it would be him, because I can see how he meets her needs in ways I'm unable to.

I'm not ignorant as to my nature; I am a very dark person, and that darkness tends to rub off on anyone who spends time with me. Carson is immune, mostly because he's grown up in a cutthroat business world with white-collar sociopaths at every turn. Elia is able to handle my darkness, as I've seen, but I don't think she could do so indefinitely without losing parts of herself; parts that she needs and *I* need. Her warmth, kindness, and empathy are like beacons of light to me—I can't stomach the thought of tainting her and making those qualities dim.

That's where Carson comes in. Our friendship has always perplexed people, because in many ways we're opposites. He is the light while I am the darkness. There's no denying that Carson has his own dark parts, but those are mere *parts* of him that don't make up the whole of who he is. Those are parts that were placed there by his cunt of a father and the brutal world of the elite he was raised in. He can be sneaky and has an excellent mind for strategy, but overall, Carson is light. My darkness is something I was born with; it *is* me.

Elia needs both of those things. The twisted darkness, and the broken light. Neither Carson nor I are capable of delivering that to her on our own, but together... together is a different story.

"So, we share her. We both date her," I propose.

Carson looks lost in thought. "How would it work? Technically, I mean."

I lift a shoulder. "You spend time with her, I spend time with her, *we* spend time with her, together."

Carson scoffs. "That's all you've got? Where's the meticulous planning I normally see from you?"

"I can't plan until I've seen her response and gotten a sense for how she feels about it," I retort.

"What about the media and tabloids?" Carson asks. "This could be bad for business, not just for us but for her. Imagine the judgement and scrutiny she'll come under if it becomes common knowledge that she's dating two men. You saw the pictures Scarlett uploaded to social media, and at the time that was no more than petty speculation meant to smear Elia's name and image—if it comes out that she's with both of us, things could get much worse."

This is a problem I've considered. "There are a few ways to deal with that. My suggestion would be to take control of the narrative; turn the tides against anyone who might look down on us—call them prejudiced or slanderous, make *them* the villains. I know a few reporters who owe me favors, and I'm sure you do, as well. Our status and sway in certain circles should be enough to protect her from any accusations of immorality or other bullshit. If cornered, we could also point out the many other high-profile people who practice polyamory, who will then be compelled to issue statements of support."

Carson tilts his head to the side, considering. "You really have thought about this, haven't you?"

I nod. "Yes. There's no way to avoid judgmental students on campus that might try to villainize Eliana—because, let's be honest, women always take the blame for perceived immorality—but you and I would both be there to protect her from such things. And if anyone attempts to disparage my character… well, few would be stupid enough to try, and someone who does will learn just what makes me such a dangerous opponent."

Carson starts warming to the idea, albeit slowly. "My father would try to break it up once he learned of it—"

"Your father has a harem of women around the world and has several sexual misconduct allegations that he's paid to keep off the tabloids. If he wants to tangle with you, pull the trigger on your blackmail. Take over the empire." I don't add that Carson taking a more central role in his business would give me more time with Elia; that might sow unnecessary discord in what's turning out to be a very productive conversation.

Carson winces. "Exposing him would inevitably drag my mother through the dirt, which I refuse to do. She's innocent, she doesn't deserve all the bullshit that will hit her if he gets into trouble. Besides, I don't want to take over business yet. I want to finish Greywood, travel, *live* before my life becomes consumed by his empire."

I know this has been a worry for Carson; we've discussed it at length before. One of his greatest fears in this life is turning into his father. Not just in the moral sense, but in the married-to-work sense.

I shrug. "So delegate. Appoint a board of people you trust, keep the majority share of your dad's companies. You don't have to get consumed by work like him, he chose that path; you have more options. I know for a fact there are students in the business program who are loyal to you and have great potential. Run the show from the background, let other capable people take the wheel. Ian Vargas has an appetite and knack for the work, you could always use him."

Carson lets out a grunt. "I'll figure that out when it comes time to pull the proverbial trigger on my father."

"It doesn't have to be proverbial. You want him gone, I can make that happen. I have friends in low places."

A half-smile forms on Carson's lips. He says, "I've missed you, man. Competing has been a whirlwind and gaining Elia's affection faster than you has been great, but losing our friendship hasn't been fun."

I frown. "Don't get sentimental on me."

Carson snorts. "Wouldn't dream of it."

"Are we in accord?" I press.

"On sharing Elia? I say give it a go. As long as you can assure me that you won't set your deadly sights on me. I've seen just what a possessive motherfucker you can be, and I have a feeling that possessiveness is magnified tenfold when it comes to Little E."

I consider him for several moments before inclining my head. "I'll keep myself in check. Now that we have that out of the way and you're no longer number one on my shitlist, I have information regarding our friendly neighborhood serial killer. I had a contact who used to work in forensic psychology create a profile on him based on all the known information of victims. What she sent me speculates that the killer is a middle-aged man with raging mommy issues and a serious sadistic streak."

"Which describes half the men in this fucking state. That's not much to go on, Seth."

I lift a shoulder. "She also speculated that the killer either lives or works on campus, given how easily he managed to pick up Scarlett in broad fucking daylight. In the last weeks I've been working on a program for my computer that'll comb through records of faculty and students, looking for any childhood incidents that might hint to our killer. I finished it yesterday and plugged it into a couple data bases, I should have results of any flagged individuals by tomorrow night."

In my waking hours, when I'm not obsessing over Elia, I'm obsessing over the danger she's in and how I can make that danger go away. The thought of someone else putting their hands on her, potentially hurting or *killing* her in some heinous way, is enough to make me lose hold over my sanity. I intend to find the motherfucker who's terrorized campus and put an end to him myself.

Carson blinks a few times. "I've almost forgotten how helpful it is to have you on my team. You're kind of unstoppable, you know that?"

I smile cruelly. "I do know, it's what makes me so efficient. I don't think my program will narrow us down to one killer, but it should gather a pool of suspects that will, more likely than not, include the killer. It's not a sure thing, but it's a start, and I'll work from there."

"Do you need any assistance from me?" Carson questions, taking another sip of his drink.

I shake my head. "No. With these sorts of things, I work best alone."

Carson nods. "Yeah, I've picked up on that. You do you. Now, in terms of Elia, how are we approaching that conversation? The one making clear that choosing both of us is an option?"

I want to correct that choosing either both of us or just me are Elia's *only* options, but decide that's something best kept to myself. People tend to be much more content when they believe they have choices, and my Little Muse didn't appreciate the one time I stated my intent to own her, so I won't push the topic.

"I can tell her in the morning. Or you can tell her when you shadow her next—I don't care who the news comes from, as long as it's soon. Each time she's with me, I can sense guilt hanging over her like a storm cloud. I don't like the way it weighs on her, dims the light in her eyes, and makes her hesitant, so it needs to go," I say calmly.

Carson's eyes widen as he stares at me.

"Holy shit," he says. "You actually care about someone else's emotional state."

I frown. "Why is this such a surprise? If I didn't care about Eliana, I'd have either killed you or set up a scheme to have you exiled to another continent to get rid of the competition. Instead, I'm here extending an invite to a three-way relationship."

Carson gives an astonished laugh. "It's a surprise, Seth, because in our years of friendship, I've never seen you have regard for another person's feelings—not even mine. The fact that you care this much about her means you've already taken the fall. You're in love with her."

He hit the nail right on the head. I *am* in love with Eliana, and I realize how much I dislike being in love as a concept. I care about another's wants, desires, and emotions more than I care about my own, which I've never experienced before. I think about her more often than I think about anything else, including work and even art. I want to spend all my time with her, because she makes that time brighter and more interesting.

"Don't pretend like you aren't," I say with a scoff. "Falling for her was always an inevitability for both of us, not a question. It was only a matter of time."

Carson appears contemplative. "I think I am," he admits quietly. "She's exhilarating. Enlivening. She's *everything*, Seth."

I very much share the sentiment. Eliana is everything that is right in this world, bright and shiny and so goddamn invigorating it's impossible to not want her.

"I know," I tell him. "So, let's keep her."

CHAPTER FORTY-EIGHT

Elia

A warm flutter along the back of my neck is what pulls me from my sleep. I stir a little in the comfortable bedding, sighing and leaning into the sensation, which I realize is a pair of lips trailing kisses along my nape. A strong arm is draped around my waist, with fingers drawing patterns on my bare stomach. I pry my eyes open, greeted by darkness streaming through a window on the wall of Seth's bedroom. I feel a slight sting from the many bite and scratch marks that were left on my skin through the course of the night as I roll over to face Seth.

He's laid out on his side, eyes that are more grey than hazel this morning watching me. After our first two rounds of sex last night, he woke me an additional *three times* throughout the night. I'm ready to curl up and sleep through the day, but I need to be back on campus in time for dance.

Seth greets, "Good morning, Little Muse."

I let out a small hum. "Good morning. What time is it?"

"Time for me to get a refill," he responds, rolling me to my back and straddling me.

I put a hand flat on his chest. "Not if it makes me late."

Seth's lips kick up at the corner. "It won't make you late, it's barely five in the morning." He takes my hand from his chest and pins it beside my head before repeating the gesture with my other hand, leaving me immobilized beneath him. His eyes glimmer with intrigue as he stares down at me in the compromising position, pinned down and naked.

"What should I do with you now?" he asks, his voice throaty.

Feeling sore all over the place, I say, "Whatever it is, please be gentle. I need to dance for the next six hours, and if you go at me with the same vigor you did last night, I won't be able to. Then you'll lose access to my body during weeknights."

Seth's eyebrows furrow. "That's not going to work for me. I won't be losing access to you, period, so I guess I'll have to be nice with you this morning."

He brings one of my wrists up to his lips to brush a kiss over my pulse point, then does the same with my other wrist before releasing them. His hands begin roaming my body with the gentlest of touches. He starts by running his fingertips up my bare arms, raising goosebumps on my skin. Then he drags the backs of his hands across my collarbones, before reaching lower to cup my breasts in his palms. They're covered in bite marks of his, and my nipples stiffen into tight peaks as he brushes his thumbs over them. His hands sneak down further south, but instead of going to my pussy they stroke over the skin of my thighs, all the way down to my knees before coming back up.

Then, Seth boldly cups my pussy in his hand and a finger nudges at my entrance. A breath hisses out of me as a stinging ignites down there, but it only takes a moment for the sting to subside into a faint, tingling burn.

A smile creeps onto Seth's lips as he watches my expression. "You *are* sore," he observes. "That probably shouldn't please me as much as it does, but I want you to feel me for the rest of the day, Little Muse. I don't, however, want to hurt or impede you in any way, so I think the best course of action here is to kiss the pain away."

"Mmm," I hum, back arching as he circles the heel of his palm over my clit. "I can get on board with that."

"If I could, I'd spend eternity with you like this," Seth says, leaning down to skim his teeth up the column of my neck. "Worshipping you, fucking you, tasting you. Everything and more."

My body lights up at his words, even as my thoughts dampen. I feel like I'm betraying Carson with Seth, and I feel like I'm betraying Seth when I'm with Carson. I've tried to brush away the thoughts of the damage I could be causing, to convince myself that this competition was their choice so it's not my fault if they aren't enjoying it, but a niggling sense of guilt always comes for me.

"I had a conversation with Carson while you were asleep last night," Seth rumbles in my ear. I tense beneath him, and my hands fly up to clutch his shoulders. He pulls back; I stare at him with wide eyes, waiting for him to continue.

With Seth, conversation can mean any number of things—he's told me about some *conversations* he's had where the other person did not walk out of the room alive. Granted, those people don't sound like they deserved to live, but Carson does. The thought of Seth hurting him because of me makes all the arousal leech from my body, replacing it with fear.

Seth lets out a low chuckle. "I didn't kill him, Little Muse, so you can stop giving me that deer-caught-in-headlights look. We talked about our arrangement, actually. I've been angling to add a third option into the mix and needed to see if he was on board. Luckily, he was."

"What third option?" My words end on a moan as he slides two fingers inside of me, scissoring them and rubbing against my hyper-sensitive walls.

"The option where you can choose both of us, if you want to," Seth murmurs before taking my earlobe between his lips and nipping at it.

My mind starts to fog up with pleasure, but his words are too important for me to get lost in physical sensations, so I clutch the hand Seth's using to torture me to keep it in place as I stare up at him.

"What do you mean?" I ask cautiously, even as excitement starts to whirl within me like a tornado.

I've been hoping, *praying* that some easy resolution to my conundrum would present itself; either Seth or Carson or both of them suddenly having to move away for business dealings, an earthquake devastating the area and creating new priorities outside of romance, some end-of-the-world event that would, in essence, absolve me of my responsibility to choose. I don't *want* to choose between Seth and Carson; I like both of them. Hell, I'm already feeling a lot more than just *liking* them, I might be starting to fall for them. If Seth's giving me the opening to choose both of them, then that's the answer to my prayers that I've been waiting for.

Then again... that might open a door to a whole slew of new problems. If I were to choose both Seth and Carson, I'd potentially be putting them both in compromising positions for their business. I don't know how polyamory is regarded among the upper crust, but I don't think the wealthy and elite are a particularly accepting bunch. Aside from the damage a three-way relationship could cause to *them*, I can't ignore the perils it would present to me, as well.

Scarlett put up the disgusting Instagram post *before* I'd even really been with either Seth or Carson, when we were all still in the them-stalking-me phase without much reciprocated attention. What sort of posts would I be looking at if we were all out in the open, together? That could draw the sort of criticism that would end my career, all over something that could still just be a game to the two men I'm caught between.

I don't *think* it's a game to them, I've sensed connection deepening on all ends, but I don't know that for sure. I haven't talked about what comes next with either of them, I've been focused on enjoying the present as much as I could before it came to an inevitable, fiery end. It still could go to a fiery end, except there will be much more at stake if I truly invest.

"I mean that you can now choose both of us, Elia. All of us, together." He pauses. "What are you thinking that's making your nose scrunch up?" Seth asks me, tilting his head to the side.

"I'm thinking about what this means," I respond honestly. "I'm thinking about what comes next; what comes later. I try to think several steps ahead, because that's the only way I've survived this long. So, tell me, Seth, what are the next steps? Even if I choose both of you, what comes next? What comes when one or both of you get tired? What will become of my career when I get called a whore for being with two men, especially when I don't know exactly where that relationship could be heading? What I'm thinking is that, at the end of everything, I could get stuck shouldering a shitstorm of the century on my own along with a broken heart."

Seth stares down at me, his eyes blazing with intensity. He slowly lowers himself to the bed beside me, curving an arm around my waist and using it to roll me to my side so we're facing each other. He props one of his arms beneath his head to hold it up while using his free hand to stroke through my hair.

"Let me tell you the next steps as I see them," he says calmly. "I want you, Eliana. Today, tomorrow, *forever*. I'm not someone who really forms attachments with other living beings, but I can say with total certainty that I've grown attached to you past the point of no return. Even if you turn your back on me, I'd never let you go. I'll always be your shadow, watching and coveting and protecting. From what I've seen of him, Carson's equally as enamored with you, otherwise I wouldn't have brought up the idea of both of us getting you to him. This isn't going to end, Little Muse. You would never be left alone to face harsh tides, because I'll be there to protect you, as will he. Tell me you understand that."

His words are spoken with such sincerity and earnestness, I can't discredit them. I'm hesitant to believe something so good could be ripe for the taking, as life has taught me to be, but I also want it *so much*.

"I understand."

Seth nods, cupping my cheek. "Good. You need to remember that we have a lot of reach and influence when it comes to media. If people try to attack us, we'll use some friendlier reporters to drive a positive narrative. Nothing has to be decided today, Little Muse. I'm not telling you about the third and newest option to pressure you into a decision, I'm just telling you it's now an available path."

I lean into his hand, sighing. "Thank you. I need to think, probably talk to April, figure out my best move."

Seth arches an eyebrow. "You make a point of talking to April about your going-on's with us?"

I smile a little. "She's a good friend. I like her a lot, and she was the one to first bring up the idea of choosing both of you. I think you might like her."

Seth lets out a low chuckle. "April... isn't she the girl Ian calls Sugarplum?"

I did hear Ian refer to April by that nickname, which I'd guess comes from the Sugarplum variation in The Nutcracker. The endearment sounded like a taunt from his lips, so I don't think he calls her that to be nice.

It's curious that Seth knows Ian. Not too strange considering Ian's friends with Carson, and Carson is obviously good enough friends with Ian to ask him to swing by dorms at night while I'm out, so maybe Ian and Seth met through Carson. It seems dangerous for someone like Ian to be friends with someone like Seth; I suspect they're both cut from a similar antisocial cloth, so that must be a recipe for chaos.

"He does call her that, though I don't think it's to be nice," I say, tilting my head to the side. "How do you know Ian?"

"I met him through Carson," Seth replies. "Carson's been trying to get me to come work at his dad's company with him, and Ian already works at the company with him, so we've crossed paths a few times. I enjoy Ian, he has a similar sense of humor to me."

"Is that the sense of humor where you both find skinning kittens funny?"

Seth strokes his thumb over the apple of my cheek. "No, Little Muse, it's the kind of humor where we both derive a certain joy out of breaking people."

I feel my chest tighten at that. I know there are dark parts of Seth that he tries to keep on a leash around me, and I accept those parts, but sometimes he says things that unnerve me.

"But you don't find joy in that with me, right?" I ask quietly.

Seth's eyebrows furrow and he shakes his head resolutely. "No. I like you exactly as you are, Eliana. I don't want to break you. If anything, I want to build you up as high as you can go and watch you shine beside me. I told you this once in the archives and I'll tell you again, I have zero desire to hurt or toy with you, outside of the sexual sense of those words. I don't want to tarnish you; I want to preserve you. I take *very* good care of my belongings, unlike Ian, who would sooner destroy them."

"Are you calling me one of your belongings?"

Seth bobs his head up and down. "At the risk of you storming out to go revenge-fuck Carson again, yes. Not because you're an object to me; that couldn't be further from the truth. Most people *are* like objects to me, I'll admit that, but not you. You are very much a person, a person I am very fond of and have decided to keep."

I sigh. "You know you're kind of pathological, right?"

His thumb moves down my cheek, and then presses against my lips before pushing into my mouth. At the same time, he slides his other hand back down to my pussy, and circles my clit, sending a small tremor of pleasure through my system.

"I do know that," Seth says. "I also know that you can handle it, which, aside from the expression you wear when you orgasm, is the most incensing, erotic thing I could possibly imagine. Now hush and let me have a taste of you. Then I'll drive you to campus."

Chapter Forty-Nine

"Your pas de deux with Sean is shaping up beautifully," April tells me, taking a long drink from her water bottle.

We've just finished up with dance for the day and are seated by the wall of mirrors on the floor of the studio we're using for Pandora's Box, catching our breaths. The room's mostly cleared out, and Carson got called into work for the morning, so he isn't sulking in the corner as usual.

"I'm trying," I tell her. "I was thinking about asking him if he wants to allocate a few extra hours a week to work on our duets."

I have three big variations with Sean; the meeting, the wedding, and after I've opened the box and permanently screwed up the world. The wedding is the most difficult and longest variation, and I suspect it'll take a lot of work for us to perfect it. It's filled with several complex and tricky sequences, so it'll probably need some legwork outside of class times.

"Go for it, but I'd suggest you tell your stalkers first, or they might assume he's competition and kill him off. Have you seen the way Carson glares at Sean when he's here while you guys are practicing?

That shit is *priceless*. Since Seth is known as Greywood's resident genius/psychopath, I assume he'll be even more intense about it. Have you all figured out what you are yet?"

I bite my lip. "No official titles, but I spent the night with Seth last night, and there were some developments. We, um…"

April waves an impatient hand. "Fucked like rabbits, I'm sure. What else?"

Feeling my cheeks burn, I murmur, "At some point while I was asleep, Seth went to Carson's apartment—they live in the same building—to talk. This morning, he told me there is now an option three, one where I can choose both of them."

April's jaw drops. "You *bitch*," she says. "I'd be green with jealousy if I didn't adore you. Oh my god, you actually managed to snag *two* of Greywood's finest! Tell me you chose them, and now you three are in a steamy, sexy, hot-as-fuck—"

"Those are all synonyms," I point out.

April continues on as if I hadn't spoken. "Mind-blowingly incredible, orgasmic, stars-bursting-behind-your-eyes relationship?"

I let out a laugh. "Not yet, no. I haven't made any decisions."

"Don't linger around for too long, you two, this studio will be getting used for a class in fifteen minutes," Sander's voice sounds from the doorway. April and I both turn our heads to the entrance simultaneously to see our director and choreographer peeking his head in with a raised hand. He says, "Good work this morning, ladies. I'll see you in evening rehearsal tonight, where we'll build on The Wedding some more."

"Thank you, Mr. Sanders, I'll see you tonight," I say with a smile.

"We'll clear out of here in just a second," April tags on.

Sanders nods, gives us a final wave, then turns and strolls away.

April turns back to me and frowns at me, like I'm an alien she can't make sense of. "What do you mean you haven't made any decisions with your men? You already know what you want to do, and now you can actually do it—have both of them. What are you waiting for?"

I shrug. "To wrap my head around it, I guess. This is just a lot all at once, April. I want both of them, yes, but I don't really know what a dynamic with all three of us would look like. I mean... what if we're together, and we go out, and spend the entire time getting judgmental stares from passersby? What happens if we ever move in together? How many beds and bedrooms would there be? Would we sleep together? Would I go out on dates with both of them at once or one at a time—"

April leans forward to clap a hand over my mouth. "Okay, Jesus, I get it, you have some concerns. Take a second to stop catastrophizing and think it through." She releases my mouth, leaning back with a thoughtful expression. "I think you need to keep in mind that those two are uber-powerful men with a lot of reach. I doubt many people would have the balls to talk shit about Carson Ajax or Seth Balor, and if you're their public object of affection, then people will think twice about bad-mouthing you, as well. From what I've seen, Elia, they're pretty enchanted with you. Granted, I've only gotten glimpses of Seth, but the way he looks at you... it's like you're a sliver of light in his lifetime of darkness. I'm pretty sure the dude would conquer the world if you asked him to."

I feel my shoulders slump. It just feels like there's an endless number of open-ended questions, with answers I'll only get if I dive in head-first. I'm not really one to dive headfirst into anything—I am very, *very* cautious by nature, and I do an agonizing amount of deliberating before choosing a course of action.

Last year, I was stuck on my final choice between Greywood and Juilliard for months, and only ended up choosing Greywood on the day of the deadline. I made pros and cons lists, created excel spreadsheets analyzing the success rate of graduates for both programs, and spent about a month poring over every tiny detail before finally deciding to go for Greywood.

That was for college; now I need to decide if I should give a three-way relationship a try, which would have a huge impact on my life *and* totally destroy my personal no-dating rule. But since that rule has already been eradicated in the last weeks, considering I spend the little free time I have with either Seth or Carson, it's not as much of a consideration.

I think back on what ended up acting as the nudge for me choosing Greywood and recall that it came down to my tours. I'd used some of my savings to be able to tour both Greywood and Juilliard, and I liked that Greywood was in a more nature-heavy state and offered a very cohesive and open campus life. It was that tidbit of experiencing what Greywood life would be like versus Juilliard life that ended up tipping me over the edge. Maybe an experience is what I need with Carson and Seth, too. Go out with them *un*officially and see what that might be like—see how they play together and if a three-way relationship is even feasible.

"I think I know what to do," I say resolutely.

April arches a questioning eyebrow at me. I give her a grin, pushing to my feet and grabbing my backpack. She stands as well and walks with me to the door.

"Don't keep me in suspense," April says. "What is it?"

I bite back a smile. "Try both of them out together."

***

I run into Carson on my way back to my dorm from class. He looks like he's heading out of his dorm room as I'm striding down the hall towards mine. A wide smile stretches his lips as soon as he sees me, and I can't help but reciprocate it. I come to a stop in front of him, craning my neck all the way back to meet his icy eyes.

He says, "Hey, Little E. Miss me already?"

I make a *pfft* sound. "I saw you yesterday."

"Then you spent the night with Seth," Carson points out calmly. "Considering his generalized lack of interest in female pleasure during sex, I figure you might've been left a touch unsatisfied."

Oh. Carson's blatant sexuality no longer jars me as it once did, but what Carson's saying about Seth not being interested in a woman's pleasure during sex does. I've fooled around with Seth at least a dozen times before last night, and each time *was* focused on my pleasure. A good amount of the time he wouldn't even let me touch him to get him off; I've always been the focal point for him.

"There were, um, no problems in that department," I murmur.

Carson's eyebrows raise. "Well, what do you know. Miracles really are possible. You should know, Princess, that I've literally never seen Seth care about another person, certainly not enough to prioritize their needs above his own, but last night he showed up at my place with a proposition of us *both* getting you just to make sure he'd be able to keep you. You must've worked some kind of dark magic on him—on me, too, now that I think about it." He pauses and tilts his head to the side. "Are you a witch? Or a fairy, maybe? You know, one of those magical tricksters?"

A giggle bursts out of me. Carson's so ridiculous, so lighthearted, it's impossible not to laugh around him. "No, I'm not a witch or a fairy. I'll have you know, I am one hundred percent human. Now, are you done being silly? Can we talk?"

Carson winces. "Those aren't usually the words a man wants to hear from a woman, are they?"

I roll my eyes and say, "It's nothing bad, just a conversation. I have questions, I'd like answers."

I take his hand in mine, stepping closer. Carson instantly twines our fingers together, and a soft smile curls his lips when he glances at our hands. "Your hands are so tiny, like the rest of you. If you didn't have enough fire to fill a volcano, one could think you're an easy target. Alright, Little E, we'll talk—but I just got a message from Seth that local PD got a partial print from the killer and some other stuff regarding our campus menace, so can we talk later?"

I instantly go on high alert at his words. "I'm coming with you. We can talk on the way."

Carson hums, tugging me closer. "Is that so? What's in it for me? Seth wants you out of the loop until we have something concrete to go on."

That irks me a little, but I already know Seth is very controlling by nature. That's one of his quirks that I'll really need to learn to live with if there's any chance of me giving a relationship with him a go.

I don't fault him for being the way he is; since learning more about his childhood, a lot of his tendencies that seem diabolical without context have started to make sense. He plans as many steps ahead as possible because he learned to do so when living in a horrible situation, same as me. He has darker inclinations and a knack for ruining lives because there was a time where his life was ruined by his own father. He doesn't care about most people, doesn't really connect with others, because nobody came through for him when he needed it most. There are some parts of him, a certain darkness that I suspect he was born with, but a lot can be explained by his difficult upbringing.

I don't mind if he tries to control me as much as I should because I can see it's an instinct for him. I just can't let him think he'll *succeed* in controlling me like he does others. If he wants me, then he'll have to understand I'm not a doll he can put on a shelf when he's working and keep things from, especially when those things pertain to something like the serial killer stalking our college campus.

I tell Carson with a saccharine smile, "You get to not find out just how hard I can knee you in the balls for trying to leave me at home like some helpless damsel. I may *look* small and sweet, but so do some of the most poisonous flowers, and they're the deadliest."

Carson blinks at me. "Wow. I think you just threatened my life in a roundabout way, which shouldn't have turned me on, but it kind of did. Have time for a quickie in your dorm before we go? I'll only be thirty minutes, tops."

I give him my most unamused look.

"Fine, twenty," he amends.

I sigh, glancing around the hall to see if anyone else is witnessing Carson's sheer lunacy. They aren't, the coast is clear, thank god.

"Okay, ten, but that's the final offer. Ten minutes, at least one orgasm. Do we have a deal?"

"No," I snap, withdrawing my hand and folding my arms. "I have rehearsal in three hours, which is how long you and Seth have to catch me up on whatever you've been doing behind my back and explain why I haven't been looped in."

Chapter Fifty

C arson's eyes twinkle with mirth as he takes my hand again, using it to pull me down the hall. "I'm pretty sure Seth left you out of it because he didn't want to stress you out. As for why I didn't say anything, it's because I didn't know anything until I talked to him last night. We haven't exactly been on friendly footing recently, what with competing for you and all, so he hasn't bothered to keep me in the loop either." He pauses as we step into the elevator, where there's a couple lip-locked in the corner. Once we reach ground floor and exit the building, Carson goes on, "All I know is that Seth had a friend put together a potential profile on the killer, and he used that profile to create a computer program that'd scan the pool of suspects."

"What pool of suspects?" I ask.

"Campus," Carson responds. "Seth's friend determined that the killer is most likely someone who either lives or works on campus. So, Seth's doing his computer magic to see what he can dig up."

We come up on the parking lot, and I spot Carson's blue Tesla in a corner parking spot by the exit. As we walk up to it, I ask, "Is there anything Seth *can't* do?"

"Be a fucking human being," Carson replies. "He's not very good at that. The dude's a walking corpse most of the time, colder than the polar ice caps. Which is why you have me, Little E." He opens the car door for me, then closes it before getting into the driver's seat.

Well, this is as good a time as any to press Carson for his view on our potential situation. I ask him, "Does sharing me with him really not bother you?"

Carson twists his lips, taking a beat too long to consider. It makes me nervous that he might not be as cool with this situation as he's letting off.

He says, "It did at first, I'm not going to lie, but not as intensely as I expected it to. When I see you dancing with Prince Gardener—"

"Sean," I correct, frowning.

"—I'm ready to catch a first-degree charge. But when I knew you'd fooled around with Seth, I was more irritated that he was getting ahead of me in our race than actually upset that you'd been with him. Maybe it's because I already know you're such a handful, it would take the both of us to contain you, so I don't mind the extra help. Not with Seth, at least. Anyone else, though, I'd kill."

"I think Seth might beat you to that," I say, thinking out loud.

If Carson gets murder-happy seeing me dance with Sean, there's every chance Seth might assassinate my dance partner before opening night. It's probably best if I keep Seth away from Sean for as long as I can.

Carson snorts. "You're right. Know what? Whoever tries to hit on you, I'll just unleash Seth on them. It'll feed the sadist in him and keep my hands clean. What do you think, Princess?"

"That you belong in a psychiatric ward," I quip. "You are not *unleashing* Seth on anyone. Also, we're having an actual conversation, so if you could keep your inner mental patient dormant for just a little longer, I'd appreciate it."

Carson mimes zipping his lips and throwing the keys out of the window, which makes me smile.

"How would it work mechanically with the three of us together?" I question.

Carson smirks. "You have enough holes to accommodate us. It might be a stretch, but we'll make it work."

I give his head a light smack, one that would be a lot harder if he wasn't driving. "I don't mean the sex."

He rubs his head, shooting me a lascivious smile. "Why not? That's fun to talk about. If, like you implied, Seth actually knows how the female body works and managed to make you come, that means double the satisfaction for you and an extra pair of hands to keep the ratio in check for me."

I groan. "Keep a lid on it for five seconds, Ajax, or I will pull your ear so hard it'll rip clean off. I don't care that you're driving. What I mean is how would the *dynamic* work? Would we go out in public? If so, where? What would we do?"

Despite my best efforts, I can't help but think about what it would be like with both of them in bed. Carson's crude as hell, though he's technically right that I *do* have more than one hole, but I can't wrap my brain around having both of them at once. A few images flash through my mind, possibilities of how we could all even fit together, and the pictures my brain conjures are at once insanely erotic and more than a little terrifying. I've never had any interest in a threesome; frankly, I didn't even have much interest in sex alone before meeting Carson and Seth, so I'm woefully uneducated and unprepared for what I might theoretically be in for.

It's more than a little ridiculous, but I can't stop from pulling out my phone and shooting a text to April. She's a very openly sexual person—as best as I can tell, she's already made her way through three men and two women in the time since we got to campus. Fridays and weekends when we're not hanging out she's usually out and about with her newest side piece, and tells me the type of stories that damn near blister my ears when she gets back. If there's anyone I know who I could ask about sex stuff, other than the two men hell-bent on keeping me, it's her.

> **Eliana:** *Theoretically, what would a three-some look like? In terms of positions and stuff.*

As soon as I hit send, Carson speaks again. "I think we'll have to play the *dynamic* by ear, Little E. Go with whatever feels good, so to speak. Seth and I hang out often when we aren't stuck fighting about a girl, and we're actually pretty good friends. He threatens to kill me a lot, but I'm sure he'll keep that on the downlow around you."

"Good to know," I say drily. "What do you think us going out would look like?"

I'm embarrassed to talk about this so openly and frankly with him, but I feel like the best way forward is to lay everything out on the table. I'm only being this bold because I know that both men want me as much as I want them, and I'd like to test the waters to get a visual of what that particular future might hold.

Carson shrugs. "I dunno. We *could* do some boring couple shit like minigolf, but I think we're more interesting than that. We'd probably drive up to that mountain you liked and go for a hike, either pack dinner with us or grab some afterwards, then come home for dessert? My place, preferably, because my bed is bigger than Seth's, therefore

I am better than him." He nods resolutely. "Yeah, that sounds like a good night to me."

The way he says *come home for dessert* makes me believe that *I'll* be the dessert, but I set that thought aside for later. I try to picture having an outing with both Seth and Carson. I've gone out with them separately on several occasions, and the dynamics are different with each of them. Seth keeps me on my toes, and spending time with him is dark, carnal, intensely interesting, and sometimes a little uneasy. Carson is light, funny, and very go-with-the-flow. They're both also gods in bed, which is a definite perk, but I don't know how our personal dynamics will play together.

My phone buzzes in my lap; I unlock it and see that April's responded to my questions with some pictures.

The pictures are of stick figures, three of them, in some very interesting positions. It looks like April drew them out on a notebook page. The first drawing is of one stick figure with long hair and tits—me, presumably—on all fours with one male stick figure in front of me and one behind me. The next picture depicts one of the male stick figures lying down, the female stick figure straddling his waist, and *another* male behind the girl, straddling the vertical man's legs. I feel my cheeks burn as I realize the implications behind that one... having them both inside me, at once, in both of my holes down below. That thought is overwhelming and a little frightening but also kind of arousing.

The final drawing is of the two male stick figures, on their knees facing each other, and the female stick figure directly in between them. Following the images comes another text.

April: *Does that answer your question?*

Carson asks, "Who are you texting? Wait, let me guess, April."

I say with a laugh, "Who else? She's my only real friend on campus." I have plenty of *acquaintances* within the dance program and in my art history/ English/ language classes, but nobody I'd consider close to a friend. Maybe Chloe, but I don't know her all that well yet—we both have really busy schedules.

"Hey, *I'm* your friend," Carson says with a pout.

"You are not my friend, Carson, you're a prospect," I respond dryly. "Totally different category."

Carson appears to think on that for a moment, then nods. "Okay, fair enough, but can't I be both? I can be your best friend *and* someone you fuck."

"I'm pretty sure that's referred to as a boyfriend for most," I point out. "Or a fuck-buddy, but I don't really do those."

Carson perks right up, sliding me a hopeful glance. "So, I'm your boyfriend? Cool, I can work with that."

I roll my eyes, letting out a long sigh. "What you are, Ajax, is absolutely insufferable. I have to admire the people who spend time with you on a regular basis; those are the real saints."

He grins. "I'll take that as a compliment. What were you texting April about?"

"None of your business," I say sternly.

Carson's grin turns mischievous. "Oh, was it something sexy? Are you guys exchanging nudes to compare or something?"

"No! What is *wrong* with you?" I snap.

"Do you want that list numbered or alphabetized?"

"Sometimes, I'm really not sure how to respond to you."

Carson chuckles, reaching over to take my hand, intertwining our fingers just like he did back in the dorm. "That's fair. You're not the only person who's a handful here, Little E. I can guarantee you, though, if you want me to go down for a nap and give you some reprieve, your best bet is letting me taste you. With a full stomach and content in the knowledge I've properly taken care of you, I might actually calm down for a while. Maybe. We'll see how it goes."

We pull into Carson's building's underground parking lot. He parks the car, then rounds the hood to open my door before leading me to the elevator.

I ask, "Can I say hi to Mewlius?"

Carson laughs lightly. "Sure, Little E. You know, I think my cat likes you more than he likes me. When I came back to the apartment to check on Caesar after you'd spent the night, the little furball kept looking around like he was waiting for you, then proceeded to ignore me when you didn't magically appear."

I chuckle. "Cats are like that. Notoriously uninterested."

"Kind of like you with me, at first," Carson quips. "Not that I let that deter me. Seth didn't, either. Obviously, we were both right to not feel deterred, as now we're here."

"'Here' being a limbo where I still haven't made a choice?" I question pleasantly.

Carson shakes his head, sliding me an affectionate glance. "You've already made the choice, love. You just haven't worked all the details out in that pretty head of yours, so you haven't yet verbalized your choice."

He's right. He knows he's right, I know he's right, and Seth is probably thinking something along the same lines—that it's only a matter of time before I fully give in. While that may be the truth, and I am strongly inclined to just dive in and see where things go, I can't *not* be cautious. I need to sample before I make a purchase.

Instead of saying that, I say, "Princess, Little E, now love. You're a big fan of terms of endearment, hmm?" I don't mention just how tingly it makes me to be called *love.*

Carson grins. "You can actually tell how I feel about a girl based on the names I call her. You're the only woman in my life to have earned yourself nicknames and endearments, Little E, so you should be pleased."

I say drily, "Ah, so the other women in your life had to settle for one or the other? Nicknames *or* terms of endearment?"

"Usually just terms of endearment, and never genuine ones," Carson assures me. "I called girls sweetheart when we were hooking up. Mainly because I didn't really remember their names most of the time."

"Because you're a man-whore," I remark flatly.

The elevator opens with a ding; I follow Carson to his apartment, waiting impatiently for him to unlock it so I can cuddle with my favorite cat.

"I *was* a man-whore, though I really prefer the term rake," Carson corrects. "Sounds a little less douchebag-y, a little more aristocratic and respectable. Now, though, I consider everyone who came before you as practice. At least I learned plenty of tricks to keep you happy."

Although his dating—well, more like sleeping around—history doesn't really endear me, I like the way he's framing it, even if I don't like the fact that he's slept with enough women to fill up the Atlantic. Sometimes I do get flashes of insecurity. He has a lot of experience, which leaves me feeling like I might be lacking in his eyes. Not because he ever gives me the sense that I'm not satisfying him—he is very generous with praise, which I like a lot—but because I worry that I'm not exciting enough for him, or even if I am *now*, I won't always be.

Carson opens the door and lets me into his apartment. I drop my backpack by the front door, smiling as Mewlius runs right up to me as soon as I've stepped inside and stands on his hind paws to sink his claws into my jeans. He meows loudly, demanding my attention, and

I happily indulge him. I bend down and scoop him into my arms, cradling him to my chest like a baby.

I've spent a little more time at Carson's apartment in the last weeks, but I haven't stayed the night, and each time I'm here I end up cuddling Mewlius until Carson pries us away from each other.

Carson disappears into the kitchen while I take Mewlius to the couch, sinking into the corner cushion and settling him on my lap. He stretches and yawns, then curls up into a little ball and falls right to sleep. Carson emerges from the kitchen with a bottle of beer for him and a bottle of root beer for me. Since learning it's my favorite soda, he always keeps it on hand for me.

He drops onto the couch beside me, uncaps the twisty top off of my root beer and hands it to me, before taking a long pull from his beer before setting it on the table in front of us. Then he slings one arm around my shoulders and uses his free hand to draw his phone out of his pocket.

I watch him, wondering if I'm really enough for him, if being here is the best course of action. I don't know if I have the sort of skill it takes to keep Carson around long-term, and I refuse to make any commitment without seeing the potential for a future.

"I'm letting Seth know that you're here with me and would like to be read in," Carson informs me.

I nod, leaning closer to him. Even when I'm feeling uncertain, perhaps especially then, I like to be close to him. He drops his phone, then turns his full attention to me.

"You're tense," he observes.

I feel my shoulders droop a little. "Just a lot on my mind," I tell him honestly.

He arches an eyebrow. "Like what?"

I shift in my spot, feeling a little nervous. Still, I think it's better to get everything out in the open, so I blurt, "I don't know if I'm going to be enough for you long-term. I mean... you've obviously been around the block plenty of times and sampled every flavor available, probably more than once. I have not done that. My experience in bed is a fumbling time when I lost my virginity, and then learning how to get my ex off just so the sex would be over quickly. I'm not the most beautiful girl on the planet, I barely have tits, and I don't really have the experience to make up for my other imperfections." I feel my eyes start to sting, and mortification washes over me as I realize I'm about to cry. I try to force the tears down, my voice turning a little wobbly as I continue. "What I'm saying is that I don't want to invest in you only to come up short down the line. So, if there's any chance that what we have is a passing infatuation for you, something you'll get over in the future, you need to tell me now so that I can move on without getting my heart broken."

Carson stares at me for several long, intense moments in silence. I take a sip of my root beer to try to distract from the heat of his stare, because the longer he looks at me without talking, the more afraid I grow that my words have credence. That there's a chance he isn't ready for anything serious and is just having a bit of fun with me. None of his actions have led me to believe that, especially since he moved into dorms with me, but I don't want to assume only to set myself up for failure.

Carson takes my root beer bottle from me and sets it on the table. Then, he picks up Mewlius from my lap and sets him on the floor, prompting the cat to hiss at Carson, *loudly*. Carson abruptly takes a hold of my arms and hauls me onto his lap.

I stiffen, not because I don't like the position, but because this isn't a response I expected from him. I look into his eyes as his arms circle around my waist harder than usual, as if holding me tightly enough will cement me in place.

He tells me, "I need you to listen to me very carefully, Eliana. Can you do that? Listen and believe what I have to say?"

I nod, and his grip relaxes ever so slightly. He tells me, "I want you *desperately*, for as long as you'll have me. Which, if things go according to plan, will be forever. This is not a passing infatuation for me—it's a compulsion, quite possibly an obsession. It's not going away. The way I feel for you hasn't lessened at all in our time together, in fact it's only grown into this raging, uncontrollable monster within me that screams for you. I want you enough to tolerate having Seth as a permanent fixture in my life and, potentially, home. I want you enough to tear this world apart for you. That's not going anywhere. *I'm* not going anywhere. Are you with me so far?"

Feeling absolutely enamored with him, I nod and relax in his hold a little.

Carson continues, "As for you feeling like you're not good enough for me, the truth of the matter is that *I'm* not good enough for *you*. I was a die-hard rake, Little E, which means I know a million ways to make you scream, but it also means sex was always meaningless, a fun and satisfying way to pass the time, until you. I've never felt any connection during it, not the way I do with you. If you want total honesty—"

"I do," I interject.

"—I often feel like you'll look at me like I'm damaged or spoiled goods because of how much I've gotten around. I don't feel good enough for you, but that isn't enough to stop me from keeping you. I'm not a bad guy, but when it comes to you, I am a selfish bastard. No two ways about it. The next time you start wondering if you're good enough for me, the real question you should be asking yourself is if I'm good enough for you. We both know the answer is no, and we both know I'm gonna keep you, anyways. Got it?"

Now my eyes are stinging for a reason that isn't a fear of rejection. I wind my hands in his hair, scraping my fingernails along his scalp the way I've learned he likes. "You're demented if you think you aren't good enough for me," I tell him with complete sincerity. "You are. You have a beautiful heart, Carson. I don't care if you've gotten around, so long as you no longer feel any need or desire to get around."

"I don't," he confirms.

I lean forward to brush my lips against his. Before we can really get to kissing though, his doorbell rings three times in quick succession, and then a thunderous knock sounds on the wood.

Carson smirks. "And that'll be the other guy you've managed to capture. Good thing I already know him, or I would have to get rid of the competition."

"I'm pretty sure he's had similar thoughts about you, even while knowing you," I say with a wince.

Carson laughs, long and loud. "You're right. It's probably good for my health that Seth decided the best way forward involved me. Otherwise, I might be breathing through a tube, if at all."

CHAPTER FIFTY-ONE

I climb off of Carson's lap and watch as he stands and strides towards the door, opening it. Seth walks right in without being invited, a black laptop clutched in his hands and a somewhat crazed expression in his eyes. When those eyes land on me the glint of insanity recedes, leaving calm, if not somewhat empty, hazel orbs.

Seth walks directly to me, ignoring Carson's muttered, "Good to see you too, asshole," and draws me to my feet. He leans down to kiss me, and I startle, jerking back slightly. I don't know how I feel about kissing Seth right in front of Carson, mainly because before this morning, I've been careful not to touch one of them in front of the other.

Seth frowns as he pulls back, looking down at me. "What is it?"

I lift a shoulder. "Habit, I think. This is very new."

Seth nods slowly. "It is new. We should all get used to it. If Carson gets miffed at us kissing, how's he going to feel when I'm balls-deep inside of you in front of him?"

Tingles *explode* in my belly at that, making my breath hitch as I realize just how much his words turn me on. The idea of having sex with Seth in front of Carson, Carson being an observer rather than an active participant, is as hot as the idea of somehow taking both of them at once.

I stand on my tiptoes and give Seth a proper greeting kiss, then pull back and glance over his shoulder to see Carson's response. He's leaning against the entryway wall, his expression is totally serene, and there's even a glint of desire in his eyes as he watches me with his friend. He pushes away from the wall and starts walking across the room to me. Seth hears the footsteps and glances over his shoulder. I watch his reaction carefully as he watches Carson's approach. Seth's body tenses ever so slightly for a beat before relaxing. He steps aside when Carson stops in front of me, passing me off to Carson without a fight.

Carson grins down at me. "My turn."

He leans down and teases my lips with several gentle brushes and light touches before finally giving me a real kiss, with tongue and passion, undeterred by the fact that I just kissed Seth with as much tongue and passion. He ends the kiss with a nip to my bottom lip. When I look to Seth for his reaction, I see a storm swirling in his eyes, a mixture of danger and desire. As if there's a part of him that doesn't like seeing me with another man, but he's keeping that part on a leash for my sake.

While I'm somewhat nervous that he might lose hold of that leash at one point or another and things could take a turn for the worst, I'm also relieved that he doesn't seem terribly distressed or murderous over watching me kiss Carson. It mostly looks like he's just getting used to the sight.

Maybe this could work. I can't make that determination after two minutes of us all sharing a space, but I do feel hopeful.

Carson drops down to the couch, on the corner cushion, then pulls me down to the one next to him, leaving space for Seth on my other side. Seth doesn't hesitate to take the silent offer, seating himself as close to me as humanly possible and planting a hand on my thigh. He gives it a squeeze before releasing it and opening his computer, setting it up on his lap.

As he clicks and types away, he starts talking. "You remember Kira, Little Muse?"

I do remember her as the remarkably elegant, eloquent, and well-dressed woman from his art show. Kira was there with Sergei, who is obviously involved in some very dark and nefarious business dealings. Seth once told me he had professional help in taking care of his father, some part of me has to wonder if Sergei was part of that.

"From the art exhibit, yes," I reply.

Carson says, "You've introduced Elia to Kira? That means you've introduced her to Sergei, as well, which can't be a good thing."

Seth pauses in typing on his laptop, and casts Carson a bored glance. "Kira and Sergei attended my art show a few weeks back. Neither of them would ever hurt my Little Muse, because they know her significance to me, and they know what I'm capable of when I'm displeased." He looks back to me and goes on, "Kira sent me the profile we were talking about not long after the show. I used the information in it—"

"To create some mega computer program, I've been caught up," I interrupt. "How did Kira determine that the most likely suspect pool is people on campus?"

Seth replies, "Accessibility. The killer took Scarlett in broad daylight, and she disappeared without a trace. Somebody who doesn't know every nook and cranny of Greywood wouldn't have even attempted, let alone succeeded, in pulling that off. My program has given me a list of names of people who have the sort of issues Kira speculated were driving the killings—unresolved trauma with female mother figures. There are about a dozen people, ten students and two faculty, who could fit the bill. There's one member of faculty in particular who caught my eye, and I think he'll catch yours, as well."

Seth turns the laptop to face me, and I feel myself go very still as I take in the image that's pulled up on screen: it's a picture of *Mr. Sanders.* My blood runs cold as possibility after possibility flies through my mind, each more daunting than the last.

"What the fuck," I whisper, feeling discombobulated.

I've only known Sanders for a few months, but not once have I gotten dark vibes from him. He's cheerful and upbeat, and although he has a very intense and corrective teaching style, there's nothing about him that's menacing or frightening, nothing that makes me believe there's any chance of him being the killer.

"Sanders was raised by his maternal aunt, who he had a very contentious relationship with, by all appearances," Seth informs me. "He ended up in the hospital a few times with diagnoses of broken bones, but social services never took him away from his aunt." Seth flicks his gaze over to Carson, and they appear to have some sort of silent exchange. Then, he goes on, "His aunt's still alive, by the looks of it, living in the same trailer park where she raised Sanders."

I give my head a shake, trying to collect my scattered thoughts. "If Sanders was the killer, wouldn't he have started with the person who traumatized him? His aunt?"

Seth inclines his head. "In most cases, serial killers start with relatives and family members, or other people close to them. Not always, but most of the time."

"So, it can't be Sanders," I say, my tone more hopeful than I intend for it to be. "I've spent a lot of time with him during dance, and not once have I felt unsafe or like he was hiding something. Not a single time, Seth."

Seth sets aside his laptop and puts a hand on my thigh, turning my full attention towards him as his thumb rubs circles on the material of my jeans. He says, "Little Muse, killers and other people who engage in dark crimes usually have a face they wear during their normal life. It's only when they're committing the crimes that the normalcy falls away, and the darker parts of them take the lead. You wouldn't be able to tell who the killer is from spending time with them, because they won't *be* the killer during those times, they'll be the person that they are 99% of the time. It's the 1% that's revealing, and killers rarely let anyone see that small, dangerous part of them unless they don't plan on letting that person live."

Cold sweeps over me as I listen to Seth's words, feeling more and more uncertain and unsafe. It doesn't escape me that he seems to know a lot about this, understands the psychology that could drive a serial killer. I can't forget the fact that Seth himself is a murderer, so he'd have a better understanding of one than I ever could.

The possibility hits me that the sort of dual personality Seth's describing is something he experiences himself. I'm not sure if that's the case, since I've always received dark vibes from him, but that could be his version of normal, hiding the true darkness beneath.

"How do you know all this?" I ask him, my voice a murmur.

He tilts his head to the side, sensing my trepidation, and doesn't appear to like it. His hand on my thigh grips me a little tighter, as if he's afraid of me slipping away from him. It reminds me of the night he confessed he'd taken human life before, when he tried to scare me with his words while holding me so tightly I could barely breathe.

Seth says, "I know because I have an unhinged side of me as well, Little Muse."

Carson snaps, "Don't scare her."

Seth stares at me while he replies, "I'm not trying to scare her, I am being honest with her. Eliana knows she has nothing to fear from me, because even the most unhinged parts of me are devoted to her and interested in protecting her. She knows that my wrath would never get turned in her direction, that she'd never be in danger with me because I'd use every inch of my insanity to protect her." While he speaks, he steadily leans closer to me, until his face is hovering an inch away from mine. "You do know that, don't you, Little Muse?"

His expression is unguarded, allowing me to glimpse the madness that lives in him, and reminding me that while Seth isn't entirely sane, I also don't need to fear his darkness getting unleashed on me. He's never hurt me, never given me any reason to feel unsafe. He's just such a dark person, I think I'll occasionally get unnerved by him. That doesn't mean that I need to be afraid of him. The only time he's ever even gotten rough with me is during sex, and he gave me fair warning beforehand along with a safeword to get out of it.

I nod, reaching my hand up to ghost my fingers over the curve of his jaw. "I do know that," I tell him honestly. "Sometimes you scare me, but that's because there are parts of you I'll never fully understand, though I accept them. I'm more scared of what I know you're capable of than you yourself."

"And you know that my capabilities will only be used to protect you, never to exploit you," Seth says, his voice silky and entrancing.

I notice that he's trying to do the thing to me that he does to the rest of the population; lull us into a susceptible state that's not unlike hypnosis so he can control us. I don't think he even recognizes that he's trying to lightly manipulate me right now, doing so must be second nature to him. I know that I can't let him get away with it and need to hold my ground against him. He has to learn to have discussions rather than simply lull me over to his way of thinking.

"I do know that," I clip. "What you should know is that I'm not agreeing with you because you're using that hypnotizing voice and trying to pull me under your spell, I'm agreeing because you've proven to me that you won't hurt me. So, you can cut the whole siren routine of singing to enslave me; it won't work."

It *might* work, but not for long. I'm not as vulnerable to the spells Seth weaves as the rest of the population because I know him. My thoughts might temporarily go hazy when he uses his allure on me, but they don't stay that way for long.

Seth's lips quirk and he leans down to brush them against mine. "You can't blame a tiger for its stripes, Little Muse."

"As long as you understand I'll only tolerate so much of your bullshit before pushing back, that's fine," I say honestly.

Another faint brush of his lips across mine. He darts his tongue out to run against my bottom lip, then nips at it with his teeth, before saying, "I do understand that, and that's what I like about you. You don't take my shit, you push back. It's fucking intoxicating."

That sends a rush of pleasure through me, and I give him a kiss before pulling back. "Back to the topic of discussion; if the PD got a partial print from Scarlett, couldn't they just cross reference it with Sanders's fingerprint?"

"He doesn't have one on file, and they have no probable cause to arrest him and get his fingerprint in the system," Seth says irritably.

"Could they bring him in for an interview without arrest?" I question edgily. It might be best if the police get on top of this sooner rather than later, because while I don't want to believe that the killer could be Sanders, I admit I have no way of knowing for sure. The best way to find out might be to get him interrogated.

Seth shakes his head. "They could, but that would be a mistake. Bringing him in for an interview or interrogation would create suspicion, and if he is the killer, he might bury incriminating evidence lying around his office or home."

"What about the stuff you've dug up on Sanders?" Carson asks. "Could you pass it onto the police?"

"It'd be useless," Seth says dismissively. "The information I have has not been attained legally, and even if I handed everything over, it wouldn't be enough for them to do anything but speculate. Lots of people have mommy or daddy issues without becoming serial killers."

Carson grunts. "There's also the fact that Sanders has been teaching here for years, yet bodies have only started dropping this year, which makes it possible that he *isn't* the killer. There are a lot of variables that could mean he isn't the killer, but there's also the slim possibility that he is."

I let out a quiet groan. "I have rehearsal with him in two hours."

Carson stares at me like I have two heads while Seth lets out a low, dark chuckle, as if I'm an adorable, mischievous, naive creature he can't help but pity.

"You want to attend rehearsal led by a man who has possibly racked up two kills since the beginning of the year?" Carson questions, his tone dripping politeness that thinly veils disbelief.

"*Possibly* being the operative word," I point out. "We don't know for sure. This is the biggest production of my life, there is literally no way I can *not* attend. Rehearsal will be full of people, so even if he is the killer, it's not like he'll pull anything. Regardless, mean girls are the killer's MO, and that's not me."

"No, you're too nice for your own good," Seth says silkily, his thumb rubbing circles over my thigh. "You need someone mean to protect you."

I arch an eyebrow at him. "And you're that person?"

Seth stares into my eyes with unwavering steadiness. "Yes, Elia, I am that person. You're not going to rehearsal, not with the danger hovering over your head. I'm not taking any risks with your safety."

I give him a sweet smile. "We should hash this out right now, Seth, so we don't start anything on the wrong foot. You do not control me. I will listen to your advice and respect your words, but you are not my boss, I do not obey you unless it suits me. If you don't want me to go to rehearsal, you can voice that opinion, but there is absolute jack you can do to stop me. Are we understood?"

Seth's eyes glimmer with interest even as they simultaneously darken. "I hear you. Now hear *me*. You know me, you have a better idea than most of how I operate. You should know that one of my key functions is protecting my belongings. You are my most precious possession, so there is nothing I won't do to keep you safe, including tying you down to a bed if that's what it takes to make you stay put."

Several emotions pass through me at lightning speed: irritation, frustration, endearment, arousal, and something of a thrill at the threat Seth makes. I'm annoyed with his attempt to control and contain me, while I also understand it's in his nature to be dangerously protective and possessive.

Carson says, "I have to admit, I don't *not* like that idea. What do you think, Little E? Feel like getting tied to a bed today?"

The thought is kind of titillating and something I'd expect to be right up Seth's alley, but being tied up to miss rehearsal doesn't interest me. I try to consider how I can voice my thoughts in a way they won't instantly get shot down—it seems like my best bet is being honest. If I can get Carson and Seth to see that trying to steam roll me will never achieve their desired results, especially Seth, maybe we can get somewhere.

"Only if you feel like getting castrated," I tell Carson. "I am going to rehearsal. I came here today to get a feel for what a dynamic between the three of us would look like. If I leave under the impression that you two will try to control me and I'll be wasting time trying to mitigate that, it will be enough to tell me I don't want to spend my time here."

That makes both of them fall quiet for several moments. Seth glares at me, seething, while Carson looks more contemplative.

Carson says lightly, "Well, we wouldn't want to give that impression, would we, Seth? Doesn't seem like it would be productive."

Seth flexes his jaw, still glaring at me. "I'm not sending you into danger." His voice softens, as does his expression. "I can't, Elia. Please don't ask me to."

It registers that while he's pushing my limits, I might be pushing one of his, as well. I take a moment to try to see this situation from Seth's point of view, taking into account what I know about him; namely, that he doesn't connect with or get attached to people easily and he outright admitted he's formed an emotional attachment to me. That means all his darkness and intensity will be turned towards keeping me safe. I'm asking him to forgo one of his basic instincts in favor of compromising with me, and if I want him to play ball, I need to choose my wording carefully.

I'm surprised to find that I don't mind how tricky Seth is. I don't mind having to adjust my approach to suit him, in fact figuring out how to make the puzzle that he is click seamlessly with me is kind of interesting.

I put my hand on top of the one he has resting on my thigh. "I understand—"

"You don't," he says, threading his fingers through mine. "If something happened to you, I'd set this continent on fire."

To be *that* important to someone, so valuable that they're willing to go to extreme lengths to protect or avenge me, is heady.

"I'm trying to understand," I amend. "But you need to work with me here, Seth. I'm a creature of compromise. Pandora's Box is a big deal for my career, and missing out on it would be detrimental. At the same time, I wouldn't love the idea of attending class led by a killer, so what's a middle ground we can find?"

Carson whips his phone out of his pocket, clicks around on it, then places a call, holding the phone up to his ear. I turn to face him, arching a questioning eyebrow, only to be hit with one of his classic smug grins in response.

I hear faint echoes of the call being picked up and someone talking on the other end of the line before Carson says, "Hi, Moira, this is Carson Ajax calling. So sorry to bother you after work hours, I was just wondering if my position as Eliana Pierce's shadow extends to your new production of Pandora's Box. My father was asking about how it's been shaping up, and I'll admit I'm personally very curious to see how it's going. Would it be too much of an imposition if I attended rehearsals?"

It's a pointed effort to keep my jaw from dropping. Carson's entire approach and every word is tailored to appeal towards a woman in Moira's position; he's playing on her vanity and need to market her department's newest ballet, and he's doing it in such an eloquent manner that Moira would have no reason to suspect he's calling for anything *but* curiosity and an update for his father.

Sometimes I forget that Carson can be as manipulative as Seth, because he is so damn charming and charismatic.

Moira says something I can't quite hear, then Carson responds, "I'm so glad to hear that, thank you. So it would be alright if I started dropping in on evening rehearsals? Yes? Excellent, thanks so much.

I'm sure I'll have a glowing report to pass on." He pauses, then says, "Alright, sounds good. Take care."

He hangs up, then turns his full attention to Seth. "Now our lovely Elia will have protection with her at rehearsal."

I turn to Seth to gauge his reaction. His eyes are narrowed in consideration, lips pursed. After a long moment of silence, he says, "Fine." His eyes meet mine. "I am capable of compromise, Little Muse. I just won't *like* to compromise where your safety is involved."

I smile at him. "I don't need you to like it, I just need you to do it. See how beneficial it is?"

Seth shakes his head. "Since the alternative was you, tied to a bed, unable to stop me or Carson from playing with you however we feel like, no, I can't say I see the benefit of compromise." He pauses to sigh when I give him an expectant look. "But I do like making you happy and comfortable, so I guess I'll learn how to live with it."

Carson asks from my other side, "What do you think of being tied up, Little E? Interested in it?"

Considering the fact that my nipples pebble each time either of them bring it up, I'd say that yes, I am interested, but I'm equally nervous. Seth's restrained me plenty of times when we fooled around, and he manhandled me when we had sex to the point where I might as well have been restrained; it's been hot as hell each time. A bit terrifying because I can see just how excited he gets when I'm physically incapable of doing anything but taking what he has to dish out, but since what he has to dish out is often a delicious balance of pain and pleasure, I haven't minded so far.

"She likes it," Seth answers for me, sliding his palm higher on my thigh.

Chapter Fifty-Two

"You usually come the hardest when your movement is restricted. Have you noticed that, Elia?" Seth murmurs.

I bite my lip, nodding my head as heat starts traveling through my body. Seth senses it, and a smile overtakes his lips. "I like it, too. I like touching you when you can't stop me. I like making you come when you're helpless."

Carson lets out what sounds like an astonished puff of laughter. "You *like* making a woman orgasm? Since when?"

"Since Elia," Seth replies, not looking away from me. "Have you seen the way she lights up? It's riveting."

"The times Seth and I have shared a girl, I did all the legwork of making sure she enjoyed herself, too," Carson tells me. "Seth is usually the type to treat women like dolls who are there for his pleasure."

Seth shrugs, totally unabashed. "That's what they were; a means to an end." His eyes flit over my face, and his hand moves from my thigh to my stomach, sliding upwards until he's cupping one of my breasts in his hand. "You, however, are very different, Little Muse. You aren't a means to an end; you *are* the end. You're my endgame, not a doll.

Although I don't mind treating you like a doll on occasion, and only because I know you like it, you know you're much more valuable to me than that. Don't you?"

What I know is that I'm starting to get wound up, sandwiched beneath them, listening to them talk dirty about the things they'd like to do to me. I try to picture what it must have been like for other girls in my position; probably one hell of a wild ride, and a painful one if Seth had no interest in their pleasure. I'm sure Carson would have softened that blow, he's known as a very generous lover, but girls who have been with Seth probably know the true meaning of an animalistic, intense, not altogether enjoyable time. The fact that I'm the first one whose enjoyment matters to Seth gives me a sense of power that I like a lot.

"You have two hours until rehearsal," Carson says thoughtfully. "Not enough time to do anything major, especially since you still need to eat, but enough time for some fun. Are you up for some fun, Little E?"

I turn my head in his direction and nod, once. I am up for a little fun, and I'm very much on board with getting a glimpse of what having both of them at once might look like.

Carson opens his mouth to respond; the words are lost in translation as Seth practically yanks me onto his lap and fuses his mouth to mine. I clutch his shoulders tightly, gasping into his kiss, feeling the outline of his erection press into my stomach. He's not in the mood to be anything resembling gentle, and everything about him advertises that. The way his teeth nip at my lips hard enough to hurt, the bruising grip he has on my waist, and the fact that it feels like he's trying to devour me whole all tell me he is not in a mild mood. Probably because I just challenged him and won. The good thing for me is that I don't need him to be gentle; I like him when he's feeling a little vicious, too.

I feel warmth at my back, and a whispered breath across the back of my neck precedes warm palms sliding around to my front and cupping my breasts. Carson squeezes the mounds in his hands, which are trapped between my body and Seth's while kissing my neck, all the while Seth continues stealing the breath from my lungs. My entire body lights up like fireworks on the Fourth of July; heat pools between my thighs, my nipples start to ache as if demanding attention, and I can't stop myself from lifting my hips so I can grind against Seth's erection.

"That's it," Carson breathes in my ear, and his hands slip under my shirt to trace the outline of my bra. "Grind on him. Take your pleasure, Little E, you deserve it."

His hands slip under the cups of my bra and his fingers start brushing across my nipples, making them tighten further. I moan softly into Seth's lips when Carson pinches my nipples, which makes Seth's grip tighten on me. He starts controlling my movements, grinding me into him harder and making me moan again, louder.

When my head's spinning so much I think I might pass out, he tears his mouth away from mine only to sink his teeth into my neck with an animalistic growl. The bite isn't soft, it's hard enough to sting and burn and it's a wonder that he doesn't break skin. A loud noise edged with pain escapes me, but it turns into a whimper when Seth sucks at the mark he made. He pauses in grinding me against him to tug up the hem of my shirt.

Carson steps back long enough for Seth to pull my shirt over my head, then his heat is once again at my back. Seth's hands move to the zipper and button of my jeans while Carson's run along the back of my bra, teasing my skin lightly before undoing the clip of my bra. He slides the straps down my arms, tossing the bra aside, and Seth's eyes turn a piercing bright green when they fall on my naked breasts.

His view is obstructed when Carson cups them again, this time squeezing a little harder before pinching both of my nipples at once, making my back arch and breath hiss out of me as a jolt of pain joins the pleasure mounting in my body.

Seth finishes with my jeans. "Stand up," he commands.

Feeling a little off-balance, I climb off him, stumbling to my feet. Carson steps back to make room for me but doesn't let go of my breasts, skimming his teeth along the back of my neck as Seth yanks down my pants, lifting my legs one at a time to help me step out of them. My panties are ripped off with one harsh yank before he pulls me back down onto his lap. One hand rises to wrap around my throat while the other slides between my slippery folds down below. Three fingers plunge into me at once, making my head fall back as a low cry spills from my lips.

My head hits Carson's chest, and I crack my eyes open in time to meet his icy blue ones, which watch me with a deep interest as well as curiosity. He grins down at me, twisting one of my nipples *hard* at the same time that Seth's thumb finds my clit. My eyes slide shut again as Seth rolls the pad of his thumb over my clit while finding a steady pace to thrust his fingers in and out of me. A familiar knot of tension forms in my stomach, and I feel a fine sheen of sweat coat my body as it's worshipped by two men who have already learned it so well.

"Oh, fuck," I whimper as Seth curls the fingers inside me upwards, finding the spot that makes my whole body tense in anticipation. I force my eyes open when Seth releases my throat, in time to see Seth swat one of Carson's hands away from my breasts, and lean forward to suck my nipple into his mouth. The pleasure of his hot, wet mouth makes an answering rush of arousal spill out of me down below, which in turn makes him speed up the action of his finger on my clit.

"You ready to come yet, Princess?" Carson asks, using his free hand to sweep my hair away from the curve of my shoulder and leaning down to scrape his teeth over it.

I nod my head with a whimper, feeling my orgasm creep closer and closer to me, scattering my thoughts.

Seth's teeth bite into my nipple hard, and his free hand raises to wrap around my neck again. He pulls back, stares into my eyes, and says, "You don't get to come until you've begged very prettily."

Carson lets out a low whistle. "Cruel. I kind of like it."

I know it's because I won the argument with Seth earlier, which makes him all the more intent on getting back at me. Since he won't actually hurt me or employ any of his countless revenge methods on me, it looks like I'll be getting sexually tortured each time we have a disagreement, which I don't think I'll mind all that much. It feels really, *really* good, and if this is what it takes for Seth to blow off steam, I can handle that.

My mouth falls open when Seth runs the nail of his thumb right down my clit, scraping it and adding a stinging burn that creates an edge of panic which adds to the pain and pleasure. A long, high-pitched whining sound I didn't know I was capable of making escapes me, and a small smile curls Seth's lips. It's an evil smile, one that tells me he really likes playing with me like this. His hand on my neck tightens, cutting off the sound and restricting my breathing.

I open my mouth and manage to squeak out a single word, "*Please.*"

Seth tightens his hold on my neck and shakes his head. "Not yet." His thumb presses down on my clit, hard, while the fingers inside me tickle the top of my channel, overwhelming me with sensation until I want to crawl out of my skin.

Feeling desperate to get the orgasm that's hovering *just* out of reach, I crane my neck backwards and train my gaze on Carson, silently pleading with him. Seth might be feeling testy, but Carson should be more amenable to giving into my silent request. His lips stretch into an amused grin that silently transmits *you should know better than that* when his icy eyes meet mine. It's a grin I'm familiar with from when we're having sex and he feels like torturing me a little, too. *Shit.*

"Don't turn those pleading eyes on me," Carson says. "I'm quite enjoying this scene. Since it's Seth's hand on your pussy right now, your orgasm is his to give. You'll get it when he's ready."

Seth uses his grip on my throat to turn my eyes back to him, and I can see from his expression that he's not very happy that I turned to Carson for reprieve. His fingers give me several hard, punishing thrusts while his thumb backs off my clit. His hand on my throat eases, allowing me to draw in several free gulps of air. I feel light-headed and dizzy, drunk on attention and pleasure, like a pliable puddle of goop these men can maneuver in any way they please.

And they do. Seth pulls me in for another kiss, dominating and ravaging my mouth. Carson releases one of my breasts and slides his free hand down my back and over my ass. He runs his fingers between my cheeks, reaching forward to gather some of my wetness before rimming the bud of my ass with his index finger. My whole body tenses and my orgasm creeps a little closer, but still remains out of reach.

"I'll be fucking you here soon," Carson murmurs in my ear, sending a shiver through me. "Shh, don't get tense. That won't help. Relax for me, Little E. You know I make things good for you."

I *do* know that, but I also know that my back hole is simply too small for his cock. Before I can tell him as much, Seth tightens his hold on my neck again, leaving me back to fighting for each and every breath. Tears spark up in my eyes when his thumb returns to my clit, at the same time that the tip of Carson's finger breaches my ass. It feels strange, slightly uncomfortable, horribly taboo, and yet so hot I almost come.

Seth must sense it because he pulls his hand away from my pussy and then slaps me twice, right over my swollen clit and folds. He releases my throat in favor of taking my chin in his grip and training my eyes on him. Then, he thrusts his fingers back into me, and tells me, "Beg."

I obey. "Please, Seth—" I cut off as Carson's finger slides deeper into my ass. "Fuck, shit, *fuck—please let me come!*"

Seth cuts off my air again. "That was good," he tells me, eyes glinting with satisfaction. "Very good. *Almost* good enough to work."

He runs his tongue along my lips while continuing to torture me below. When his nail scrapes over my clit *again*, the tears building in my eyes spill over. Seth's gaze flares as he leans forward to lick them up, making a noise of pure pleasure that makes me very nervous.

"I like the taste of your tears," he murmurs. "I'll have more of that soon."

My lips part on a gasp that I'm unable to take as Carson thrusts his finger in and out of my ass, setting a much slower pace than Seth's fingers, which are still torturing my pussy and clit.

"I think we've pushed her enough. Are you ready to let her come?" Carson asks.

"That depends on how she begs. Are you ready to beg me just right, Eliana?"

I nod, and he releases my throat. My voice is hoarse as I blab out a plea, adding a lot of *pleases* and *pretty pleases* to try to entice him. It seems to work, because Seth gives me a single nod of his head and his thumb on my clit speeds up until I feel like I'm about to explode.

"Good girl, now come."

My body obeys; my back arches and my head falls against Carson's chest as my inner muscles squeeze and convulse. I suck in a long breath that's released as an ear-piercing scream and I feel every single one of my muscles tense and spasm as an orgasm of cosmic proportions sweeps me into its hold. It feels like it goes on forever, my inner muscles clench around both Carson and Seth's fingers, the sense of incredible fullness drawing out my orgasm until every drop of strength has seeped from me.

CHAPTER FIFTY-THREE

I slump forward, falling onto Seth's chest, panting. He pulls his fingers out of me, as does Carson, and I let out a small whine at the sensation. I feel raw and vulnerable after that whole scene, so I hold Seth tightly, laying the side of my cheek against his chest. He's always so strong, confident, and capable, right now I want to draw on some of his strength after feeling like my soul was sucked out of me by that orgasm.

Seth must sense that, because he wraps his arms around me and pulls me tighter against him, stroking one hand along the ends of my hair while the other rubs up and down my spine soothingly. I feel the couch dip as Carson takes a seat beside Seth, then turn my head in his direction to look at him, gauge his reaction. He looks riveted, like he enjoyed what just happened as much as I did, which is a relief. While blowing my mind, our little three-way-encounter also alleviated my fear that Seth will go for Carson's throat in any shared sexual scenario. He won't; instead, it looks like he'll channel any darker energy into torturing me.

"Now *that* was fucking hot," Carson murmurs, staring at me, eyes glinting with intrigue. "Didn't know you liked it that rough, Little E."

"Only with me," Seth replies, leaning his head down to brush a kiss over my forehead. "I give the pain, the intensity, the overwhelming sensations. You, Carson, make them more bearable. Yes, I think our arrangement will work out quite nicely."

I hum in agreement, still too tired to force words past my lips. I don't want to make Carson feel left out, though, so after a few min-utes—when I'm no longer incapable of moving—I reach for Carson's shirt, tugging on the hem. "Gimme."

He cracks a smile, looking amused. "You like wearing my shirts, Little E?"

I nod, though he already knows that. I always ask for one of his shirts when I'm over here; they're soft and warm and so big on me the hems often fall to my knees. They also smell like him, and I swear I can even feel his energy on them. I like wearing Seth's clothes just as much and for the same reason, but since he's the one I've been clinging to, I figure it makes sense to give Carson more attention.

Carson says, "Whatever you want, Princess, all you have to do is ask." He lifts his shirt up and over his head, revealing his well-toned chest and abs, making a spike of lust course through me yet again. I release Seth so I can pull on Carson's shirt. Seth lets go of me long enough to let me pull on the material; instantly, Carson's scent and warmth surrounds me, along with the feeling of sunshine that always seems to accompany him. I let out a happy sigh, then glance up into Seth's eyes to see *his* reaction.

He appears content in the way I've only seen him when he's paint-ing, playing with my body, or just got done with either. He doesn't seem offended that I reached for Carson's shirt instead of his; in fact, he actually looks a little satisfied, like events are playing out exactly the way he anticipated.

"You okay?" Seth asks me, stroking his fingers through my hair and pulling it out from under Carson's shirt before once again clasping my waist.

I nod, a little drowsily. Having one of them at a time was always intense, but what just took place transcends intensity and moves towards total annihilation territory. I enjoyed it a lot, though. The dynamic was weird at first, literally being trapped between them while they both worked over my body, but the weirdness quickly melted away into such an erotic scene I get the sense I'll be having wet dreams about it for the foreseeable future.

Seth inclines his head. "Good. Are you hungry?"

I blink a few times, trying to remember the last time I ate. I grabbed a muffin between my dance classes and English/ language ones, but other than that, I haven't eaten anything today. Although I'm not hungry, I know I should be, so I nod.

"My Little Muse has a problem with taking care of herself properly," Seth says, addressing Carson. "Not eating or sleeping enough. That's going to change, Elia. Now that you're ours, you will be well taken care of."

I feel a frown furrow my eyebrows. "Now that I'm yours? I don't remember agreeing to that. I'm still in the test-drive stage."

Seth and Carson share a look of faint amusement, some silent communication passing between them that annoys me.

"You are ours, Little E," Carson says. "You don't have to admit it yet, though, I can be patient."

Seth fists a hand in my hair, tilting it back and forcing me to meet his eyes. "I'm not so patient," he says, the words edged with aggravation. "Get on board, Eliana. Having things with you left unsolidified will drive me insane, and strangely enough, I don't think you want an insane version of me unleashed on the world. I'm not sure humanity would survive that."

"You're crazy," I say, the words coming out affectionate.

A pleased smirk curls his lips. "Thank you."

"Pretty sure that wasn't a compliment," Carson says, standing up. He asks, "What are you in the mood for, Little E? We can order takeout or I can whip something up. Have you had any protein today?"

It's markedly strange having another person care more about my needs than I do, care more about things like my nutrition and sleeping schedule than I ever have, but it also feels good. Like there's finally someone—someones—in my life to watch my back and help me out. The sensation is a foreign but welcomed one.

"I only had time for a muffin between classes," I murmur.

I turn my head to look at Carson, in time to see him pull his phone out of his pants. "I haven't done grocery shopping recently, so my fridge isn't well stocked. I'll have my housekeeper fill it up tomorrow, that way I can cook for us soon. For now, any cravings for takeout, Little E?"

"You're not going to ask me?" Seth questions, faint amusement coating the words.

"Nope, this decision goes to Elia."

"I don't care," I say.

"Chinese?" Carson asks.

I frown. "We had that the other day, so no."

"Indian?"

I shake my head. "Too heavy, I have dance in..." I glance at the clock on the coffee table, "just over an hour."

Carson sighs. "Okay, how about Japanese? Sushi?"

"It'll take too long," I reply.

"You sure you don't care, Little E? You're shooting down my offers," Carson says dryly while Seth chuckles.

I laugh, too, seeing my own ridiculousness. "Fine, um... is there a soup or salad place nearby? I can't dance on a heavy stomach, but I do need some fuel before evening rehearsal."

Seth frowns. "I don't think that's enough."

I shrug. "It's something light or nothing at all. I can't *not* eat before rehearsal, I don't want to pass out, but I also don't want to get cramps."

"There's a little café with soups, sandwiches, and salads that delivers," Carson says. "Does that work, Princess?"

The way he emphasizes *princess* tells me that he also thinks I'm being a touch ridiculous with my indecision, but he'll humor me because he's fond of me.

I nod. "Yeah, that sounds good. Thank you."

After a little more back and forth, Carson places an order. I'm still too boneless to move, so he joins Seth and me on the couch and clicks on the TV. After the men find out I haven't yet watched Game of Thrones even though I've read the books, we settle on starting on the fantasy TV show. Halfway through the first episode, I'm filled with intrigue and horror when the food arrives. Carson sets it up on the coffee table, and I finally climb off Seth's lap to eat. Seth doesn't appear to like this change, as I've noticed he prefers to be touching me at all times, but he doesn't voice any protests, probably because he doesn't want to interrupt my eating.

It makes me feel warm and fuzzy inside to know there are now two people who care a great deal about my wellbeing and are invested in protecting me and keeping me healthy, especially when I often don't do a great job of that myself.

Once we've eaten and finished the first episode of the show, which I enjoyed far more than I thought I would, I pull on my clothes and Carson drives me back to campus while Seth sulks off back to his apartment.

I start to get a little apprehensive during the drive, thinking about Mr. Sanders, trying to remember if there was *ever* a time I noticed anything off or unsafe about him. There are periods during rehearsals when he gets irritated and a little snappy, and he can be pretty harsh with corps dancers who don't keep up their standards, but he's never been anything but kind and helpful to me, April, and Sean. Then again, we're his leads and some of the best and most ambitious dancers in the company, so we generally don't give him reason to get snappy.

Outside of those instances when he gets crude with corps, though, or the drill-sergeant persona he always takes on when teaching the finer points of technique, he's perfectly cordial and pleasant. Nothing's ever struck me as off about him.

I trust Seth's instincts and words that even if Sanders were the killer, I probably wouldn't know, which only makes me more nervous. Carson senses my anxiety and reassures me that he'll be with me every moment, that he'd never let any harm befall me. He walks with me from the parking lot to dorms, where I change into my dance gear and grab my dance bag, and then over to dance headquarters. The building is mostly empty as the only students or faculty here past 5pm are usually company members who get cast in whichever upcoming production is being worked on at the time.

I run into Sean on my way into the building, who gives me a warm smile. "Hey Carson, Elia. Ready to dazzle everyone with our duets?"

I grin at him. "Only if you are. Just be gentle when lifting me, yeah?"

He laughs, the sound edged with faint embarrassment. "I'm used to taller girls who are a bit heavier as my dance partners, you always feel like a freaking feather. I'll be more controlled."

I reach out a hand to squeeze his shoulder, letting him know I'm not terribly worried or upset about it, just aware that he has a propensity of using too much strength during our lifts, which can make the variations a bit jerky and unnatural. Not to mention that it throws off my balance.

Carson slips an arm around my waist, pulls me away from Sean and into his side. I can practically feel the possessiveness radiating off him, and when we step into the stairwell, I glance up at him. His gaze is shuttered, he's glaring at Sean like he wants to plant him in the ground, and his hold on me is steel-like. *Goddamn men and their territorialism.*

Sean also notices Carson's tenseness, and says, "I don't swing that way, man. She's all yours."

That causes Carson to relax significantly; his hold on my waist loosens, his eyes lose the edge of danger, and his face relaxes. He even gives Sean a small smile.

"Good. I don't think Little E would've been very happy if I landed her dance partner in the hospital."

I smack Carson's chest before trotting up the stairs. "Stop being ridiculous, I'm not a piece of meat to growl over." Pointedly ignoring him, I switch over to talking ballet with Sean, discussing our variations and personal progress on our solos.

When we reach the studio where rehearsal's being held, I see the space is already mostly filled, with only a few corps members and Sanders absent. April smiles brightly at me as soon as I walk in; her gaze bounces between me, Carson, and Sean, and her smile turns mischievous. I leave Carson in his usual seat by the piano, then give Sean one last smile before making my way over to April.

She says, "Looks like things are going well in paradise. Have you sampled your two lovers together yet?"

I laugh. "We just talked about it this morning."

She winks at me. "And you're rocking a post-orgasm glow, and Carson's now attending evening rehearsals. Earlier, I sent you diagrams on how a threesome works. Spill."

I bite my lip, before telling April in vague detail about the delightful scene that went down just a little while ago. April's eyes brighten as she listens, and at the end, she says wistfully, "Lucky bitch. God, that sounds amazing; two men who are obsessed with you worshipping your body at once. You should rent your boys out, Elia, they'd make a fortune."

A startled laugh escapes me at that. "Absolutely not. They're mine; only I get to know what being with both of them is like from here on out."

"And she's already possessive," April says, amused. "So, is it solidified? Are you guys official? Can I start rubbing the dance bitches' faces into the fact that my best friend has been tamed and claimed by two of Greywood's most eligible?"

"I haven't been tamed," I say, frowning. "No, things aren't official yet. It's only been a few hours since you've last asked—"

"And you got the orgasm of the century from both of them, so I thought that meant things were settled. Obviously, you're still holding back, which means you're afraid. Don't be, Elia. I've seen how Carson looks at you. He's obsessed. Just let it happen."

"I will," I tell her. "I just need to get a better feel for the dynamic before I commit."

She arches an eyebrow. "Do they know that?"

I frown. "Yes. They're giving me time, but I think in their minds, things are solidified." At least, judging by that silent exchange they had earlier.

April opens her mouth to respond, but is cut off when Sanders walks into the room. I try to keep myself from outwardly stiffening as everyone turns their attention to him and he starts rattling off orders. I look him over as he speaks, wondering what the odds are that we're all sharing a classroom with a psychotic killer. I can't know for sure one way or the other, but even the possibility sets me on edge. I don't *think* it's Sanders, but I wouldn't stake my life on that.

I glance over at Carson, who's eyes are glued to Sanders, as well. Even if Sanders is the killer, I know I'm safe with Carson here; every fiber of my being believes he will protect me, so even though I'm a bit uncomfortable, I'm safe. I take my spot at the front of the room, right before the wall-length mirror, and get started on rehearsing.

Chapter Fifty-Four

The rest of the week passes by without any further incidents. I have evening rehearsal with Sanders again on Thursday, and again, Carson accompanies me. He's far laxer about my dancing with Sean now that he's confident that Sean poses zero threat to him.

When I'm not in classes or rehearsals, my time is commandeered by either Seth or Carson. If they were insufferable stalkers before, now they're like a missile target-seeking system that's been locked onto me. I barely get any time alone; when I'm in my dorm doing homework, Carson persuades me over to his dorm so we can study together, often with promises of food and orgasms. He does his best to distract me from my homework, but I don't let him; I don't let him touch me period until my assignments are done, which winds him up so tight that he tackles me once I'm finally done. When I'm not with Carson in either of our rooms, I'm at his apartment building, either in his place or Seth's.

I spend Wednesday night over at Seth's apartment, having dinner with him and Carson. Since I have a no sex during the week rule, all I do is pose while Seth paints, watch some TV with them, and then I share Seth's bed with him while Carson heads back to his apartment for the evening.

Friday comes around, bringing with it the promise of an exciting weekend. Seth and Carson informed me they'd be taking me out tonight, something I see as the official test-drive for the three-way relationship idea, which I'm really starting to warm towards.

Each time I'm with both of them, I relax a little more because the dynamic—though deeply strange—somehow works. Carson tempers Seth, Seth tempers Carson, and I temper both of them. Still, I've only seen that we work in private; I need to know we work in public as well before committing.

After classes on Friday, I text a group chat I've started with both men, asking how I should dress. Seth texts back that he prefers me without clothing while Carson tells me to bundle up because we'll be outside for part of the evening. I still want to look nice for them because I suspect the evening will probably culminate in a passionate three-way, so I tug on my nicest pants and the only cashmere sweater I own, one that an old ballet master gave me when she saw me shivering backstage because I didn't have any sweaters that fit me at the time.

Then, I knock on Carson's dorm door. He opens it a moment later, smiling down at me and greeting, "Hey, Little E. You ready?"

I shrug. "You refuse to tell me where we're going so I can't say for sure, but I think so."

A secretive glint flashes through his eyes, and his smile turns sly. "Sorry, Princess, you'll be kept in the dark until we're there."

I don't know where *there* is, and I also know that asking won't get me very far, so I simply sigh. "Fine. Are we picking Seth up on our way?"

Carson shakes his head. "No, Seth's already at the destination, setting up. Grab a warm jacket and bring your snow pants just in case, it might snow tonight."

Feeling more and more curious, I swing back into my dorm room to grab the items, before following Carson downstairs and to his car. I try to pester him during the drive to give up the final destination, but he deflects each time with a sly smile. When I realize he won't give anything away, I try to focus on mile markers and the direction we're heading in to figure out where we're going; I think we're driving in the same direction as the mountain Carson took me to a while ago, but it's dark out so I can't tell for sure.

Carson tells me, "Don't sulk, Princess, it's beneath you. Relax, trust that we'll take care of you, and go with the flow."

"You make this sound like a trust building exercise kids do at summer camp," I say, nose wrinkling.

Carson arches an eyebrow. "Isn't it? Not the summer camp part, but the trust-building-exercise part?"

I suppose it is. I need to get a feel for whether or not I can trust Carson and Seth out in public, together with me. I fall quiet, my mind drifting back to the implications of our relationship and what it'll mean in the future if I decide to commit. This isn't just a big deal for me; it'd be a big deal for both of them, as well. Carson more so than Seth, because he has an empire to eventually take over and a shitty father who might breathe down his neck on account of his life choices.

"Will your dad have a problem with us and Seth?" I ask Carson, feeling my brows furrow at the thought.

Carson's lips thin and his expression turns dark, which makes me feel bad for broaching the topic in the first place. I don't want to bring his mood down when we're on our way to our first *official* date.

"Probably," Carson starts, "but he won't be able to do anything about it. My father's a very bad man, Little E, who's done a lot of bad shit to many people. There are certain things I could easily blackmail him with to get him to stay out of my business. I'd prefer not to go to war with him, but I will if I have to, and I'll be the last man standing at the end of it."

That makes my chest tighten and mood darken. I don't want to be the cause of more contention between Carson and his father; their relationship is already strained as is. Carson understandably hates his dad, and it sounds like Ajax Senior has little love for his son in return. From what I've seen, the status quo between them is tense distance; I don't want to be the cause of anything getting worse.

I tell Carson, "I don't want to make things harder for you with your father. I know he's an asshole of epic proportions. If you need to hide me in order to avoid his scrutiny, I won't be mad."

Carson scowls. "Fuck that, I'm not hiding you, Little E, I'm going to flaunt you with all the pride I feel for knowing you're mine. If Dad has a problem with that, he can test how deep my patience runs. Hint: I have none when it comes to him."

I can't help the small giggle that bubbles out of me, and the tension in my chest subsides. Carson turns his car onto a smaller road that takes us up the canyon we hiked not too long ago, making my curiosity kick into overdrive. I didn't know there was an official road for cars to go up it. The trees are covered in white powder, lit by the occasional lamppost on the side of the road.

"It's so pretty," I say on a sigh. "God, I love winter."

Carson chuckles. "Just wait till we get there. *That's* real beauty."

"Stop teasing me!" I whine. "It's only making me more impatient, and eventually I'll start yanking your ear out of annoyance."

"No need for that, since we're here," Carson says, pulling his car off to a small clearing on the side of the road. It looks like a makeshift parking lot, with snow shoveled to the tree line, making space for cars. There's a single lamppost that illuminates a trailhead, which is glowing with fairy lights hanging from trees. I let out a soft gasp of excitement as I take them in; they make everything in the vicinity look like it glows. The deep green of the winter trees—pines, spruces, and firs. The bright snow, thick and fluffy. Carson's features, which look luminous and positively beautiful.

"Did you guys put those there?" I ask.

"Seth did," Carson responds, opening his door. I open mine, too, and hop out, practically bouncing on my toes with excitement. This isn't exactly a public outing like I expected, but I like it. I like the privacy, I like not having to worry about judgement or bullshit, and I absolutely *love* that Carson and Seth put their heads together and set up something that's literally *perfect* for me.

Carson takes my hand, smiling down at me. "You like them?"

I nod animatedly. "I love them. Do they lead to our destination?"

Carson inclines his head. "They sure do. Let's go, Little E."

We embark on the trail leading into the thick forest. My boots crunch over the snowy ground, and I zip up my jacket for extra warmth. The cold is particularly biting this high up in the mountains, but Carson's warmth along with my coat and the excitement burning me up inside keep me nice and toasty.

I gaze at the fairy lights as we pass them; some are hanging off the pine tree branches while others are wrapped fully around them. I'm not sure how the lights are even on, as there are no electrical outlets up here, so they must be either wireless or solar powered. Seth must've been out here for hours just setting these up.

The walk down the trail takes about fifteen minutes before the narrow snowy path lets out into a large clearing scattered with picnic tables. The clearing oversees the most gorgeous view of the canyon; a picturesque setting boasting of three snow covered mountain peaks and thousands of trees, all visible beneath the beams of the moon. On the picnic table in the center of the clearing is a white dining cloth, atop which sits a collection of opened Tupperware containers filled with many different dishes. This arrangement must've taken Seth all afternoon.

Seth stands in front of the table, eyes glued to me, his expression tinged with faint anticipation.

I speed up my pace, letting go of Carson's hand, then leap into Seth's arms, wrapping him in a hug. This is so gorgeous and so tailored to my tastes, I'm almost lost for words.

"This is amazing. Thank you," I whisper in his ear.

He squeezes me tightly. "I'm glad you like it. I've agonized all week over what to do for our first date. You should be glad Carson decided to go with my idea rather than executing his own; if it were up to him, we'd be eating burgers at a diner right now."

I grin, letting go of Seth and stepping back. "M's diner is awesome, but this is even better. Seriously, I'm deeply impressed. Thank you."

Seth plants a kiss on my lips. "You're welcome. Now, I didn't know what you'd feel like eating—your appetite is more mercurial than me in an art craze—so I picked up the usual orders from all the restaurants you like."

Carson plops down on the bench beside us. I take a seat next to him, looking from the food options to the scenery beyond and back, feeling warmed down to my very soul and so happy I'm practically bursting with giddiness. Seth takes a seat on the other side of me, then starts interrogating me on which foods I'm hungry for, loading a paper plate accordingly.

He grabs beers out of a cooler at the end of the table for himself and Carson, a root beer for me, and we all start eating together. While we eat, we talk about everything and nothing; world politics and economics, the current dealings in Carson's company, Seth's art projects, my upcoming performance of Pandora's Box. Carson mentions Sean being my dance partner to Seth, though he refers to him as Prince Gardener rather than his actual name, and Seth looks ready to commit murder until I tell him Sean's gay.

Then, he says, "Let's hope that's enough to protect him from your allure. If he falls into it, I'll be delivering a very clear message that you're off-limits."

CHAPTER FIFTY-FIVE

W e stay at the picnic table for nearly two hours, talking long after we've finished eating. I manage to convince Seth to let me glimpse his first painting of me soon—which he says is almost finished—and we confirm that Carson will be modeling with me for the second painting. I'm excited to hear that it'll be a reimagining of Mars and Venus, even more excited that Seth's looking forward to painting me and his friend.

It's only when the temperature abruptly drops and I start shivering that we finally start packing up, preparing to head down the mountain. Seth closes all the Tupperware containers, packing everything into a picnic basket, while Carson tosses our paper and plastic dishware into a trash bag and I fold up the table cloth. Then, we start on the trail back towards the parking lot.

"How long did it take you to get all these fairy lights up?" I ask Seth. "How are they lit? There can't be any outlets up here."

Seth glances around, not looking anywhere near as impressed as I am with his work. "I finished up the last of them this afternoon, but I started on Wednesday after school once I told Carson we're doing our date up here. They're solar-powered; during sunlight hours they soak up the sun and then automatically turn on when it's dark. I made them myself, since all the solar-powered fairy lights on the market are unreliable jokes."

"You *made* fairy lights for our date?" I ask, awed.

Seth scoffs faintly. "It wasn't difficult. I've made other light systems that are solar powered before, I just modified some designs and reapplied them here."

"I'm really, really impressed right now," I tell him. "You're totally getting lucky tonight."

Carson says from the other side of me, "All of us are getting lucky tonight, Princess. Now, since I know one of your concerns is seeing if we can behave ourselves in public, we're stopping by an ice cream store for dessert before going home."

I turn a smile to him. "Thank you. Both of you. Tonight has made me really happy." Happier than I've ever been, in fact. Being with them feels like it completes me. Carson is the gentleness, softness, kindness, and light that I need to keep positive; Seth is the darkness, intensity, and complexity that keeps me fascinated. Neither would be on their own what they are to me together, and I realize that I made my choice as soon as Seth gave me option number three at the beginning of this week; I'm keeping both of them. The last few days of indecision were simply because I needed to check a few boxes to feel comfortable and safe, but there's no way I'm giving up either of them. I don't want to; I don't think I could even if I did want to. They've become integral to me, and while that idea is frightening, it's also liberating because I know I can rely on them and trust them. They've proven that to me repeatedly.

Once we're back at the makeshift parking lot, Seth leads me to his car, citing that since I drove here with Carson, it's his turn to have me in his passenger seat. I don't argue, and neither does Carson, who doesn't seem to mind, which relaxes me even more.

The ride down the canyon is taken in comfortable silence. Seth turns on a quiet classical aria, Mozart's Queen of the Night. I hum along to the music, enjoying it, enjoying being with Seth even more.

"I really, *really* like you," I tell him earnestly. "You better be serious about me, because I'm getting in deep here."

Seth gives me an irritated glance. "I've already told you how serious I am about you, Eliana. If I thought you'd say yes so soon, there'd already be a ring on your finger. I'm not backing away, even if you choose to. We're a done deal; I've already fallen for you, and I don't want to go back. You breathe life into me, how could I not want to keep you forever?"

My breath hitches at his casually spoken words, but more specifically, the part where he said he's already fallen for me. I know the implications behind those words, but since he didn't outright say that he loves me, I don't know if that's what he means.

The idea is ridiculous. It's far too fast, too soon; I don't even know if Seth has the emotional capacity to love. From what I've seen, his emotional range is limited to contentment, lust, anger, and the occasional snippets of joy—usually when he's sexually torturing or painting me.

"You have an interesting way of saying really sweet things in that faintly insulting tone," I observe, smiling a little. "It only makes them more profound because I don't think you realize how much they mean in the first place, and I know you're not lying."

"I don't lie to you, Little Muse," Seth says, casting me a quick glance from the corner of his eye. "Everyone else in this world, yes, but not you."

"Why?" I ask curiously.

After all, Seth has no obligation to be honest with me; I probably wouldn't even be able to tell if he was lying. He's too smooth, too well-versed in deceit, so there's no reason for him to be candid with me, but I think that he is. He's told me things that could get him arrested and a lifetime sentence in prison, and trusted that I'd keep them to myself, which I have and will continue to, because I don't really see his actions as crimes. Criminal, sure, but not necessarily bad, as they often function to serve the greater good. I don't know if Seth realizes that he does great favors to the victims of the terrible people he hunts; he just likes to hurt and torture and kill bad people, unaware that in doing so, he's protecting many others. Some of his activities might make me uncomfortable, but since he confines his darker tendencies to the worst of the worst, I don't mind.

"Because you don't need me to lie to you, Eliana," Seth says. "You can handle the truth. That's one of the things I like most about you. Most people need to be told a pretty lie to keep their lives nice and comfortable, but you're okay with the *un*comfortable. You might not love it, but you don't hate it, either. You can handle me better than anyone I've ever met."

My thoughts flicker back to the first time we met, at the museum. At the time I thought the run-in was purely coincidence, but now that I know Seth better, I understand there aren't really coincidences with him. He plans everything down to the finest detail.

Now's as good a time as any to test out his honesty. I believe him when he says he doesn't lie to me, but I also want to know for sure.

"The first time we met, at the museum," I say. "Was that an accident?"

Seth's lips quirk. "Of course not, but you already knew that. You know how I work; you had me figured out after our first conversation.

First time in my life that's happened, by the way, which is why I was riveted."

I didn't know that for sure, but I think some part of me suspected, because I do know how Seth works. I also like how much *he* likes how I can see him for what he is and handle that, especially because I imagine that's a novelty to him. Seth's gone through the majority of his life being misunderstood and mislabeled, which has made him immune to judgement, but also lonely.

"I have another question," I inform Seth.

He arches an eyebrow, not taking his eyes off the road. "What are you waiting for? Ask. I'll tell you the honest answer, even if I don't think you'll like it."

I feel my cheeks burn. "Carson mentioned that you, um...well, that you didn't ever care about getting girls off during sex."

Seth nods. "That's true."

"But with me you seem focused on my enjoyment above your own," I point out.

Another nod. "Also true."

I frown. "Why? Why would you care with me when you didn't with them?"

Seth smiles, and the smile is edged with darkness and cruelty. "Because I didn't give a shit about any other girl, Elia. They knew what they were in for, I was very clear from the beginning that the sex was going to be on my terms to meet my own ends. If they happened to enjoy it, good for them, but my focal point was myself because I was seeking a satisfactory release. None of them were really people to me, just warm holes to get myself off in. You are a person to me; more, you're my Muse. I want you content, happy, and satisfied, so I naturally focus on you before me. Besides, you never look more beautiful than you do mid-orgasm. Except when you've come a few times and start to get panicked and overwhelmed; that's even better."

I blink a few times. "That's sweet, dark, and twisted, all at once. It's pretty impressive how you can manage to make me feel turned on, treasured, and a little scared all at the same time."

Seth tips me a wink. "It's a gift. Stick around, maybe I'll teach you."

I shake my head. "No, I'll leave the craziness to you and stick with whatever sanity I still have."

Seth shrugs. "Probably for the best, anyway. You might be able to handle my brand of crazy, but I don't know that you could channel it."

"I love how aware you are of your own abnormality," I say fondly. "It's strangely endearing. You're totally comfortable with who you are and how you function, despite knowing that you're singular in your uniqueness, your ways of thinking and handling things."

"That's because I don't seek acceptance from the masses," Seth tells me. "Frankly, I couldn't give less of a fuck what most people think about me. You've proven to be the sole exception to that rule; I care very much what you think about me, Elia, which is deeply strange."

I reach over to squeeze his shoulder. "Is that your roundabout way of asking me what I think about you?"

He appears amused by that. "Perhaps. If you'd like to tell, I'm all ears."

"You first," I say.

Seth's silent for several moments, thinking. Finally, he says, "In a lifetime of darkness, you're the first rays of light I've seen or felt. Not like the sun, that's far too bright for me...but if I'm the darkness of night, then you're my moon and stars."

I blink several times after he says that, feeling choked up. Again, he doesn't speak the words with a great deal of kindness, but they're still profoundly meaningful.

I tell him, "You take away my fear of the dark. You chase away my nightmares, because I've never met anyone scarier than you, yet I know I don't have to be afraid of you. I always feel safe, coveted, and protected—albeit occasionally on edge—with you. You make me feel like I'm invincible and capable of taking on the world."

Seth smirks. "We *could* take on the world together. I'll be the king, you be the queen, Carson can be the court jester."

I slap his shoulder. "What if I want Carson to be king?"

Seth takes my hand in one of his and places it on his thigh, intertwining our fingers. "Then I'll be your dirty little secret. I don't care what the optics are, Elia, so long as I have you. I don't care if I have to share you with Carson," he pauses as I give him an accusatory stare, then amends, "Okay, I might not love having to share you, but I'll do it if it means I get you. That's how much you mean to me. Honestly, if you ever tried leaving me, I'd probably trap you in a castle somewhere until you're feeling more agreeable." A slow smirk spreads on his lips, just evil enough to make my nether regions tingle. "My pretty little captive, the things I'd do to you."

"As long as they don't hurt too much, you can still do them to me with or without the castle-captive scenario," I point out.

Seth squeezes my hand. "I wouldn't hurt you in any way you wouldn't like, in any way that wouldn't ultimately lead to pleasure. I don't want to hurt you; I want to cherish you."

Feeling my heart squeeze, I assure him, "You do. I want to cherish you, too. If I'm ever not, you need to tell me so I fix it, okay?"

He chuckles. "Okay, Little Muse. Likewise. Traditional affection eludes me, so there will probably be times when I don't properly show you how much I treasure you. I will do my best to avoid that, and I think Carson being part of our relationship will benefit me because he'll also keep me in check, but if you're ever feeling down or like I'm not making clear just what you are to me, promise to tell me so *I* can fix it."

"What am I to you?" I ask.

We stop at a red light at the base of the mountain. Seth takes the opportunity to look into my eyes and tell me, "Everything, Eliana. That's what you are to me: fucking *everything*."

At that, I can't help myself; I take advantage of the red light to lean forward and kiss him, winding my hands into his hair. I never would've thought someone like Seth, the type of person I usually stay *far* away from, would become this important to me. The excitement that bursts through me at his words is what really tips me off that I've already crossed the point of no return, both with him and with Carson. I'm already in love with them.

CHAPTER FIFTY-SIX

The ice cream store Seth and Carson take me to is a cute, quaint little shop with a huge display of dozens of ice cream flavors at the front of the store, and a seating area that's mostly full in the back. I'm still feeling a little raw from my conversation with Seth and the realization that followed it, so I push away thoughts of love and the pain it could potentially cause and instead focus on my enjoyment of this moment, this time with them.

Carson bumps my shoulder with his as we wait in line to place our orders. "What are you thinking of getting, Little E?"

I crane my neck to look over the display case, feeling overwhelmed by the many options. After staring for a few seconds and bathing in indecision, I say, "I don't know. What's good? You've been here before and I haven't, so it's your job to guide me in the right direction."

Carson looks amused. "I think you came to the wrong guys if you're trying to stay on the garden path, Elia."

Seth lets out a dark laugh from the other side of me that tells me he concurs.

I roll my eyes. "I'm not expecting you to keep me on the holy path, I'm asking what ice cream flavor you'd recommend. In case you can't remember from each time we eat together, I can be a little ambivalent."

"Understatement of the century," Carson mutters, giving me a playful glare when I stand on my tip toes to smack the back of his head with my hand. "Careful, Princess. I told you the first time we met, naughty girls get punished."

"I'm looking forward to it," I say, surprising all three of us.

"Oh, hey, Elia!"

I turn my head to the left, looking farther into the shop, when I hear Sean's voice. He's walking towards me with a smile on his face, wearing a fanny pack over dark jeans and a white button up. It's so weird to see him without his usual dance gear, I blink a few times as I step away from Carson and Seth to accept a half-hug from Sean.

"Hey," I say with a smile, stepping back. "It's weird to see you off campus."

Sean laughs. "You, too," he admits. "I almost didn't recognize you without the leotard. Or maybe it's because your companions were hiding you from me."

Carson's been a lot calmer about Sean since finding out he's gay, but Seth hasn't yet been introduced to my dance partner, and when I glance over my shoulder and see the death glare he's aiming at Sean, it makes me stiffen.

"Sean, you already know Carson, the other one is Seth," I introduce, waving at my men. Then, I tell Seth, "Sean's the Prometheus to my Pandora in Sanders' upcoming show."

Hold on, when did they become my *men?* Even in my inner thoughts, that strikes me as a little strange. The change must've happened around the time I realized both of them already have pieces of my heart in the car.

Sean nods at Carson. "Good to see you again." Then, to Seth, "Your reputation on campus proceeds you."

"As does yours," Seth purrs, taking a hold of my arm and pulling me into his side. "Eliana talks about what a wonderful dance partner you are all the time."

I'm tempted to stomp on his foot because I have never once told Seth anything about Sean, so I recognize his words as a way to set Sean at ease so he can pull more information out of Sean. He really wasn't kidding when he said I'm the one person he doesn't lie to, whereas I can see that everyone else is free game.

Sean chuckles. "I try my best. I'm just glad we got paired again—I have literally never danced better than the Sleeping Beauty performance at the beginning of the year."

"Right, you were Prince Gardner," Seth says.

I dig my nails into his arm, trying to silently tell him to be nice.

"You're an amazing dancer," I tell Sean honestly. "You're definitely going places, and I'm glad I can help you shine. You deserve to."

Sean grins at me. Then, his eyes flick between Seth and Carson, somewhat curiously. I don't offer an explanation because I have not yet officially agreed to anything, although odds are I will by the end of the night.

"You guys should join us," Sean finally says when nobody else speaks. "A few company members have commandeered one of the back tables—we can pull up some extra chairs. Since Ajax's father is one of Greywood Dance Co's biggest patrons, and Seth is an acclaimed artist himself, you'll be right at home."

I smile. "Thank you for the offer." I don't accept or decline, because I'm pretty sure Seth is a few seconds away from taking Sean by the throat, and I need him to rein it in before I can trust him around my company members.

Sean nods, then says, "The cookie dough's the best here, if I do say so myself." With that, he turns and walks towards the back of the store.

Just then, we step up to the cashier; I order a small cup with one scoop of coffee ice cream and one of cookie dough, as per Sean's suggestion. Carson swipes his card, then we stand off to the side to wait for our order.

"Elia doesn't have the parts it takes to attract Sean, so if you could tone down the death glares you're still sending him, maybe Little E will stop looking like she's about to throw up," Carson tells Seth.

Seth blinks a few times, then looks down at me. I don't know if I appear nauseous, but I am a little nervous, and not just because of Seth's glares. I wanted to test Carson and Seth out in public, but now that we're here, near people I know and interact with daily, I'm not so sure. Especially since those horrible photos only circulated around the dance company a few weeks ago. I'm not Seth; I have to care what other people think about me, because those sentiments can directly impact my life.

Seth's brows furrow as he stares down at me. "Don't be afraid," he tells me, stroking his index finger over my cheek. "As long as nobody tries to take you from me, they're safe."

"So if another guy ever hits on me, they're not safe?" I ask dryly, grateful for the distraction from my thoughts.

Seth lifts a shoulder. "People are going to hit on you, Little Muse, you're too eye-catching for them not to. So long as they leave when you turn them away, I won't feel the need to deliver a message. I can't guarantee safety for anyone who tries to stick around to keep pestering you, though."

I feel a smile pull on my lips. "I'm weirdly okay with that."

Seth nods. "I'm glad to hear that, but even if you weren't, it wouldn't change the facts."

Carson scoffs. "Christ, you're an asshole, Balor. How can you stand him, Little E?"

"Because he's not an asshole to me," I say sincerely. Not usually, anyways.

Carson thinks for a moment before nodding. "Fair enough. Hey, can you make him stop being an asshole to me?"

"I'll stop being an asshole to you the day you stop being annoying," Seth informs him flatly.

Carson pouts playfully. "Considering my breathing around you is sometimes enough to annoy you, that means never?"

"Correct," Seth confirms.

I can't help the giggle that escapes me. I wonder if this is how they were before they met me when they hung out together; teasing and poking at each other, shooting the shit light-heartedly with the occasional threat thrown in by Seth. I can definitely picture that, though I'd never picture them at an ice cream shop—it seems too light an environment for Seth.

Carson wraps his arms around my waist, then moves me in front of him, putting me between him and Seth. "Shield me, Elia, I'm scared of the big bad wolf."

"What you are is a child trapped in the body of a man," Seth retorts, looking like he's holding back an eyeroll.

"Considering I'm half your size, I don't know if I'd make an effective shield," I point out.

"You could try throwing her at me to distract me, though. That would work," Seth offers.

"I am not a shield or a baseball to be tossed around, thank you very much," I reply.

"True," Carson responds simply, squeezing my waist. He leans down until his mouth is right by my ear and says, "But I'm not gonna lie, it's kind of hot to manhandle you. I like how small you are, it makes you easy to maneuver."

I feel a blush crawl up my neck at his words, because I also like being manhandled. I never thought I'd find it as hot as I do; frankly, they both have a habit of doing things I never thought I'd find erotic, but enjoy when they're the ones doing it.

"I like it, too," I murmur.

Our order is called out from the counter, and I step away from Carson to accept my ice cream cup. Carson got the largest available sized cup with several different flavors, and I'm not surprised to find he has a bit of a sweet tooth. Seth, on the other hand, got the same size as me, with one scoop of chocolate and one vanilla. That's fitting for him; black and white.

"Would you like to go sit with your dance friends?" Seth asks me after we've grabbed spoons and napkins.

I worry my lip between my teeth, unsure. I don't think Sean will judge me if he finds out I'm with both Seth and Carson, but I don't know about the others sitting at the dance table. I'm certainly not ashamed of my men, but I also don't want to *be* shamed by anyone. Still, I understand that if I'm going to really give a relationship with them a shot, I might have to deal with some judgement. Hopefully not great amounts, but some.

Seth taps my nose with his spoon. "Stop thinking, start talking. Yes or no?"

"Yes," I finally say, mentally steeling myself.

Carson smiles at me, while Seth simply nods. Tension gathers in my shoulders as we walk to the back of the shop, approaching my dance crew. There are about six dancers there; a mixed bag from all different years, though I recognize all of them. Sean smiles at me, then motions to a few empty chairs at the corner of the table. April isn't here, which is a shame, but probably means she's out with her flavor of the week.

I take the center seat available while Seth takes the one on my right and Carson sits to my left.

Chloe, a fellow freshman I've spoken with a few times, and someone I like—she was one of the Gen Z dancers in Sleeping Beauty and has two solos in Pandora's Box—smiles at me.

"Hey, Elia," she greets kindly. "Who are your friends?"

"Boyfriends," Seth corrects, which makes me stiffen in my seat. "Seth Balor."

Carson, rolling his eyes at Seth, also introduces himself. It's an honest to god struggle not to shrink down into my seat with discomfort as I flick my eyes around the dancers, searching for reactions.

A wide smile spreads on Sean's lips. "I fucking knew it. Good on you, Elia. I'll try to pretend I'm not jealous."

Brianna, seated on the far end of the table, curls her upper lips as she looks between me, Carson, and Seth. "Guess Scarlett wasn't wrong, after all."

She was one of Scarlett's closest friends—though *friend* might be a bit of an overstatement. Loyal foot-bitch is more accurate. Brianna tried to get close to Scarlett in order to heighten her own status, and for a time, it worked, until Scarlett fell from grace and promptly disappeared.

Instead of feeling shame or embarrassment at the stroke of judgement, I feel irritation, because it really isn't anyone's place to disparage me for my decisions.

"Envy isn't a good look on you, Bri. You had a fucking orgy last weekend where three guys rode you at once, so do you really want to cry wolf?" Sean asks, giving Brianna an annoyed look.

Cheeks reddening, Brianna shuts her mouth and crosses her arms, then pulls her phone out of her pocket and pointedly turns her attention to it. I bite my lip to hide my laugh, and when I look around the other members of my dance company, I see that most of them don't look like they care one way or another, which makes me relax.

"I might be okay with Prince Gardener after all," Seth murmurs.

Chloe gives me a soft smile, raising her spoon to me in salute. "Whatever makes you happy, sis."

After that, the evening goes by nicely. I eat my ice cream and chat with my fellow dancers about the upcoming production. Carson turns the charm up to 100, making easy friends with everyone seated at the table—everyone except Brianna, that is, who leaves a few minutes after Sean's clapback. Seth's mostly quiet, content as an observer, and I actually enjoy myself. It eases a lot of my worry over judgement; especially when I realize that Brianna's condemnation didn't even hurt me, it just annoyed me. I'm good at ignoring annoyances.

An hour of chatting lightly and laughing later, the group disperses, and Carson drives me back to his apartment building rather than dorms, which I don't have it in me to complain about. Tonight has already been a resounding success, and I look forward to seeing where it goes.

We decide to spend a few hours posing for Seth's painting, the reimagined Mars and Venus, which is how we both end up on Seth's couch, laid out across from each other, both half-naked. Although I'm still getting paid for my time—*bonus!*—the no-nudity clause in my contract with Seth has gone lax. I can't really complain, since dynamics have shifted quite a bit over the last weeks. Carson is leaned back on his elbows, head resting against one of the couches' arms, staring at me so intensely I can't stop blushing.

I'm laid out in the opposite direction, wearing only a bra and panties, with one arm beneath my head, clutching my side of the couch, and my head turned towards Seth where he sits in his usual spot before an easel. My legs are tangled up with Carson's, covered with a sheet, and I feel at once ridiculously sexy and slightly embarrassed at the position, probably because Carson's stare transmits a thousand dirty things, and each time Seth looks at me, it's with so much heat in his gaze it makes everything inside me tighten.

"Is this going to be one of your demonic, dark paintings?" I ask Seth, curious.

Although he's nearing completion of the first painting he started of me, and now he's working on this one, I still haven't seen any of his work, though I know I will soon. I already know he's an incredible painter, talented beyond comprehension, so I'm not sure why he hasn't let me see his paintings of me so far—it can't be that he's nervous. It could be because of how much I've been pestering him.

"All my paintings are dark, Little Muse, but this one won't be demonic," he tells me. "I'll show you the first one as soon as it's done, but I think this one will far eclipse it."

Carson says, "It's because I'm in it, right? Anything featuring me must have god-level beauty."

Seth rolls his eyes. "Act your age, Carson, not your shoe size."

Carson grins. "You know what they say about big feet."

I sigh. "Are you ever not...*this*?"

Both Carson and Seth respond at the same time, "No."

I nod. "Fair enough." After a pause: "Can we break? I'm thirsty."

"What a coincidence, so am I," Carson says, giving me a lascivious smile.

I kick him lightly. "Don't be gross. Seriously, we've been here for upwards of two hours. My muscles are starting to tense." I turn to give

Seth a pointed look. "If posing for you interferes with my dancing, I will be pissed."

Seth smiles. "It won't, all you have to do if you need a break is tell me. I've gotten plenty for tonight, anyways." He sets down his paintbrush and stands, examining the canvas, before giving a satisfied nod, seemingly to himself. While I untangle myself from Carson and get to my feet, Seth picks up the canvas and takes it to a closet in his bedroom, where he's told me he leaves paintings to dry.

I wander into the kitchen, familiar with the space from the last weeks, and grab a bottle of water from the fridge, downing half of it in four gulps. I'm not *just* thirsty because we haven't taken breaks, I'm also a little hot and bothered from getting stared at by two of the hottest men I've ever encountered, both of whom are mine.

Warmth at my back precedes two strong arms wrapping around my waist, and I sigh with contentment, leaning back into Carson's hold. Because I'm already wet, ready, and turned on from the last hours, I press my ass into his erection, smiling to myself when I feel it jump against my lower back.

"Careful, Princess," Carson growls in my ear. "I'm already planning on devouring you, keep up the teasing and it'll only get worse."

CHAPTER FIFTY-SEVEN

The thing is, *worse* with him means more sex, which I am perfectly happy to instigate, so I roll my hips against his erection again. That's all it takes for Carson to spin me around, grip my waist, and lift me into his arms effortlessly, making me giggle. I wrap my legs around his waist, arms around his shoulders, and skim my teeth up the side of his neck, liking his answering shudder of arousal.

"Seth," Carson calls out. "I think our woman needs to be taken care of."

God, I love hearing that. The *our woman* part. I'm completely set in my decision to have both of them, especially because today was the last leg of the test run I needed to see if things between all three of us could really work. They can—my greatest remaining concern was judgement in public, and even when Brianna got a little judgy, it didn't hurt me; it only pissed me off, which tells me all I need to know.

"Then bring her to the bedroom," Seth calls back.

"You ready to get wrecked, Princess?" Carson murmurs in my ear, before nipping at the lobe, making my fingernails curl into his shoulders.

"Very much so," I say, surprised at how breathy my voice comes out. I clutch onto Carson tightly as he walks me through Seth's apartment and into the bedroom, where Seth's already seated on the edge of his bed, staring at me with sheer, stark hunger filling his gaze.

A touch of apprehension makes my chest flutter; I'm not exactly sure what sex with both of them at the same time will look like, and that makes me nervous. I *think* I can take it, I certainly want to take it, but I'm also a little scared. That fear is overshadowed by desire, though, as well as trust. I trust both of them deeply, trust that they won't do anything I won't like or push me too far. Seth certainly likes to test my limits, but even he eases up if I need him to.

Carson sets me down on my feet, and I get a brief glimpse of him shucking his pants before Seth pulls me onto his lap and drinks deeply from my mouth, kissing me with one of his hands tangled in my hair and the other kneading my ass until I feel dizzy and woozy and am on the verge of passing out. He pulls back and stares at me with bright green orbs. His ever-changing eyes never fail to fascinate me, and I love seeing them light up green because that usually precedes me getting fucked to within an inch of my life.

"I want you to take both of us at once," Seth murmurs. "I also don't want to hurt you too much or go too fast. Soon enough you'll find out what it's like to have your ass and pussy filled at once, but not yet. You aren't ready yet, so we're going to take things a bit easier."

I relax a little at his words, and at the reaffirmation that he takes my wants, considerations, and limits into account above his own, which I treasure, especially because I know I'm the first he's done that with.

"Stop hogging her," I hear Carson mutter behind me, before he plucks me right off of Seth's lap, stands me up, and turns me around. My arms automatically wind around his neck and I lean into him.

Carson kisses me, no less intensely than Seth did, but a little more tenderly. While, with Seth, it sometimes feels like I'm getting consumed, with Carson it's different. He can consume me and treasure me in the same breath—it's evident the way his fingers skim up and down my body, the way one of his hands gently cups the back of my head, massaging the base of my skull, and the way he holds me like I'm made of glass and he's afraid to break me. His lips are full and soft, moving over mine, his tongue is playful, and everything about him is *light*. He really is like the personification of the sun.

I feel his erection press into my stomach more firmly, leaving a sticky spot on my torso, which only makes this whole thing hotter. I like getting him worked up, like how much power I can exert over him with something as simple as a kiss.

I startle when I feel Seth's hands slide along the waistband of my panties before tugging them down my legs. Like he did the other day when I was sandwiched between them, he lifts my legs one at a time to help me out of them. I jump when I feel his teeth sink into the left cheek of my ass, tearing my mouth away from Carson's with a low cry and resting my head on his shoulder, holding him tighter.

Seth releases the bite with a chuckle, tracing the sore skin with his hand while I cling to Carson. Seth's the one who brings the pain to our dynamic, but it's softened by Carson's presence, which is more playful and less animalistic.

"I like seeing my marks on this perfect ass," Seth rumbles, before brushing a kiss over his bitemark. I peek at him over my shoulder, seeing satisfaction glitter in his eyes as he stares at me.

"Here's what's going to happen now, Little Muse," he tells me, his voice an octave deeper than usual. "I'm going to feel your mouth wrapped around my cock while Carson gets you nice and wet. Then,

I'm going to hold you down the way I like to while he fucks you. You got any problems with that?"

I shake my head. I don't have any problems with that at all. Through all the times we've been together, I've never gotten around to giving him a blowjob—he's always too greedy for other things. I want to suck him, to blow *his* mind the way he's blown mine way too many times. If Carson's working me over at the same time, I'll consider that a bonus.

I look back to Carson with questioning eyes, silently asking if he's okay with this.

He smiles at me, brushing a few stray strands of hair from my forehead before answering my wordless inquiry. "We talked about what we'd do beforehand, Little E. I'm good with it if you are."

I didn't think I'd like the idea of them talking about what they'll do to me behind my back, I thought it'd be weird, but it isn't. In fact, it's kind of liberating. I don't have to do any of the math for this situation—all I have to do is go with the flow.

I give his lips one last kiss before turning around and looking to Seth. The sheets rustle as he scoots up farther on the bed until his back's resting on the headboard. His eyes darken when Carson flicks off the clasp of my bra and slides the material off of my arms, leaving me naked and bared to both of their gazes. The stark attention from both of them, knowing that these two *incredibly* powerful men are both deeply attracted to me, is invigorating. It makes me feel powerful in turn.

"Crawl to me," Seth commands, his muscles tensing in anticipation. He strips off his paint splattered sweats and briefs with one quick motion, and his cock springs up, pointing towards the ceiling, swollen and engorged, the tip glistening, which makes my mouth water.

I get on my hands and knees on the bed, hearing Carson suck in a harsh breath at the sight, and slowly crawl my way up the mattress until I'm directly in front of Seth, my face eye-level with his cock.

I pause for a moment as memories of less-pleasant scenarios like this flit through my mind, then internally shake myself to force those thoughts away. This situation isn't anything like times with my ex—with him, I learned the quickest way to suck him off in order to avoid having sex as often as he wanted to. I never *liked* doing it, mainly I blew him so he'd leave me alone. With Seth, I very much want to suck him—I want to see what he tastes like, find out what gets him to lose his mind, but I also don't want to be stuck in memories.

I wrap my hand around the bottom of Seth's length, feeling the thick appendage jerk in my hand. Even Seth's cock is a reminder of how wildly different this situation is. My ex had a small cock, not even five inches, that always smelled sweaty and disgusting and looked wrinkly and pathetic, sort of like a bot-worm. Seth's cock, on the other hand, is nearly twice that size and a thing of beauty. It's as powerful and masculine as the rest of him.

"Talk to me while I'm doing it," I gently request of Seth. "Tell me what you like. Praise me." Those are all things I never got from my ex—he just grunted and sweated and the whole experience was always nasty. I think if I hear Seth's voice it'll help me stay in the present.

Seth's eyes narrow for the briefest second, and I see him register that something's driving my request as he flicks his searching gaze over me, his eyebrows creasing with concern.

"You don't have to if you don't want to," he tells me, sternly. "I'll never make you do anything you don't like."

"No, I do," I assure him. "Just... I need to hear your voice. Please."

Seth reaches out to stroke his hand through my hair, and I nuzzle into his touch like a kitten. I like it when he's soft with me, but I like his intensity even more.

"Of course, Eliana. Whatever you want. Whatever you need. All you have to do is ask," Seth says.

I nod, silently shoving away bad memories, then turn my attention to the task in front of me, tightening my grip on the base of his cock, liking the hiss that draws from him. I brace myself on one elbow planted on the mattress, keeping my ass in the air as a lure for Carson, then focus on Seth.

I jerk him off a few times, pumping my hand up and down his length, watching as he hardens even further as more blood rushes to his extremities, turning his tip a purplish color. He has a particularly prominent vein running along the underside of his shaft, and I decide to start there, leaning forward to run my tongue along it. Seth lets out a low curse and his hand slides into my hair, fingers lightly scratching my scalp. He doesn't try to control my movements at all, though, like he's content to let me explore and see what I do. I take him into my mouth, just the tip, and suck the drop of his precum off. He tastes slightly musky and distinctly masculine, with a hint of salt that bursts on my tongue. I like that more than I thought I would.

Seth lets out a low groan as I take him a little farther in my mouth, sucking hard enough for my cheeks to hollow. The noise invigorates me and restores my confidence, which wobbled under the pressure of bad memories. It makes me keen to get him off, to show him that he's not the only person here good at oral. I know how to use my mouth for mind blowing pleasure, too.

I hear the rustling of sheets behind me, feel the mattress dip as Carson also climbs onto it. His hands slide over my ass before he tugs my legs further apart, making me tense in anticipation as I suck Seth harder. When Carson braces one hand on the small of my back while the fingers of his other hand slides through my slippery folds, I let out a low moan around Seth's cock, which only gets louder when Carson's middle finger finds my clit.

"Fuck, Elia. Just like that," Seth growls. "So fucking good. Your mouth is heaven."

His praise makes me shiver with pleasure, though that shiver could also be brought on from the way Carson slides two fingers into my pussy, slowly starting to pump them in and out, making my belly tighten.

I take more of Seth's length in my mouth, bobbing my head up and down, keeping the suction firm, and start jerking him off in time with my movements. Noises spill forth from him, one after another, low moans and groans that set me on fire as much as Carson's hand. Each sound of pleasure from Seth feels like praise that makes me want to do even more.

Though it might kill me, I take Seth as deep as I can manage, trying to relax my throat to see if I can take him all the way. After a moment, my gag reflex kicks in; I tilt my head back and let his cock slide out of my mouth, swallowing a couple times and blinking as tears spring into my eyes.

Still, old habit has me murmuring, "Sorry."

Seth lets out a breathless, dark chuckle. "For what? That's fucking *amazing*, Elia. So goddamn hot I'm about to blow like a thirteen-year-old."

I can work with that. With renewed vigor, I lean down and suck him back into my mouth, taking him deeper with each pass but not trying to kill myself over it because he seems to *really* like what I'm doing. All the while, Carson alternates between rubbing my clit and thrusting his fingers inside me, driving me wild, making me suck Seth harder. I let go of Seth's shaft to move my hand down to his balls, testing the weight before tugging on them *ever* so gently.

Seth barks, "Fuck." The tendons in his neck strain against his skin and he clenches his jaw. "I'm about to come. If you don't want to—"

I cut off his words by sucking even harder, opening my jaw wider, taking him deeper. I'm certainly not a quitter, and I want to taste him. Everything he has to give me. One more tug on his balls is all it takes; he explodes with a shout, legs shaking, shooting jet after jet of warm, slightly salty come down my throat. His hand in my hair tightens, nails scraping at my scalp harder, which I really like. I love making him lose control. I swallow down every drop, even though the volume is a little intimidating—he just keeps coming, so I keep swallowing, all the while Carson works me over harder and faster until I feel like I'm losing my mind. Just as Seth's orgasm ebbs and I swallow the last of his load, my own orgasm begins. Seth uses his grip to tug my head off his softening cock, and a low moan spills from me as Carson pulls his fingers from inside me to rub my clit *furiously*, setting off a round of convulsions in my pussy that makes me aware of just how empty my channel is.

Before I can ride out my orgasm, Carson abruptly flips me over, shocking the breath out of me, and uses his hands on my hips to drag my body down the bed.

Seth kneels above me and gathers my wrists in one of his hands, pinning them above my head, and I look up into his eyes to see them glimmering with both satisfaction and dark anticipation.

He leans down to kiss my forehead. "You did very well, Little Muse. That was very good."

The compliment makes me feel warm and fuzzy, and I smile up at him softly, feeling very accomplished and treasured.

My attention is quickly diverted when Carson spreads my legs, moving his hands to grip the backs of my thighs and pushing them up until my knees are nearly resting on my shoulders. I meet his eyes, which are practically glowing an electric blue and shining with mischief.

"I think you deserve a reward for that, Princess," Carson tells me, slowly stroking his thumb over the soft skin of my thighs. He lifts his hips to press his erection along my slit, making me gasp.

"She definitely does," Seth agrees, staring down at me. "Make it good, Ajax. Live up to that shiny fucking reputation."

"My pleasure," Carson replies.

My hands tug against Seth's grip as Carson slowly starts sliding into me, and as always, it's a stretch. I'm used to the burn, though, and I've come to crave the sensation, even if it hurts a little, because the pain is quickly eclipsed by pleasure. My eyes bounce between Seth and Carson, between hazel-green eyes and blue eyes, and I bite my lip, unsure where to look or who to focus on. Being between the two of them is overwhelming in a *really* hot way, making me want more.

"You labored over Seth's cock so nicely, Princess," Carson says, and the words draw a groan of pleasure from me. "Now you're stretched out for me, taking what I have to give, letting Seth hold you down while I enjoy this gorgeous pussy. Such a good girl."

Carson releases one of my thighs to cover the top of my mound with the heel of his palm, pressing down on my clit and making my eyes roll into the back of my head. Before my leg can relax or straighten, Seth grabs it in his free hand, making my eyes snap back open as he cuffs his fingers around my ankle and stretches my leg over my head, opening me up further for Carson. There's a slight prickle in my muscles at the position which only heightens my need as Carson starts sliding in and out of me with long, deep strokes, letting me feel every inch of him.

I feel another, stronger orgasm creeping up on me, raising goosebumps along my body and making my muscles tense as my stomach clenches. Carson feels it, too; he speeds up his strokes and starts rubbing his palm along my clit, before lifting his hand and replacing it with two fingers that zero in on the sensitive bundle of nerves, spreading my wetness over it and gliding across it, up and down and back and forth and going in circles that make me moan loudly.

His thrusts speed up more, and I see the veins in his arms pop as his body also tenses on top of me, which tells me he's close. I think he might've actually gotten off on fingering me while I sucked Seth as much as I did.

He grits his teeth and rolls his neck before asking in a gravelly voice, "You ready to come, Princess?"

I nod, feeling my orgasm creep closer and closer, aided by his fingers on my clit and his cock sliding so deeply inside of me I can almost feel it in my throat. Carson's nails dig into the thigh he's holding while his fingers speed up their motions until I think I might pass out from pleasure alone.

"Then come. Let me feel this hot, tight pussy squeezing around me—" he cuts off with a groan as I start to come with a loud cry, my legs shaking, yanking at Seth's unyielding grip on my hands to try to find something to ground me. Seth only tightens his hold on both my wrists and my leg, shaking his head at me immovably, which just makes me come harder and louder. My orgasm sets off Carson's; I sense it in the way his thrusts speed up, becoming jerky and uncontrolled, before he goes still and I feel him twitching inside of me with his own release. A moment later he falls on top of me, his softening cock sliding out of me as he releases my thigh, resting his head on my breasts. Seth releases my leg, too, gentling it down on the mattress before also letting go of my wrists. He massages the area he gripped tightly with his fingers, which feels soothing and gentle.

I try to get my racing heart under control, letting my eyes flutter shut and feeling my body slowly calm. My pussy feels tender and well used and there's a fine sheen of sweat coating my body, but I don't mind. I like knowing that I pleased both Seth and Carson and got incredible pleasure myself in turn. Carson slowly rolls off of me, which makes me whine and reach for him, cracking my eyes open to look at him.

He smiles down at me. "Not going anywhere, Little E, I just don't wanna crush you."

He curls his arm around me and tucks me into his side, at the same time that Seth scoots down the bed and wraps an arm around my waist, also holding me. I slide my feet between Seth's warm calves and rest my head on Carson's chest, feeling totally content and *so* complete, like I'm exactly where I need to be. I'm always cuddly after sex, and I love getting cuddled by both of them. Double the warmth, double the contentment.

Seth slides his palm up and down my spine in a gesture that always soothes me, leaning forward to press a kiss on my shoulder.

After a while, Seth asks me, "Why'd you tense earlier? Before you blew me, it looked like you went somewhere else for a second."

I let out a long breath, pressing a kiss to Carson's chest before rolling over to face Seth, who adjusts his hold on me to press me up against him. I wouldn't usually want to answer his question or talk about it, but I trust him and want to be open with him.

"Bad ex," I murmur. I've already told Carson about him when we were trading secrets, but I didn't go into much detail, and I don't think I've mentioned it to Seth. "Trust-fund brat who thought money equated rights to do whatever he wanted. We were together for most of my senior year, mainly because I didn't want to deal with the blowback of a breakup. He had a really high sex drive, but sex with him always disgusted me—I couldn't stand the feel of his grubby, fat fingers grabbing at me and his smelly, gross dick inside me—so I learned to blow him just so I wouldn't have to deal with as much sex. Got pretty good at it." I stop talking when I see Seth's eyes start to darken with anger, and quickly add, "It wasn't forced, or rape. Not really. I mean, I never said no because I'm pretty sure he wouldn't have listened, and I didn't want to turn into a victim. I just figured out how to handle him as often as I could without having to...you know."

Seth's grip tightens on me and he lets out a long, dark breath, shaking his head. "Consent is a spectrum, Little Muse. There's an important little thing called *enthusiastic* consent. If your mouth says 'yes' or 'fine' but your body says no, a man should know to back the hell off. What's his name?"

I shake my head, burying my cheek into his chest to hide from the question.

"It doesn't matter," I mumble against his skin. "I've moved on. So has he, I expect. It's in the past." I look up to meet Seth's eyes. "You help me forget." I glance at Carson over my shoulder, who looks equally tense, though less murdery. "Both of you do."

Seth exchanges eye contact with Carson, and some hidden conversation seems to pass between them. I put a hand on Seth's chest and say, "Please don't do anything crazy. I don't want to think or talk about him, I just want to forget."

Seth gives me a dark smile filled with hidden meaning that I'm too tired to try to decipher. "I won't do anything more or less crazy than what I always do. Thank you for telling me, Little Muse. You don't have to worry about him or anything harming or hurting you ever again." He puts his hand on top of mine, then pulls me closer to leave a lingering kiss on my lips.

His words are coded and he doesn't exactly tell me that he'll go after my ex but he also doesn't tell me that he won't. I don't want anything good for my ex, but I also don't want to be the cause of harm to him. I just don't want to dedicate that sort of thought or effort to him. If Seth does it on my behalf, though... maybe that's alright. I'm not usually one to stick my head in the sand, but this situation might be the exception. I wouldn't complain if some accident befell my ex.

"I know I can't stop you from being you, and I don't want to. Just don't kill him. I don't want that on my conscience," I say against Seth's lips.

Seth pulls back to stare down at me. He's silent for a long moment, before he finally purses his lips and inclines his head. "Fine. I won't kill him. I'll just make sure he can't use certain appendages ever again."

I'm strangely okay with that, so I sigh and relax, resting my head against Seth's hard chest. Despite the darkness of the conversation we just had, I feel so warm, so complete, so full with joy and love and that sense of profound rightness I think I could burst.

My eyes start to flutter closed as I laze in both of their attention. Carson's warmth at my back, his hands stroking over my side. Seth's warmth and strength at my front, his heart that I can hear pounding beneath his chest.

"I love you," I say dreamily. "Both of you. So much." I mean to say the words in my head, but instead they sneak past my lips, which makes me tense and snap my eyes back open. I didn't mean to make a declaration of love right here and now, but it's just what I felt. What I feel with both of them, towards both of them.

Seth shifts his position sideways so he can lean his forehead against mine while staring deeply into my eyes, letting me see everything held in his. Affection, *so much affection*, protectiveness, and a darkness that I've come to crave. "I love you too, Eliana. You should already know that, though. You're it for me."

I practically burst with happiness at that, trying to lean in to kiss him, only to be yanked away when Carson spins me around to face him. His blue eyes are wide, a little wild looking.

"Look at me when you say it, Little E," he growls. "Tell me again."

I lean closer to him, wrapping an arm around his chest. "I love you, Carson. More than I ever thought was possible."

Carson takes my lips in an impassioned, wild kiss, curling his body over mine and pressing a thigh between my legs.

"I love you too, Little E," he pulls back to breathe. "So much sometimes I think I'm going crazy. Now, let me show you how much. Gotta keep that ratio in check."

CHAPTER FIFTY-EIGHT

"**M**ichelangelo was the most enlightened artist of the renaissance, and you cannot make me think otherwise," I tell Seth, somewhat stubbornly. "In fact, he might've been a bit *too* enlightened, considering the fact that he had a propensity to go into creative crazes, and almost *all* of them were while he was working on his most intense religious pieces—he locked himself in the Sistine chapel while painting the ceiling."

"You don't need to mansplain renaissance history to me, Little Muse. While he might've been *one* of the most enlightened minds of the time, he is not *the* most enlightened," Seth returns. "Broaden your horizons, Elia—shall we talk about DaVinci? Or Caravaggio, who inspired Rembrandt?"

I frown at him, reaching for my root beer to take another sip. I usually enjoy getting into art debates with Seth, but today I'm a little stressed out about rehearsal, Sanders throwing tantrums on a near daily basis—a side effect of the show being a month out from its early December debut—and April being somewhat withdrawn recently, probably courtesy of the fact that Ian has been trailing her on campus and screwing with her head. I've restated my offer to have Carson fire him and Seth come for him, but she always declines, and tells me her recent quietness is because she's focusing on the upcoming production.

Sensing my mounting stress, Seth has sequestered me away in his apartment. I'll admit, it's kind of adorable the way he has an almost petulant disdain for anything that makes me uncomfortable. He constantly seeks to rid my life of any and all complications, because he'd prefer for my attention to go to him instead of worries, and I can't be as attentive to him when I'm stressed or thinking about other things. A spread of my favorite foods laid out on his dining room table is both a kindness and a reminder of his hatred for my habit of undereating.

Carson's working late tonight, so Seth is taking full advantage of having me to himself.

"Caravaggio was a baroque painter, not a renaissance painter, and DaVinci's religious beliefs are still a source of debate—we kind of went over that the first time we ever spoke," I remind Seth.

He shrugs. "Religion and enlightenment don't always walk hand in hand, Elia. Someone can be enlightened in many ways—science is as enlightening as religion, as is math, and all the higher studies of technical arts. DaVinci was an excellent mathematician, and brilliant engineer, and a stunning artist—he was enlightened in all three fields."

I sigh. "You know how irritating it is to be around someone who's as versed in the Renaissance as I am? Usually, *I'm* the best source of knowledge on that particular period of history in my vicinity and social circles."

Seth casts a pointed glance at my nearly full plate, which has two sushi rolls on it, along with an abundance of ginger. "I'm not seeing you eat. I'll only debate Renaissance with you if you eat."

I roll my eyes, but pick up a piece of tuna sushi, dunk it in soy sauce, and pop it into my mouth. Seth gives me a satisfied nod before speaking again.

"I'm quite well aware that, generally speaking, you're very knowledgeable about the Renaissance. You are not, however, omniscient, and while we agree on many points, I also have a few viewpoints that might come in handy. Davinci's my favorite artist of that time, of course I have a great deal of knowledge of him. I would most definitely refer to him as enlightened, in many ways that others weren't." He pauses. "You know, your little rant on the renaissance when we first met was the thing that really drew me to you. It's what enlightened *me* to the fact that there were many facets of you; I was bewitched by the way you walked around, calmly ignoring me, casual as you please after I'd irritated you."

I smile at the memory. "You were being an asshole; I didn't feel like dealing with that. I also sensed that you were the type to get off on a reaction, so I didn't think feeding into your bullshit would get me anywhere."

Seth inclines his head, looking contemplative. "Typically, yes, I would've gotten some satisfaction from getting a reaction out of someone. In your case, though, your utter lack of reaction was what pulled me right in. You figured me out quickly, then proceeded accordingly. It might've worked to put me off if I wasn't so fucking fascinated by you."

I tilt my head to the side, growing curious. I know that I caught Seth's interest right off the bat, but I don't understand exactly what it is about me that drew his attention. I didn't do anything crazy or act in any remarkable way—I rambled like the off-balance idiot I was in that moment, then made a joking comment about dumb girls in horror movies and walked away.

"Why were you fascinated by me?" I ask. "I mean, I'm not complaining about your fascination anymore as it's turned out to be quite beneficial to me, but I'm still pretty confounded by it."

Seth takes a bite of his food, chewing and swallowing thoughtfully before washing it down with a sip of his own drink—white wine. I watch his adam's apple bob, then find my eyes straying down to his thick, corded forearms with bulging muscles and veins, his tight shirt that molds right to his six pack, before forcing my eyes back up to his. It really isn't fair to have to be in the presence of someone who has ethereal beauty the way Seth does; if I was a less confident person, his looks might make me insecure because he's simply too gorgeous to exist.

"There were a lot of things that pulled me in. You had a depth of knowledge on one of my favorite art periods, a sense of humor that was tinged with darkness, shadows in your eyes, and a way of looking at me that made me think you were seeing *through* me. It also struck me that you were a pretty flexible person—not just physically, but with your personality. After feeling insulted, most girls would've told me off and tried to leave. You didn't. You just popped your headphones into your ears to drown me out, then proceeded on with your day as if I didn't exist. When I tried to get to you in the museum lobby, you basically told me to go fuck myself without telling me to go fuck myself. Was it any wonder I got enamored?"

I guess not. I exhibited a set of behaviors that made him very interested, because they went against his expectations of how other people would behave when faced with the sheer force of his personality. He anticipated that his provocations would lead to reactions; in giving him none, I only got more of his interest. It's kind of a twisted and backwards situation, which is what one should expect from a man like Seth.

"For most people, it would be odd, but you're not most people."

Seth's lips quirk. "Neither are you, Eliana. Neither are you."

I eat another piece of sushi before Seth can prompt me to, then say, "You lured me here tonight under the guise of showing me the first painting you worked on of me. I'm not seeing any painting, which is a problem for me."

Seth smiles. "Is that so? Well, you not taking care of yourself is a problem for *me*. Fix my problem and I'll fix yours."

I can't hold back an eyeroll. "You're like a nagging grandmother who thinks her grandkids are malnourished unless they're overweight."

Seth shakes his head. "No, Little Muse," he disagrees. "I'm the person who won't tolerate you not taking care of yourself, because you belong to me, and I take good care of my belongings. Always. So, if you prove an inability to do it yourself, that prompts me to step in and pick up the slack. Finish your food, then I'll show you the painting."

I'll never admit out loud just how heartwarming it is when Seth gets worked up over my wellbeing, but it always makes me tingly. He's right that I have a habit of neglecting some of my basic needs, probably because of the childhood and early adulthood I had where my needs weren't treated like needs, but like privileges I had to earn. I've gotten better at taking care of myself, but not as much as I should.

We talk a little more about art history, even touching on how the Black Death threw a wrench in the development of renaissance art, while I finish the food on my plate, and then let Seth coax me into eating a few bites of other dishes because I know taking care of me settles something in him. I'd never have anticipated Seth to be a natural caretaker, considering the self-admitted enjoyment he takes in destroying things, but he is when it comes to me.

Finally, Seth retreats into his bedroom closet where he stores his paintings, before bringing out a canvas. He makes me close my eyes while he settles it on an easel, which I do, mainly because I don't see the point in arguing—I've accepted that he's a control freak. Despite having a controlling nature, though, he listens when I tell him he's going too far and adjusts accordingly, which is all I need.

When he finally tells me I can open my eyes and approach, I do, eagerly. Then, a soft gasp escapes me as I get my first good look at the canvas.

Seth used oil paint to portray the most gorgeous depiction of me, lying on a forest floor with a restful expression, surrounded by nature and flowers. It looks like he took some inspiration from the Venus paintings but did an entirely new take on Venus. The background of the painting, outside of the abundant, lush forest floor I lie on, is dark and dismal and withered; swirls of angry purples and dark navy's combine to create an almost apocalyptic appearance, and there's a demonic hand dipping downwards from a dark red sky, reaching for me. I have to admit, I am absolutely *stunned* with his skill and precision.

"Holy shit," I breathe, stepping closer to the painting. "You are unreasonably talented."

Seth chuckles. "No, Little Muse, you're just unreasonably gorgeous and ridiculously inspiring. You don't mind that, aside from the little stretch where you're laid out, the painting has my usual edge of darkness?"

"No," I say emphatically, shaking my head. "It's amazing. The juxtaposition between dark, dismal, and frightening and light, living, and beautiful is absolutely stunning. This is a twist on a Venus painting, right? Sleeping Venus?"

Seth lifts a shoulder. "In part. Venus, one of the Greek muses, a saint... the interpretation is up to the viewer, but the message should be clear; you're the slice of brightness in an otherwise unpleasant setting. That's how I see you, how I feel about you; a drop of light in this miserable fucking world that makes it a whole lot more bearable."

"You need to stop saying sweet things like that," I murmur, my voice faintly choked up. "It makes it difficult to resist you."

Seth wraps his arms around my waist. "So don't."

I sigh. "I told you there'd be no sex tonight—I have a very intense dance day tomorrow, and you've proven that you don't get the concept of taking it easy. This painting is touching and gorgeous and darkly magnetic and I'm very grateful you showed it to me, but that won't change my decision."

Seth sighs. "Sometimes it's irritating that you stick to your rules and convictions with such precision. Not many people do."

I grin, turning around to face him. "That's part of why you love me."

He nods, not bothering to deny it. "Very true." He leans down to kiss me nevertheless, and I let him. I love it when we kiss, love feeling swept up in the storm that is Seth. Frightening, intense, sensual, and addictive.

"You're still sleeping in my bed tonight," he says, pulling back. It's not a question, more of a statement that makes me arch an eyebrow at him.

"Am I, now? You might want to rephrase before I decide I'm not in the mood to deal with you."

He clenches his jaw, but then says through gritted teeth, "Will you stay with me tonight?"

I squeeze his biceps. "Yes, I will."

His jaw relaxes, his lips tip up at the sides, and the way his eyes brighten makes me melt into him, wrapping my arms around him and resting my head against his chest. He embraces me in turn, wrapping one arm around my waist and using the other to run his hands through my hair, a favorite pastime of his.

"I'll respect your no-sex rule for tonight, but you said nothing about fooling around," Seth murmurs, using the bedroom-tone that never fails to make my body tighten and belly flutter. "I'm going to feed you dessert, Little Muse, then you are going to be my dessert."

CHAPTER FIFTY-NINE

An hour later, I realize that Seth wasn't kidding when he said I'd be his dessert tonight. He's in the mood to take his time with me; after eating my pussy for the better part of an hour, making me beg for an orgasm until I was actually crying for it, he finally gave me a release that left me shaking, yet not wholly satisfied.

He straddles me on his bed, fully clothed while I'm naked, and kisses me so deeply and thoroughly I lose whatever breath I have left.

When I feel cool silk slide around my wrists, knotting them together, I'm still so boneless and limp it takes me a moment to realize what he's doing. By the time conscious thought returns to me, I look up to see that my wrists are above my head, tied together firmly, with the other end of the rope attached to a conveniently placed spindle on Seth's headboard. Above them, the demonic version of Vitruvian Man stares down at me, almost like a taunt.

"Now *that* is a pretty picture," Seth murmurs, drawing my attention back to him. I gape up at him, lips parted and eyes wide, struggling to comprehend exactly what's happening right now. I am astonished at his gall and the fact that he must've planned this out far in advance; everything he does is thought out meticulously.

"I kind of want to paint you like this right now," he murmurs, reaching up to palm my breast and circle my nipple with his fingers. "Then again, I'd also like to spend the rest of the night playing with you. Hmm."

"Seth," I start slowly, blinking up at him. "What the hell?"

"Hell is not being allowed to touch you," Seth murmurs. "Hell is not being allowed to fuck you, Little Muse. This, however... this is closer to my version of heaven."

He's talked about tying me to his bed on numerous occasions, I always assumed we'd eventually end up here, I just didn't expect it *tonight*. Certainly not right now, without discussing it beforehand and agreeing to it. I should've expected that Seth would work on his own timetable; he likes surprising me. He also likes it when I'm confused and a little scared, when anxiety and uncertainty is thrown into the mix.

"You know your safeword, Eliana," he says lowly. "Until I hear you say it, I'm going to play. And since you told me I can't fuck you tonight, I am going to play *hard*."

He stares at me for several moments, his gaze challenging, practically *daring* me to say my safeword and put an end to this before it begins. I don't, though. I'm surprisingly turned on by being immobilized, completely beneath his mercy, even more so than I usually am when he's rough with me during sex. Ultimately, I know I'll always have a way out—a single uttered word puts a stop to all of this. I want to see where he takes me tonight.

After all, I did agree to stay with him, and I know spending the night with Seth always involves a certain degree of intensity. He's prone to doing things that startle me, shock the hell out of me sometimes, but he never takes things too far. I've never once actually *had* to say my safeword, which makes me trust him all the more.

"Okay," he says after a few beats of waiting for me to protest. "Let's get started. I'm in a particularly playful mood tonight, Little Muse. I'm going to introduce you to some toys that I think you'll like very much, until you don't. Until they become too intense, and you beg me to take them away." He nods, slowly. "Yes, that's what I'd like to hear tonight."

"Toys?" I repeat, tensing.

"Mhm. I was on a website the other day while fantasizing about you. I'll admit, I might've gotten a bit carried away with my purchases. I'm eager to test them out." Again, he pauses, waiting for me to protest. Even though I'm growing nervous, and it's on the tip of my tongue to put a stop to all this, I don't. *You trust him, Elia. He's never betrayed that trust*, a voice in my head reminds me.

I give him a single nod; a slow smile of pleasure spreads on his lips. "Very good." From his pocket, he pulls out—oh Jesus, a *blindfold*. He doesn't ask or wait this time—he reaches up and fastens it around my head, slipping the cool, thick silk over my eyes, robbing me of my vision. My breathing turns harsher as my other sensations heighten in the absence of sight. I can feel the warm silk sheets beneath me, hear Seth shuffling forward on the bed. The sound of the bedside drawer opening echoes like a gunshot through the room, and I hear him pull out several items, some of which make clattering noises kind of like keys on a keychain.

I hear him drop whatever he took out on the mattress beside me, feel the slight dip on the sheets, making my breath catch. Seth cups my breasts in his palms, teasing my nipples with his fingers until they've hardened into sensitive buds.

"I've wanted to see these pretty little pink nipples decorated with bejeweled clamps for some time," he murmurs lowly. "Tonight, I'm going to make that happen, Little Muse. I'm going to make several visions come true, starting with this." He firmly cups my breast in his palm, and a sharp pinching feeling descends on my nipple as he fastens what must be the clamp he talked about over it, making me cry out and jerk my wrists against the binding. Shooting pinpricks of intense pain course through my breast, robbing me of the ability to think as pain overwhelms me.

"Shh," Seth soothes. "You can take it, can't you? The pain will subside in a second, breathe."

I follow his directions, inhaling deeply, waiting... and after a minute or so, the pain does subside, replaced by a numbness. I let out a low whimper as Seth circles his finger around my clamped nipple.

"Better?" he asks.

After a slight hesitation, I murmur, "Better."

He repeats the motions on my other breast, clamping my free nipple as well—again, he soothes me through the pain until a strange, aching numbness overtakes my entire chest. It feels weird, not altogether pleasant, but I can't deny it's very erotic. I can feel renewed wetness between my thighs, arousal gushing out of me. *Guess I'm more into the kinky stuff than I ever could've fathomed.*

"I'm going to tie your legs open now," Seth tells me in a deep voice that feels as smooth as whiskey, yet carries the same burning bite as the liquor. "I want your pussy totally exposed, achingly vulnerable while I torture it. Okay?"

Again, I hesitate for a moment, considering. Again, I remember the fact that Seth, despite being dark and very kinky, never tortures me more than I can handle. He tends to show me new heights as to how much I'm able to take, but he keeps himself leashed. I'm curious about the toys he spoke of, curious to see where he's going with this. I know that, at the end of the day, this will probably mean several orgasms for me, which I'm definitely okay with.

"Yes," I tell him.

I can practically feel the satisfaction radiating off of him as the sound of him shuffling down the bed echoes through the air. I expect him to tie my ankles to the bedposts—instead, he surprises me once again by using what I suspect to be belts to bind my legs together, keeping them bent with my calves molded to the backs of my thighs and my feet just under my ass. Then, he spreads them so that the outsides of my legs are resting on the bed, and loops what feels like more silk beneath the belts, using it to hold my legs in position, presumably tying them to the wooden siderails of the bed. I can't close my legs and I can't even straighten them—the bottom half of me is completely immobilized, and my pussy is stretched wide for him.

"Fucking *stunning*, bound and completely at my mercy," Seth muses, his voice barely more than a growl. "This is better than anything I could've imagined, Little Muse. You are a *vision*. My bound Venus, spread out like the loveliest sacrifice for the darkest of predators."

A low whine escapes me at his words as a deep ache starts up in my pussy, demanding to be satisfied. I'm more wound up by this than I ever thought I could be by bondage, and I know we're just getting started. Seth hasn't actually done anything beyond clamp my nipples and ready me for whatever he intends to do to me, and the anticipation is both riveting and absolutely unbearable.

Two fingers glide through my slit, drawing a low moan from me and a growl from Seth. "Already sopping wet," he hisses. "What's turning you on so much, Little Muse? Being bound and at my mercy? The clamps? Or is it just the fact that *I'm* doing this all to you?"

"All of that," I cry as he pinches my clit between two fingers and tugs on it. Tingles break out over my skin, making me restless with the need to reach a climax.

"Believe me, Elia, this is turning me on beyond anything I could've comprehended, too," Seth mutters, his voice strained. "If you could just see yourself now... pussy spread so wide for me, clit swollen, tits clamped—I'm about to go off in my pants."

I hear him rise from the bed, feel the mattress lift a bit without his weight, and then... then his footsteps sound as he walks away from me. That's what actually makes me afraid more than anything else; this whole scene is enjoyable, albeit almost hovering on the edge of too intense, when he's right here with me, but as I feel his warmth subside, panic sparks within me.

"Seth?" I call out. When he doesn't respond fast enough, I cry, "Seth!"

Footsteps return, just as he says, "I'm not leaving you like this, Little Muse, just had to grab something." His palm, cooler than it was before, smooths up my navel to trace around my breast as he once again joins me on the mattress. Instantly, some of the tension seeps out of me, and the edge of panic subsides.

"Don't leave me," I whisper.

He makes a noise low in his throat that sounds somewhat like an admonishment. He shifts until I can feel his body leaning over me, and his soft lips brush over mine before giving me a kiss. "I won't, Eliana. Ever. Certainly not like this. Even if you begged me to leave you, I wouldn't be able to—I don't have it in me. Now, hush, and let me get to work."

His words are proprietary and spoken with a dangerous edge, one that probably should make me fearful, but instead they soothe me. I don't want him to ever leave me—at this point, I'm not sure how I'd survive without him *or* Carson.

He pulls back and cups my pussy again, slowly rubbing his fingers up and down my slit before circling over my clit, drawing a long, languid noise of pleasure from me. He works me over until I'm just on the cusp of an orgasm, and then pulls away.

"Not this again," I whine.

He chuckles. "Yes, this again. I love hearing you beg, Eliana, and you are going to beg for me a *lot* tonight, for many different things. In fact, I'm switching your safeword tonight. If you want me to stop, you're going to have to *beg* me to stop."

"W-what?" I stutter.

"You want me to stop, beg very prettily for me to stop," he repeats, sounding very pleased at the idea. "I'll know if you actually need me to stop before even you will, Little Muse, I know your body very well at this point—I'd say better than you know it yourself. Do you trust me?"

"Yes," I respond. He's never given me a reason not to trust him, but he's also never replaced my safe word with begging. He always has me beg for him, ever since the first time we had sex, but that felt like a game, before, while now it'd be my only way out.

"How would you know to stop?" I ask, a slight shake in my voice.

"Because I know you. I know all your noises, I know your limits, I know your breathing patterns, and I know what you look and sound like when it's getting to be too much." He pauses for a beat, letting that sink in. "So, tonight your safeword is begging. Trust that I'll know when you actually need me to stop. Yes?"

"Okay," I reply quietly, somewhat hesitantly.

"Mm, that's my good girl," Seth says, approval coating his tone, which feels like a warm blanket descending over me and makes me more confident, both in myself and in him.

A low noise cuts through the air, like a buzzing, which is the only warning I get before Seth presses what feels like a bulbous silicone object to my pussy, instantly drawing a startled cry from low in my throat. It must be a vibrator of some sort, something I've never tried but heard of from friends, and the sensation it causes is achingly intense, especially with the way I'm bound and spread for Seth. He moves the toy up and down my slit before circling it over my clit, and noises far beyond anything I've ever made before are pulled from me. The sensation is pure, uninterrupted pleasure, so intense I can barely handle it, but Seth is a man on a mission. I shriek when he thrusts three fingers into my channel, which he answers with a low groan.

"I can already feel you tightening around my fingers, Little Muse," Seth mutters, the words barely audible over the noise of the vibrations. "So fucking hot, so wet..."

My back arches and I try to wriggle out of the way of the pleasure that's already too much, though I don't really want to stop it—it's too much *and* not enough, so good I can barely form a coherent thought. The clamps on my nipples jiggle as my body starts to shake, sending renewed bursts of pain through my breasts and making clanking noises that draw a noise of masculine pleasure from Seth. Just when I'm about to detonate, Seth turns off the toy and pulls his fingers out of me.

"No, please—" I cut off, shaking my head and breathing deeply, not even sure what I'm asking for. Edging me to the cusp only to pull me away is a favorite pastime of Seth's, and it never fails to make me plead mindlessly.

"Hmm?" Seth questions, running the toy over my slit, tantalizing me even though it's turned off. "You know what you need to do to get what you want, my gorgeous muse. Beg."

He turns the toy back on for a split second, only to turn it off again. "Seth, please!" I cry. "I'll do *anything*—"

"Anything," he repeats, amused. "Good."

I feel a thump on the bed as he drops the toy, making disappointment overwhelm me. It's quickly replaced by confused anticipation when I hear the cap of a bottle open, then a squirting noise. He presses something against the bud of my ass—*a butt plug?* I guess he really is going all out tonight.

I make a high-pitched whining noise as the tip of the object, coated in a slick substance that must be lube, breaches my ass. It stings and burns, but the pain's different from when he clamped my nipples; more intimate and uncomfortable.

"What I really love about this position is how all of you is spread out for me," Seth says conversationally. "Including this tight little ass. Since I'll be fucking it soon, Little Muse, believe me when I say you'll be grateful for the practice. Now relax for me."

Breathing harshly, trembling all over, I squeeze my eyes and clench my hands into fists, but try to obey him and relax. It's difficult, considering the most I've ever had in my butt is a finger or two—plenty of threats for more, but never the actual thing.

"Come on, Eliana, you can do it. Breathe deeply, push out." As I follow his directions, he manages to slide the plug farther in, and I make a panicked noise at the burning sensation—it hurts. Not terribly, the pain isn't enough to overwhelm the pleasure still lingering from the vibrator, but it's more than I anticipated. "We're almost there, Little Muse. Just a bit farther. Do you need to stop, or can you take it for me?"

After several moments of silence, I give a nod. "I can do it."

"Yes, you can," he agrees, tone warming. "You're my strong girl, aren't you? You can take anything I have to dish out." With one final push along with a bit of twisting, he seats the plug fully inside me. The end of it is thinner than the rest, like a little pole, and I can feel an uncomfortable fullness deeper inside me. Though strange and foreign, it isn't bad—just something that I expect will take some getting used to. "Now, since you were such a good girl, you're free to come."

The vibrations return to my clit; combined with the pressure in my ass and the way Seth immediately thrusts his fingers back into me, my orgasm sweeps over me almost instantly. A hoarse shout is ripped from my throat, my toes curl, my back arches, and I instinctually struggle against my restraints, trying to get away from the vibrator that's already proving to be way too much. Seth simply circles it around my clit faster, not giving me reprieve; drawing out my orgasm for so long I feel like my pussy's on fire, and the rest of my body starts to ache from the way I'm pulling at my restraints. After what feels like an eternity, when I'm on the verge of begging him to stop for real, he turns it off and tosses the toy aside, pulling his fingers from my channel, leaving me a panting mess.

"Now, that," he cuts off with a harsh chuckle, "was one of the hottest fucking things I've ever seen. Only thing that could've made it better is having my cock deep inside you as you came; you nearly broke off my fingers, Little Muse, that would've felt *incredible* around me. Since you made it clear that's off the table tonight, I guess I'll just have to satisfy myself with feeling that a few more times with my fingers deep inside you rather than my cock."

"A few more times?" My voice is hoarse and shrill.

"Yes," Seth agrees. "Until you beg me to stop, Eliana. Until I'm convinced you really can't take anymore."

Oh, shit. Seth's playfulness is mixed with his usual darkness, the fact that he always enjoys testing my limits and setting new limits for me. I try to catch my breath and prepare myself for whatever else is to come; as if sensing that I need a moment, Seth rubs his hands up and down my inner thighs, massaging them while murmuring praise in a low tone. He knows I love getting praised, that I *need* it, and he always gives it in spades. Even when he's doing a lot, satisfying his own dark urges and desires, he still makes things *very* good for me, still meets all my needs and helps me through the sensual torture.

I hear a noise of the front door opening and closing; instantly, I tense up, all of the calm accumulated from Seth's massage and words dissipating in favor of panic.

Chapter Sixty

"Shh, that must be Carson back early," Seth soothes. "Looks like he couldn't wait to get back to you, left work early to come see us. Think he'll like seeing you like this? Tied up like the most beautiful, helpless muse in the world? Spread open and ripe for torture, with a plug in your ass, clamps on your nipples, and your clit swollen and the prettiest red?" Seth pauses. "Think we should give him a show?"

"Oh god," I murmur. When Seth says *a show*, it could mean any number of things.

Before Seth can elaborate, I hear Carson's footsteps carrying him closer to the bedroom; they stop, and a faint, "Holy fuck," slices through the silence like a scythe.

I'm embarrassed as hell at the idea of being found like this—trussed up and thoroughly tortured, awaiting more torture at the hands of Seth's sadistic idea of pleasure. At the same time, though, something about this is extremely hot. Getting caught by Carson like this is hot—it's not like I'm doing anything wrong, just deeply unconventional.

"Carson," Seth greets lowly. "Didn't expect to see you until tomor-row."

"I came back early, figured I'd drop by." Carson's voice is still faint, still somewhat shocked. "What... the hell is going on in here?"

Feeling more embarrassed and turned on than I ever have, I mur-mur a weak, "Hi."

I can practically feel Seth's nonchalant shrug, punctuated by the slight rustle of his shirt. "I'm having some fun. Care to join?"

"I... *fuck* yes. Little E, are you... good?"

"I think so, yes," I reply. I'm almost glad I can't see anything right now, because if I had to look Carson in the eye, I might die from embarrassment.

"Eliana's a bit drugged on pleasure right now," Seth says. "She's fine. You can join or you can watch, Carson, but I'm going to get back to work. Since my Little Muse told me I can't fuck her tonight on account of her having a long day of dance tomorrow, I'm settling for playing with her."

So that's why Seth's going to such extremes; when I tell him he can't have something, he finds another way of satisfying his urges. I told him he couldn't fuck me tonight, so he's torturing me tonight. So much so that I'm almost tempted to let him fuck me if that'll make him ease up.

I gasp as Seth twists the plug in my ass around, letting out a low whine. "Please, just give me a second. I feel like I'm burning up."

"Burning up," Seth repeats, cupping my pussy in his palm. He lets out a low hiss, then says, "You are, aren't you? Can't have that, we need to cool you down." I hear the clinking of something, I'm not sure what, and then Seth asks Carson, "Would you like to do the honors?"

I don't bother asking what he's talking about; if Seth wanted to tell me, he would've. I think a big part of his enjoyment of tonight is how

I can't see anything that's coming, all I can do is lay back and take it. I am physically incapable of anticipating or participating.

Slow footsteps sound—Carson's—as he makes his way over to the bed. I can hear his breathing, picture his astonishment over coming to Seth's apartment, probably to say hello after his late night, only to find *this*.

"Little E…" he trails off with a low groan, and I feel his hand cup my cheek. A moment later, his lips descend over mine, softer and gentler than Seth's but no less consuming. He cradles my face as he kisses me with reverence, and when he pulls back, I'm once again breathless and terribly turned on.

I only get a moment's reprieve, hear the noise of shuffling along with some whispers too quiet for me to make out, before something shockingly cold and slick slides over my pussy, making me yelp and twist in my bindings.

"Just some ice, Little Muse," Seth says lowly, amusement coating his tone. "You did say you were burning up, didn't you? I think you should thank us for cooling you down."

His words mean that he won't stop or take the ice away until I've thoroughly shown my gratitude for this twisted interlude. This must be what Seth walked away to get earlier—ice from the freezer. *Always thinking ahead.*

"Thank you!" I squeak, still twisting. "Oh god, it's too cold—please, Seth, too much!"

"I'm not the one rubbing the ice over your hot little pussy," he says, sounding even more pleased. "You aren't even going to be able to tell who's where and doing what, are you? Which pair of hands is on which part of your body. That must be horribly confusing."

"Carson," I say hurriedly, "I'm cooled down—*oh my fucking god,*" I cut off with a hoarse cry as fingers push the cube of ice inside of me, leaving it there. It's so cold it burns against my over sensitized and overheated inner walls. I feel tears burn my eyes at the overload of sensation everywhere, but it still isn't *bad*, just too much.

"I never saw the appeal of things like this before," Carson says, sounding intrigued. "Now I think I'm starting to get it. You are *so fucking beautiful* right now, Eliana, it honestly hurts."

"She is, isn't she?" Seth agrees, sounding pleased at his handiwork. Someone's palm—*Carson's? Seth's?*—rubs over my pussy again, fingers teasing my clit, before lowering and jostling the butt plug inside me, once again making me squeal.

"Poor Little Muse, getting tied up and tormented," Seth purrs. "We're not done yet, though. I want a few more orgasms out of you before I'm satisfied, and now I have Carson to help me work you over. I'm really starting to warm to our arrangement."

This whole situation is a mindfuck as much as it's physically over-whelming, because without my vision, I can't tell who's touching me. While that should turn me off or make me nervous, it only turns me on further, makes me more excited. I must be as screwed up as Seth is to be feeling so liberated right now.

The fingers circling my clit speed up; more fingers from a separate hand, I think, thrust inside me. The ice cube's melted but my channel is tightened from the cold, which draws a low groan that I instantly recognize as belonging to Carson. "You don't have to beg with me, Little E," he says, his voice sounding strained. "But you are gonna come when I tell you to, aren't you?"

I nod my head vigorously, already on the cusp of another orgasm. The clamps on my nipples are pulled, *must be Seth and his enjoyment of torturing me with pain as much as pleasure*, and I let out a long whine, tossing my head from side to side.

"Come," Carson says; I helplessly obey. Again, I orgasm, this time from the cleverness of his knowing fingers as he works me over—this orgasm is longer than the last one, slower yet no less intense, and it leaves me trembling and whining in the aftermath, unable to control my body or my voice.

"Good," Seth says, plucking at my clamp again and sending more pain coursing through my breasts. "Carson, why don't you liberate Eliana's nipples from those clamps and kiss them better?"

Shuffling sounds as they switch positions. I get the sense that Seth only spoke to Carson aloud for my benefit, so that I'd know what was coming, though I don't know why. The clamps can't hurt coming off as much as they did going on.

I'm quickly proven wrong. Seth once again presses the toy to my clit, sending vibrations coursing through my entire body, at the same time that Carson releases one of my nipples. For a moment, the numbness remains, but then a deep, aching pain courses through my breasts along with intense pins and needles as blood rushes back into my nipple. I scream at the pain, along with the vibrations insistently coursing through my clit; shriek even louder when Seth's fingers slide back inside of me, thrusting in and out at a feral pace, and Carson lowers his mouth to my breast, encasing my tortured nipple with wet heat. The warmth of his mouth helps the pain and intensifies the pleasure, which on its own is becoming painful. Unable to stop myself, too mindless to beg, I come again, yanking desperately at my bindings. Seth doesn't let me ride out my orgasm; he pulls away the toy, then spanks his hand over my clit several times.

"You didn't beg me to come," he says, his tone dripping displeasure. "Bad Little Muse. You know how it goes with me, Eliana; you *will* listen to instructions."

"I'm sorry," I gasp as he spanks me again, even harder. Again, tears burn at my eyes, both of confusion and sheer overwhelming sensation, along with the deep-seated feeling of vulnerability. I hate that I displeased Seth, that he's not praising me or calling me his good girl or good Little Muse; I need him to be nice with me.

"Please, Seth, I'm sorry," I whimper, my voice wobbly.

"Good, then you won't forget next time," Seth mutters darkly.

Carson releases my nipple with a pop, making me gasp, then asks, "Are you good, Little E? You need to stop?"

I shake my head. Even though this is all too much, more than I thought I could bear, I'm taking it and it feels *really* good. Pain intermixes with pleasure so thoroughly I'm mostly incoherent, but I don't need to stop yet. I think I will soon, though, and hopefully at that point I still have a voice to beg Seth with.

"Do her other nipple," Seth says flatly. "Eliana, you better fucking beg this time." Then, his fingers are back inside me, this time giving me angry thrusts that still feel absolutely amazing despite being just on the edge of what I can handle, and Carson slowly releases the clamp from my other nipple, once again closing his mouth over the peak to soothe the pain, while Seth brings the toy up to my clit, this time on a *higher setting*, with vibrations even more intense.

"Please, please, please," I chant repeatedly, shaking my head and yanking at the silk holding me in place.

"No," Seth says. "Not yet. You better fucking hold it, Eliana."

He curves his fingers upwards inside me, moving the toy faster over my clit, making it damn near impossible for me to hold it, especially when both of my breasts are aching with pain and he's taking me to the very heights of pleasure.

"Seth—I need..." I cut off with a low moan, clenching my teeth. "Please!"

"Closer, but not quite enough," Seth says, dark amusement once again dripping from each syllable. "*Really* beg me, Eliana, better than you ever have."

I follow his instructions, letting out a ramble so jumbled I'm not sure he understands it, with a lot of pleases, begging for him to let me come because I really can't hold it anymore.

"There's my good girl, now come," he says lowly.

Nuclear explosion. As my orgasm sweeps me under, I see stars bursting behind my eyes, feel my whole being get set aflame, like it's being repeatedly torn apart and remolded. Dimly, I feel the tears that have threatened multiple times fall through, soaking my blindfold. All sensibility and thought escapes me; all I'm capable of doing is coming with a scream that belongs in a horror movie, and full body convulsions that I can feel even in my fingertips and toes. It takes an eternity for me to come back to myself; it takes me even longer to realize that I've already been released from my bindings and am clinging to Seth's chest, tears staining my cheeks and his shirt. The blindfold's off, and in the light of the evening I feel more vulnerable than I ever have, more in need of his strength.

"Shh," he hushes, running his hands over my hair and my back, holding me tightly and peppering little kisses over my face and head. "You're okay, Little Muse, aren't you? You took everything like such a good girl. *My* good girl." As I tilt my head up, lips trembling, he leans down to kiss them once, twice, then three times. "Easy, Elia," he soothes, rubbing his nose along mine. "Breathe."

I inhale several deep breaths, my tears slowing and sobs dissipating, leaving behind a sense of exhaustion that weighs heavily on me.

"Was that too much?" he asks. "Too far?"

I shake my head. "No, it was good, just a lot. I'm okay now."

He visibly exhales at that, arms tightening around me, leaning down to kiss my forehead and murmur soft reassurances along with words of praise. I glance around, looking for Carson; before I can ask, Seth says, "He's just getting a washcloth for you in the bathroom, Elia. He's not leaving you, and neither am I."

I cling to him tighter, resting the side of my cheek against his chest.

Even as I try to regain my bearings, I realize it's impossible; I'm like one raw, pulsing, vulnerable nerve after that scene, and I need Seth's stability in place of my own. Little tremors still run through my limbs, aftershocks of the overload of pleasure. Seth continues giving light praises and assurances to me, planting kisses along my forehead, cheeks, jaw, and neck, holding me tightly to him as if he needs me as much as I need him. I'm so caught up in his hold and sweet words that I startle when I feel the bed dip under Carson's weight, not even having heard him come out of the bathroom. I look over my shoulder when I feel him brush a kiss over the slope of my spine, exhaling a shuddering breath.

"You okay, Little E?" He questions softly, meeting my gaze with his own. When I nod, a slight grin spreads on his lips. "Good. Turn around and spread your legs for me."

"Never heard that before," I quip, though my voice is still wobbly.

Carson chuckles. "I just want to clean you up, love. Come on." I follow his instructions, wincing when I feel the warm washcloth in his hand run up and down my sensitive flesh. Then, I turn a glare on Seth. "My no sex rule was because I didn't want to be sore tomorrow; I'll *definitely* be sore now."

Seth lifts a shoulder, unashamed. "That was the hottest thing I've ever seen or done, so I'm not going to apologize, Elia. I will, however, help you with the soreness." After Carson's done and leaves to throw the washcloth in with the dirty laundry, Seth kneels between my thighs, drawing a whimper of fear mixed with anticipation from me—he doesn't touch my pussy, though, instead he grips one leg and slowly starts digging his fingers into the muscles, massaging them. He goes all the way from my calves to my thighs—when Carson returns, he props my upper half against his chest and also starts massaging my shoulders. I let out a soft sigh, feeling my body relax.

I know I'll still be sore tomorrow, I'll probably need to put band aids on my nipples, but I'm not upset with Seth; I learned new things about what I like and am capable of because of the way he worked over my body. I never knew I was so tolerant of pain or into things like nipple clamps—maybe that's because I never would've been into it if it weren't for Seth. He's twisted and morphed my idea of pleasure and enjoyment, something that might worry me if I didn't enjoy his sensual games and love him so much.

After they've thoroughly relaxed me, Carson cuddles with me while Seth takes a shower—Seth offers for me to join before disappearing, but I honestly don't think I can stand right now, let alone shower, so I tell him I'll take one in the morning.

Carson doesn't mind the way I cling to him and rest my head on his chest, enjoying the sound of his heart hammering away beneath my ear; doesn't take issue with just how much I need physical contact, especially after intense sexual play like what just occurred. I need to feel treasured and loved and *safe*, and while Seth is good at providing that, he isn't quite as good as Carson whose very energy is relaxing to me.

I release a sigh of contentment and snuggle closer to Carson. Then, because I'm irritated at there being a shirt separating us, I murmur, "Take off your shirt. I want to feel you."

Carson's chuckle shakes his chest beneath my head, but he doesn't protest or rebuke. Instead, he gently rolls me off of him, rips open the buttons of his collared button-up, sending several flying across the room, shrugs out of the tatters of his shirt, and then pulls me back on top of him. My head resting on one of his pecs, I trace the other with my index finger, loving the feel of his muscles rippling beneath my touch.

"Did you ever think you would be here?" I ask him. "Sharing a girl with Seth, being okay with it?"

"No," Carson replies, easily. "Never, Little E. But that's because I'd never met you. Now that you're here, and you're *mine*, a lot of things have changed. I would've done whatever it took to have you, to make you mine. Sharing you with Seth is no hardship; especially not when I get to walk in on situations like I did tonight. Sexiest thing I've ever seen."

I smile faintly. "Were you into this kinky stuff with others?"

"Not really," Carson says. "I mean, I liked to get rough sometimes, but nothing like Seth's predilections. I'm definitely starting to see the appeal, though. Playing with you is more invigorating than I ever could've imagined, especially when you're bound and unable to do anything but take it. I like that a lot more than I anticipated."

I let out a soft snort. "Glad that I can be of some amusement."

Carson leans down to press a kiss against my forehead. "I'm glad we found our way to each other. You're my favorite thing in this world, Elia."

"You and Seth are my favorite people in this world," I tell him. "I love you both, so much I can barely understand it."

"Good, because I love you too," Carson tells me.

CHAPTER SIXTY-ONE

The following week, I'm running the usual drills in my second dance period of the day, the one class I don't share with April. It's not yet the time when the Pandora's Box dancers get separated out from the rest of the dance students—that's still about an hour away, and I'm not looking forward to observing even more of Sander's tantrums. He's been increasingly irate, as the opening date for the show is fast approaching.

The day after I spent the night with Seth and Carson, doing things that *still* make my cheeks flame when I think about them, I wasn't dancing my best as my mind was firmly in the gutter; I received a thirty-minute lecture after the end of rehearsal on the merits of perfection from Sanders. I fixed my form the next day, and everything was smooth sailing from there on. I'm still on the fence as to whether or not Sanders could actually be the killer stalking campus; when he's having his tantrums, I start to wonder, but then I recall that all artists are temperamental. Carson only shadows rehearsals that happen in the evenings, since I convinced him that even if Sanders is the menace that frightens every female fine arts student on campus, he wouldn't pull any moves in broad daylight with a building full of witnesses.

"Eliana," the teacher, Mrs. White, calls out, pulling me from my thoughts. "Since you're the sole person in this class who doesn't seem weighed down by sheer incompetence, could you head to the basement for me? Third door on the right of the hall is where we keep supplies, grab the box of colored stretch bands so I can get the rest of these would-be professional dancers up to speed."

I feel my cheeks heat as I glance around the class, seeing envy burning in every single other student's gaze as they glare at me. Even Sean looks a little bitter, but at least he has the decency to glare at the floor instead of me. Chloe, stationed at the back bar, is the only one who gives me a soft, encouraging smile and nod. I think I'm liking her more and more; she's really nice. She's hung out with me and April a bit more since the night in the ice cream shop, and we've become good friends.

I clear my throat, inclining my head at Mrs. White. "Of course. I'm glad my dancing is up to standards; I have no doubt we're just having a bit of an off day today. After all, each student in the Greywood Dance Co. has proven to be outstanding."

I say the words in hopes to alleviate some of the disdain that the teacher's favoritism is bringing to me. It doesn't appear to work, unfortunately, it just makes my dance instructor glare at me for daring to praise the pupils she's just insulted, though the ire amongst my classmates does seem to ease minutely.

"Less talking, more moving," Mrs. White snaps. "Be quick about it."

I incline my head. "I'll get right on it." I grab my sweater from where it's lying up against the wall, pulling it on as I hurry out of the room, down the hall, and into the brightly lit stairwell.

I've never been to the basement of HQ; it's generally a no-student zone. Usually, only instructors make it down here—something to do with a past student stealing supplies. As I get to the bottom landing of the stairs, a sense of foreboding sweeps over me, raising the hairs on the back of my neck and sending nerves fluttering through my belly. I frown, trying to shake off the strange feeling as I push through the metal entrance door and head right into the basement.

The area is damp and dark, and I wrinkle my nose as the smell of mildew assaults me. I slap along the wall beside the door until I find the light switch to the space, flicking it on. I'm greeted with a hallway made of cement, a few lightbulbs hanging from the ceiling to illuminate the space. Something feels profoundly wrong here, though that could also be my personal dislike of basements; I've always found them creepy and eerie. Figures that I'd be the student sent to rifle through this one.

Inhaling a fortifying breath, I follow Mrs. White's instructions, walking down the hall until I've reached the third door on the right. I swing it open, then flick on the lights, which once again reveal a single bare lightbulb swinging from the ceiling, casting a dim glow on several shelves with piles of odd-out supplies. Trying to find the box of stretch bands the teacher told me about, I look over all the shelves, which house a host of odd-out items.

One small plastic bin in particular catches my eye. It has a weird mix of items: a broken-in pair of pointe shoes, a paintbrush, and a red scrunchie. I frown as I step closer to it, lifting the lid on the container and pulling it off the shelf to look inside.

My sense of foreboding grows, and a heavy weight settles on my chest. Feeling like I'm doing something wrong by snooping, I quickly toss the bin back onto the shelf, only to startle when the wooden shelf shifts downwards, sending the box sliding to the floor, where the meager contents scatter. A metal click sounds from behind the shelf, followed by what could be gears turning, before the entire wall swings inward, revealing a separate room. Fluorescent lights automatically switch on from above in the hidden space, casting light on a small room that looks the size of two jail cells put together, with grey cement walls.

My breath catches in my throat, and I take a step backwards when I see there are splatters of what looks like a brownish red substance on the walls, the same color coating the floor. There's a rusted over drain in the center of the room, and in the corner, there's a kennel that's big enough to hold a large dog, with a padlock hanging from it.

Jesus fucking Christ. I think... I think the rusty brown color is *blood*. Holy shit, *shit, SHIT!*

I'm pretty sure I just stumbled into the kill layer. A hidden room with dried blood and a *cage*, which on second glance also has dried blood on it. Seth's computer program was right, the killer must be Sanders. Worst of all, he's been doing his killing right fucking *here*, under the building where dozens of dancers are in and out every day.

The paintbrush and the shoes... those must be mementos taken from the dead girls. Paintbrush for the painter, pointe shoes for Scarlett. The red scrunchie belonged to her, too, I realize. I remember joking with April that Scarlett was like Heather from that old movie with her damn scrunchie. *Dear god.*

I pull my phone out of my pocket, but instead of dialing 911, something compels me to call Seth. I'm terrified right now, and he's the scariest person I know, capable of chasing away any of my fears because whatever I might come up against, he's seen and done worse. There's a strange comfort to that.

He picks up after three rings. "Elia?" he greets, my name more a question, probably because I never call in the middle of the school day.

I don't even respond to texts until my dance classes are over and I'm headed to my art ones. "What's wrong?"

"I…I—I," I cut off my mumbling to inhale a deep breath, steadying myself. "I think I just f-found Sander's kill layer." My words are little more than a horrified whisper, and I can practically hear Seth's alarm. Rustling sounds on his end of the line as he starts moving.

"Where are you?" he barks.

"HQ basement." I manage to force the words through stiff lips. "T-third door on the right. There was a shelf… a box with some items that looked weird…the shelf caved inward and now there's a hidden room and *ohmyfuckinggod*—"

"Eliana, listen to me very carefully. Shut the room, get out of the basement, go outside where there are people, and call 911. I'm across campus, I'll be there in ten minutes."

I hear echoing footsteps in the hall behind me, the swift sounds of them falling with the weight of a hammer cracking bone.

"Someone's coming," I whisper.

Then, functioning on sheer instinct, I hang up the phone and try to pull the makeshift door to the trap room closed. I'm not fast enough, though; before I can pull the entire weight of a shelf attached to a wall shut, I hear a feminine sigh sound from behind me.

I spin around, coming face to face with Moira. My initial relief that it's her and not Sanders is destroyed when I realize that Moira does not look surprised at the room behind me. In fact, she looks *disappointed* as she gazes inside it, shaking her head. Just like that, a whole lot of facts click into place.

Sanders was never the killer, it was Moira. I don't know why or how, but I do know it's her. If it wasn't she'd be as horrified as I am at the room I found, or at least curious to see a hidden room in the basement of her department's headquarters. Instead, she looks mildly inconvenienced.

I start noticing things about her that I haven't before. She's always struck me as stern, aside from the times she was being charmed by Seth or Carson, but now I realize her grimness wasn't the mark of a ballet master, her expression has always held a disdain bordering on anger. Moira really didn't like Scarlett after she pulled the social media stunt, and she might've seen Scarlett as an impediment to her company, as a problem to be rid of. I don't know what the deal was with the fine arts student, other than she was a mean girl, and now I'm realizing that the reason Moira's always been kinder to me is because I'm one of the few genuinely nice people in the company. I suspected there was some favoritism in play, and there was, but not in the way I assumed. It's not because I'm one of her best dancers, it's because I'm not actively mean.

"Well, this is unfortunate," Moira says. "You know the expression 'curiosity killed the cat'?"

I try to stuff down my fear long enough to say, "I won't tell anyone. I haven't seen anything."

Moira tuts. "But you have." Slowly and leisurely, she walks up to the fire alarm on the side of the door and pulls it. Instantly, loud alarm bells start to blare, and my initial shock is overshadowed by realization; with the fire alarm going, everyone will vacate the building. She'll have ample time to *lock me in that fucking room* and do god knows what.

Moira raises her voice to be heard over the alarm as she slowly starts walking towards me, shaking her head sadly. "This is a true waste, Eliana. You had great potential to be my star pupil, greatest success story. In truth, I have no wish to kill you—you're one of the few good eggs. But, considering what you've seen, I can't very well let you live."

I look around frantically, searching for any item I can use in my defense, while Moira continues speaking. "The kindest thing I can offer you is a quick death. You haven't earned pain." Her expression morphs into anger. "Not like those other *bitches*. Flaunting themselves around campus, making a mockery of the fine arts, taking pleasure in grinding others in the dirt."

I need to keep her talking for as long as possible. The longer she talks, the more time Seth has to get here. He won't care if the fire alarm's pulled; in fact, he'll probably see that for what it is—a diversionary tactic. There really are perks to having an insane boyfriend.

"Scarlett really was cruel," I say, my voice choked with fear. "Did she… did she remind you of someone?"

Moira stops walking, and her eyes fog over with memories. She gives a shiver of disgust and her upper lip curls with disdain.

"She did. In fact, she was quite the replica of the reason why I never became a principal dancer. I attended Greywood, you know, on principal track. I was set to dance on the greatest stages of the world until my competition, a stuck-up little bitch named *Amanda*, arranged for an accident that put an end to my career before it even began. She could have been Scarlett's twin. As was that horrid painter that terrorized my students last year."

My eyes land on a glinting object, sitting on a shelf not far to the left of me, *a hammer*. Three steps in that direction and I'll have it in my grip, be able to wield it against Moira. I've never hurt a living being—I don't even like killing flies—but this situation is extreme, and it calls for an extreme response. I'll knock Moira out, get the fuck out of here, and let the police take care of the rest.

"I'm so sorry that happened to you," I say shakily. "Amanda shouldn't have done that."

Moira nods her agreement. "She shouldn't have. Just like Scarlett shouldn't have been so cruel to a company member who she could've instead mentored. Killing her was a necessity, the company needed to be cleansed of her."

"H-how did you do it?" I ask, eyeing the hammer and considering my options.

"Easily," Moira replies. "I lured her here under the guise of an official talk. Took her to the basement, locked her up, and got a container of blood from her. Then, went back to her dorm room and made quite a fuss, throwing around the blood and knocking over items. By the time someone discovered the scene, Scarlett and I were both long gone." A soft smile curls her lips as she reminisces, and I have to swallow down the bile rising in my throat. Moira's eyes sharpen on me. "You shouldn't have gone snooping." She sighs. "Let's get this over with. I'm sorry, Eliana, truly."

She turns her attention away from me, taking two steps to the right to grab something from a shelf; I lunge to the left and pick up the hammer, spinning around and holding it in front of me with a shaky grip, only to feel cold wash over me as I see that the item Moira picked up is a *knife.*

She frowns at the hammer. "Don't be silly, dear. You won't hurt me. I told you I wouldn't hurt you, either. A quick cut to your carotid, you'll pass out within a few seconds, and never wake up. It'll barely even hurt."

"You're fucking psychotic," I whisper. "How could nobody have seen that before?"

Her features twist with anger and she takes a step towards me. "Don't be rude, Eliana, not when I'm doing you a kindness. Be a good girl and put the hammer down, or I'll be inclined to think you're mean, as well. Believe me when I say, you do not want that. Mean girls suffer."

When I don't move, staying in place with my hammer ready to swing, Moira kicks out her leg in a lightning-quick ballet move that sends the hammer clattering to the ground, then lunges at me with the knife. Startled, I revert to my basic instincts, which are well-honed thanks to a lifetime of ballet training. She sweeps her arm out, attempting to stab me in the neck, I duck under the blow and move to the side, only for my back to meet a row of shelves. *Shit.*

Moira swings the knife again, this time low, and searing pain explodes in my stomach as she leaves a deep gouge on it. The breath gusts out of me and I yelp, folding my arms over my stomach, only to startle when I feel them get wet with blood. A *lot* of blood—she cut deep.

"Look what you've made me do," she snarls, her eyes wide and glinting with a mania I'd have never anticipated from her as she looks at the blood seeping through the wound, staining my leotard.

She swings the knife, once again aiming for my throat; I block it by holding my arms up in an x-shape in front of my neck, hissing as her blade slices through my forearms like butter. Then, I use all of my strength to shove her back, sending her falling to the floor, run to the hammer and pick it up. When I turn around, Moira's already back on her feet, features twisted with rage as she glares at me.

She runs across the space to me, and I move on sheer instinct. I block her knife with my hand, letting out a cry as it stabs straight through my palm, then swing the hammer at her temple. It connects with a sickening, nauseating crack; she falls to the ground like a stone.

For a moment, I'm terrified that I might've killed her, but then I see the shallow rise and fall of her chest, as well as the fluttering of her eyes. Her head lolls around on the ground as she groans. Before she can wake up and resume her attempts to kill me, I turn and stumble out into the hall, leaving a trail of blood behind me. The cut on my stomach is bad, and each of my steps make more blood pour from it. The knife is still embedded in my palm, but I don't dare remove it for fear that I'll sever something that'll make me bleed out. The diagonal cut on my arms also stings and leaks, but it's the most minor of my injuries.

Just get out. Get to the stairs and get out. I've been put through the wringer many times by harsh ballet intensives, getting to the end of the hall and to the stairwell should be a piece of cake, bleeding or no. I can't make it, though. Dizziness overwhelms me and the noise of the screeching fire alarm is quickly surpassed by a rushing sound in my ears. I cling to the cement wall with my good hand to stay upright, hissing and whining from the pain radiating throughout my entire body. *I think...* I think I might actually die down here, in this cement hellhole, trapped with the psychopath that's brought terror to campus all year. *What a way to go.*

CHAPTER SIXTY-TWO

The door to the hallway slams open, hitting the wall with a loud bang; I squint as a figure emerges, sprinting down the hall. A familiar head of dark hair and wild-looking hazel eyes makes me let out a shuddered breath of relief, because it's Seth. He came for me. I was right to call him, I know he'll always come for me.

On the tail of my relief comes more blood and more exhaustion. My vision blurs further and I start to keel over, what little strength I still have failing me. Seth gets to me just in time, catching me as I fall, panic radiating off of him as he takes in my wounds.

"Sanders is outside—*who did this to you?*" he demands. He cradles my upper body to his chest, hands shaking as he bunches up the corner of my sweater and presses it to my stomach, hard, drawing a moan of pain from me. My legs kick at the cold cement aimlessly, and I want to burst out of my skin if it means getting away from the agony.

"Moira," I manage to force out. "I knocked her out, but not for long." Another set of footsteps echo through the hall loud enough to be heard over the alarm, and I blink hazily as Carson appears beside me. Seth must've called him on his way.

Carson swears loudly, looking panicked while Seth's expression has transformed to sheer fury, a look I'm pretty sure he wears when he kills. He takes the wrist of my injured hand, examining the knife sticking through it. The gesture makes me whimper again as tears of pain and accumulated fear start to leak from my eyes.

"Shh, Princess, we'll get you better soon," Carson attempts to soothe me, though his voice is shaky and uneven and he looks nothing less than horrified at the sight of my blood.

Seth gentles my hand back down, then tells Carson, "Call the cops, take her upstairs, and get an ambulance, I need to take care of that psychotic old bat."

I know what he means by *take care of,* and although my thoughts are hazy, I also know I can't let him. If he kills Moira, there *will* be evidence—he doesn't have enough time to clean it up in whatever manner I expect he usually does. Carson already has his phone out and is dialing the police, they'll be here soon. If they get here to see a dead Moira and Seth near her, they'll assume the worst. He can't claim self-defense as she didn't try to slice him up like a Christmas turkey, so he'll go to prison for a long time. I can't lose him.

"No," I whimper, grabbing at Seth with one hand, leaving blood smears on his crisp white shirt. "Don't."

He frowns at me. "Nobody who hurts you gets to live."

I don't have it in me to explain my logic out loud—I just don't have enough energy to. Instead, I feel more tears roll down my cheeks as I beg him, "Please don't leave me. Please. I need you."

That seems to work. His expression softens just a touch as he reaches his bloodstained hand up to wipe away my tears. Then, his features harden with frustration and he lets out a curse.

"*Damn* you, Elia. *Fuck.* Okay." He inhales a deep breath, seeming to steady himself, and then scoops me up in his arms and stands. I clutch onto him tightly just in case he changes his mind, but he doesn't. My plea works. He wasn't kidding when he told me he can't deny me anything.

He turns and starts walking briskly towards the entrance of the hall, to the staircase. Over his shoulder I see Carson doing the same while speaking rapidly into his phone, his expression strained as he glances at the streaks and puddles of blood I've left behind. He follows behind me and Seth, rushing forward to open the stairwell door for Seth and casting me a concerned glance.

Knowing that I'm safe, and that there's no way Seth will let go of me now, I let my eyes flutter shut and succumb to the pull of darkness.

***

Seth

Hours later, I pace in the waiting room of the hospital while Carson sits in a chair propped against the wall, pale-faced, head in his hands. Moira's been taken into custody, and the police have already begun doing a forensic analysis on the hidden room my Little Muse had the misfortune to find.

Moira sang like a bird as soon as she was taken in; that could have something to do with the fact that I managed to bribe my way into getting a minute alone with her in the interrogation room while Elia was in fucking *surgery* because of her, and made it very clear to the old bat that prison could not protect her from me. She nearly killed my most precious belonging, which means I will very much enjoy making her life into a living hell. Repeatedly. I have contacts in low places that can easily facilitate such things, regardless of whatever hole she spends her life rotting in.

Apparently, Moira's been killing for some time, though she only took her nefarious activities to Greywood's campus this year, after discovering the perfect hidden room to conduct her killings. The painter who she killed at the beginning of the year had pulled a nasty prank on a boy in the dance company last year, a prank that resulted in him having to get surgery and sit out for the rest of the season. As for Scarlett, she was gearing to shoot the company's reputation to hell with her bullshit, so psychotic Moira figured that the best thing for all would be to kill her. I've already tapped into the PD's computer system and read the transcript from the interrogation that took place right after I left Moira to come to the hospital—the crazy bitch is certifiably insane and under the impression that her killings were righteous.

The only reason my program didn't flag her as a potential perp is because she never told anyone about her problems with the Greywood student who gave her a career-ending injury; instead, Moira locked that shit up, and later decided to avenge herself by cleansing her world of mean girls.

She'll be going to prison for the rest of her life, and I don't intend for her to live long. Just long enough to get tortured repeatedly until she's broken in body and spirit, a lamb ready to slaughter.

"You're making other people nervous," Carson says on a sigh, lifting his head from his hands to look at me and motioning around the waiting room. There are only a few other people scattered around the small space, but they are giving me anxious looks, as if I'm a loose cannon ready to blow.

I clench my fists and force myself to take a seat beside Carson, cracking my knuckles and then my neck. I won't calm down until I've heard from doctors that Eliana's fine and seen for myself that she's okay.

When Moira sliced Eliana's stomach open, she went deep enough to also skim one of Elia's kidneys, hence the surgery to sew things up and make sure there are no lasting problems. The surgeon assured me it should be a simple, uncomplicated procedure, that damage was minimal, but words aren't enough to calm me down.

By some miracle, the knife through Elia's hand didn't hit any veins or tendons, even though the blade went clear through her delicate skin. She'll need physical therapy to restore full functionality, but beyond that, she should be fine.

"Little E fought like a fucking champ," Carson says, probably in an attempt to lighten my mood. "Nearly cracked Moira's skull with that hammer."

My lips twitch at the reminder that, although Elia is a kind soul, she has a steel spine and will do what it takes to get by. My woman's a survivor through and through.

"She got sliced up for the effort," I growl, a frown creasing my brows and curling the corners of my mouth down.

"Yes, but she'll be fine. The doctors already told us that. If all goes well, she'll be back in dancing shape with plenty of time to spare before Pandora's Box opens."

That was Eliana's greatest worry before she went into surgery; she demanded to know when she'd be back to dance. Though her hand will be in a wrap for a couple weeks, and she'll be off her feet for two weeks while her stomach heals, she'll be good as new rather quickly. Things could've been much, *much* worse for her. That's the thought that keeps getting to me; this could've gone sideways in a million different ways, and my muse could've been taken from me. I was an inch away from never holding her warm body to my own, never kissing her luscious lips, and never being able to drink in the fact that she exists and belongs to me ever again. She would've simply been...*gone*.

"Excuse me, gentlemen," a woman's voice calls from the doorway. I'm up from my seat in a millisecond, closing the distance between myself and the doctor dressed in scrubs—one of the members of the surgical team for Elia.

"How did it go?" I demand. "Is Eliana okay?"

"Eliana is going to be just fine. The surgery went off without a hitch, we are very optimistic about the patient's recovery. She should be waking up in the next hour or so, if you'd like to wait in her recovery room—"

"Yes," I growl.

Carson, stepping up beside me, offers the doctor a charming smile. "Thank you, doctor. If you could offer us a list of what to look out for through the duration of her recovery, we'd most appreciate it."

"I'll have my PA get back to you with a packet of instructions in the next few hours," the doctor responds. "For now, we'd like to keep Eliana for overnight observation—we don't anticipate any complications, but it pays to be safe. If you'll follow me, I'll take you to the recovery room."

She glances between Carson and I, probably wondering as to our relationship to Eliana; the only reason she doesn't have the nerve to ask is because we've just paid the costs of Elia's surgery and stay here in full and up front. Carson's last name, which is plastered on several major hospital wings around the country, and my own last name and reputation also probably help the doctor keep her curiosity to herself.

I follow her through brightly lit linoleum halls, past several shared and private rooms, until we stop in front of a room labeled Recovery Room 5.

"Don't wake her, and please don't overwhelm her once she wakes up; she needs rest, but I'm sure familiar faces will be of comfort," the doctor says. "I'll send my PA to you shortly." She turns and walks back down the hall, out of sight.

I push open the door to the room, feeling my heart clench at the sight of Eliana, surrounded by monitors, laid out on the hospital bed, looking so very innocent and vulnerable in her slumber.

Chapter Sixty-Three

Elia

Consciousness is slow to return to me. My senses trickle back one-by-one from their slumber—first, I hear a faint beeping of a monitor, the murmur of low voices around me. Then, an astringent scent of something uniquely unpleasant and overlaid with lemon-scented cleaner burns through my nostrils. After that, I slowly start to feel things; initially, the stiffness of the sheets covering my legs, the uncomfortable mattress beneath me, and finally, pain. Both in my hand and along my stomach, low pulses of pain that intensify with each breath I take, until they become overwhelming. That's what triggers the memories to come crashing into my mind like a flood; *the hidden room, Moira, my fight with her, getting my stomach slashed and hand stabbed, Seth and Carson appearing just as I was sure I'd die in that horrible basement.*

A low groan rumbles out of my chest as the pain gets stronger, growing so consuming I want to do anything to escape it. My eyelids feel heavy and my mouth feels dry, and an unpleasant sense of nausea is settled in my stomach, rising into my esophagus with each pulse of pain.

"Oh, shit, something's *wrong*." Carson's voice drifts across my consciousness, and I half expect it to be a figment of my imagination. If Carson's actually here, though, and not just a hallucination, I'll feel a whole lot calmer and safer.

"Nothing's wrong, you idiot, she just had double surgery on her abdomen and hand. I'd be worried if Eliana *wasn't* in pain—*that'd* be concerning. Little Muse, can you hear me?" Seth's voice confirms Carson's presence as well as his own, and makes me all the more determined to face them, talk to them, and ask for something to help alleviate the unbearable pain.

I force my eyes open, millimeter by millimeter, grimacing at the bright light of the room and blinking repeatedly. Everything's blurry at first, meshing together into a discombobulating blob, but eventually, shapes and colors start to distinguish themselves within the mess. White walls, navy blue sitting chairs, a chart hanging on the wall opposite to the bed with a diagram of a human body. Then, the most relieving sight I could possibly wake up to; Carson sitting at the end of the hospital bed I'm lying on, Seth seated in a chair to the right, elbows braced on the mattress.

Weakly, I murmur, "Hi."

Both of them look disheveled and like they've seen better days; Carson's hair is unruly, there are dark circles under his eyes as if he hasn't slept for a while, and his shirt is buttoned the wrong way. Seth looks a little more put together, his hair smooth and clothes right, but I can see the lines of strain in his face and body.

"Hey, Little E," Carson greets with a soft smile, reaching out a hand and gently resting it on my leg. "How are you feeling?"

I grimace. "Shitty."

"You're going to need to be more specific, Elia," Seth says, eyes running over my body with piercing intensity. My legs are covered in a hospital blanket while the upper half of my body is clothed in a beige hospital gown tied together at the front.

"My stomach hurts a lot, and my hand... let's not even start," I clarify. Pain shoots up from my hand, into my wrist and over my arm with insistent waves that grow stronger with each second that passes. I look to the side, seeing that my injured hand is wrapped in a bandage that has small bloodstains on it—not a pleasant sight.

Seth reaches over to the table by my bedside, clicking a red button that rests on the smooth surface beside a bottle of water and tray of food. "A nurse should come soon, we'll get you something for the pain."

"What happened after I passed out?" I ask. "With Moira? Please tell me she's in jail."

"She is," Seth confirms. "She will stay there for the rest of her miserable life, which I expect won't last very long. She confessed everything to police shortly after being taken in; there are renewed investigations going on in accordance with her confessions. She'll never be able to hurt anyone again, Eliana, that I can guarantee you."

I exhale a deep breath, relief washing over me, dulling the worst edges of my anxiety. I'm more relieved that Seth didn't go back to kill Moira than I am about her being locked up; I knew she'd get put away for her crimes, but I didn't know if Seth would let her live long enough to go to jail. I'm glad that he did, that he listened when I begged him to stay with me and didn't end up implicating himself in a murder.

"How was surgery?" I ask. "Did everything go well? How long will recovery be? Will I be well enough to dance for the opening night of Pandora's Box?"

"Surgery went off without a hitch," Seth assures me. "It was successful. Recovery time will be about four to six weeks for your wounds to heal enough for you to get back to rigorous physical activity. I've fielded calls from Sanders and the entire dance company, all of whom were very worried when they heard about what happened. Sanders is actually pushing back the opening of the show, it'll now be debuting just before winter break, so you'll definitely have enough time to recover and get back to the final weeks of rehearsal before hitting the stage. Right now, all you need to worry about is getting well."

Hearing the door to the room open, I try to sit up instinctively, then gasp as the pulses of pain turn into overwhelming waves that I'm no longer able to handle, and fall back onto the bed, blinking rapidly as tears well in my eyes.

"Don't move," Seth growls. "You just got out of abdominal surgery, Eliana. You want to move, tell me and I'll slowly adjust the bed."

He clicks a button on the side of the bed, which causes it to slowly rise into a sitting position—the motion is still painful, but not as unbearable. A nurse bustles into the room, wearing scrubs with flower prints. She's young, maybe in her thirties, and has a bright smile pasted onto her face.

"Hello, Eliana," she greets. "It's good to see you awake. How are you feeling?"

"Pain," I say, my word little more than a moan because the agony is starting to reach obscene levels. "So much pain."

"Yes, that's to be expected," she replies, stepping around the bed without sparing a glance for Seth and Carson and checking on the monitor attached to a clip on the index finger of my uninjured hand. "The good news is that all of your vitals look healthy, and the surgery went just as expected. I'll go grab a morphine drip and set it up so we can alleviate some of your discomfort. In terms of next steps, we'll keep you here overnight to monitor your vitals and ensure everything continues looking good." She pauses to glance at Seth and Carson. "Only one visitor is allowed for overnight stays, I'm afraid, so one of your, um, *friends* will need to leave."

"I'm staying," Seth and Carson say at the exact same time, both with equal amounts of conviction. They glare at each other briefly, and a small laugh escapes me which quickly turns into a wheeze and then devolves into a coughing fit. My eyes water again, and the nurse says something about grabbing the morphine before leaving the room.

"Breathe, Elia," Seth says, putting a gentle hand on my shoulder and rubbing circles over it soothingly. "In and out, nice even breaths."

I focus on following his instructions, and slowly my breathing levels out, coughs subsiding, though my stomach now feels like it's on fire and the throbbing in my hand intensifies with each beat of my heart. Thankfully, it doesn't take long for the nurse to return and set up an I.V. that's set to alternate between a morphine drip and saline mixture that'll rehydrate me. The first dose of morphine is quickly administered, and the worst of the pain dulls into something more manageable as a pleasant fuzziness dampens my senses and makes me, quite oddly, so incredibly happy to be with Seth and Carson, despite the unfortunate circumstances. They showed up for me, they're coddling me, they're proving that they'll be with me through highs and lows, and gratitude fills me until I'm bursting with it.

"I love you both so much," I say once the nurse leaves, smiling mildly as I look between my men, who are both undoubtedly my favorite people in the world.

"You're high as a kite," Seth says dryly, looking me over with a faint smile tugging on his lips.

"Probably, but it feels good, and I love you," I reiterate, before looking over at Carson. "I love you just as much. For different reasons, but just as much. You're my light; he's my darkness. I need both and I adore you both. Have I said that?"

Carson chuckles quietly. "You have, Little E. You've said it plenty. You're adorable when you're loopy."

"You're adorable, especially when you're fighting over me with your cat," I reply, before my eyes widen. "Oh my god, can you bring the cat here? Mewlius would totally protect me against any and everything, and he'd give me an extra ser—sera...*serotonin* boost."

"I think you should sleep right now, Little Muse," Seth says, amusement lacing his tone. "The more you sleep, the faster you'll heal."

"Okay," I agree readily, because the fuzziness clouding my brain is quickly turning into the pull of sleep, drawing me away from the pain and into a beckoning slumber. "Please don't leave. Either of you." I pause, frowning. "Or, I guess one of you has to..."

"We'll find a way to both stay," I hear Carson assure me, though my eyes are already drifting shut.

Chapter Sixty-Four

I stay in the hospital for two days all in all before getting discharged. Then, Carson and Seth take me home to Carson's apartment—both because I continue requesting to see Mewlius and because Carson has a bigger bed and a spare bedroom, giving all of us plenty of space.

For the week after my discharge, I'm under orders to stay on bedrest and only walk around very slowly and for a short bit each day to keep my blood circulation healthy; Carson and Seth both wait on me hand and foot, making me feel like a princess and even a little smothered, though I love it. After living a life where I always had to take care of myself, could never rely on another to show up for me, it's deeply meaningful to have not just one but *two* people who are there for me 100%. I end up in tears countless times because of it.

By the second week, I'm allowed to walk around more, much to the consternation of both of my men; Seth gets especially grumbly when I want to get out of bed to walk around the apartment, so much so that Mewlius claws at him a few times for growling at me. Seth threatens to euthanize him; I threaten to castrate Seth, which is the end of that discussion.

The third week is much better; I go to the hospital to get the stitches out of my stomach and wrist, and have a very awkward interaction with the nurse where I question when I'll be able to return to certain physical activities, such as sex and some exercise for dance. Carson and Seth both refuse to touch me until I have an all clear from the doctor, which happens on week four, when I return to school and classes.

It's a chilly day when I finally step foot back on campus, the temperature close to zero, but I feel especially upbeat and practically exuberant as I walk down the familiar path to dance HQ, hand in hand with Carson. I won't be able to participate in all of the dance activities just yet, but I should be able to do most of them, which is good enough for me. As we near the building, though, a fine shiver starts up in my limbs—not just from the cold but from the flash of memories that cascade through my mind. The basement, Moira, the knife she wielded, nearly dying...

"Hey, Little E, what's going on?" Carson asks as I come to a stop mid-stride, staring up at the building that I've grown attached to in the last months, one that now feels irrevocably tainted.

He gently wraps his arms around my waist, pulling me towards him, running a soothing hand up and down my spine.

"It's just... Moira..." I trail off, shaking my head.

Understanding flashes in Carson's eyes and he nods, pulling me closer until we're chest to chest, resting his chin atop my head. I let out a shuddering breath, trying to regain my bearings and calm my racing heart.

"It's okay, Elia," Carson murmurs, kissing the top of my head. "We don't have to go back today. We can hole up in my apartment instead; I promise good food and multiple orgasms." I let out a small laugh at his words, knowing that both he and Seth would probably much prefer it if I were confined to their apartment rather than free to roam in the wild, where they worry I could get hurt again.

"No, that's not necessary," I murmur against his chest. "Just hold me like this for a bit and I'll be good."

Carson complies, planting more kisses along my head and squeezing me gently, murmuring reassurances that he'll never let anything happen to me and that I'm safe into my ear. It helps calm the worst of my anxiety, and after a few minutes I step away from the safety of his arms, taking his hand again and resuming the walk to the dance building.

Inside, I take the elevator instead of the stairwell up to the second floor. Stepping into the hallway where most of the studios are at once feels like something I've done countless times and entirely new because I now know of the horrors that this building was home to.

All of my worries fall away the moment I walk into the dance studio where warmups take place, though, and am instantly ambushed by a flock of dancers, all of whom talk over each other to ask me how I am and tell me that they missed me. April and Sean are leading the pack, of course—April pulls me away from Carson and into her arms for a tight embrace, murmuring that I better not scare her like that again. Sean's next, hugging me tight—earning a warning growl from Carson that we both ignore—and telling me how much he's missed having me as a dance partner. Then comes Chloe, who gives me a brief hug and kind smile, followed by half a dozen other dancers that I'm pretty sure are only being nice because I almost died, and also knocked the menace that's been haunting our dreams unconscious, which led to her detainment and arrest.

After a while of talking, we fall into our usual groups for warmups; I keep my stretching minimal, mindful of the surgical wound on my stomach, which has sealed up but won't be fully healed for another week or so. April, Sean, and Chloe sit around me, also stretching, and catch me up on everything I've missed, which isn't much; more tantrums from Sanders, more bullshit from Brianna, and a whirlwind of rehearsal and preparation.

Half an hour later, Sanders stalks into the room, a clipboard in hand. "Alright, children, I'll need my Pandora's Box dancers to convene in studio 7 after first period, from here on out your second period onward belongs to me—*Eliana!*" He cuts off when he looks up and sees me. "You're back, thank *god*. Are you better? Healed? Healthy? Ready to make my show into the vision it's meant to be?"

"Better, yes; healed, almost; ready to make your show into the vision it has been from day one? Always." I reply, getting to my feet.

Sanders nods with approval. "Flattery will get you everywhere, especially when it's so well executed. I'm glad you're better, positively exhilarated to have you back with us—rehearsals haven't been the same without you. Pandora's Box students: you know the drill and focus points, I'll see you in ninety minutes."

Sanders strolls out at the same time that the teacher strolls in, and my day of dance commences.

***

The following week is a flurry of rehearsals, preparations, and trying to get Carson and Seth to stop babying me long enough for sex, which is a difficult task in itself. Since I'm cleared for all dancing activities by doctors and back to full swing with rehearsals, I expect for them to be onboard, but they aren't.

I insist on moving back to dorms, much to the displeasure of both of my boyfriends. They like having me close, and while I enjoy spending time with them, I also like my independence. The return back to dorms also moves me closer to April, where I can keep an eye on her and have more time with her, which is a big bonus. I spend a lot of time with both her and Chloe in the final two weeks leading up to the opening night; we start frequenting the campus café, which has reasonable student prices and delicious winter themed coffees. I also spend several nights a week either at Seth or Carson's apartment, but relish my hours on campus, especially now that I'm no longer constantly living in fear.

The week before opening night, April, Chloe and I are all hanging out at the campus library, each working on our respective homework. Chloe's taking biochemistry-track classes in addition to her classes for the dance program, so she has four textbooks laid out on the table around her, along with two notebooks. April has a French textbook she's reading and taking notes from, while I have two art history textbooks and an extra book on The Renaissance.

Greywood's library is its own gigantic building, with thousands of books on three seperate floors, along with many study areas. We're using a study space on the second floor of the library, a small nook hidden in the back of many rows of shelves consisting of old science and math books.

"You three look like you're hard at work." I raise my head to look at the newcomer; Ian Vargas leans against one of the bookshelves, arms crossed over his chest, looking devilishly handsome and very dangerous in a black button down and beige slacks. "Eliana, good to see you're back on your feet. I understand that you're the reason Carson took two weeks off of work—management wasn't pleased."

I encouraged Carson to go back to work in the days after my surgery, to not shirk time at his company for me, but he refused, adamantly stating that he wasn't going to leave my side until I was better.

"Management, as in his father?" I question, arching an eyebrow at Ian. "It sounds to me like he's got that handled."

"It does sound like that, lucky for all of us," Ian agrees, his lips tilting up in a beautiful yet entirely humorless, flat smile. His eyes shift to April, who hasn't bothered looking up from her reading. "Sugarplum."

"Assface," April returns, still not looking up from her book. "I'm surprised you managed to find your way through a library—illiteracy was always one of your limitations."

Ian's smile widens, and this time, there does appear to be a spark of some sort of emotion on his face, though I can't quite place it. I frown at him, wondering yet again whether I should set my boyfriends on him; ask them to keep Ian away from April. I would, if I believed April needed my help or protection; as is, I really don't think that she does. She seems more than capable of holding her own against any threats that might come her way, and there's little doubt in my mind that Ian is a threat, though I'm not sure what kind of threat he is to her. Not physical, at least not from what I've seen, but there's something profoundly off about their dynamic.

"Not all of us can make being a nerd look so delicious," Ian says in a low-pitched tone, licking his lips.

April *still* doesn't look up from her reading, while Chloe lifts her head to give Ian a startled and jaded look, seeming uncomfortable with his presence.

"Don't you have a hole somewhere to crawl back into?" April asks. "Or, better yet, a ride to hell to catch? I'm sure they're missing you down there. A demon like you looks a bit out of place in civilized society."

"Hilarious," Ian replies tonelessly. "Anytime you want a demonstration of my demonic prowess, do let me know. I'd love to unleash every bit of my hellishness on you."

Chloe's lips part and her eyebrows hit her hairline, while shock also ripples through me. Ian has a very strange, not altogether sane style of flirting that's alarming to both me and Chloe, yet doesn't seem to leave even the faintest impression on April, which makes me wonder just what Ian must've done to April in the past to make her so desensitized to him.

"Eliana, I was just here to let you know that Carson's waiting for you in front of that quaint little program dorm building. He's growing increasingly worried the longer it takes for you to return, especially since you aren't answering your phone."

I frown. "You're telling me this *now* instead of when you first got here? Is there any humanity lurking behind the veneer you wear, or are you really just a lizard hiding in human skin?" While I speak, I start gathering my textbooks and notebooks into my backpack. I also check my phone, which has been on do not disturb, seeing two missed calls and a bunch of texts from Carson. I quickly tap out a reply, telling him I'm at the library and heading his way now.

Ian shrugs. "Why would I spoil his fun? He should know you well enough to know that if you aren't at the dance building or campus café, you're here."

That finally causes April to whip her head up and glare at Ian, while I frown at him.

"Why exactly do *you* know that?" I question crisply, standing and swinging my backpack over my shoulder. "We're not friends."

"Quite right, I don't have friends," Ian responds. "It does pay to be well informed in the life I lead, so I ensure I always am."

"Stay away from Eliana," April hisses.

"No need to be jealous, Sugarplum, my only interest in your little friend is the fact that she's making my boss lose his fucking mind."

"I'm *not* jealous," April snaps. "Merely worried for the wellbeing of my friend."

Ian yawns. "She's under the protection of not only Carson Ajax, who's my direct superior, but also Seth Balor. I'd prefer not to cross Carson, but I make a point to stay in Seth's good graces—or as close to good graces as that man has."

Carson texts me back, telling me to hurry up because he has a surprise for me. I quickly say my goodbyes to April and Chloe, then make my way out of the library.

Ian stays behind, probably to taunt April more—something I'd be worried about if I didn't have complete confidence in her ability to handle herself. If it came down to it between Ian and April, I have no doubt that April could take care of herself; she has a knack for wiping the floor with people who underestimate her.

CHAPTER SIXTY-FIVE

"Oh, *fuck*," I whimper, tugging at my wrists, which are firmly pinned to a pillow above my head by one of Seth's hands. After a very nice evening at a local Italian restaurant, he and Carson took me home—this time to Seth's apartment—stripped me and got to work on my body. The sheer deluge of pleasure I'm always showered with, especially with both of them at once, is overwhelming and yet not enough. They stoke a fire in me that burns brighter with every sensual touch, but never reaches the peak unless one of them is inside me.

While Seth's torturing my nipples with his teeth, biting down with increasing pressure, Carson's between my spread thighs, eating my pussy like a man starved. I shake my head from side to side, tugging at my wrists again, then wincing and hissing at a sliver of pain that travels through my mostly healed hand.

"Bad girl," Seth says, tone coated with warning as he pulls back and lands a slap on my breast, right over my tortured nipple. "Hold those hands still, Eliana. The only person who gets to hurt you is me—you do not hurt yourself, *ever*. Are we clear?"

"Yes," I whimper. "Yes, we're clear. I'm sorry, it's just—" I cut off with a hiss as Carson hikes my legs over his shoulders, then spears his tongue inside me while sliding two fingers into my ass. A long, loud moan is ripped from my chest as my back bows and my toes curl. Seth's lips quirk at my reaction, eyes sliding down my body. "Maybe you're not ready to take both of us tonight," he says, contemplatively.

"I am!" I exclaim, louder than intended, because I've been aching for this—to feel both of them inside me at once—for so goddamn long. They've both done their fair share of work to prepare me—a few days ago, Carson fucked my ass for the first time. The pain intermixed with pleasure, especially as Seth fingered my pussy and tortured my clit, was an experience beyond anything I've ever felt before. It hurt without a doubt, but it also ignited one of the strongest orgasms of my life. I need more desperately, want everything that they have to give me.

"Then keep. Fucking. Still," Seth says, his tone coated in silky menace. I feel my brows draw together in both pleasure and agony as Carson suckles on my clit, feel my impending orgasm grow that much closer with the gesture. Seth tilts his head to the side, a slow smile pulling at his lips as he watches my expression. He drags the tips of his fingernails over my breasts, around my nipples, before scraping over my sensitive nipple. That edge of pain is all it takes for my orgasm to hit me; a cry escapes me as Carson's fingers thrusting in and out of my ass speed up their pace and he bands an arm around my stomach to hold me still as he sucks on my clit so hard my back bows and it almost hurts. In the aftermath, once Carson's pulled his face away to offer me a mischievous smile with glistening lips, I pant heavily, wondering how I got so lucky to have two men who are both deeply dedicated to my pleasure and satisfaction.

Seth slowly releases my wrists, massaging them and lifting my hand, which has been downgraded from a full splint to a simple wrap, examining it keenly.

"Does it hurt?" he asks me.

I shake my head. It hurt a tiny bit when I was flexing it hard while tugging on my wrists, but it's fine now.

"You sure?" he prods. "You know how displeased I get when you lie to me, Little Muse."

"I'm positive," I tell him. "Please fuck me."

Seth's gaze heats even further while Carson releases a low, rumbly chuckle.

"Here's what's going to happen," Seth says after a long beat of contemplation. He shifts his position on the bed so that he's laying down beside me. "You're going to ride me—impale that gorgeous, wet pussy on my cock, with your elbows braced on my chest, while Carson works his way into that tight little ass." His filthy words make a flush cover my body head to toe, and I nod emphatically, quickly climbing over Seth to straddle his waist. He's already naked, and his cock is hard as it presses up against my pussy, the tip of it nearly reaching my belly button. I'm always amazed that I can manage to take his full length inside of me, though there's yet to be a moment where it doesn't hurt at least a little.

I brace my hands on his chest, leaning heavily on my uninjured hand—Seth tsks in disapproval.

"Uh-uh. Elbows here, Eliana," he says, tapping his pecks. Feeling my cheeks flame even brighter, I fold over him to rest my forearms where he indicated.

"My weight doesn't hurt?" I ask him.

He chuckles. "No, Little Muse, you're light as a feather." He reaches down with his hands, using one to lift my ass while the other lines up his cock at my entrance. A breath hisses out of him as I start lowering myself onto his length, feeling my inner muscles stretch to accommodate him, my position making him hit places inside of me that send stars bursting across my vision. "That's it," Seth breathes. "Just like that. What a good girl you are, Elia."

His praise practically makes me preen as I lift myself up his length before lowering once again. Seth lifts his hips in time with my downward motion; I gasp in pain as he bumps the top of my channel.

"Easy," Seth says, stroking his fingers over my cheek. "You can take it."

I hear the opening of a bottle behind me, followed by a squirting sound before Carson's hand slides over my ass, coating my hole with lube. He works two fingers back into me, then adds a third, all the while I slowly ride Seth. His fingers are a stretch, but it's less of pain and more discomfort; I'm worried that I won't actually be able to take both of them, but I also trust their technique. When it comes to anything sexual, Carson and Seth are both gods—I know they'll make it work, and that they'll never push me farther than I'm capable of going.

"Ready, Little E?" Carson questions from behind me. I stop riding Seth and glance over my shoulder to see him also straddling Seth's legs, cock fisted in his hand, shiny with more lube.

I nod, then turn my head back towards Seth, breathing deeply in preparation for what's to come. The tip of Carson's cock pushes against my ass as he grips my waist; I gasp in pain as he begins to push forward and the tight ring of my hole stretches too wide to accommodate him. The sting is intense, pain radiating through my ass and up my spine. I whimper; Carson stills his movements at once, running a hand through my hair.

"You good?" Carson asks me. I can't manage anything but another whimper in response as I can *feel* his cock rubbing up against Seth's through the thin layer of skin within me separating them—I feel so much pain, so much fullness, that it begins to overtake the pleasure and I squeeze my eyes shut, trying to fight back oncoming tears.

When I don't answer, Carson prods, "Elia, you need to talk to me, love. Are you okay?"

"Overwhelmed," I manage to squeak out, "but okay, yes. You can keep going."

Carson strokes a hand over my spine soothingly, doodling nonsensical patterns, murmuring words of praise in between his own grunts as he resumes pushing forward. After a few moments, it all becomes too much; I let out a whine that's pure pain, and once again Carson stops his movements. I feel a faint brush against my nipple—Seth's fingers getting to work pinching and soothing it—as his other hand lowers to my clit and begins rubbing slow, tantalizing circles.

"Look at me," Seth says. "Show me those gorgeous eyes—there we go," he breathes as I force my eyes open. A few tears fall out of them and onto his chest, making Seth's lips tilt down. He likes seeing me cry during sex, but only if it's from pain *and* pleasure; he can tell that right now, it's just pain, and I can see how much he dislikes that.

"Take a deep breath for me, Little Muse," he says. "Focus on my hand on your clit—relax for us. You're doing very well. I'm proud of you." I nod, trying to direct all of my focus into the insistent circles his fingers are drawing over the most sensitive spot on my body while inhaling deep breaths. After a minute or so, the sensation of pleasure from my clit starts to overtake the pain everywhere else, and I feel my body begin to relax, inch by inch. Carson continues rubbing my back soothingly, while Seth plays with my clit with one hand and my nipples with the other, using everything he knows about what gets me off to help me overcome the pain. A quiet moan slips out of me; Seth responds with a satisfied smile, then nods at Carson over my shoulder.

"We're almost there, Little E," Carson says, his voice lined with strain as he begins pushing forward into me once again. After what feels like an eternity and two full feet of his cock, accompanied by an enormous stretch that would be too painful if it wasn't for Seth's work, I feel Carson's body heat up against my ass and thighs as he finally seats himself fully inside me. Tears are still freely flowing from my eyes, but they're no longer from pure pain; they're from pleasure and fullness.

"You did it," Carson murmurs, reaching up to squeeze my shoulders. "Such a good girl." He moves his hands to my waist, then uses the grip to lift me while moving forward; Seth's cock slides out of me while Carson's stays in. Carefully controlling both our movements, he then lowers me onto Seth's cock while sliding his own length out of me, leaving my pussy filled while my ass only has his tip in it. He continues the languid motions, in and out in contrast to Seth's position, leaving one of them fully in me at all times as the other pulls out. I clutch onto Seth's shoulders and just hold on for the ride, allowing myself to be maneuvered like a rag doll, part of me actually getting off on it. This doesn't feel quite as good as the other things we do—it's too overwhelming to be purely pleasurable—but I like the feeling of being completely owned and surrendering myself to them.

Both of my men know what they want and have no hesitation taking it, even as they both bathe me with words of praise and adoration. Soft whimpers and whines escape me, high pitched and quiet—I feel so full I can barely let out an audible moan, all of the sensations are just too much.

"I'm about to come, Little E," Carson breathes, lifting me almost all the way off Seth in time with another thrust. "You ready?"

I let out a quiet moan and nod vigorously, wanting to know that I satisfied him, to feel his pleasure. After a few more measured thrusts, it happens; I feel him twitching inside of me, his cock swelling and stretching me even more as heat bathes the inside of my ass. With a kiss planted on my shoulder, Carson withdraws, leaving me sweaty and exhausted, slumped over Seth.

"Now it's our turn, Eliana," Seth grits out, the speed of his fingers on my clit increasing, making my wrung-out body tighten once more. "Ride me, baby, and make both of us come."

Even though I'm limp and beyond tired, I brace my forearms on Seth's chest more firmly and resume sliding myself up and down his length, panting with effort and exertion. I can feel Carson's come seeping out of my ass as I work myself over Seth's cock harder, while Seth continues rubbing my clit.

"Come for me, Elia," Seth grits out, scraping his fingernail down my clit. The burst of pain draws a groan from me; unable to help myself, I come with a cry, choking on it as my body shakes with pleasure. Seth grips my hips and slams me down on him one final time; I feel him pulsing within me in time with my own convulsions as he also reaches his orgasm. I slump over him as we both recover from our climaxes, my breathing heavy and eyes fluttering shut. Seth draws me higher on his body, making his length slip out of me, and peppers kisses all over my lips and cheeks reverently as his arms close around my waist. I feel Carson's lips on my shoulder as he tells me what a good girl I am, how well I took both of them, making my chest warm with contentment.

After a while, Seth gently rolls me off of him, laying me beside him; Carson heads to the bathroom, then returns with a warm washcloth to clean me up.

"You good?" Seth asks me, stroking his thumb over my cheek.

Unable to conjure up any words, I simply hum in response, which makes a soft rumble of laughter bubble out of his chest.

"Speechless. I like that. Get some sleep, Little Muse, you need the rest before I take you again."

CHAPTER SIXTY-SIX

Carson

After Eliana's fallen asleep, I hold her close to me, stroking her hair, staring at her and drinking in the fact that she exists. The fact that she's irrevocably *mine*. I've claimed every part of her that there is to claim—every hole in her body, but more importantly, her heart. It's deeply satisfying to know that it belongs to me, so much so that I don't even mind the fact that I have to share it with Seth.

"Your father's called you on six separate occasions," Seth comments quietly, rubbing his thumb back and forth over Elia's bottom lip, gaze glued on her even as he addresses me. "You're going to need to take care of that. I don't want him storming in and trying to cause any disruptions—you know I don't take kindly to anyone who upsets my muse."

I let out a long sigh that ruffles Elia's hair, leaning close to nuzzle it and breathe her in. Breathe in the fact that she's here, she's ours, and she's safe from any harm that might ever come to her. I know with a deep certainty that, while Seth might be the more violent member of our trio, anyone who treads near her with ill intent will also find themselves on the wrong side of a battle with me, and I will not hesitate to shed blood when it comes to her protection.

"You have the file on him ready to go?" I ask quietly, stroking a hand up and down Elia's bare spine. "Everything I'll need to keep him in line?"

"I have for weeks," Seth returns flatly. "You know this. You've been hesitating to pull the trigger on your blackmail for too long, and now we've reached a critical point. Take care of him, Carson, or I will."

Our versions of *taking care* of someone vastly differ. While, for me, keeping someone down with information I have on them or their loved ones will generally suffice, Seth prefers to be totally rid of threats before moving forward. As in, they're dead and buried in the ground so he can dust off his hands and never have to worry about them again. While I am in no way a fan of my father, or an advocate that he even *deserves* to live, his death would heap a lot of pressure onto me that I'm just not ready for. I need time to solidify my place in his empire and appoint a trusted team of people to run different parts of it before I take control; I don't want to work so much that I'll barely have time with Elia.

"I'll call him and make it clear where we stand," I say. "You think he knows about Eliana?"

"The news of the attack on her made waves not just through the state but through the country," Seth returns. "There's footage of us carrying her out of dance HQ—footage that I was too distracted to suppress before it went viral. It'd be a fucking miracle if your father *didn't* know about us. Why else would he call repeatedly?"

I let out a long sigh in response, shifting even closer to Elia, absorbing her heat and the lightness that emanates from within her—the sort of light that can never be tamped down or dulled, because it's fundamental to her soul.

"I'll do what needs to be done," I mutter into her hair. She's passed out in the way she only sleeps after a long bout of uninhibited sex and multiple orgasms; I'm pretty sure a freight train could crash into the wall right now and she'd still sleep through it.

"Now," Seth enunciates.

"Right now? But I'm cuddling—"

"*Now*," Seth repeats more firmly.

"You suck the fun out of everything," I grumble, even as I move to stand. I pick up my discarded boxers and pants, pulling them on, not bothering with a shirt as I grab my phone off the bedside table and head into Seth's living room. A glance over my shoulder before I exit shows a peek of Seth pulling Eliana into him, laying her head on his chest and closing his arms around her, staring down at her with a softness in his eyes that I've only ever seen appear in her presence. *Possessive motherfucker.*

I know damn well that the only reason there's actually room for me in the relationship, and Seth hasn't decided I'm a problem that needs to be *taken care of*, is because he determined that Eliana loves me as much as she loves him, and he'd never do anything to upset her. It's possibly his single redeeming quality.

I close the door to the bedroom, then drop onto the couch, pulling up the call log on my phone. There are several missed calls from my father over the last month—all of which I've ignored and pushed to the back of my mind, deciding I could deal with them later. Although he's an asshole, Seth's right; this is something that needs to be dealt with now, if only to get it out of the way.

It's not too late for a call in New York, where my scumbag sperm-donor currently is, according to company gossip. I click on his number, then hold the phone to my ear. As it rings, I decide that this is not a conversation I want to have sober, so I stand and make my way into the kitchen.

After six rings, my father picks up. "Carson," he says, sounding agitated. "Good of you to *finally* call me back."

"Father," I greet, my tone flat. "To what do I owe the honor of six calls from you? It's more than you've called me in the years I've been at Greywood."

A pause ensues, during which I can feel the anger from my father, even though we're hundreds of miles away, speaking over a phone.

"What's this bullshit that I hear about you being in a fucking *menage* romance with some trailer park trash girl?"

I dig a bottle of Seth's nicest bourbon out of a cupboard and reach for a glass. "The trailer park trash girl you're referring to is one of this country's star dancers, a very bright and talented young woman who also happens to be my girlfriend."

"Girlfriend," he repeats with a crude laugh. "Is that the label you give every girl you're fucking these days? I don't give a shit where you sow your oats, but any relationship you have with her will be ending now, or I will ensure that wannabe ballerina will never step foot on any reputable stage. Do you know the fucking *embarrassment* I've had to deal with? Hearing of you and that psychopathic artist, Seth Balor, both supposedly *dating* such an unsuitable girl? The coverage has been—"

"I'll stop you right there," I interrupt, pouring a glass. "Eliana is going to be my wife one day. That is not a question, it is a factual statement. If you want to discuss trashy women, why don't we talk about the actress you've been fucking behind Mom's back—actually, it would be right in front of her wide-open eyes."

Another pause. "Don't you *dare* disrespect me! A man's private dealings are *private,* but you are publicly *flaunting* this gold digger—"

"Speaking of gold digging, we can also talk about the three super-models who you paid off in the last years after your *private dealings* resulted in assault reports," I snap, swirling the dark liquor in the glass. "Or, better yet, the four secretaries in the last decade that ended up in the *hospital* after you attacked them, who you didn't even bother to pay off—you just settled for ruining their lives. When I had *my* people speak with them, it sounded as if they were all happy to band together and bring a very public lawsuit against you. Individually, you could squash their voices and bury reports with bribes to the right people, but four women together? I wonder what that'd do to your image."

"Don't speak to me that way!" Father roars, losing his temper. "I made you, boy! I fed you, clothed you, educated you—"

I laugh. "I'm sorry, I think you're confusing your role with Mom's. *She* raised me. *She* clothed me. *She* made me into the man I am today, and she taught me ideals that your mother never bothered to teach you," I snap. "Listen to me very carefully. In the morning, you will receive a file via email with a case that I'm sure any lawyer will happily take to knock you down several pegs—all the way into a prison cell. That's just from four women that were easy to find—imagine what I'd stumble upon if I *really* decided to dig into your proclivities?" I pause, letting that sink in. "Here's what you're going to do if you don't want to have a nice long stay in a prison complex. You will keep your fucking head down. You will stop your affairs. You will stop taking out your baseless rage on innocents. I have eyes on you, don't doubt that; if you step a toe out of line, that file's going to the authorities. If you try to sabotage Eliana, that file's going to the authorities. Basically, if you do *anything* to even *mildly* irritate me, that file's going to the authorities. Your time of being a horrific tyrant is over. Do your fucking job, prep your empire to pass onto me, and stay the *fuck* out of my business, or else I won't stay out of yours." I take a sip of the liquor, enjoying the way it burns a path down my throat, filling my senses with smoky, rich, woodsy flavor. "You should've paid more attention to me, Father. Then you might've realized that I'm not just a useless playboy; I'm the biggest threat in your life." I hang up with a click, feeling like a ten-ton weight has been lifted off my shoulders.

My father's been the shadow looming over my shoulder for my entire life; a constant palpable threat and bane of my mother's existence. Someone I've hated since I can remember, someone who was the very model of who I *don't* want to be when I grow up. I'm under no illusions that he'll try to fight back against me and take back control, but he won't succeed. I won't allow it. He doesn't hold the power anymore, and knowing that I'm the one who took it from him is empowering beyond anything I've ever felt.

Soft footsteps sound behind me; before I can turn around, a soft pair of slim arms close around my waist and a warm body presses up against my back. I feel my lips tug up as I take one of the tiny hands in my own and bring it up to my mouth for a kiss. "You should be asleep, Little E," I murmur, turning around to face her. She is so beautiful it makes my heart ache; especially with her eyes still glazed from her orgasms and her skin still flushed. She's wearing one of Seth's shirts which comes down to her mid-thighs, but I glimpse the bite marks I left on the succulent flesh, which are already darkening into bruises, making me smile.

"I missed you," she murmurs, pressing her body against mine again. "Seth said you were having an important conversation with your father. I know you don't like him. Is everything okay?"

I nod, pulling her up into my arms and setting her on the counter, beside the bottle and glass of bourbon. "More than. He won't be able to bother us." I rub my nose against hers, breathing her in. "Where's Seth?"

"Painting," Elia says mildly. "He's finishing up another piece, giving us time to talk. He's remarkably well behaved these days."

"Mm," I hum, running my lips over her cheek. "You sore?"

She nods her head up and down. "Very."

A twinge of regret pangs through my chest at the idea that I hurt her. Pain is Seth's trade; pleasure is mine. He hurts, I soothe. I don't like that I might've inadvertently hurt her. Little E's been hinting that she wanted to experience both of us at once for some time, and I was happy to comply, but I'm not happy if it leaves her in genuine discomfort. I pick up her bandaged hand, dropping kisses over the soft wrap covering it.

"I'm sorry if it was too much, Little E," I say quietly.

She kicks at my leg with one of her tiny feet, glaring at me. "Don't be. I wanted it, I liked it. I like the soreness; I'll remember you each time I move for the next few days. It's hot."

I feel my cock harden yet again at her words. "Fuck, Elia, you can't say shit like that. Now I want to fuck you again."

She laughs lowly. "I don't think I can take anymore tonight. If you want, though, I can blow you." She bats her eyelids at me when I pull back to look at her, lowering her hand into her lap. "Suck you like your good girl, swallow every drop."

A low groan escapes me at the visual she paints. As much as I've learned all her weak spots, the things that make her purr and scream and come uncontrollably, she's also learned me quite well. We're a fantastic match in the bedroom, just like we're a power couple outside of it. Elia has a fair few kinks that I'm happy to indulge, but I think my favorite one is her praise kink. She loves being called my good girl, loves it when I shower her with words of adoration, as much as I love to give them.

"You are my good girl, aren't you?" I ask her, leaning down to press a kiss to her lips. "So sweet, so soft, so perfectly *mine*. I think I might be obsessed with you, Princess."

"Join the club," Seth says, silently strolling into the kitchen. I glance over my shoulder to see him regarding me and Elia with furrowed eyebrows, seeming displeased that he's not part of our moment. "You should be asleep," he says to Elia, stepping up beside me and placing a palm on her thigh. "I thought I wrung you out properly. The more you sleep, the faster you'll heal."

"It's barely ten p.m.," Elia says with a laugh. "Besides, I'm hungry."

Seth and I share a glance, knowing the conversation that always ensues on the rare occasion when our girl actually *gets* hungry. I've learned by now that her past eating disorders culminated in a few lasting effects; first, she can't eat when she's anxious; second, she rarely ever *gets* hungry, which is why Seth and I both keep an eye on her food intake religiously, even when she makes it damn difficult with her indecision.

"What do you want to eat?" I ask Elia.

Her features twist with adorable confusion. "Um... I don't know. Food."

"Chinese?" I offer.

"No."

"Japanese?" Seth says with a sigh.

"No, we had sushi a few days ago."

"Burgers?" I suggest.

"Too heavy."

"Soup?" Seth counters.

"Too light."

"Indian?" I question, trying to hold back a laugh. We go through this ordeal every time that Elia declares hunger, and at this point I find her indecision endearing.

"No."

"Enough," Seth growls. "We will choose; you will eat."

Eliana's eyes sparkle with laughter and her shoulders shake. Sounds good. Oh, wait, I know, I want—" she cuts off when Seth leans in to devour her lips with his own, silencing her midsentence. One of her hands slides up his arm to clutch the side of his neck, and she lets out a soft moan that makes me harden even more. In the beginning, watching her with Seth was somewhat irksome; at this stage in the proceedings, it's erotic as hell. Seth nips her bottom lip before pulling back, which makes her pout adorably.

"You never follow through, Eliana, so I am going to choose, then I am going to feed you," Seth says immovably. When she opens her mouth, he goes on, "No, don't protest, I know you well enough to know how it goes."

Her bottom lip sticks out in a pout, but she acquits, "Fine. You don't have to be so mean about it."

"Mean or sensible?" Seth asks, arching a questioning eyebrow.

"Both," Elia replies, far more decisive in her words than she's ever been about her eating.

"You're right, Little E, he's a meanie," I say solemnly. "I'm not, though, which means you love me more. Right?"

Elia lightly smacks my chest, shooting me a glare. "Both of you have my whole heart, as you know. It's not a competition."

"Everything's a competition," Seth and I disagree *in unison*, the words escaping us at the exact same time.

Elia blinks a few times, looking back and forth between us, shrinking back on the counter. "I feel like I've created a monster by bringing the both of you together like this. You're starting to scare me."

Seth smirks. "Good."

I shrug. "As long as we acknowledge that my dick is bigger than Seth's—"

"Oh my god, you're not in a measuring contest," Elia says, shaking her head.

"We could get the measuring tape out if you really feel like backing your statement," Seth says, staring at me with a challenging glint in his eyes.

"No!" Elia snaps emphatically. "No way, I am not sitting through that." She pushes me aside with her good hand, then hops down from the counter, shaking her head. "God, the two of you are just *wrong*. I'm going to go take a shower."

"I'll join," I say. "Seth can figure out what we're eating in the meantime."

Seth shrugs, bringing his phone out of his pocket, though his eyes linger on Elia as she slips past him. "I'm going to want dessert later, Little Muse," he says. "Be ready to feed me."

A flush crawls up Elia's neck, but she doesn't turn to look back at him as she strides off. I follow behind her, mouthing at Seth, *mine's bigger*. I see a glint of irritation spark in his eyes just as I turn my back on him, hoping to god that he doesn't decide to grab a knife from the knife block and lunge at me with it.

In the bathroom, Elia turns on the shower while I strip off my pants, then pull the shirt she's wearing over her head, leaving her gloriously naked. Creamy skin, perky breasts just big enough to fill my palms tipped with rosy nipples, a thatch of trimmed blonde curls between her thighs that make my mouth water. Everything about Eliana is like an aphrodisiac to me, and every day with her I wonder exactly what I've done to deserve her in my life.

I take Eliana's hand in mine, gently removing the metal clips holding the bandage in place and unwrapping the cloth, taking care to roll it up as I go. My lips curve downward at the sight of the angry red scar that rests in the center of her hand—I fucking *hate* the fact that she was hurt, *stabbed,* and there was nothing I could do to protect her at the time. I lift her hand, pressing one kiss on the scar, then a second.

"It's okay, Carson," Elia says softly. "I don't even technically have to wear the bandage anymore—"

"You're wearing it for another week," I say immovably. She gets twinges of pain without it, and Elia being in even the barest bit of pain irritates the hell out of me. I drop one hand to her stomach, running my palm over the slightly raised scar tissue there with a sigh, shaking my head.

"Carson," Elia says quietly. "I'm fine. You got me out of there and paid for surgery that I needed. You saved me. Don't blame yourself for not being there when this happened—you ran across campus to get to me."

"You were fucking *stabbed,* Little E," I say, frowning as I nuzzle her palm with one of my hands and run my thumb over the scar on her stomach with the other. "How can I not feel like I failed you?"

Elia presses her body into mine, her softness melting into my hardness. "You're not magical—you can't teleport. You did, however, save me when I could've bled out on a cold basement floor." She pauses to shudder; I release her hand and stomach in favor of slipping my arms around her waist and resting my chin on her head. "Don't blame yourself for anything that happened. You can't be my shadow twenty-four/seven—"

"Debatable," I argue.

"—but you are an excellent boyfriend. You've gone above and beyond for me at every turn, in ways nobody else ever has, aside from Seth." She pauses, and I feel her throat work as she swallows, nuzzling my chest with her lips. "So stop blaming yourself, or I'll kick your ass."

I feel my lips quirk. "Kick my ass, hmm?" I lift her up by her waist, wrapping her legs around me, prompting her to squeal. "I think we'll just have to see about that." I carry her into the shower, mindful of the wet floor, and press her up against the wall, leaning my head down to drink leisurely from her lips as warm water bathes both of us from all three of Seth's shower heads. After a thorough taste of her lips, I reluctantly set her on her feet, then lather my hands with the scented shampoo Seth keeps on hand for her—though the one I bought her *is* better—and start working my hands through her thick mane of hair.

"I want to take you to meet my mom," I tell Elia. "Or invite her here. Either way, I want you to meet her. I think she'll love you."

Elia startles, tilting her head back farther to look at me. "Are you sure? That's a big step, will she feel weird about... you know, Seth?"

I shake my head. "She's met Seth before on breaks. She likes him well enough. My mom is literally the least judgmental person on this earth, in stark contrast to my father. She'll be happy as long as I'm happy, and I really do think she'll adore you. Maybe even as much as I do."

Elia softens at that. "In that case, Carson, I'd love to meet your mom."

EPILOGUE

Elia

The next week passes in a blissful haze. I continue to heal and continue to rehearse, putting long hours into preparing for Pandora's Box. Both Seth and Carson continue in their attempts to get me to move in with one of them; I continue to hold firm against them, preferring to stay in Greywood dorms, especially as dance becomes more and more demanding. It's easier to not have to drive to campus in the morning, and as much as I love being with both of them, sleeping over at one of their places usually means I'll be going to dance with a twinge of soreness the next morning, since I'm not as good at observing my no-sex-before-dance rule as I should be, so I reserve that for weekends.

At long last, opening night of Pandora's Box rolls around. I'm a jitter of nerves throughout the entire day, wondering if I'm actually worthy of the role I've been given and if I'll manage to do it justice. I linger close to both April and Chloe throughout the day, sticking by them through dance classes in the morning, then taking the afternoon—while I'm excused from my usual classes on account of opening night—to prepare with them. We have a light lunch at the campus cafe, then head over to the theatre for preparations with the cast hours in advance. We go through a few cast traditions, games made up by past Greywood dance co. members, before splitting off at 5:30, an hour and a half before the show begins and an hour before patrons begin to arrive, in order to get into costume and makeup.

April and I share the star's dressing room this time around; we invite Chloe to join us, since she's a soloist in the show, but she says she plans to get ready in her own little nook that she's found in the bowels of the theatre.

I have many costume changes throughout the show, as my story is told over time—some of those changes even happen on stage, which will be challenging from a technical standpoint, though it's well-rehearsed—so I lay out each costume that I'll need to do backstage, then set to work doing my makeup.

In my first variations and scenes, I'm a young, fresh-faced woman just created by the gods, so as I'm putting on subtle eyeshadow and nude lipstick, I chat with April about everything and nothing. As Zeus, she wears a much more elaborate costume with most of her visible body being covered in a silver-blue, shimmery paint, so she has more work to do.

After a while, though, conversation wanes. I finish with all my preparations at 6:30, just as patrons are filing in, which gives me half an hour of free time; the worst possible thing for pre-performance jitters.

Anxiety takes hold of me, starting at my chest and then spreading through my body like a sickness, making me at once feel weighed-down by dread and as if there's a swarm of insects angrily buzzing around my chest, all heading in different directions. After a few minutes of trying to read my Stephen King book while April does her makeup and listens to classical music through headphones, the stillness becomes too much; I can't stand it.

What if I'm not meant to be a dancer? What if I'm not good enough? What if I fail on stage, in front of hundreds of patrons, and prove that I'm not cut out for a creative life? The taunting questions and doubts rattle around in my mind until they're unbearable, prompting me to stand from my squeaky chair and head out into the hallway, wanting to walk off the worst of my anxiety. April's so focused on applying liquid eyeliner that she doesn't even notice me, leaving me free to slip out.

The hallway is surprisingly calm considering the sheer chaos that opening nights always breed; there are plenty of stage crew members and technicians milling about, though they're quiet and know to keep out of the way of dancers. I wander up and down random halls, taking care to steer clear of getting too close to the stage, even though I know it's curtained off.

That's when the *truly* insidious thoughts set in, as my mind seems committed to tormenting me until I'm too frozen with fear to perform well. I start to wonder about the longevity of my relationship with Carson and Seth. We've had somewhat of a whirlwind romance between us, and while I don't doubt that they believe they're sincere with the promises they've made to me, I start to wonder if that all could be connected to my stardom when it comes to dancing.

It's not unreasonable to assume that, had they not seen me dancing as Aurora, I wouldn't be where I am with them—had they not initially been in a competition, maybe they wouldn't have pursued me the way that they did. It's possible that, despite everything we've been through, I'm a novelty in their lives that will eventually wear off.

It isn't long before I find myself at the very back of the theatre, in front of the emergency exit, breathing harshly and having to ward off an oncoming anxiety attack. Logically, I know that my invasive thoughts are just that: invasive thoughts, ones I shouldn't give any credence to. Emotionally, however, I can't seem to get enough air into my lungs or even *think* about dancing.

I push open the emergency door, desperate to get some fresh air, sagging against the metal door and trying to regulate my breathing. The back exit lets out into an alleyway behind the theatre, poorly lit, which is why I hear Seth before I see him.

"Well, this certainly makes finding you easier," he says, his words accompanied by echoing footsteps as he walks closer. I squint my eyes, opening the door a little wider, letting the dim glow from within the building illuminate Seth.

"You look like you've seen a ghost, Little Muse," he says, sounding amused as he stops in front of me. "It's cold out here, Eliana, what are you doing?" He tilts his head to the side, examining me, brows furrowing as he does. "What's wrong?"

His proximity alone is enough to chase away the worst of the anxiety that plagues me. I don't respond to his words; instead, I grab his arm and pull him inside the theatre before burying my face in his chest and wrapping my arms around his waist, breathing him in, trying to soak up his strength and the comfort of his presence.

Seth's muscular arms close around me, pressing me tightly to his chest, and I feel him drop a kiss on the top of my head. "What's wrong, Elia?" he questions again, reaching one hand up to cup the back of my neck and massage it, loosening the corded muscles there.

I pull back to stare into his eyes, giving my head a shake. "Just... catastrophizing, as usual. Opening night nerves are bad for my anxiety."

Seth's brows draw together. "What the fuck do you have to be anxious about? You're the best dancer in the company."

"But what if I wasn't?" I ask quietly, deciding it's best to voice my thoughts instead of letting them eat me alive. "What if you hadn't seen me dancing on stage?"

Seth lifts a shoulder. "Then we would've met another way. Greywood's campus might be big, Little Muse, but we were always meant to meet. The pull between us is too strong to be overcome by space or time or tens of thousands of other people who attend Greywood. Why do you ask?"

"Would you still love me if I wasn't a principal dancer?" I question.

"I'd love you regardless of what you did. It isn't your ability when it comes to dance that draws me to you, Elia, though I'll admit I enjoy finding uses for your flexibility. It's *you*. Your personality, your heart, your empathy, the light that shines brightly from within you. That's what I love about you—everything else I can take or leave."

His words make the ball of anxiety that's been building within me start to deflate. The horrible feeling in my chest subsides, replaced with warmth and adoration, both for Seth and the other man that makes me feel like the center of his world. Before I can open my mouth to ask where Carson is, several bangs rattle the door; Seth rolls his eyes, giving his head a shake.

"And that'll be the other person you managed to ensnare." He keeps one arm around me while using the other to push open the door, and Carson slips inside, smiling at me brightly.

"Hey, Little E. I was hoping I'd manage to find you before the show—whoa!" he cuts off as I release Seth and jump into his arms instead, hugging him tightly.

"Would you still love me if you hadn't seen me dancing Aurora a few months ago?" I ask him.

Carson's expression changes from pleasant surprise to irritation within the span of a heartbeat. "The fuck? Of course I would, where is this coming from?"

"Our girl's feeling a little insecure pre-performance," Seth explains for me, crossing his arms and leaning against the brick wall a few feet away.

"Just a lot of bad thoughts swirling around in my head," I say, dropping my head against Carson's chest. "Both of you being here helps."

"What thoughts?" Seth asks. "We have twenty minutes before you need to get in place for the show; plenty of time to run through and disbar them."

I inhale a deep breath, then let all of them loose. "What if what both of you feel for me is temporary, and I'm left with nothing once you turn away? What if I'm not as good a dancer as everyone seems to think, as *I* think I am? What if I fuck up the show tonight and embarrass Sanders? What if the sky falls down and the apocalypse starts?"

Carson lets out a deep breath that rustles the fine hairs on the back of my neck. "What I feel for you isn't temporary, it's certainly not going anywhere. You *are* an incredible dancer, but that's not what defines your worth; you're so much more than *just* a dancer. You won't screw up tonight, you've worked too damn hard, but even if you did, it wouldn't change anything; I'd still love you, Seth would still love you."

"As for the apocalypse question, the sky won't fall down on us—the most plausible scenarios are an EMP knocking out all the power in America, a nuclear war beginning, or an economic crash of epic proportions leading to the end of civilized society. In any of those cases, you'll have me to protect you, and short of a nuclear bomb killing us—in which case I'll find you in whatever afterlife exists—I'll make sure all of us are fine," Seth adds.

I let out a half-laugh, half-sob. Trust Seth's cynical brand of realism to make me feel better when my anxiety feels like a noose slowly closing around my neck. That's what I know about him, about both him and Carson; they make the world more bearable and less scary for me. Seth will always call the situation how it is, not bothering to spare anyone's feelings by sugarcoating things, which is perversely calming because I know I can trust his words, even when inner doubts try to get the best of me.

Carson, on the other hand, is there to soothe and bring light into my life when my anxiety tries to dim it, as evidenced by the soft way he smiles at me and runs his thumb up and down my throat. "Little E," he murmurs. "Come thick or thin, you have us. That'll never change." Seth pushes away from the wall and gracefully stalks up to us, coming around behind me and taking my shoulders in his hands. I feel dwarfed between them, and there would've been a time when this scenario could send my panic into overdrive. Now, though, it makes me feel safe, treasured, and a little turned on as erotic memories start to cloud my mind.

"Tell any negative thoughts to go fuck themselves," Seth tells me simply as I crane my neck backwards to look at him. "Later, I'll fuck them out of you myself, but we regrettably don't have time for that now. Go dance your heart out, Eliana, not because you have to in order to prove yourself, but because you can, and you enjoy it. We'll be in the lobby waiting for you afterwards."

He drops a kiss on my forehead before Carson pulls me to him for a soft, brief kiss on my lips that leaves a smudge of nude lipstick on his bottom lip, and then the two are gone, taking with them any anxieties or doubts and leaving me ready to own the stage.

Come what may, success or failure, ease or difficulty, I know I'll always have two incredible men there to catch me when I fall and help me stand back up again.

Afterword

Thank you for reading Muses and Monsters!

I'll confess, when I started this book, I meant for it to be a love triangle. I was curious to see which man Eliana would choose; Carson, the guy who gives this book elements of a rom-com, or Seth, who would make it a dark romance. I was very surprised and somewhat irritated when Elia chose both, because it meant I had to figure out how to write a menage, why-choose romance. Lucky for me, these characters made it very doable.

Elia is not my usual brand of heroine. I generally write overly strong, in-your-face heroines who will fuck someone's shit right up if they make a misstep. I had to find other ways to connect with Elia, because her kindness and sweetness were foreign to me. We ended up connecting through the shared experiences of an eating disorder and a horrific ex, and I absolutely loved getting to know her. Like Seth observed, Elia is strong, and her strength lies in her fortitude. Her ability to bend and bend without breaking, to take the punches as they come and go with the flow. It's what made the why-choose, menage elements here possible.

I loved Seth's single-minded obsession with Eliana. Loved Carson's devotion and his playfulness. Loved the way Elia loves both her boys with such fierceness and fire, it could light up an entire world.

I hope you loved this book as much as I did.

Next book in Greywood Elites, Primas and Predators, is live! It's April and Ian's story, and let me tell you, it is one *hell* of a wild ride.

About the Author

Rose likes to write about complex, oftentimes twisted main characters who grow stronger together on whichever journey they take. Watch out for sexy morally grey heroes and sharp, intelligent heroines within settings ranging from fantasy to academia to the underworld of organized crime.

When Rose isn't writing or listening to the whispers (or shouts) of her characters in her mind, she's drinking coffee, throwing herself at anything nature-related (especially in the winter, when there are no spiders or mosquitos to attack her), and reading.

If you'd like to connect with Rose, join her Facebook group: https://www.facebook.com/share/1AgAcE5efaztPjLq/

To stay updated on her upcoming releases, you can visit her website and/or subscribe to her newsletter: https://rosegravestone.com/

If you're interested in reading her works-in-progress (pre-edits and re-writes for publishing) she has a Patreon where she posts chapters of books she's working on: patreon.com/rosesreaders

9 798990 505858